LONGITUDE

LONGITUDE
A NOVEL

Cárlos Cortés

University of the Philippines Press
1998

This is a work of fiction. Any resemblance to actual persons, living or dead, is purely coincidental.

Published by the University of the Philippines Press
and the UP Creative Writing Center

Philippine Copyright © 1998
by CÁRLOS CORTÉS

All rights reserved. No copies can be made in part or in whole without written permission from the author and the publisher.

ISBN 971-542-154-7

PHILIPPINE WRITERS SERIES 1998
LIKHAAN: Sentro ng Malikhaing Pagsulat

Editorial and Production Supervision:
Gémino H. Abad and *Laura L. Samson*
Cover Design:
Bones Calleja
Book Design:
Mariposa Clemente
Set texts and titles in Palm Springs, Eras Book, Prose Antique & Dauphin

Printed in the Philippines by the UP Press Printery Division *for my mother, Josefina B. Cortés (1927 — 1995)*

Já no largo Oceano navegavam
As inquietas ondas apartando;
Os ventos brandamente respiravam,
Das naos as velas concavas inchando:
Da branca escuma os mares se mostravam...

Now in broad Ocean navigating
The restless waves parting;
The winds softly blowing,
The ships with their concave sails billowing,
The white foam of the waves following...

—Luis Vaz de Camoëns, *Os Lusiadas* (i, 19)

Contents

Foreword   xi
Preface   xv
Prologue   xxi

Iª Parte
    O Mundo Novo   1

IIª Parte
    No Outro Mundo   93

IIIª Parte
    O Mar Pacifico   191

IVª Parte
    O Mundo Velho   299

Epilogue   395
Afterword   397
Gazetteer   399
Endnotes   401
Bibliography   407

Leste-Oeste: Livro Emque dà Relação do Que Viu é Ouviu no Viagem

Dedicado a la memoria de mi seignior, Dom Fernão de Magalhães é Mesquita, capitão-mayor do primeiro Armada de Maluco, cavaleiro comendador del Orden de Sanct Iago de la Espada, fidalgo da cota de armas é geração que tem insignias de nobreza

por la lengua da Armada, su esclauo Harith de Sumatra, que siguirio no mas cuenta

En Ricca Duoro

En casa do Xavier Lourenço de Gusmão, Año MCCCCLXJX
A costa da Maria Brigida de Cortesão, livreiro

Longitude: Book Which is the Relation of What I Saw and Heard on the Voyage

Dedicated to the memory of my master, Dom Fernão de Magalhães é Mesquita, Captain-General of the first Armada de Moluccas, Knight Commander of the Order of Sainct James of the Sword, armigerous gentleman of the class entitled to the insignia of nobility

by the interpreter of the Armada, his slave Harith of Sumatra, who followed him unreservedly

In Ricca Duoro

In the house of Xavier Lourenco de Gusmão, Year MCCCCCLXJX
At the cost of Maria Brigida de Cortesão, bookseller

Foreword

THE MANUSCRIPT TRANSCRIBED HERE was handed to me, as an afterthought, by a woman who had hired me as a scuba diver. At that point I had made several dives with my partner, Beatrize Clemente, but we still hadn't found what we were looking for.

It all began when Beatrize called me up: a woman she would identify only as Madame R. had engaged the services of her two-woman diving services company but Beatrize's partner, Vivian Abadilla, was in Palawan with some German clients. Would I fill in for the nonce? We were to look for an underwater cave in Mactan Island. You know, the cave where Lapulapu hid Magellan's body...

I did not listen to the rest of it. Beatrize had inveigled me into half-assed ventures before, but this one sounded rather flaky.

Well, I couldn't not go, of course. And she knew it. We made several dives. At the critical point—and this happened on every dive, without exception—it always fell to me to hold firm, despite Beatrize's increasingly frantic hand signals, and make certain we observed the 100-foot depth limit.

The oldtimers swear that Mactan is shaped like a mushroom, connected to the seafloor by a thick stalk. Not once did we reach the part where it supposedly slopes inward, nor did we ever find anything remotely resembling the underwater entrance to a cave.

When Madame R. returned from an overseas trip (I had not even known she was abroad), Beatrize took me to meet her. A most gracious lady, svelte and sophisticated, not at all dismayed by our lack of success. I recognized her at once. I had never met her before, but I had heard of her and seen her from afar. Who hadn't? She looked just like her pictures in the society pages, only lovelier; a hint of subtle perfume added to her allure. I pegged her at 50 or a little less, and Beatrize said that was probably right. It wasn't until much later that certain of Madame R.'s detractors assured me she was closer to 60.

Beatrize extolled the feasibility of deeper dives. There was a secret to it: you had to use a special mixture of helium and oxygen. If you got the proportions exactly right, dives as deep as 300 feet could be done. The trick was to prebreathe the mixture for an hour before a dive. Nitrogen purging was the key. Helium didn't form bubbles in the bloodstream. No way you could get the bends. What's more, the decompression period would become a whole lot shorter. No longer a matter of hours. The entire ascent, believe it or not, would take but a mere 30 minutes.

I found the technical details extremely boring and entirely unconvincing. Madame R. herself seemed neutral to the idea. Talk turned to the purpose of the dives: the search for Magellan's remains. If his bones ever turned up, I said, I expected the forensics experts to find evidence of the leg wound from his Morocco campaign of 1514. It had lamed him and left him walking with a limp. And there would be the injuries received in the Battle of Mactan. If we were lucky we might find his shield, which should have his coat of arms, and perhaps a ring or a medal with the insignia of the Knights of Santiago.

Madame R. seemed impressed with my knowledge, and began to wax nostalgic about the good old days: 1972 for example, when she entertained good old Sammy Morison, who was retracing Magellan's voyage for a book he was writing. She went to her library, and fetched her autographed hardbound copies of Admiral Morison's The European Discovery of America. There was Volume I, subtitled The Northern Voyages, AD 500-1600, published in 1971 by Oxford University Press in New York. I was even more interested in Volume II, The Southern Voyages, AD 1492-1616 (O.U.P., NY 1974), as it devoted 7 of its 31 chapters to Magellan's voyage. Morison, she told us, had been accompanied by his wife-cum-literary editor, Priscilla, and a Colombian couple from Bogotá, Mauricio and Josefina Obregón. They had flown into Mactan in the Obregóns' private plane. Maurice, himself a historian, was the pilot, and Josie the co-pilot. Josie also functioned as Sammy's photographer. Madame R. never suspected Priscilla was suffering from cancer; the following year, 1973, she was shocked to hear that Priscilla had died of it.

Then there was 1975, when Madame R. hosted a dinner for Captain Allan Villiers, his wife Nance, and photographer Bruce Dale. Villiers too was following Magellan's track; the article he wrote about it appeared in the National Geographic. Madame R. again excused herself to look for the magazine. It was the June 1976 issue, and there indeed was an article by Villiers, "First Voyage Around the World."

She had saved the best for last. Most intriguing of all, she told us, was the visit of a refugee from East Timor. This was late in 1975, that troubled time, with the Portuguese pulling out, East Timor turning from colony into independent state, and Indonesia bent on annexation.

The man, one Tristão Lopes-Pelea, was on his way to Portugal by a circuitous route. Darwin, Australia, was too obvious, as were Port Moresby and Singapore. He had brazenly transited two Indonesian cities, Ujung Pandang and Manado in Sulawesi, to get to Labuan, Malaysia. He then slipped into Jolo and made his way via Zamboanga to Cebu.

Tagalog-speaking military men had appeared at Madame R.'s door and politely showed her a warrant for Lopes-Pelea. She went back to the patio and informed him of it. He reached into his bag and she flinched, thinking he would pull out a gun and take her hostage. But all he took out was a sandalwood box. He asked her to keep it for him, then went to face the music.

She later heard he had been deported; she did not know where. She never heard from him again. As for the box, which was slightly larger than a cigar box, it contained a manuscript, a thick sheaf of foolscap with the dunce's hat watermark, just like the sheets Bob Cratchit in the Dickens story clerked on. The unknown scribe, who had a fine, flowery hand, had used quill and inkpot. Everything was in Portuguese. On the first page, actually a flyleaf, was a short note datelined Oé-Cusse 1816 claiming it was an accurate copy of a manuscript hidden in a bahar of cloves shipped from Ternate to Macao in 1619. A Jesuit priest had brought it to Malacca circa 1630. It was found among his possessions after he was killed by Dutch artillery fire in 1641. The priest's faithful sacristan, a Malay whose great-grandfather had been baptized by Francis Xavier, had entrusted it to a Portuguese factor fleeing to Timor.

Madame R., relying on her command of Spanish (she also spoke excellent French and passable Italian), attempted an English translation. She soon found that Portuguese was a different language altogether. Giving up the idea of a line-by-line translation, she instead simply made notes: a précis of each chapter. Then she put it away. For the last twenty years it had lain forgotten.

Beatrize blurted out that I was a writer, that is when I wasn't being a beach bum or a shallow-depth scuba diver, and before I could shush her Madame R. had said yes of course, now she remembered where she had seen my name before...hadn't I written a column for a newspaper? Wasn't that my short story in a recent issue of some magazine?

Suddenly, by those trivial achievements I had become, in her eyes, eminently qualified...in short order I was yoked, and the task of translating the manuscript (still smelling faintly of sandalwood) placed squarely on my shoulders. Beatrize must have been glad of the chance to replace me with someone who didn't mind breathing helium. I had always thought that stuff was strictly for balloons.

With the help of Madame R.'s notes, the thickest Portuguese dictionary I could find, and a promise of substantial remuneration for my efforts, I managed to translate the manuscript. I often altered the syntax, usually by transposing subordinate clauses. Whenever in a quandary, I merely picked out the key words and used them in whatever English sentence I could formulate. My habits were after all those of a fictionist, not of a scholar.

My infidelity to the Portuguese original did not bother me, as I had seen at once that the document was almost certainly a clumsy fake. It purports to have been published in 1569 in Ricca Duoro, a mythical place. I can stand delusions of grandeur in an author, but not anachronisms. In the very first chapter is a reference to Enkidu fighting a bull in Nineveh. That allusion to Sumerian mythology seems less likely of a 16th-century man, be he ever so knowledgeable about things esoteric, than of a 19th-century one who has heard of the archæological discoveries of the Assyriologists. In the same chapter, near the end, may be found the word "sabotagem," from the French word sabotage, which was not coined until the Industrial Revolution, when a factory worker threw his wooden shoe, or sabot, into the machinery to make it come to a grinding halt.

As for the rest of the manuscript, none of the subsequent chapters could suspend my disbelief. The author's erratic style (which I tried my best to homogenize) is simply too artificial, too sophomoric.

Only a sense of duty forced me to complete the task. When I submitted the finished work to Madame R., cracking a weak joke about how I should have opted for breathing helium, she merely smiled. She then casually remarked that the best version of Magellan's story hadn't been told by any writer. It had been sung by Yoyoy Villame.

Preface

On longitude

The technical problem of finding longitude must have quite perplexed Magellan in the 16th century. Several methods of estimating longitude were available to him, Ptolemy's not being the first and Ruy Faleiro's not being the last, but he must have understood that no reliable system could be possible without an accurate timekeeping device. By 1714 the problem had become sufficiently acute for the British Parliament to offer a reward of £20,000 toward its solution. Not until 1763, when the English horologist John Harrison invented his chronometer, was the problem of longitude finally considered to have been solved.

The novel Longitude

Longitude is a work of fiction and to see it as anything else would be a mistake. In general it remains faithful to the historical events it chronicles, with certain gray areas having been colored by my speculations, conjectures, and personal biases. Where the accounts differ or contradict one another, I have chosen the versions that, from my own analyses, I deemed most likely.

People

The first-person narrator is a man most historians and commentators consider despicable. However, as the only Asian aboard a European armada, his unique viewpoint has its advantages. As might be expected, Enrique in the pages of this novel eventually avails himself of the opportunity to justify his treachery. This must not be taken to mean that the author condones his dastardly deeds in any way.

Several persons too minor to be named in the historical accounts have been given suitable appellations: Capitão Diogo Coutinho, Botyok, Sri Ubulokob, Kulnarit Sungvornyothin, Rintap, &c. Sri Parameswara has been nicknamed Sri Harimau.

Some authorities count 20 Frenchmen in the Armada de Maluco. Mitchell counts only 16, the other four being Breton. Mitchell and Morison both count two Irishmen in the Armada, the latter identifying them as Guillen Irés and Juanillo Irés. By adding Guillermo de Lole (whose name I transliterate as William of Loughrea) I assert, at the risk of being the first to do so, that there were three Irishmen in the fleet.

Pigafetta's elevation to knighthood has been advanced by some four years, as he did not join the Order of the Knights Hospitaller of St. John of Jerusalem (also known as the Knights of Rhodes and later as the Knights of Malta) until 1523.

Albo's association with Piri Re'is, considered probable by Morison, could not have begun before 1524.

Master Andrew's participation in Cabot's 1497 voyage to Newfoundland is pure conjecture.

Places

The hometowns of the crewmen are given as they are spelled in the Spanish rosters. Some of those spellings are really rather quite farfetched: "Lila de Groya" for the Île de Groix, "Napoles de Romania" for Naples, "Enveres" for Antwerp, "Medyoenburque" for Edinburgh. For such spellings as "Bruz," "Monaym," "Estric," "Silvedrin," "Agan," or "Cruesic," I still am not certain what towns were being referred to.

I have accepted Morison's identifications of many places in and off South America, and Freitas Ribeiro's identifications of the Pacific isles Magellan called "San Pablo" and "Tiburónes." I have likewise accepted Sitoy's identification of "Mazaua."

The suggestion that Pigafetta garbled Pacijan as "Gatighan" and then confused it with "Ticobon" (which Morison thinks may be Himuquitan Island) is from Jose Vicente Braganza, SVD, in his book *The Encounter* (Manila, 1965).

Measurements

Most dates are in the Julian calendar. The narrator is usually careful to equate dates in other calendars to the Julian. He also keeps the civil day, which begins at midnight, rather than the nautical day, which begins at noon.

My chronology of events in Patagonia may differ slightly from Pigafetta's, as he seems to have confused the two Feasts of the Holy Cross.

The standard unit of length is the legua, here considered to be 3.18 nautical miles (3.66 statute miles).

Two prime meridians are quoted. Albo's, Hierro in the Canaries, is 18°10' west of Greenwich. Pigafetta's, the Papal Line of Demarcation, (the amended one, 370 leguas west of the Cape Verdes) is approximately 45°30'W if measured from La Sal or Bõa Vista or 47°30'W if measured from Santo Antão.

Ortography

Of the variant spellings to be found here, some are used inconsistently, as was the practice in medieval times.

By way of homage

Inserted in Pigafetta's classic eulogy of Magellan is an understated plea. How poignant this petition really is becomes apparent only when its background is understood.

In his *Primo Viaggio Intorno al Mondo*, which is apostrophized to his lord, "the Most Illustrious and Very Excellent Seignior Phillippe de Villiers de l'Isle Adam, Renowned Grand Master of the Knights of Rhodes," Pigafetta implies—very obliquely, by remaining vague or silent on certain subjects; by recounting tall tales (the cloud that daily sends water down the tallest tree, the bird that never stops flying) to distract attention from the fact that he has glossed over the drama of the captains' cabal and the subsequent mutiny; by never once mentioning Elcano's name; by averring that a sovereign such as the King of Spain would value his book more than silver or gold—that influential persons in the Spanish imperial court have prevented him from denouncing the men who betrayed the Captain-General of the Armada.

He also realizes that attempts will be made to influence history's judgment of Magellan.

In this he was correct.

As Morison notes, over the centuries "many efforts have been made in Portugal to denigrate Magellan, and in Spain to promote the fame of Elcano over his."

For most of his book, Pigafetta writes in a droll, factual style. The contrast is evident when he rises to the heights of eloquence:

> "Recognizing the captain, so many turned upon him that they knocked his helmet off his head twice, but he always stood firm, like a good knight, together with some others. Thus did we fight for more than an hour, refusing to retreat farther. An Indian hurled a bamboo spear into the captain's face, but the latter immediately killed him with his lance, which he left in the Indian's body.
>
> "Then, trying to lay hand on sword, he could draw it out but halfway, because he had been wounded in the arm. When the natives saw that, they all hurled themselves upon him. One of them wounded him on the left leg with a large cutlass. That caused the captain to fall face downward, when immediately they rushed upon him with iron and bamboo spears and with their scimitars, until they killed our mirror, our light, our comfort and our true guide. When they wounded him, he turned back many times to see whether we were all in the batels. Thereupon, beholding him dead, we wounded retreated as best as we could to the batels, which were already pulling away. But for that unfortunate captain, not a single one of us would have been saved, for while he was fighting the rest retired.
>
> "Among other virtues which he possessed, he was more constant than ever any one else in the greatest of adversity. He endured hunger better than all the others, and, more accurately than any man in the world did he understand dead reckoning and celestial navigation. And that this was the truth was seen openly, for no other had so much natural talent, nor the boldness to learn how to go around the world, as he had almost done."

Then the quiet plea:

> "*Spero in vra Illma s^a la fama duno si generoso cap^o non debia essere extinta neli tempi nost*" ["I hope that through (the efforts of) your most illustrious Lordship the fame of so noble a captain will not become extinct in our times."]

Acknowledgments

Terima kasih to María Victoria Kapauan, whose æsthetics, literary sensibilities, computer expertise, and unsolicited criticism were invaluable; *muchas gracias* to Miss Aurora Basa of the USIS Library in Cebu City; *ug daghang salamat* to Mrs. Sagrario D. Taghoy of the Lapulapu City Library.

Thanks too to Dr. Resil Mojares, Director of the Cebuano Studies Center at the University of San Carlos. *Muito obrigado* to SDJ, TM, JBL, NB, BS, CG, HL, TB, and JD II.

The Trinidad leading the way out of San Lúcar de Barrameda.
Background: the Duke of Medina Siodina's castle.
Picture digitized from a 1976 painting by Björn Landström.

Prologue

"WHEN THE WORLD WAS FLAT AND CIRCULAR," my father told me, "its circumference was known to be 6,600 parasangs."

A parasang was a day's walk and that distance, the size of the world, seemed to me beyond comprehension. Many years later, when I had learned the white man's ways, I converted it into miles: 22,500.

"In the very center of the world was the mountain of Meru, standing 18,000 parasangs tall, so high it grazed the moon. It had three peaks: one of gold, one of silver, one of iron.

"Near Meru the people of our race founded their first kingdom, the Kingdom of Funan, in the year Vikrama 35 of the true calendars.

"Our first ruler was Liu Yeh, or Willow Leaf, a virgin queen. Funan was founded by a woman, and we have always been proud of that.

"Funan was invaded by a prince of the Pallavas, Kaundinga Varman, who was a Brahman from Kanchi. The prince took Liu Yeh in marriage, and she was fruitful and brought forth many sons.

"After three hundred years in Meru, Funan moved its capital to Langkasuka, in Champa.

"After four hundred years in Langkasuka, the Kingdom of Funan was conquered in the year Vikrama 762 by the new kingdom of Sri Vijayâ, from Chenla. The Sri Vijayâ peoples went south, to Sumatra, and made Palembang their capital. The last King of Funan, a descendant of Liu Yeh, fled via the Bandon region to the island of Jawà. He gave his family the name of Shailendra, or King of the Mountain, so that his descendants would not forget their blood.

"In the year Vikrama 805 Sri Vijayâ sent an embassy to the Emperor of the Han, in the days of the T'ang Dynasty, and was acknowledged in the official rolls as the Kingdom of San-fo-t'si.

"In the year Vikrama 818 Sri Vijayâ conquered the Malayu lands from Temasik all the way to the Moesi River, and Bangsa Island, too.

"In 821 Sri Vijayâ conquered the Kingdom of Taruma and seized control of the Sunda Strait, so that it controlled as well the seaborne trade between Xanglei on one hand, and Champa and Chenla on the other.

"In 887 Bhanu, a descendant of Liu Yeh, married the daughter of Rajah Sanjaya, the ruler of a minor kingdom in Central Jawà that worshipped Shiva. The Shailendras practiced Mahayana Buddhism, but Bhanu's respect for his wife and for Hinayana Buddhism stood him in good stead with his father-in-law. Rajah Sanjaya, then in the twentieth year of his reign, appointed Bhanu his Bendahara, or Grand Vizier.

"The Shailendras had reestablished themselves. From then on, for the next two centuries, the real power was in the hands of a Shailendra bendahara, with the Jawà rajah on the throne a mere figurehead. Both positions were lifelong and hereditary. Each man, rajah or bendahara, was succeeded at death by his firstborn son. Side by side they ruled Central Jawà, rajah and bendahara. The bendahara would stay on after the death of the old rajah to serve the next one. Or the rajah, losing his old bendahara halfway through his reign, would turn to the son. Always, they were in the shadow of the powerful Kingdom of Sri Vijayâ, by whom their little kingdom was considered an ally.

"Rajah Sanjaya was succeeded by Rajah Panagkaran, who sat on the throne from 895 through 915. Bhanu was succeeded by Dharmatunga, who was called Vishnu, and who was Bendahara from 910 through 917. He it was who began the building of the magnificent temples at Borobodur.

"Rajah Panagkaran was succeeded by Rajah Panungalan, who reigned from 915 through 935.

"In 917 Vishnu was succeeded by Indra, whose true name was Sangramadhanarmajaya. His tenure was as long as his name. He was Bendahara for thirty years, until 947. Eighteen of those years were under Rajah Panungalan, and the remaining twelve under Rajah Warak, who reigned from 935 through 954. In 947 Indra was succeeded by Samaratunga, who remained Bendahara for twenty years.

"Rajah Garung was on the throne from 954 through 973. In the last six years of his reign he was without a Shailendra at his side, for Samaratunga upon dying in 967 was not succeeded as Bendahara by his son. Rajah Garung was obliged to elevate one of his datus to the post.

"Samaratunga's son, Bulaputra, could not assume the lowly post of bendahara in Jawà, for he had been born a prince in Sumatra. His mother was the Princess Tara, only child of Sri Dharmasetu, the Rajah of Sri Vijayâ. There being no other heirs, Sri Bulaputra succeeded his grandfather as Rajah.

"The Shailendra dynasty had done it. This was its revenge on Sri Vijayâ. Now it had placed its own king on the throne of its old conqueror.

"Sri Bulaputra graciously gave his sister's hand in marriage to Rajah Garung's son Pikatan. (Her name was Pramodavardhani and she was called Sri Kahulunan, 'Her Majesty the Queen,' because she had been born a princess.)"

THE SHAILENDRAS WERE ON THE THRONE of Sri Vijayâ for the next five hundred years, but for the last century of that were merely vassals of the Maja Pahít. Then the Maja Pahít conquered Palembang in the year Vikrama 1512. The last of the Shailendras held out on Temasik. That small island soon fell, and they fled by sea. My father could not even remember their names. But in only a generation a Shailendra boy, the one known as Sri Harimau, or "Lord Tiger," had grown up and married a Maja Pahít princess. Marriage to a royal gained him the megat title of parameswara. Sri Parameswara founded a new kingdom, Melaka, in the year Vikrama 1536.

I was born in Melaka in the year Vikrama 1628, which year I later learned to translate as Anno Hegiræ 899, and still later as Anno Domini 1493. I was the son of a warrior, seven generations removed from the ancestor who shielded Sri Harimau in Palembang. The Sultan then reigning, Mahmud Shah, was the seventh of Sri Parameswara's line, descended from Liu Yeh, a true Shailendra, a King of the Mountain, a Tiger of Malayu.

1ª Parte
O Mundo Novo

1 Farewell, All Ye Tauromachian Faithful 3

2 Al-Wadi al-Kibir 12

3 In Manzanilla Heaven 16

4 Armada de Maloques 26

5 Vma Mesa Sem Maçapão 35

6 Mare Tenebros 43

7 Teneriphe Tripe 52

8 No Le Pidiesen 61

9 Ventos Gerais, Rudos Marinheiros 69

10 Doldrums, Sodomy in the 76

11 Æquinoctials 85

I

SAGO PALMS MELT, my dream fading, into the dawn. To the east, a sky the color of last night's wine. I stretch awake and yawn, such a lovely day, foul vapors in the mouth, effluvia in the eyes. Skull crawling with cocoanut beetles.

Ungodly hour, this. Too soon Monday. Already time to get up and bathe.

Civilized men don't do this. Not for them the unhealthy early morning bath. Not in these latitudes. Here, they don't even wash daily. This land is a land won back from a race whose beliefs demanded frequent ablution. Reconquest having made the ways of the enemy abhorrent, in this realm men and women seldom bathe. They stay unwashed with a vengeance.

Too cold, the icy water shocks me, makes me jump and hoot. Too much the barbarian I shiver, touch of wind and old longings quickening my blood.

And then to church, cleansed if not absolved I must go to church with them today. Not my will but theirs, yet their will be done.

In my heart I abjure their bearded gods, but it has not been given me to betray the least sign of constancy to my own true gods, the gods of my land and my fathers. And so I steal into the pantry and eat hurriedly, before they awaken, as unlike them I have no stomach for fasting. The cold bath always puts a keen edge to my hunger. Let them fast if they so wish, unto the twelfth hour as required, that they might partake of the ritual food at their ceremony. They think mere bread a sacrifice, they cannot an entire animal immolate and so shed rich blood and thick, to a High Mass they bring thin bread and thinner wine, no better than their offerings for Low Mass, how then should the grace of their Lord be upon them?

Nor is it to be at the new cathedral, the one completed but this year after the labor of a century, that stupendous building fronted by a court of orange trees, so vast the Notre Dame Cathedral of the Faranghis (whom they call the Franks) could fit inside it, so dominating the eye is drawn to it for leagues around, so total an impression no one calls it by its formal name, the Cathedral of Sancta María de la Fede. Always it is simply "La Catedral." They boast that "all who see our cathedral will think us mad!" and indeed, to give madness its due, I had supposed our High Mass of Farewell would be at no less than the Cathedral, with its five aisles and Colón's tomb, the better for all the world to see. Surely this voyage we are embarking on is mad enough.

But our Mass will be at a little church instead, the one just off the dockyards, across the river. Here be mad men gathered in this mad city for a voyage of madness, and they choose a sensible church when Europa's biggest and maddest cathedral could have been theirs for the asking!

It is just as well. My head spins when, inside the Cathedral, I gaze at the ceiling of its nave: a sky unto itself. True, a basilica is being built in Roma, over San Pedro's tomb, that will be bigger. Whether it will be madder still remains to be seen.

I have suffered from vertigo in the spire of the Cathedral. Its name, La Giralda, comes from the giant bronze weathervane atop the belfry, a figure of La Fede: a woman wielding sword and shield, bigger than life. The shield catches the wind, so that La Fede wheels around to face the adversary wherever he may be. She tops the highest structure in the city, for the belfry, the *TVRRIS EBURNEA*, was built on top of a minaret. That minaret, and the hundred marble columns surrounding the platform on which the Cathedral stands, are all that remain of the mosque Abu Yusuf Yakub built. The mosque, as everyone knows, was built on the ruins of a Visigoth church, a basilica of San Vicente. What few care to remember is that this basilica was itself preceded by a temple to Venus Salambo.

Desecration then has followed upon desecration as points of view have changed. One is reminded of Mt. Moriah in Uru Salim, and the temple King Sulayman built: destroyed, rebuilt, destroyed again. Upon that hallowed mesa, where Ibrahim once prepared to sacrifice his son, now stand the El Aqsa Mosque and the Dome of the Rock; of the second Temple, only a part of its western wall remains. If La Catedral stands on hallowed ground, so too did the mosque of Allah and so too therefore did the temple of Venus. Each an abomination in the other's eye, one man's brother in the faith another man's infidel. A baptized Gentile, a nominal Mohammedan, an animist—which am I? More to the point, which should I choose to be?

From the Alcázar we skirt the Cathedral and soon reach the river. We cross the Sanct Elmo Bridge, an old makeshift pontoon affair that seems to be moving upstream. Another look, and the motion transfers to the water flowing downstream. On the other side, in Triana, the ships lie berthed at the Müelle. Nearby is the Church of Sancta María de la Victoria, in whose yard my master plans to be buried.

I feel more at home here on the poor side of the river. While the great city on the east bank of the Wad-al-Kibir sleeps late, Triana is up and about on the west bank. Its little church, with its single aisle, does not have its back to the river. It faces the waters even as it faces east. I am glad of that, for I feel disturbed in places of worship that do not align to a solstice or the æquinox, or at least to the rising of a renowned star.

I take a last look at the city once called Hispalis, and later Ixvillia. There is the Arsenal, where they worked on our ships, and there, the Torre del Oro. There is the Ayuntamiento, there the Arenal, gateway to the Alcázar. That was where we stayed. A decagonal palace, full of patios, pavilions, fountains and gardens. How I gaped the first time I saw it! I wandered through all of it, through the triple Arches of the Peacocks, the Patio of the Lions, the Salón de Ambajadores, the Patio de Montería, the Salón de los Reyes Moros, the Patio de Yeso, the Patio de las Doncellas, the Patio de las Muñecas, Pedro the Cruel's bedchamber, Ysabel la Católica's oratorio. And the gardens! Palms, magnolias, orange and cypress trees, myrtle and roses. Wild trees of apricot, peach and almond, planted by the Sultan al-Mutamid after he married a Varangian princess who complained that she missed snow. Now, in their season, peach and almond blossoms carpet the ground with a pureness more fragrant than snow.

In the Alcázar I could never stop marveling at the curving arches, the stuccowork of filigréed arabesques, and the shadowy arcades that led to marble baths. They evoked, as they must have been meant to, pleasant oases in the midst of sere deserts.

My master went to live in the Alcázar after his wedding. It was where his bride and her family lived. There a son was born to him, even while he oversaw the outfitting of the ships.

I lived there too, in the servants' quarters.

I look at all of it now from the opposite bank. They hold me in thrall to their majestic grandeur, those edifices standing resplendent across the river. Their ramparts, towers, and crenellated battlements, reflected upside down on the water, seem suspended in empty space. Several have moats, the water for which has been diverted from the river. Across these, they lower drawbridges.

The grandées all live there on the east bank, graciously consigning the dockworkers and the gitanos (a nomadic people who have camped here for the summer every year since the Reconquista) to Triana.

In these parts the Wad-al-Kibir, or Guadalquivir as they spell it now, flows south by southeast. The rising sun gleams off the water and down the aisle all the way to the altar. Were it the height of summer the sun's first light would shine straight down the center of the aisle. Today, because we are in the month of August, between the summer solstice and the autumnal æquinox, it favors the Gospel side. Still, it is good enough. It must be why the bishop says Mass with his back to the congregation. If he faced us, the sun would surely blind him in its golden glare.

I had begged to be excused but my master was insistent, quite adamant that I attend. "Do not forget," he told me, "the vows you made when you were baptized with water." Yesterday I had slipped away from Sunday Mass, thereby incurring a mortal sin. For now my heart is black and should I die this very moment (*simbako!*) my soul would drop straight down through earth and rock into the fires of Hell. It then would not be very politic for me to absent myself again. I must try and look devout.

My master has always been devout. Quite deeply devout, I should say, knowing whereof I speak. And ever since that boy king of theirs, the one who speaks only French, appointed him Captain-General my master has also become very pious. It lit a fire in him. He is a changed man now; these days, he burns with an intense energy. I have been a baptized Christian myself for eight years all told, since he acquired me, but it is not something I take very seriously. Only because I am in a foreign land and must pay due homage to the local deities do I come to this Mass.

This religion I shall never understand. They admit the existence of only one God (denying all other gods) who they say is actually three. That is either a profound conundrum or bad mathematics, and none of their priests can explain it. A mystery, they say, beyond the ken of human understanding.

If they have only one Supreme Being they certainly have a great number of lesser gods they call saints. The mother of their God is one of these. She was a human who begot a God, and subsequently became a saint. I have never heard of such a thing before. Gods have been known to beget humans, but not the other way around. Which is how it should be.

If one man may be born a God, why cannot other men be born saints? Martyrdom seems to be the only way to sainthood. Despite this, their calendar does not lack for saints. Their holy feastdays exhaust the days of the year. This calendar, the one given them by Julius Cæsar (that sometime resident of Hispalis) is inaccurate and by this time has accumulated an error of some ten days. All their astronomers suspect this, but nary a single one has the courage to propose the necessary correction. For which of any ten consecutive days in the whole year dare any rightminded Catholic discard, which feastdays give up?

As for this man born God of theirs (or, as they prefer, God made man), he was a bearded, circumcised, pork-eschewing Yahude—a Jew. He died on a cross, and they honor this death with the ubiquitous crucifix. His resurrection led to a movement which is now a great religion, this worship of a dead Jew on a cross. It is their hatred of live Jews that mystifies me. Cristóbal de Haro for example is said to be a Jew, a converso in fact, but one who still practices Judaism in private: a Marrano. It is an open secret and must be the reason why, prominent as he is, he cannot be granted a coat of arms. Even so, he may count himself fortunate. It was only yesterday, still fresh in the memory of local men my father's age, that Tomás the Dominican, who was called Torquemada, went after the Jews of this kingdom. Here in Sevilla, which had the most Jews of any city, more even than Córdoba or Toledo, Cristóbal de Haro has escaped the Inquisition only because he is from Burgos and has a protector in the Bishop of Burgos. For a price, I daresay. Juan Rodríguez de Fonseca, even as a priest, was always wealthier than a vow of poverty might have allowed. Now he is a bishop, wealthier than ever, and has also become Chancellor of the Indies and Keeper of the Seal. His achievements include the gaoling of Cristóbal Colón and (through his agent Pedro Arias d' Avila) the beheading of Vasco Núñez de Balboa, both so their fortunes could be malversed. My master says Fonseca is the real power behind the throne. I can well believe it. The Bishop is sixty-seven while the new King, Don Cárlos Primero, is only nineteen. The boy doesn't even speak castellano. He grew up in Ghent, Flanders, where all the court spoke French, not Flemish, and never learned the Greek and Latin all schoolboys are supposed to master, though he did pick up some rough Alemán and bawdy Tuscan from the mercenary warriors who were his bodyguards.

As for me, I must endure the tedium of this long High Mass in Latin. I know when to say "Amen" and I respond with "Et cum spiritu tuo" to every "Dominus vobiscum" but those Latin prayers go in one ear and out the other like so much random noise. I learned Portuguese in a few months, after my master acquired me, and castellano soon after we moved to Sevilla two years ago, but Latin is a dessicated tongue, beyond all hope of revival. It is only for those who write learned treatises or official documents or say tedious prayers or sing songs that drone on and on. Otherwise, I fail to see how magic incantations in that extinct language will purify my soul.

Perhaps the white man's soul is different. The Xangleis and Annamese who follow the eightfold path of the Buddha tell us that the soul is reborn forty days after death, in a cycle that ends only when nirvana is attained. While eternities must be involved here, that idea has much appeal, although I cannot reconcile myself to being reborn as a toad, say, or a crow.

The Hindoos use Sanskrit in their rites, but their gods are ancient and speak only the old language.

The Arabs and the Persians, as do the Gujarati and the Atjinese, also acknowledge only one God, Allah, and call Mohammed His prophet. But they do not pray to His image nor, for that matter, before any graven image. They do praise Allah five times a day, kneeling on rugs, bowing towards Mecca. But they do not eat pork, and they require a pilgrimage to their holy city.

The white man, though he prefers beef, relishes pork. He eats the flesh of the cloven-footed pig so as to mock his erstwhile enemy the Moor and his quondam neighbor the Jew. Mockery and torture seem so much a part of his devout character one would not think it the vestige of an earlier belief. Or so I thought until yesterday. And then, escaping from Sunday Mass, I went to the Plaza de la Maestranza. This coliseum, near the Cathedral, was where they staged the bullfights.

I expected the agile fun of the games I had seen in Portugal, where the tips of the bull's horns are sawed off and padded. Men on horseback play with the toro, dodging its horns by fractions of an inch, until eight men, the forcados, line up in a file before the bull. The leader takes its charge head on, grabs it by the horns and attempts to wrestle it to the ground; the bull knocks him down with a snort and the next man in line grabs the horns in his turn. There is much sport in it, and the bull is not killed afterwards, not even when it injures a man or a horse.

In the Spanish corrida, as I saw for the first time at La Maestranza, it is more than mere sport. The fight is to the finish. The shadow of death looms over it, certain death for the bull, and sometimes for the man as well. This is what the devout Spaniard must come every week to see: a majestic animal mocked, tortured, killed by banderillero, picador, torero. Confronting the bull is a man dressed like a high priest of old, in a *traje de luces*. The toro is the same Bull of Heaven Enkidu fought in Nineveh, the same bull that carried Europa across the seas. ¡*Olé!* chants the Spaniard, ¡*Wa Allah!* he responds to the psalm the man and the bull dance to. There is only toro, hombre, muleta. Only the matador, possessed by an atavistic *gracia*; a touch of divinity transforms him, and this he projects to his gathered fellowmen. Then the flash of the estoque, the sudden keeling over of the toro...

But yesterday the bull charged right past the red cape, and gored its foe. The crowd gasped in shock, several men came running, waving muletas to distract the bull, and soon one of them had killed it with a single neat thrust, using the fallen fighter's sword.

An ill omen, and surely it portended evil for me! Yet the ritual had ended as it should, in death, for the contest between man and bull is old. The *tauromaquía* of the Iberian peoples harks a long way back to the tauromachy of the Minoans and the Mycenaeans; they have merely imposed a civilized choreography on it, as they build cathedrals on the ruins of temples.

As for us, my people's religion flows from nature itself and, like nature, has always been so. We worship the moon, tall old trees, birds and animals, magic mountains. In all of these dwell spirits, devatas, to whom we offer food and prayer. Our priestesses, *ang mga babaylan*, lead us in the sacrifice of rice, bananas, palm wine, pigs, gold...the men pound out the rhythm on log drums and brass gongs...the girls dance naked, shyly at first, then faster and faster and wilder and...

My thoughts had wandered. I snapped awake. I must have nodded off. The concelebrated High Mass was ending. The bishop, Don Sáncho Martínez de Leyva, the Corregidor of Sevilla, stood facing us, the Armada's chaplains flanking him. My master came forward to kneel before the Bishop and take his oath. Right hand raised, left on Holy Scripture, his raspy voice rang out full and clear in that little church as he swore to serve the Emperor and bring the light of the Christian faith to the heathen. The Bishop blessed him with the mitre, allowed him to kiss the ring, and gave him the silken flag, the symbol of command. The royal standard, it bore the canting arms of León and Castilla, in quarterings of red and gold. Then my master stood and turned to face us. His knight's habit was white, with a gold-bordered cross of red upon it. Three tips of this cross each ended as a fleur-de-lys. Only the select wore the habiliments of a Knight of Santiago, and we were all justly proud of Dom Fernão. Being a Knight Commander of the Order of St. James of the Sword quite became him, and it seemed correct that all should address him formally as "comendador."

The captains and pilots came forward to kneel before the Captain-General and take their oath. They all swore to follow the course ordered by him, and to obey him in everything.

The Donha Beatriz, in a front pew beside her parents and with little Rodrigo in her arms, had never looked more radiant. Already, as I had overheard, the Doña was *grávida* again. My master had certainly lost no time.

Dom Diogo Barbosa, my master's father-in-law, wore a robe like Dom Fernão's. He too was a caballero comendador del Orden de Sanct Iago de la Espada. He too came from Portugal. He was a naturalized Spaniard, something my master had not yet become. It had been easier then. Nowadays naturalization required an act of the Cortes.

Duarte Barbosa, Dom Diogo's son, would be sailing with the Armada. Dom Diogo would be left behind, and I wondered how he felt. Twenty years ago, when he was still Portuguese, he had sailed as one of the captains under Pedro Álvares Cabral in a fleet of four caravels to Brasil, East Africa and Índia.

Amidst the pealing of the church bells, the congregation burst into song. The Bishop started down the aisle, followed by the Captain-General, to lead the procession. I exited by a side door and took a shortcut to the flagship, wondering if the Portuguese Consul's henchmen would attempt some last-minute sabotage.

In the cabin I laid out my master's wardrobe. He would be changing from knight's habit to nobleman's doublet as soon as the ships were in the midstream current.

From the quarterdeck I could see them coming. The sky above was cerulean blue, and the excitement lent a tang to the August morning air. The whole town had turned out to line both banks of the river, to crowd the crenellated parapets of all towers and rooftops, and to row little boats around our ships. I hunched down in the shade of a capstan to wait for my crewmates. In a matter of minutes they would be all over the decks and the rigging. For now, there were only the merinos on guard duty.

Suddenly, the last few minutes of waiting had become unbearable. I desperately craved a betel chew.

2

A WHISTLE BLEW. "¡O dio!" sang out the contramaestre.

"...*ayuta noy*," intoned the marineros and the grumetes in chorus as they pulled on the cables. This was the saloma or chantey used when hoisting the anchors. The men hauled away on the contramaestre's "O" and joined in on the refrain while they got a new hold on the cables.

"¡*O que somo!*"
"...*servi soy.*"
"¡*O voleamo!*"
"...*ben servir.*"
"¡*O la fede!*"
"...*mantenir.*"
"¡*O ponente!*"
"...*de cristiano.*"
"¡*O malmeta!*"
"...*lo pagano.*"

And so on, the contramaestre improvising, until the anchors were aweigh. "¡*Dejad la driza, amarrá!*" he yelled, ordering the halyards welled, coordinating movements with short toots on his whistle. The whistle hung from a lanyard around his neck; it was his badge of office.

There remained only the Captain-General's traditional command. With bated breath, everyone tensed for it.

"¡*Largüen en el nombre de Dios!*"

His raspy voice carried clearly all the way to the Cathedral. The wind shifted and the figure of La Fede suddenly pivoted to face us as if she too had been waiting for the command.

"¡*Tira!*" boomed the condestable de bombarderos. Several of our cannon fired a broadside in salute. Smoke drifted downwind.

"*¡Tira!*" yelled the next ship's bombardero. One by one, the other four ships saluted Sevilla with broadsides of their own.

The Corregidor of Sevilla, the Bishop of Burgos, the directors and officials of the Casa with their almirantes, tenientes, alcaldes del mar and alguaciles, Cristóbal de Haro, comendador Diogo Barbosa, wives, mothers, sisters, lovers, dockside prostitutes and other well-wishers waved their blessings.

Men in the waists rowed us out with long ashwood sweeps.

"*¡Dad vuelta!*" the contramaestre spurred them on.

Where the midstream current caught the ship, the pilot signalled for the foresail to be raised.

"*¡Izá el trinquete!*" ordered the contramaestre, relaying the pilot's word. He had a good strong voice, as did the contramaestres of the other four ships. They were chosen as much for their voices as for their nautical skills.

Soon the five ships were in single file in the middle of the river, all flags flying. A river pilot now took over to guide our helmsman. The Guadalquivir, placid but muddy brown with silt, was full of hidden dangers. Downstream, by the village of San Juan de Aznalfarache, were two submerged columns, all that remained of a Roman bridge destroyed in the Guerras de Reconquista. Farther down were the ruins of Moorish watermills. It took a good river pilot to get a ship past all the obstacles and through the river's tricky currents and treacherous eddies. We had hired five pilots, one for each ship. They would see us all the way down the Guadalquivir to the sea, 19 leagues away.

"*Diez y nueve leguas*," said the condestable de bombarderos, Maestro Andrés. "That would be something like, let me see, yes, threescore miles. Just about. Perhaps a fraction more." He winked at me. "That is, if el comendador will be using the legua of Cristoferens Colombo. Three and one-fifth Saxon miles, that was."

Our condestable, or chief artilleryman, preferred to be called Master Andrew, strange though that pronunciation was. He came from Bristol in Inglatierra, where they clipped all their words. He had been in Yspaña, which he mispronounced "Spain," for a long time. He spoke castellano rather well and had married a sevillana lady named Ana Estrada. Their children spoke good español with andaluz accents, but no inglés.

"Avast, me hearties!" boomed Master Andrew of Bristol, "'tis but a creek, fit only for freshwater swabs. When we taste ye salt spray, as 'pon a Brygstowe bark, then will I break out ye olde Malmsey wine!"

Calling his hometown by its old name, and reverting to the corrupted English name for Malvasia wine. It seemed that by such trivial things he revealed his inordinate pride in being the only Englishman aboard the Armada. Far was it from me to begrudge him that small chauvinism, but what of it? I was the only Malayu, surely a finer distinction.

Sevilla faded away. By the morrow we would be within sight and smell of the Mar Océano. Only now did the crew, drifting downstream in the hands of the river pilots, hunker down to breakfast. I joined them, having become hungry again.

My master stood with the river pilot at the forecastle, scanning ahead for obstructions.

The voyage was off to a fine start. Despite the delays, we were under way at last. What adventures awaited us, what perils? When Cristóvão Colom and his three ships first crossed the Ocean Sea twenty-eight years ago, it was a feat worthy of a magnificent admiral. For us, it was to be but the first leg. Our next leg, the Great South Sea, was an unknown, first glimpsed seven years ago by Núñez de Balboa who saw it from Darien, that vast sea on the other side of Tierra Firme and Nueva España. In ancient times the white man said of the Pillars of Herakles: *non plus ultra*. Nothing lies beyond. Was that true of the Great South Sea as well? Or was the Sea of Tethys, as it was still called in the mappamundo, the path to a nether world?

No one knew if passage was possible to that ocean on the other side. What secret knowledge did my master possess? He had spoken of a Strait of Anian connecting the two oceans, and the young King had believed it all. The beardless Hapsburg boy, whose lower lip drooled and whose castellano was so halting I wanted to finish his sentences for him, elevated Dom Fernão to knighthood, named him Captain-General, and gave him a fleet. My master had staked his all, gambling that the fabled paso indeed existed. Dom Fernão had a lot of guts. Don Cárlos Primero himself had, to use a Spanish word he did know, cojones. Between them they had given a whole fleet heart and soul.

Now the first Armada de Maluco was setting out for undiscovered bournes. What fates awaited us, who among us to attain glory and honor, who never to return?

In this, I stood apart from all the rest. For me, it remained only to come full circle and complete the trip begun eight years before. This would be the last leg.

It was miercules, x días de agosto, MCCCCCXJX ãs. A very fine day. This is it, I told myself. Take the long way home.

3

SAN LÚCAR DE BARRAMEDA at the mouth of the Guadalquivir was our first stop. A small town, it was not without strategic value, for it guarded the estuary of the Guadalquivir, gateway to Sevilla and Córdova. On a promontory commanding the entrance stood the castle of the Duke of Medina Siodina. The town had grown behind it, and the castle seemed to lend the town an air of grandness.

We anchored hard by the Duke's castle, so near to salt water yet so far. What I had hoped would be a quick stop, four or five days, certainly no more than a week, now became an interminable delay. The fleet was nowhere near ready to go. Preparations were only half complete. For all the grandness of its manner, our departure from Sevilla had been but a dress rehearsal. With so much to be done, would we get out to sea while the season lasted? Or would we have to reach the Great South Sea in the dead of winter? I no longer felt the same excitement, the same sense of anticipation. It would all be anticlimax now.

The tenth of August was the date yo el rey had set. He had set other dates, five or six earlier ones, and those deadlines had all come and gone. This time he had put his foot down and peremptorily ordered the Captain-General to sail by August 10, ready or not. His Most Serene Highness, hooded Maltese falcon on his wrist, meant it. He had recently been elected Holy Roman Emperor after an arduous campaign and much subtle maneuvering, not to mention straightforward bribery. The title had supposedly cost him a million ducats. Not formally Emperor until he could go to Rome for his coronation he had already, with Pope Leo X's permission, begun using the style and the titles. Still called Don Carlos Primero, Rei de Yspaña, he was now concurrently Carolus Quint, Imperator Cæsar Romanorum. The more obsequious of his courtiers, Bishop Fonseca especially, made it a point to address him cringingly as Cæsar Augustus Romanorum.

We sailed unready then, booming broadsides at Sevilla, more for show than for anything else. How they love show, these white men.

The Captain-General himself had been eager to go. He would complete the outfitting in San Lúcar, at a distance from the Casa de Contratación. When the Casa under Fonseca outfitted Cristóvão Colom's ships for the second and third voyages, it took them only about two months each time. For our Armada, still under Fonseca, they could not do anything right. The date of our departure kept being pushed back again and again, from December to March to May to July...

The Captain-General remained philosophical about it all. He knew the Casa's officials had never been more inept. He also suspected all of it was in fact a masterful act of sabotage by the Portuguese consul in Sevilla. The Casa, I once heard him mutter to Dom Diogo, was corrupt from top to bottom. "Before I went to sea," I heard him tell his father-in-law, "I worked for seven years as a clerk at the port of Lisbõa. I know how bureaucracies like this conduct business."

The consul, Dom Sebastião de Alvares, was openly contemptuous of our old, secondhand ships. "Personally," he was reported to have said, "I would not sail in them even as far as the Ilhas da Canarhas. Their ribs are as soft as butter."

My master assumed that Dom Sebastião was bribing officials in the Casa to do what they wanted to do anyway. Money meant for the Armada's supplies and food was being diverted into deep pockets. Dom Sebastião of course had to be acting under orders from Dom Manoel himself. Dom Manoel, Rei do Portuguall, hated Dom Fernão's guts.

"It goes back to the days when we were schoolchildren in Reina Leonora's court," Dom Fernão told Dom Diogo one evening in the Alcázar. "Manoel's long hairy arms reached down almost to his knees, like an ape's. He looked like a buffoon. Manoel was Donha Leonora's brother. He was a bit older than us. He wasn't part of our circle. We were close to Jorge, the Infante

Dom Jorge. Younger brother of the Infante Dom Affonso."

"Bastard brother, you mean," Dom Diogo said. "And Affonso was the Crown Prince."

"Yes. Jorge was a bastard son of Dom João II. Affonso was the heir apparent."

"And then Affonso was killed?"

"Hunting accident, or so they said. He was only sixteen."

"So Jorge was named Dom João's successor?"

"He was. Jorge was only eleven. Manoel was about twenty-three, and was Grand Master of the Knights of Christ. The King thought his successor should have more titles than his brother-in-law, so Jorge was made Duke of Coimbra, Master of the Knights of Santiago, and Master of the Knights of Avis. But when Dom João died three years later, Donha Leonora convinced everyone they could not have a bastard as King. Certainly not another woman's son. She managed to put her brother Manoel on the throne."

"And so he is called 'The Fortunate'."

"He should be called 'Manoel the Vindictive'. Meanwhile, he is King, and he's never forgiven me for those pranks we used to play on him. He won't forget we were in Jorge's inner circle, my brother Diogo and I."

"*Allors*. I know how Manoel harbors animosities. It's one reason I left Portucale. The main reason was of course to marry an andaluz lady of the Caldeira family."

"And mine was to marry a lady of the Barbosa family."

"My son, I know you would be the last to underestimate Dom Manoel's spleen. But be on guard. I fear he will send a patrol of three or four caravels just to lie in wait for you in the Mar Oceano. Beyond the Islas Canarias, I would guess."

"Ah, but I'm certain of it. That's exactly what he would do."

Our short stay in San Lúcar had now been extended to forty days. Everyone came down from Sevilla to see us off: wives, mothers, sweethearts, sisters, with their retinues of servants, footmen and maids; Sevilla's men-about-town; the more presentable of Sevilla's waterfront whores; a band of gitanos from Triana; and of course our financier Cristóbal de Haro with the Bishop's brother Antonio, Lord of Alaejos and Coca; and finally the Bishop of Burgos himself, His Grace Don Juan Rodríguez de Fonseca.

The inns and hostels were all full. The rooms at the monastery were all taken. Those of the noblemen who had cigarrales or summer houses in San Lúcar were accommodating as many houseguests as they could.

The Captain-General was of course the Duke's guest in the castle, as were de Haro, Bishop Fonseca, Lord Coca, the other captains, and some of the sobresalientes. The Duke of Medina Siodina, Don Felipe Pérez de Guzmán el bueno, was the third holder of the title. It was a fairly new duchy, granted only in MCCCCXLIIIJ. The duquesa, Doña Ysolda, loved to entertain. With so many guests, merrymaking went on every day at the castle.

They made merry, too, at the cigarrales. Many of the nobles invited their friends from the nearby town of Xérès de la Frontera—not from the wrong Xérèz, Jerez de los Caballeros. I never understood the joke.

Our main task was to complete the outfitting of the ships. We procured what we could in San Lúcar itself. The captains and maestres kept rowing back to Sevilla in the batels for more supplies. Each of the five ships had its own batel, or longboat; an officer would man it with a crew of rowers and go upriver on the flood tide. It took two flood tides to reach Sevilla. After a day of business there, they would drift back to San Lúcar. Going downriver was easier, but they always waited for the ebb tide. The five yawls made the round trip several times each. The Captain-General also chartered some riverboats for heavy items, like the additional cannon. And a team of men was sent overland to Cádiz for supplies cheapest there.

Most of the crews were given shore liberty, the Captain-General stipulating only that each man should hear Mass and receive Communion daily at the only church there, the Iglesia de Nuestra Señora la Guía.

I took to wandering the dusty streets. One day Dom Fernão's nephew, Cristóvão Rabelo, went with me. A lad from Oporto, he was a boy of ten the first time I met him, when I arrived in Portugal seven years ago. I was nineteen then, already an adult. Now he was seventeen, and his emerging beard made him seem older, older even than me. He also stood half a head taller. I was twenty-six, but my beardless chin and my Asiatic features kept my age indeterminate.

"Come, Henrique," Cristóvão Rabelo said, "we must drink and be merry."

"Speak not português, por favor," I said, "for in a small town such as this, the walls have ears. Os Mouros estão na costa." I used the Portuguese idiom for "Be on your guard"—"The Moors are on the coast."

"What does it matter?" he asked me. "No one will mistake you for a mozarabe or a gitano."

"It is not that which concerns me. Better they should mistake you for a native of Sevilla. Perhaps a nobleman, seeing that an exotic slave attends you."

"A learned slave, no less. From whom one may learn. A slave who will teach me. San Lucar must have felt like this."

"San Lúcar?"

"Or San Lucas. The patron saint of this town. You know the one I mean, the evangelist. He was also a physician. He first learned medicine from his slave Keptah."

"I am a slave, but I am no healer."

"Your learning is in other things, O esclavo. Tell me about the Treaty of Tordesillas. Which does it favor, Lusitanha or Hespanha?"

"España. Remember, Pope Alexander XI was born Rodrigo Borja. An español."

"What lands does it grant Hespanha?"

"Ah, the spiceries all the way to India east of the Padma, I mean Ganga, River."

"That much?"

"It really depends on where one puts the line of demarcation. First it was at 100 leguas west of the Ilhas do Cabo Verde. The Portugales said this left them no sea room in the Mar Oceano for voyages to Africa and India. So now it is at 370 leguas west of Cabo Verde. The Portingales however still say the measurement should start from the meridian of either La Sal or Bôa Vista. These are the easternmost islands of the Cabo Verdes."

"Where do the Spanish want it?"

"Measured from Santo Antão."

"The westernmost island. I see."

"It's all guesswork. The world is round and should have 360 degrees. But they cannot agree on how many leguas or millias a degree should have."

"And should this voyage be successful, will that permit them to determine how long a degree should be?"

"Inshallah. I mean, por la gracia de Dios."
"Yes, I had forgotten you grew up in a Muslim town."
We had come to a tavern on the waterfront. In the distance could be heard the murmur of the sea.
"Cerveja," I ordered.
"No, no," countermanded Cristóvão Rabelo, "we must try the specialty of the region. Manzanilla!"
Pewter cups were filled from a cask, using a dipper, and placed before us. A pale gold wine, it had a delicate bouquet. I took a sip. Very fine and dry. I swallowed. It went down more as an essence than a liquid. It had seemingly not even touched the sides of my throat. How could so grubby a town produce so fine a wine?
It had no effect on me. I could not possibly get drunk on something so ethereal. We ordered another round, and then another. They served small dishes to go with the wine: goat cheese, olives and raisins, a chorizo, a bit of jamón serrano, some bread.
A roving band entered and occupied the patio: two men with guitar and violin, an old woman with a drum, a young woman with castanets and tambourine, a boy with a dulcimer.
"Gitanos," Cristóvão Rabelo said. "Egyptians."
"Are they from Egipto, then?"
"Who knows? From somewhere in the East, obviously. Egypt is as good a guess as any."
The five struck up a lively tune.
"Flamenco!" Cristóvão Rabelo said, snapping his fingers and swaying his shoulders.
"Flemish?" I asked. "Why is their music Flemish? Didn't you say they're Egyptians?"
"It swaggers," he said.
I knew what he meant. I had seen those Flemings the King had brought over from Ghent, his birthplace, and they always acted like they owned España.
The band did a second tune, a slow, sad song this time. The girl sang:

> *Na janav ko dad mro has,*
> *niko mallen mange has;*
> *Miro gule dai merdyas,*
> *pirani man pregelyas.*

> *Uva tu, o hegedive,*
> *tut sal minding pash mange...*

And so on. A wistful song with many verses. Their language, I had heard, was called Romany. Some said it was an old form of pidgin Latin. But to my ear it sounded like...Prakrit. Or maybe even a corrupt Sanskrit.

I wondered how many centuries out of India these gitanos were. They must have belonged to the lowest caste, that of the Panchamas or untouchables. They would never have been tied down to any land, not even in India. They were nomads, as we all must once have been. They were not exiles in the sense that I, longing to return to the land of my fathers, was an exile. They had no land to return to.

I slumped in my seat and laid my head on the table, in the crook of my elbow. I felt maudlin. Perhaps enough of this manzanilla could get me drunk. A rustle of long skirts and, when I looked up, the gypsy girl was sitting down to join us, together with another girl, a blue-eyed blonde.

"What was that you were singing?" Cristóvão Rabelo asked.

"One of the old songs," she said.

"Un cante jondo," the blonde said.

I had thought it sounded like a raga, a bhairavi, but I said nothing.

"It sounded like a fado to me," Cristóvão Rabelo said, "but I couldn't understand it. What was it about?"

Softly, the gypsy sang a translation:

> *I have never known my father,*
> *and I have no friends;*
> *My mother is long dead,*
> *and my loved one departed angry*
>
> *You only, oh my violin,*
> *accompany me in the world...*

Another draught of manzanilla. Both girls drank, too.

"You must be from the North," Cristóvão Rabelo said to the blonde.

"Yes," she said, "I'm from Asturias."

"He is from the Islas del Ponente?" asked the gypsy, indicating me. "From the West Indies?"

"Oh, him. He was brought over as a babe in swaddling clothes by Cristóvão Colom. On the fifth voyage."

"Cristóbal Colón made only four voyages," the blonde said, "and your accent is that of a gallego. I thought you said you were a sevillano?"

"I grew up in Porto."

"A Lusitanian! You are of the enemy!"

"I am with the Armada."

"Ah, a marinero. A sobresaliente?"

"Este, un paje de escober."

"A page of the broom? Señor, surely you jest. Pages do not wear fine raiment or sit in taverns drinking manzanilla."

"This one does," I said. "He's a nephew of el comendador."

"Oh, he speaks Spanish!" said the gypsy, who herself was now speaking the lengua calo. "Ask him to say something in his native tongue."

"Puslan man nga wa'ay nagmahal," I said, "alak pa, 'day!"

They all laughed. Cristóvão Rabelo raised his mug.

"Que no beber, que le corten la cabeza!"

We drank to that.

"At least your toast was in good Spanish," said the blonde, "not in that argot of yours. Well, I drank my wine, so don't you cut off my head!"

I proposed another toast. "To a good voyage," I said. I thrust my fist towards Cristóvão Rabelo, as if to strike him, then knocked my mug back to swallow my wine in one gulp.

"Que barbaridad," said the gypsy girl.

"That's how my people drink," I said.

"Ah, yes, in the West Indies."

"No. I'm from Melaka. In the Orient."

"Isn't that the place Albuquerque captured?" asked the blonde. "How far away is that?"

"Very far. Farther east than India. Southeast of Kithai."

"Is it in the mappamundo?"

"No."

"Then it doesn't exist."

"It doesn't. I'm from a land found only in dreams."

"Maybe you mean nightmares," the blonde said. "Is yours

the land where the Cynocephali are found? Or the Sciopodes?"

"I don't think so. What are those?"

"Those are monsters, Henrique," Cristóvão Rabelo said, "that a bishop of Sevilla wrote about. Bishop Isidoro, I think it was. He wrote his book some nine hundred years ago."

"A Cynocephalos," the blonde girl said, "is a man with the head of a dog. A Sciopode, on the other hand, is an ogre who has only one foot, a very big foot. In the summer he lies down holding up his foot, so he can stay in its shade."

"Oh, we use parasols in my land. White parasols are special. Only the royals may use white parasols. It's the only way to tell them apart from the commoners."

"Is the dragon found in your land?" the gypsy asked.

"Yes. We call it the bakunawa but I've never seen one. I've seen the moon being swallowed by it, though. Once. We made much noise with our drums and gongs. We danced and prayed. And that made the bakunawa spit the moon out."

"Is not the dragon found also in the River Nilus, in Egypt?" asked the gypsy. "We call it the makara. You know, the krokodilus."

"El largato," the blonde said. "El largato de Indias."

"That's the bu-aja," I said. "I've seen a man eaten by one. I've also seen a man being eaten by a serpent. It coiled itself around him, squeezed him to death. Then it swallowed him whole."

"¡Que horrible!"

"Do you have the unicorn?" asked the blonde.

"No. We have the elephant."

"Yes, the beasts Hannibal used. What about the rukh?"

"What is that?"

"A bird. So big that its egg is taller than a man."

"We have a bird that lays a big egg, not that big, but bigger than a goose egg. This bird lays its egg in the sand, then covers it until a mound is formed. We call it the tabon."

Cristóvão Rabelo was no longer listening. He leaned over and murmured in the blonde girl's ear.

"Do you miss home?" the gypsy girl asked me.

"Yes," I said. "And raw fish. Meals eaten with sago. The sound of cicadas. The splash of girls bathing in the river."

"You have become like the white man. You like to look at the breasts of women bathing."

"Well, in my land the women show their breasts. It is not something to hide."

"Yes, I know. Among the Rom, among us, it is not something to hide, either. But these white people! They think it is something shameful."

Cristóvão Rabelo had gotten to his feet, and the blonde was going with him. I stood up, and the whole room seemed to sway. The gypsy girl steadied me, taking my arm. Why did the place lurch like the deck of a ship? Or a house during an earthquake?

Then we were in a small room, her wild heat near me. I was in a sweat, and the sweetish smell of manzanilla was breaking through my pores. She too was redolent of it, but in a different, female way. She had not bathed for some time. In Europa, of course, frequent bathing was considered unhealthy. Fine ladies in this kingdom, who might glaze their faces with the white of an egg once a week, bathed but once a month, and found that quite sufficient.

Unwashed, sweating fine wine, la gitana was an aromatic, well-ripened cheese. I had become fond of queso, milk that has died and gone to heaven. In Europa they made many varieties, and their cheeses often evoked the skin tones of their women. Like Spanish women, many kinds required aging. Odors too seemed to share an affinity between these two, and so did characters: sometimes bland, sometimes sharp; often fruity, often salty. I panted in the gypsy girl's ear, licked the lobe. "Lami-an ka, 'day?" I whispered, reverting to my native tongue, the only one for love. "Oh, yes," she moaned, "that's so good," or something like that. The words were in Romany or the lengua calo, I wasn't sure which.

"Langit na man dagway ini, 'day," I crooned.

"Uva, tu," she cooed.

A gift of tongues: ours were the tongues of nomads, or of wanderers, exploring, languages barely meeting. And as we groped for common meanings the warmth of her glowing skin was in my nostrils, a bouquet of manzanilla whose heady vapors would transport me to the clouds even as that perfume confounded my rising heathen spirit, finally bringing home to me the true essence of this land, this sunny al-Andalus I was very soon, at last, to leave.

4

ON THE LORD'S DAY, xx dias de septiembre, año de dxjx, after xl days in San Lúcar de Barrameda, we weighed anchor and sailed out with the tide. I have given the date as they write it here, in the Roman or Julian calendar. In Melaka we used the Islamic calendar, with its rotating seasons (owing to its truncated lunar year of 354 days), by which it would now be the 925th year of the Hejira. The Xanglei magnates of Melaka used the Ssu-fen calendar, and they would call this the Han year 4217, or the 150th year of the Ming Dynasty (if it still rules.)

In Melaka too the Jewish moneylender from Kalikati would have, by the calendar of his race, reckoned this as the year 5279. It was in the year 3174, he told me once, that his forebears fled Hierosuloim, Nebuchadnezzar's minions at their heels, and reached faraway Kalikati at one of the mouths of the Ganges, near the Bay of Bengal.

I have not forgotten my own people's calendar. Today would be Ligid-ligid, kaluha-ang adlaw sa buwan nga Kang-gurulsul, tu-ig Saka napúlo'g upát, tuló ka pulò ug siyám (1439). Even so, certain of my elders will have remained loyal to an older system, by which this would be the year Vikrama 1654 of the true calendars.

Would that the heavens confer trueness on all true calendars! The Julian calendar, the one I must perforce observe, is the most untrue I have ever seen. To make matters worse, it uses Roman numerals. Now, to be perfectly honest, I find Roman numbers rather tedious and quite stupid. The current year is written dxjx in abbreviation, omitting the M and substituting a D for five C's. But the slower-witted of the white men count on their fingers, forget the ellipses, and write the cumbersome

MCCCCCXIX. If they abbreviate at all, it might be to MC^{V}XIX. Both forms look pitifully awkward. Neither can be read on sight. Henceforth, I shall confine myself to Arabic numerals.

So then Sunday, the 20th of September, 1519 A.D. After 40 days in San Lúcar, we sailed out with the tide. In the lead was the capitana, or flagship. The *Trinidad* had a burthen of 110 toneladas, meaning she could carry 110 tuns of wine, a tun being a standard wine barrel. She also had the sleekest lines of any ship I had ever seen.

Next was the *San Antonio*, the almiranta and our largest ship at 120 tuns. On either side of her were the *Concepción*, 90 tuns, and the *Victoria*, 85 tuns. Bringing up the rear was the *Santiago*, not a nao like the other four, but a caravel, and of 75-tun burthen.

All five of our ships were small. The Captain-General preferred it that way. In unknown waters, ships of light draft were an advantage. Not surprisingly, many of our men had crewed on bigger ships. The maestre of the *Concepción* for example, Juan Sebastián Elcano, had once been captain of a 400-tun warship. Why was he only a maestre now? The story was that he had captured an enemy ship, but then sold it back to the enemy when the Crown was slow to pay his crew's wages. The case was still pending...

Two of the ships had masculine names, and this bothered me. San Antonio and Santiago were important saints, the latter being the patron saint of the Spanish nation, but ships were essentially female. Would these misnamed ships be unlucky?

Each ship was commanded by a captain. The captain was always an aristocrat, which also meant he was a military man. He was not necessarily a sailor or a navigator. A captain merited a salary of 6,000 maravedis per month for the duration of the voyage. If he was a King's Captain, that 6,000 maravedis would be in addition to his annual salary of perhaps 40,000 mvs.

Next in rank was the pilot, a licensed navigator who drew 3,000 mvs. a month. For a piloto de su alta, or Pilot of His Highness, as most of our pilots were, that monthly emolument was on top of his annual salary of 10,000 mvs. a year. The pilot had custody of the astrolabe, the quadrants, the cross-staff, the charts, maps and declination tables, and the ampolletas. The last were hourglasses or, more exactly, halfhour-glasses: it took thirty minutes for the sands from the upper glass to fall into the lower glass. We had eighteen ampolletas on the *Trinidad*. The other ships had at least a dozen each.

After the pilot was the maestre, whose salary was 3,000 mvs. a month. He was in charge of the cargo and oversaw all commercial details. In foreign ports, all the trading, all the buying, selling and bartering were under his supervision.

The contramaestre, who received 2,000 mvs. a month, was in charge of his crew, meaning the marineros and grumetes. Each ship had ten or twelve marineros or experienced seamen, and six or eight grumetes or apprentice sailors. A marinero was paid 1,200 mvs. a month; a grumete, 800. The contramaestre ate with his men, the only officer who did not dine at the captain's table.

Each vessel also had several petty officers: a doctor, an escribano or notary, a barber, a tonelero or cooper, a carpenter who doubled as boatwright, a calafate or caulker, a despensero or steward, an alguacil, and if possible, a chaplain.

On the *Trinidad* the cirujano or surgeon, Juan de Morales, was called el bachiller because of the degree he had earned at the Universidad de Salamanca. He was the only one who was not paid by the month. Men of his profession drew yearly salaries, and his was 25,000 maravedis.

The escribano, who was always an educated man, received 3,000 mvs. a month.

The barber was paid 1,200 mvs. a month, the same wages that accrued to the tonelero, the carpenter, the despensero and the calafate. The tonelero looked after the barrels in which we stored our wine, water and most of our food. He had staves of wood, already cut to fit, and metal hoops with which to fashion new barrels as the need arose. He also led the pumping crew which pumped out the bilges thrice a day. The despensero served the meals and waited on the captain's table. The calafate caulked the hulls when the ship was beached and patched leaks sprung when the ship was at sea.

A chaplain was entitled to 1,500 mvs. per month. We had only two, one each on the *Trinidad* and the *San Antonio*, but expected to pick up a third in Teneriphe.

The bombarderos were experts on cannon, artillery and ordnance. This was a pristine science not yet known in España.

Spanish men, whether hidalgos or commoners, preferred weapons of steel; gunpowder was considered less than honorable. All the Armada's fifteen bombarderos, three to a ship, were foreigners, mercenaries not burdened with the Spanish concept of pundonor or punto de honor.

The bombarderos were paid in gold. This took the form of Venetian ducats, a ducat being officially worth 300 maravedis, although everyone knew it fetched 375 mvs. on the black market. Master Andrew of Bristol, as condestable, was paid 5 ducats a month. The other 14 were each paid 4 ducats per month.

The alguacil or provost-marshall, who rated 1,800 mvs. a month, had a team of merinos under him. A merino was paid 800 mvs. a month. They functioned as military police and could double as assault squads.

The sobresalientes were gentlemen-adventurers, voluntary observers who shipped as supernumeraries. Only noblemen could be signed on as sobresalientes. Some were captains or pilots who came too late to secure places as active crew members. A few were knights of some order or other. Sobresalientes had no routine duties but were available as fighting men should the captain require their services.

The sobresalientes had token allowances of 1,000 mvs. a month each. Most of them were gentlemen with private incomes who did not require salaries.

There were a total of twenty sobresalientes in the Armada. The eight on the flagship included a brother-in-law of Dom Fernão's, Duarte Barbosa, and a cousin, Álvaro de la Mesquita. There were a pair of idealistic young men from Sevilla, Juan Miñez and Diego Sánchez Barrasa. There was the Angevin, or Frenchman, Petit-Jean d'Anjou, whose name was a joke. He was the biggest man in the Armada, head and shoulders above most of us, with the bulk of a bull. He was rumored to be a secret Knight Templar but he denied it, saying the Order had been disbanded by the Pope in 1312 or something.

There was also the Italian, Antonio Lombardo, or Ser Antonio Francesco Pigafetta from Lombardy, Patrician of Vicenza and Knight of Rhodes. Ser Antonio had fair brown hair and blue eyes, rather like a German, but his speech and gestures were wholly Italianate. He had been in Barcelona as a member of the suite of the Papal ambassador to Don Cárlos Primero.

Hearing about the Armada de Maluco, he wangled permission from both his superior and Don Cárlos himself to join it, and arrived in Sevilla three months before we departed. Not only was the voyage to be a great adventure, it would affect the spice trade itself. For centuries Venezia had been Europa's great entrepôt for the trade; Lisbõa had stolen some of her thunder after the passage to India had been found. Now Spain too might open a new route for the trade. Pigafetta, it seemed clear, would be submitting a report to the Doge of Venice on how the voyage would affect the spice trade.

The pajes de escober or pages of the broom were lads of good family who could expect promotion to high rank in due time. They reversed the ampolletas at the exact moment the last grain of sand left the upper glass. They sang the ditties and led the prayers. Since they were boys who had been to school (grumetes and marineros were usually illiterate), the pages were often asked by the pilot or escribano for assistance. There were four of them on the capitana, at salaries of 600 mvs. a month. Cristóvão Rabelo was the exception: Dom Fernão had somehow gotten the Casa to authorize a salary of 1,200 mvs. for him.

Last and quite least were the criados and the esclavos, the servants and the slaves, who had salaries of 600 mvs. a month. The Captain-General had four personal servants, two of whom were slaves. Captain Juan de Cartagena, however, had ten personal servants on the *San Antonio*. He was nothing if not foppish. The two other Spanish captains were almost as bad. Captain Gaspar de Quesada of the *Concepción* and Captain Luis de Mendoça of the *Victoria* had four servants each, as many as the Captain-General had, although their ships were smaller. By contrast, Captain João Serrão had only one slave aboard the *Santiago*. The names of both Mendoça and Serrão had been respelled in modern Castillian in the rosters: Mendoza and Serrano.

Captain Serrano was the elder brother of Captain Francisco Serrão, with whom Dom Fernão and I had briefly lived in Melaka in 1511. As far as was known, Francisco was still the Grand Vizier of Terrenate. This was an important consideration. The Portuguese had reached the Moluccas first, but Spain wanted them, too. Each claimed that the Hespeciarías lay in its half of the world, as demarcated in the Treaty of Tordesillas.

Of the four slaves in the Armada, I was the only brown man. The other three were blacks. Dom Fernão's second slave was Jorge el moro, who had once belonged to the Sheik of Azamor. We picked him up after defeating the Sheik in the Marruecos in 1514.

Our alguacil, Don Gonzálo Gómez de Espinosa, also had a Morrocan slave, purchased on the slave market. This man, Antón de color negro or Antón moreno, was enrolled as a grumete on the Trinidad.

Captain Juan Serrano's slave came from the other side of Africa. Serrano had acquired him there while in the service of the Portuguese King. The man was named after his current master and called João of Moçambique.

Being brown or black both meant the same thing: being not white. No one took Slavs as esclavos anymore, because Slavs were white, too; the lot of slavery was now reserved for black men or brown. I was the Captain-General's personal slave, acquired as booty in the conquest of Malacca in 1511. I was a baptized Christian. I spoke the Iberian languages well. On the crew roster I was listed as a lengua or interpreter, at a salary of 1,500 maravedis per month, as high as a petty officer's. It showed how highly my master esteemed me. My salary was higher than the barber's or the carpenter's, and almost as high as the alguacil's. The majority of my shipmates on the *Trinidad* ranked below me in the order of our salaries. Having lived two years in Sevilla, I well knew the value of the maravedi. A simple but adequate meal could be had for 3 or 4 mvs., including a cup of wine. A knight could hire the services of a squire for 26 mvs. a day and found; a young man seeking employment as a clerk in a notary's office commanded similar wages. A bushel of wheat cost 73 mvs.

In Sevilla all of us received, upon signing up, an advance of four months' salary. With this each man bought new clothes and personal supplies, paid off debts, or provided for his family. I spent most of mine on whores, the best and most expensive I could find. I always chose a white woman, a Circassian if available. The white woman, I had learned fairly early in my sojourn, always gave me my money's worth.

The capitana or flagship, the *Trinidad*, had Dom Fernão as its captain and the Captain-General of the Armada. His salary of 8,000 maravedis per month was in addition to the annual salary of 50,000 maravedis he had begun drawing when Don Cárlos Primero first appointed him a King's Captain late in 1517. It thus came up to 146,000 mvs. a year, a princely sum measly only in comparison to the dowry Beatriz de Barbosa y Caldeira had brought to their marriage: 600,000 mvs.

The second ship, the *San Antonio*, was the almiranta, although the Armada had no admiral. It was a bit confusing; the Spanish words were too repetitive. The Malay word for captain-general was laksamana but Malay usage was more exact: a fleet acquired a laksamana only when sailing to war.

All five of the ships mounted a proud array of cannon. The *Trinidad*'s broadside artillery consisted of twenty bombards, nine on the port side, nine on the starboard, and two astern. She had one extra-heavy bombard, as did the *San Antonio* and the *Concepción*. These three also had one pasamuro each, deck-mounted, as well as twelve culverin and six falconetas. The falconetas were mounted on gimbals and could be swiveled around.

The *Victoria* and the *Santiago* had bombards for their broadsides and demi-culverin for their decks. They also had sakers and minions.

Each ship's batel had two serpentinas.

The *Trinidad* carried a dismantled bergantym, or bergantina in Spanish, in her hold. This could be assembled for shallow-draft sailing when needed. She had no masts; she could be used only where trees could be cut down and shaped into masts. The bergantym was equipped with four serpentinas.

The Armada had fourteen bombarderos to supervise the operation of the cannon. Their condestable was English. Six of them were French or Breton and the other seven German or Flemish.

Master Andrew of Bristol loved to talk about the cannon, and so did his two bombarderos on the *Trinidad*, Juan Bautista de Mompeller and Guillermo Tañegui of Lila de Groya. They always found a ready audience among us. These weapons were new. Many of us had never seen cannon up close and we would probably have to help fire them. It was our duty to memorize the ammunition for each type. The extra-heavy fired an iron ball of 50 pounds which had a bore of 7¼ inches. The 20 bombards each took a 32-lb. iron ball with a bore of 6¼ inches, loaded at the muzzle. The culverin fired a 17-lb. stone ball of 5¼-inch bore; the pasamuro, a 2-lb. ball of 2-inch bore. The serpentina used a ball with a bore of 1½ inches, which meant it could be loaded with scrap iron or ordinary stones if it came to that.

In case of transfers to other ships, it was necessary to memorize the ammunition requirements of the other types. The demi-culverin used a 9-lb. ball of 4¼-inch bore. The roqueira, a 5-lb. ball of 4-inch bore. The falconeta, a 3-lb. ball of 2½-inch bore. The minion had a bore of only ¾ of an inch, for which pebbles would do.

Master Andrew needed only the slightest excuse to get into a discussion of elevation and range. "Balls," he would say, "it's all ballistics." He could not wait to test-fire the extra-heavy bombard. "And 'twill require a correction for sure," he said, "to compensate for the earth's curvature, what?"

Arcane concerns like that left the rest of us cold. We were more attuned to close combat. Many of us had had some experience of hand-to-hand fighting and it was what we looked forward to. For that we could draw on the Armada's supply of heavy armor.b We had in stock a hundred steel plastrons, or corselets. These came with armlets, shoulder plates, moriones or pikeman's helmets, and pavises or heavy wooden shields. These were for men going in landing parties.

For sailors at the rigging or at the oars there were 100 cuirasses, or breast plates with shoulder pieces. Each also came with a pavis.

The arms included 60 windlass crossbows with 360 quivers, each quiver holding a dozen arrows. We had 1,000 lances, 95 dozen darts, and 120 javelins. There were six boarding pikes. There were also 200 Swiss pikes and 200 halberds.

All of the noblemen had their own swords. Every single man had his own knife. The vizcaíno ironsmiths had also given us good copies of the new weapon the Mamluk Turks were now using, the matchlock harquebus. We had fifty of these, each with its wooden crutch. This weapon was so heavy it had to be supported by the crutch while aiming and firing. The gunner carried a length of fuse rope with him, perhaps a yard long, slowly burning at one end. He fired the harquebus by touching the smoldering end of his rope to the breech pan and igniting the gunpowder. It seemed a clumsy system, and many of the crew said so. Some of the merinos explained that each gunner was supposed to pair off with a crossbowman. The archer would cover him while the harquebus was being reloaded.

As for the Captain-General, in addition to his old coat of mail, he had two new suits of armor from Bilbao. And six spare Toledo steel blades for his sword. All six blades had been cast from the same mold, with their final quenchings as he had specified: two in oil for flexibility, two in water for strength, and two in both oil and water.

He wore an amulet, a scallop half-shell picked up on a beach near Santiago de Compostela. He had made the pilgrimage there in his youth. He firmly believed the shell had snatched him from the jaws of death at Diu in 1509. He also regarded as an amulet the gold ring he never took off his finger. As yet untested in battle, its power could not be in doubt. It had been given to him by Beatriz. Etched on its inner surface were the words *No tengo más qve darte*— "I have nothing more to give thee."

5

"*¡ENMARA EN POCO LA CEBADERA!*" bellowed the contra-maestre. Marineros moved to give the spritsail a little sheet. Spanish nautical tradition had evolved commands with unique verbs and nouns for each action, so there never was any possibility of confusion, not even when these commands were bawled out amidst the howling of storm winds. It never ceased to amaze me. The language was richer than I might have thought at first.

"*¡Alzá aquel briol!*" Heave on that buntline!

"*¡Desencapillá la mesana!*" Unbend the mizzen!

The sail unfurled by the mizzenmast, and I felt the ship pick up speed.

"*¡Amarrá aquellas burdas!*" Belay those backstays!

There remained only the mainsail.

"*¡Levá el papahigo!*"

The square mainsail, made of canvas, bore the gaudily colored eagle from the Hapsburg arms. The foresail and spritsail, also square, bore the cross of Santiago, as did the lateen mizzensail.

The royal standard of Spain, the same flag the Bishop had given to the Captain-General at the farewell Mass, flew from the mainmast, topping the gavia, which Master Andrew called the crow's nest. It bore the arms, in red and gold quarterings, of León and Castilla.

The ship's flag, with the symbol of the Holy Trinity, was on the foremast.

The Captain-General's coat of arms flew on four banners, one from each capstan. His three checkered bars of red and silver were quartered with the quinas from the Portuguese royal arms.

Dom Fernão's arms did not originally have the quinas. He traced his ancestry to a Burgundian knight who had helped Duke Eudes wrest Minho Province from the Moors some five centuries before. That knight's arms showed, on a field argent, three bars chequy, gules and argent; crest, an eagle with spread wings. Three generations ago the family became allied by marriage to the royal family, allowing them to add the distinctive feature of the royal blazon to theirs. This was the quinas, the motif of five bezants symbolizing the five wounds of the Christ. Three of the bezants were arranged in a horizontal row, with one bezant above and one below, so that all five also formed a cross.

"He's showing his true colors," I could imagine the natives of Sevilla muttering, and perhaps some of our Spanish officers, too. "Spanish armada or not, el comendador is still very much the loyal português."

Red and silver checkered bars, quartered with the quinas: really an ordinary, quite unremarkable coat of arms. But not in Spain. There it was a cognizance of peril. There it could ignite the passions of insane men. And, as we discovered last year in Sevilla, such men would rise to it with naked madness and naked swords.

It happened one morning in Triana when the flagship had to be hauled ashore because of a coming ebbtide. Nautical etiquette required a King's ship to fly the royal ensign but the King's flag and the ship's flag were still with the Casa's tailors for repainting and the Captain-General could not wait for them. He had hired forty additional men to help drag the ship in and had set the job for the lowest level of the ebbtide, which would be at dawn, at the fourth hour of that day, xxii de octobre, año de MCCCCCXVIIJ. The marineros had flown only the Captain-General's flags from all four of the capstans, leaving the masts without their prescribed flags. Sevilla being a town that never sleeps, we were not surprised to find a crowd gathered to watch the shipdragging. Suddenly someone saw that the Trinidad flew nothing of Spain, but displayed the quinas of the Portuguese King. The whisper went 'round the crowd: the Captain-General planned to hand the ship over to the Portuguese! An alcalde del mar, a man named de Alcázar, shouted: "Take down those flags and destroy them!"

Dom Fernão dropped his rope and approached the man.

"Señor Alcalde, I will have you know that those flags are not the King of Portugal's, but my own. I am the vassal of His Royal Highness Don Carlos, and Captain-General of this royal Armada. Now, if you will excuse me, Señor, I must go about my duties."

The alcalde, however, called for men to help him take the flags down. At that moment a priest who sat on the Casa's board, Dr. Sancho de Matienzo, Abbot of Jamaica and Canon of Sevilla, emerged from the Cathedral. He asked the alcalde to desist. He then went to Dom Fernão. They knew each other well enough; the priest was Dom Fernão's confessor.

"Don Fernando," he said, "it is all very stupid, I know, but I think it would be better if you took those flags down yourself."

"Dr. Matienzo, I apologize for all this trouble but I simply cannot do that. It would be an affront to me as Captain-General of this Armada. At this very moment, there is a gentleman of the King of Portugal watching us from somewhere in that crowd. His orders are to persuade me to return to Portugal, or otherwise to frustrate this undertaking in any way he can. It would place me at a great disadvantage were he to see this affront done to me."

The marineros, without waiting for an order, had prudently pulled down the flags. Leaving a ship bare of flags was against all nautical tradition, but Dom Fernão, acknowledging the fait accompli, shrugged. Then the alcalde returned, bringing in tow the lieutenant of the admiral, the lieutenant of the admiral's assistant, and the alcalde mayor of the Duke of Medina Siodina, all flanked by their alguaciles. The alcalde del mar called out:

"Seize the Portuguese captain who flies the flag of the Portuguese King!"

He came face to face with Dom Fernão.

"Where are those flags? Why have you hauled them from your capstans? I shall have you arrested for lèse majesté!"

Dom Fernão glared at him.

"I don't have to explain anything to you," he said.

The alcalde del mar grabbed Dom Fernão's shirtfront with both hands.

"Seize him!" he yelled to the alguaciles. "And all his men! Seize them all!"

Canon Matienzo gently detached the alcalde's hands from the Captain-General's ruffles.

"Do not do this, I beg of you, alcalde," the priest said. "On behalf of His Majesty, I order you to refrain from any action so contrary to the service of His Highness."

"Who are you to order me?"

With that, the alcalde and his men pounced on Canon Matienzo, some of them pulling out their swords and thrusting the points at the Canon's beard. The mob moved in.

Dom Fernão raised his voice.

"I call on all here present to formally witness that this official"—he pointed to the alcalde del mar—"is now responsible for His Majesty's warship, and may answer for it to the King himself. We have an inrushing tide, the hatches are open, and in a few minutes the ship will be swamped and should capsize."

He pivoted on his heel and walked away.

The alcalde del mar's shoulders suddenly slumped. He abjectly turned to Canon Marienzo and begged him to run after the Captain-General. That the good Canon did. Dom Fernão calmly returned, boomed a few crisp orders. We managed to pull the ship ashore in the nick of time.

Later, we found that an alguacil had stabbed the pilot Basco Gallego in the arm.

Dom Fernão wrote to the King immediately, dating his letter xxiv de octobre. He treated the incident as a huge joke. He did not mind the affront done to him personally, but protested the indignity visited on a King's Captain.

In a letter dated vi de novembre, the King acknowledged receipt of the Captain-General's letter. "Yo el rey" informed Dom Fernão he had directed the Corregidor of Sevilla, Bishop Martínez de Leyva, to investigate the matter and impose disciplinary action on those culpable, and that he had also expressed gratitude to Canon Marienzo for the latter's intercession. The letter from the King looked impressive, but I wondered how long it would take the investigation to die a natural death.

If his coat of arms was staunchly Portuguese, his name was the kind that easily turned Spanish at the border. It required but the slightest of changes: he spelled it now without the tilde.

The tilde, or wavemark, over a vowel meant that vowel carried a hidden *n* sound. This was a vestige of the old Latin endings

-anem, -onem and -anum. Thus, according to the classicists, Fernão was properly pronounced "Fernanum." My untrained ear, however, never picked up anything but "Fernan."

The Portuguese tongue was also wont to invest the letter *m* with the *n* sound. What was San Miguel in Spanish was in Portuguese either São Miguel or Sam Miguel; in all three spellings the pronunciation was identical. By the same token, the Portuguese honorific Dom was pronounced exactly like the Spanish Don. Dom Fernão became Don Fernando in Spanish, but it wasn't that simple. The Spanish tongue had the strange tendency to change an initial *f* into *h*. My master became Don Hernando as well, except that the *h* was invariably a silent letter.

Not even a silent letter could be forgotten too easily. In speaking Spanish I had to remain alert and avoid Portuguese words like fado, falar, filho, ferir, forca or fel. In their places I had to say hado, hablar, hijo, herir, horca and hiel. And this was not all. For the Portuguese cheio, chama, choro or chave I had to remember to say lleno, llama, lloro and llave. Then there were intervocalic *l*'s the Portuguese had dropped, such as those in the words voar, so, or moinho. I had to put the letter *l* back in and say volar, sol and molino.

My master's family name had to be respelled because of its Portuguese letters that did not function the same way in Spanish. The *h* had the value of *y* or *i* but of course in Spanish it became a silent letter. The *s* was often given the *sh* value, a rare sound in castellano. A nation of lispers, the Spanish made much of the *th* sound instead. Dom Fernão's surname, de Magalhães, pronounced de Magalyáensh, became de Magalhaens or de Magallayns or de Magallanes, depending on which scribe wrote it. Educated men had their own favorite ways of spelling things; there were no hard and fast rules. Sometimes an escribano spelled the same word two different ways on the same piece of paper.

The Italians in the crew knew the capitanio-generalle as Ferando de Magaglianes. To the Sicilians, he was Ferrante di Magaglianni.

The French gunners called him Fernánd de Magallanche, fair enough a rendering, retaining the same number of syllables.

To the alemán gunners, for whom everyone south of the Teutoburg Wald was Roman or Latin, he was Ferdin de Magellanus.

To the three Irishmen and to Master Andrew of Bristol, he was Ferdinand Magellan, pronounced with a hard *g*. As was typical of the English, Master Andrew corrupted both names very badly. He carelessly dropped the aristocratic *de*. He extended the given name to three syllables, like *fer-de-lance*, giving it a poisonous ring. As for the surname, why, he made him sound like a Java man from the small town of Magelang!

Of the five grades of nobility in Portugal, my master belonged to the fourth and next-to-last. He was a *fidalgo da cota de armas é geração que tem insignias de nobreza*, an armigerous gentleman of the class entitled to the insignia of nobility. As a second son he had inherited only trifles, because of which he went to the Orient at 25 to seek his fortune. In the seven years he spent abroad he fought as a conquistador in East Africa, the Malabar Coast and Malacca. Two years after his return he fought in the Marruecos, sustaining a leg wound that left him walking with a slight limp.

His elder brother, Diogo da Sousa, was given their grandmother's name so as to be able to inherit the da Sousa estates. Sometimes I wondered why my master had not been given his mother's name, de Mesquita. Perhaps he did not care for a name that sounded Moorish.

Of their three sisters, whom I saw only a few times, Tereza was married to Dom João da Sylva Tellez. Ginebra was married to Pedro Cão, a nephew of the Captain Diogo Cam who had commanded pioneering voyages to West Africa south of Cape Bojador. The youngest, Isabel, was unmarried.

Dom Fernão's parents were both deceased. He had been orphaned at 12. His father, Dom Ruy de Magalhães, had once been Alguacil Mayor of the town of Aveiro. His mother, Donha Álda de Mesquita, had taken her name from her mother, not from her father who was a Pimentel. Perhaps the distaff side of her family had been the more prominent.

Dom Fernão's great-grandfather, Dom Gil Annes de Magalhanes, had spelled the name the old way. It was his grandfather, Dom Pero Affonso de Magalhães, who first put in the tilde.

The white man's clumsy mind, the same mind that produced the Roman system of numerals, made him spell words with useless marks. There were all sorts of accents and diacritical marks that I never bothered with. There was also the ridiculous and redundant letter, the cedilla. This was the *c* with the hookmark hanging like a tail from it: ç. It indicated a voiceless *z* in the French, Italian and Portuguese, with the Spanish lisping it into a voiceless *th*. I could not think of a single example where the superfluous cedilla could not be replaced by the *zed*: açúcar, maçapão, açores; even names like Gonçalo or Lourenço or placenames like Moçambique or Luçõa. The cedilla, however, has never lacked for apologists, who stoutly maintain that it is quite indispensable. Look at words like *direcçión* or *civilização*, they always say.

My own favorite example was the name Conceição, with its three *c*'s. Each had a different function. The first had the value of a *k*, the second of an *s*, and the cedilla of a *z*. Then too, as I had seen for myself, girls named Conceição were invariably very pretty. And it seemed that all of them wore three layers of clothing, each with a different function...

For the white man, the letters *x* and *j* were interchangeable. In some regions these letters had the *sh* or *zh* sound, while in others they had the *th* sound. The frontier town of Jerez was the old town of Xérès, and it had always been known for its superb fortified wine. Master Andrew could not pronounce the wine as "vino de zheresh," so he called it sherry. When he had imbibed enough of it and had become quite drunk, it would taste very sweet on his tongue. Then he would call it sack. That was how he pronounced "seco."

Names like Xavier or Ximenes were also spelled Javier or Jimenez. The andaluz pronounced these as "Zhavier" and "Zhimenesh." The castellano, proud of his lisp, said "Have-year" and "Him-e-neth." And João had only to cross the border to become Juan.

The letters *i*, *j* and *y* were interchangeable, as were *u* and *v*. Hispania was Yspaña. Sevilla was Seuilla. Córdova was Córdoua was Córdoba. Antequera was Anteqvera. Iohan was Johan was Juan. Hierónimo was Gerónymo.

I remained the same thing in either language: un esclavo. The Portuguese, however, had a cipher for it. "Clavo" meant "nail," and nails usually had triangular heads, so "esclavo" was represented by the letter *s* and a triangle: S Δ. This cipher would function equally well in Spanish but had not gained currency in that language, the Spaniards being latecomers to the slave trade. It was said that the Portuguese used to brand these symbols on the cheeks of men abducted from the Gurne Coast: the S on one cheek, and the Δ on the other. Fortunately, my master was not given to such vulgarities.

There was an affectation no pious man could avoid, that of using Greek letters for the name of Christ. Ever since Cristóbal Colón signed his royal charter as χροFERENS Colón, every Cristóbal or Cristóvão has had to sign his name as χρο ual, the tilde over the rho signifying the abbreviation of ΧΡΙΣΤΟΣ to χρο.

In the Portuguese, at least, there had been some use for the *h* in my name, making "Henrique" sound like Yenriki. In the Spanish the *h* was a silent letter, one my name did not need. They cut off my beginning, and made me Enrique. Why couldn't they be consistent? Why did many of their words still retain that useless silent letter? Why didn't they drop it altogether?

¿Qve hay?

6

FROM SAN LÚCAR to the Canaries was an idyllic six days. Going out with the noon high tide the new moon brings, we sailed due southwest at a leisurely rate, wind on the quarter, calm cool sea. The Mare Tenebros promised to grow balmier each day in our progress from 37°N latitude to 28°N.

We hummed along at speeds between four and six knots, moderate for ships that could do nine knots when putting on airs, and twelve in a huff. There was no hurry. This was our shakedown cruise in blue water, and learning how to keep the Armada's speed uniform mattered more. Ships had individual idiosyncrasies. Merely following the capitana's course and sail display was not enough. Keeping in formation required constant vigilance, little adjustments here and there, lacing bonnets on to the sails if lagging behind, or removing one or two when the ship's bow began to nudge up under the stern of the leading ship.

On the *Trinidad*, only the marineros taking the helm for an hour at a turn had anything much to do. The sails billowing out, the decks scrubbed, the rest of us had naught but to move a halyard's nip on the block every once in a while to keep it from chafing too much in one place and wearing off.

At night the other four ships followed us by the lantern set in iron cressets on our stern. One farol was normal. If the flagship showed two it meant the fleet was to come about or wear; three was a signal to reduce sail; four, to strike sail.

Any ship that sighted land was to fire a gun.

We were divided into six watches throughout the day, changing at 4:00, 8:00 and 12:00. Each watch had eight ampolletas to reverse. In practice, that meant reversing one ampolleta eight times. These half-hour glasses were fragile and could break anytime the ship lurched. We had eighteen ampolletas and used only one, keeping the rest as spares.

Page boys on the watch had to reverse the ampolleta at the exact moment the last grain of sand left the upper glass. When the page had reversed the eighth ampolleta the watch was in its final half-hour; the watch was over when the sand ran out of the eighth.

There were names for the watches of the night. The first was the noite, or la noche in Spanish, led by the captain or the contramaestre. Under him were the minimum number of men needed to keep the ship on course: a helmsman, lookouts fore and aft, a page to reverse the ampolleta, and a couple of other men on standby, usually with their eye on the bilge pumps lest the vessel start to make water. The positions were rotated every hour.

The second nightwatch, the modorra or la modena, was led by the pilot and began at midnight.

The watch of the alva, or la diane, led by the maestre, was the watch that saw the dawn.

The Captain-General followed the practice, first done by Cristóvão Colom, of dogging the afternoon watch and splitting it into two watches of two hours each. This resulted in men being assigned to the unpopular watch of la modorra only on alternate nights.

As soon as it was light we all had to rise for morning prayers. A page in fine voice always led, standing on the quarterdeck between the chaplain and the Captain-General, who acted as his prompters.

Our youngest page on the *Trinidad*, 16-year-old Andrés de la Cruz, was the best singer. He was from Sevilla, a city where men and women break into spontaneous song during the Semana Santa processions when the statues of the Virgin or the martyred Christ pass by them. Andrés sang with all the fervor of an altar boy at la Catedral, which he had been.

> *Bendita sea la luz, y la Santa Veracruz,*
> *y el Señor de la Verdad, y la Santa Trinidad;*
> *bendita sea el alma, y el Señor que nos la manda;*
> *bendito sea el día, y el Señor que nos lo envía.*

Andrés then led the whole crew through the Pater Noster and the Ave Maria. Then the last prayer:

> *Dios nos dé buenas días; buen viaje; buen pasaje haga*
> *la nao, señor capitán y maester y buena compañia, amén;*
> *así faza buen viaje, faza: muy buenos días dé Dios a*
> *vuestras mercedes, señores de popa y proa.*

After this we broke up and went about our routine duties. The wind brought the murmur of the other ships' crews saying their prayers.

At 7:30 Cristóvão Rabelo, the page on the watch of la diane, reversed his eight ampolleta. He had to sing the traditional ditty for this. The Captain-General looked on and watched him sing:

> *Buena es la que va, mejor es la que viene;*
> *siete es pasada y en ocho muele,*
> *mas molerá si Dios quisiere,*
> *cuenta y pasa, que bien viaje faza.*

The maestre of the *Trinidad*, Juan Bautista de Punzurol, who was the captain of the watch, shuffled his slate and derrotero around and conned his helmsman through the hatch:

"No boteis."

A moment later:

"Governá la sud-oeste."

There was no real need for these orders; the helmsman was keeping steady and steering southwest. They were killing time.

Now the sands of the eighth ampolleta were running out, all eyes on it. Cristóvão Rabelo reversed it at precisely the last second, thereby turning it into the next watch's first ampolleta. Then he sang the chantey for calling on the relieving watch:

> *Al cuarto, al cuarto, señores marineros de buena parte,*
> *al cuarto, al cuarto en bueno hora de la guardia del*
> *señor contramaestre,*
> *que ya es hora; leva, leva, leva.*

The new watch captain, our contramaestre Francisco Albo, asked the course of the outgoing captain and gave that course to his incoming helmsman. Then he logged it on his slate with a piece of chalk: sud-oeste. Later, he would record it in his derrotero.

With the ship in the hands of the day watch, it was time for breakfast. The fare was hardtack, peas and salt pork, all on a trencher. I ate with my fingers, cutting up the meat with my sheath knife. All of us ate this way, each man pulling out his own sheath knife, even the officers at the captain's table. Petit-Jean d'Anjou had a beautiful knife, which he called a couteaux de breche, its handle inlaid with mother-of-pearl and its blade decorated on one side with musical notes and a motto etched into the metal in incuse relief:

ET EN ARCADIA EGO...

which meant "And in Arcadia I..."

An incomplete phrase: it lacked a verb. When I asked him about it he evaded the question and began talking about the different kinds of knives, the couteaux de chasse and the couteaux a trancher...

We drank wine with all meals, breakfast, lunch and dinner, Spanish claret, a decent if unremarkable wine. Dom Fernão had vino de Jerez at his table. Since this was breakfast, it was an oloroso. Following the Andalusian custom, he began the day with sweet sherry, "to cradle the stomach." For lunch he would have a palo cortado, usually an amontillado, and for dinner, a fino. His afterdinner wine was always a ruby or a tawny vintage, from Oporto or from Douro. The despensero would wait until Dom Fernão specified the grape, for these wines were made from four varieties: Sercial, Bual, Verdelho, and Malvasia. All of it was from the 15th century. My master had yet to taste a 16th century vintage, as he never drank port that was less than seventeen years old.

High noon was the time for the pilot's shot of the sun. Piloto de su alta Estêvão Gomes stood on the poop deck and braced his astrolabe between his knees. Since the ship was heading southwest, he turned a bit to his left until he faced exactly south. He adjusted the alidade, or pointer bar, until the shadow cast by its upper button aligned with its lower button. He did not sight through the dioptra or the pinholes of the buttons; those pinholes were for shots of stars only. He noted the number indicated on the upper half of the circular scale: that was the sun's meridional altitude. He put the astrolabe down and took the watch captain's chalk and slate. Subtracting the sun's altitude from 90° gave him the zenith distance. He opened the derrotero and turned to the declination tables at the back pages. Having found the declination for that day, September 21, 1519, he added that to the zenith distance. The sum was our latitude, in degrees north of the æquinoctial line.

The Captain-General had been watching all this, and now he asked the pilot, "Did you use addition?"

"Yes, of course, mi capitán," replied Gomes. Aside, he made a wry face, but the Captain-General did not see it. "We haven't crossed the æquinoctial line. Once we are south of it, I'll use subtraction."

"What result did you obtain?"

Gomes showed him his computations on the slate.

"Thirty-five degrees and a fourth north."

He meant 35¼ degrees, or 35°15'N. Dom Fernão nodded.

"Very well. Prick the card."

Gomes turned to the card, which had ruled lines on it for latitude and longitude, and pricked a pinpoint hole in it as his estimate for our noontime position.

Cristóvão Rabelo made the call to the noonday meal:

> Tabla, tabla, señor capitán y maestre y buena compañía,
> tabla puesta; vianda presta; agua usada para el señor c
> capitán y maestre y buena compañía.
> Viva, viva el Rey de Castilla por mar y por tierra!
> Quien la diere guerra, que le corten la cabeza;
> quien no dijere amén, que no le den á beber.
> Tabla en buena hora,
> quien no viniere que no coma.

In the afternoon we watched the birds flying about, some of them following us for short distances. One of the sobresalientes, Antonio Lombardo, seemed very interested in them. I knew he came from Vicenza in the Kingdom of Lombardia, that he was a Patrician of Vicenza and an Ene Aca, but he looked so young and naïve. Later I found out that he was 25, my junior by a year. I learned that Ene Aca, or N.H., stood for Nobilis Homo, but that he appended those initials to his name only in legal documents. I learned, too, that he was something of a writer. Like all stylish writers, he signed his name in different ways: Pigafletis, Plegafetis, Pagaphetta, Pigafetta. In all of those versions, he was entitled to be addressed as Messere.

"Would you look at that!" exclaimed Ser Antonio Francesco Pigafetta.

A bird dove into the sea, then rose back into the air with a fish in its beak. All at once another bird swooped down on it, forced it to disgorge its prize, and made off with the stolen fish.

León Pancaldo, a marinero from Savona in the Genovese Kingdom of Liguria, turned to Ser Antonio.

"That bird ate the other bird's *merde...*er, *caca!*"

"A bird eating another bird's shit! Iesú Maria!"

He crossed himself, touching left shoulder before right.

"But you saw it with your own eyes. And don't use the holy names in vain."

"I beg your forgiveness. What do you call those birds?"

"The first one was a gaviota. The shit-eater was the cagassela."

"A gull, he means," Master Andrew said. "And the eater of ordure was the boatswain bird."

He flickered his eyebrows at me. He knew the bigger bird had forced the gull to disgorge the fish, but was willing to let León Pancaldo take the credulous Lombard for a ride.

The Captain-General happened by.

"Portuguese fishermen always look for the pardela," he said. "When they see this bird swooping down into the sea and catching fish, they know that is where the sardines are. The pardela eats only sardines. Of course, at night they look for the ardentia, the luminous glow a school of fish gives off."

"A phosphorescence, you mean, commendatore?"

"Precisely."

"There is another bird you might see sooner or later," Pancaldo told Ser Antonio. "What was it called, do you remember, Maestro Andrea?"

"The stormy petrel," replied the Englishman.

"Oh yes, the stormy petrel." Pancaldo grabbed Ser Antonio's arm. "Do you know what is remarkable about that bird? It has no anus, and no feet. It never stops flying. The female lays its eggs on the back of the male. When they hatch, the chicks fall off and learn to fly just before they hit the water."

"I must see this bird sometime," Ser Antonio said.

"Oh, you will," Master Andrew said. "Not to worry."

"Somewhere past the Canaries," León Pancaldo said.

"Oh, and I'm looking forward to our stop in the Fortunate Isles. These are the islands the ancients called the Hesperides. Where Hercules found the golden apples..."

"Yes," León Pancaldo said, "the same golden apples Juno tossed on the floor to influence the judgment of Paris. But the Romans found only dogs on those isles, and that's why they're now called the Canary Islands. No apples. That was just a myth. Did you know those islands have no springs of water, and no wells at all?"

"How do the people there obtain water to drink, then?"

"Each day at noon a huge cloud comes down and hovers at the top of the tallest tree. There is in fact only one tree tall enough to reach this cloud. Its leaves collect moisture from the cloud. The natives have arranged the leaves so that the dew funnels into jars they have placed by the roots around the trunk. And that is how those natives, the Guanches, obtain their water. Were it not for that cloud, they would all die of thirst."

"And you have seen this with your own eyes?"

"I have never been there. This will be my first visit. But you may ask any sailor who has been there. He will swear to the truth of it."

At dusk, all hands were called to evening prayer. It began with the page boy of the watch, Juan Antonio Genovés, trimming the binnacle lamp in the forecastle. As he walked down the deck to bring the lamp to its iron cressets in the stern, he sang:

> *Amén. Dios nos dé buenas noches, buen viaje, buen pasaje haga la nao, señor capitán y maestre y buena compañía.*

The other pages, Cristóvão Rabelo, Andrés de la Cruz and Rodrigo Gutiérrez now joined Juan Antonio for the round of prayers called the doctrina cristiana.

We said the Pater Noster. I knew it well enough, but I happened to be next to Master Andrew, and I realized he was saying it in another language: "Our father, which art in Heaven, hallowed be Thy name..."

This was followed by the Ave Maria and the Credo. Then the Salve Regina; for some reason, this was always sung. Master Andrew was always badly out of tune, as were about half the men on board. It would have sounded more pleasing if Andrés de la Cruz had sung it solo, but by tradition everyone had to sing this song. Both Padre Valderrama and Dom Fernão would glare at anyone whose singing was not loud enough, and exhort him to sing by making waving motions with their palms.

Now came the ships' salutes to the Captain-General. First was the *San Antonio*. She maneuvered as close as she dared to the flagship, her bow only a few feet from our stern. Her captain, Juan de Cartagena, who was also the Veedor General or Inspector-General of the Armada, stood on the foredeck and hailed out to Dom Fernão on our poopdeck:

> *Dios nos te salve, señor capitán-general, y maestre, y buena compañía.*

"How goes it?" asked Dom Fernão.
"All is well," reported Cartagena.
"Very well. Follow my lantern. Carry on."

The *San Antonio* fell back, and soon the *Concepción* came forward and maneuvered into place. Captain Gaspar de Quesada repeated the ritual word for word.

When the *Victoria* drew near, I saw that the man on her foredeck was not Captain Luis de Mendoza but Basco Gallego, her pilot. Then I remembered that Gallego was in command. Captain Mendoza had boarded a fast caravel and gone ahead to Teneriphe in the Canaries. He was the tesorero, the Fleet Treasurer, and was to purchase supplies for us there: firewood, pitch for caulking, salted meat and salted bacalhao or codfish. These were all cheaper in Teneriphe. Pilot Gallego performed the ritual salute, also word for word.

The last ship, the *Santiago*, closed in for her salute. Captain Juan Serrano hailed the Captain-General exactly as the others had, and received the same orders: "Very well. Follow my lantern. Carry on."

The page Rodrigo Gutiérrez made the dinner call.

After eating, we lolled around and idly watched the changing of the watch. The outgoing page reversed his eighth ampolleta and sang:

> Bendita la hora en que Dios nació,
> Sancta María que le parió
> San Juan que le bautizó.
> La guarda es tomada,
> La ampolleta muele,
> Buen viaje haremos
> si Dios quisiere.

Half an hour later the page of the new watch reversed his first ampolleta and sang the ditty for it:

> Una va pasada, y en dos muele;
> más molerá, si mi Dios querrá
> á mi Dios pidamos, que buen viaje hagamos;
> y á la que es Madre de Dios, y abogada nuestra,
> que nos libre de agua de bomba y tormenta.

Master Andrew was drinking uisgebaugh from a flask. He offered me a nip, and I fell back reeling from its potent but smooth and smoky flavor.

"Yon ditty did not refer to the ampolletas, boyo," he laughed. "It was about whiskey shot glasses, and the god was Bacchus!"

But I hardly heard him. I was leaning over the side and looking at the water. It shone with some inner light, millions of little points of light. After a long spell of no body of water save the Wad-al-Kibir to look at, I was at sea again. It was even more beautiful than I remembered, with a phosphorescence riverine waters never acquired.

I wrapped my gown of coarse serge around me, pulling the hood over my head. I adjusted my loose serge trousers and my long woolen stockings. Kicking off the leather shoes with the silly gilt buckles, I went to lie down in a corner right there on the deck. Just before I fell asleep, I thought I heard the wind whistle through sago palms.

⚓

7

TENERIPHE LOOMED AHEAD, not so much an island as a mountain at sea, so tall it rose through the clouds and past them, its peak poking through and emitting thin smoke. It seemed as if the clouds had formed from the smoke.

"That's the Pico de Teide," Duarte Barbosa told Ser Antonio, "an active volcano."

"Twelve thousand feet," said Master Andrew, "if she's worth an inch."

"We're seeing only the half of it," Dom Fernão said. "The other half is submerged; the island is a volcano that rose straight from the seafloor. As are many of the islands east of Malacca. Is that not so, Enrique?"

"None as tall as this, mi comendador," I said. It seemed strange to be speaking Spanish. We had always spoken Portuguese, at least whenever Spaniards were not around. For Dom Fernão, of course, Portuguese was merely what he spoke in the streets of Oporto or Lisbôa. His family had always spoken castellano, the language of the educated classes in all the Spains and in Portugal.

"I hope it doesn't erupt while we're here," Ser Antonio said.

"Not if you observe the holy office every day," the Captain-General assured him. "Hear Mass, receive the Sacrament."

Dom Fernão went aft to the quarterdeck and relieved the officer of the watch. He wanted to con the helmsman himself. I remained at the forecastle. We were steering straight into a solid wall of rock. Nearer and nearer it came. Collision was inevitable. Then I saw the cleft in the rock.

The tide surged through the narrow passage and swept us inside, into a wide bay. Ahead lay the wharf, and behind it the Spanish colonial town of Santa Cruz.

Captain Luis de Mendoza and his team were there to meet us at quayside. The Captain-General summoned the captains and maestres to the *Trinidad*. After hearing Mendoza's brief report he gave orders and assigned tasks. The maestres returned to their respective ships, assigned contingents to load the goods already stacked on the dock, others to procure supplies still at the warehouse, still others to stand watch duties. Those granted shore leave were ordered to hear Mass and receive Communion daily.

The five captains were still in the *Trinidad*'s stateroom, and I was in my master's cabin, polishing his armor, a daily task. I could hear them through the wall.

"Now that we have completed the first part of the voyage," said a voice, "it is only proper for us to assess our ships and men. From the homeland to the Canaries has been a fairly easy six days, ample time for us to observe our Armada under sail. Have you any remarks on the first leg of the voyage? How went it on your vessel, Captain Quesada?"

Such a speech should have been given by the Captain-General, but now I realized the voice was Cartagena's.

"On the *Concepción*," reported Quesada, "everything was normal. My contramaestre is a vascongado who has gone whaling as far as the coasts of the Labrador and Terra Verde. My marineros are all experienced sailors, including Juan el sordo. They had no trouble adjusting the *Concepción*'s speed to conform to the rest of the fleet's. As for my grumetes, they are learning fast. Already, most of them are now as knowledgeable as the marineros."

"Very good. How about your crew, Captain Mendoza?"

"The procurement of supplies here on Santa Cruz went about as well as might be expected. As for the *Victoria*, my pilot reported nothing out of the ordinary."

"Serrano?"

"A very good voyage, Don Juan. The caravel *Santiago* answers the helm well. She's a delight to handle. Better in some respects than a nao, if I may say so."

"Magallanes?"

Dom Fernão cleared his throat. I could not understand why he had kept silent through it all. Cartagena was acting like a Captain-General, and treating Dom Fernão like a subordinate captain.

"A routine trip on the *Trinidad*. Nothing of moment to report."

"Good," Cartagena said. "We are making fine progress, and the whole crew is desirous of setting out to sea again. When we resume, we shall follow the course agreed upon at the Casa, in Sevilla. This meeting is adjourned."

I heard them getting up to leave. As soon as they were gone I went out to look for my master. Why had he allowed Cartagena to usurp his prerogative?

The Captain-General was pacing the dock, overseeing loading operations on all five ships. I sensed that questions would not be welcome.

Making sure that Francisco de la Mezquita was there to attend to the Captain-General's needs, I slipped away and explored the streets of Santa Cruz. It was a new town, founded only a quarter of a century before, on an island that had until then been largely uninhabited. The townspeople were all white, mostly Spanish, although a few might have been Portuguese, and some Flemish. When the King left Flanders to take up the Spanish crown, many Flemings had come with him. Some of them were eventually persuaded to settle in the island colony.

I saw no Guanches in Santa Cruz. There must have been a few in Teneriphe, but most of them were native to the island of Lanzarote. The Guanches were supposed to be of Berber stock, like some of the tribes I had seen in the Marruecos. Others claimed they were the remnant of the race that had sunk with the island of Atlantis into the Ocean Sea.

My feet led me to a nondescript tavern a few streets from the waterfront. There were men from the Armada inside. I ordered a cup of the local wine. It was tawny, almost the color of urine, the heavy urine of someone who has not bathed for a whole week. I twirled the liquid in my cup, enjoying its bouquet, then took a sip: good strong taste, rough finish, a slightly burnt aftertaste that sang to me of rebirth in virgin volcanic soil.

I nodded to a couple of men I knew, Martín Magallayns of Lisbõa, distant cousin to Dom Fernão and a sobresaliente on the *Concepción*, and Antão Fernándes from Oporto, now Antonio Hernández of Sevilla, a servant to Captain Mendoza on the *Victoria*. In the corner were three crewmen I did not know.

"You may join us, Henrique," Magallayns said. "Have some more wine. Here, try some of this tripe. It's good."

He signalled the serving wench, and a bowl of soup was put before me.

"The cook here comes from Galicia," Fernándes said. "He makes a superb caldo gallego."

I tasted the soup. It was indeed very good. It was rich with kale, squid, tripe, pork slices, pig's trotters and young turnip leaves: a whole meal in itself, with some bread.

"The callos," said Fernándes, referring to the tripe, "have been cooked beforehand in oil, garlic and pepper. The kale was cooked in lard. And the locon con grelos have been scrubbed scrupulously clean."

"Gallegos really know how to cook tripe," Magallayns said.

"We have something," Fernándes leaned forward, "to tell you. It's important. You must tell Dom Fernão."

"Later, Antão," Magallayns said. Drinking is more important, even if we must drink the horsepiss they make here."

"That's exactly what it looks like," I said. "And its aftertaste is of volcanic soil, wouldn't you say?"

"No," Fernándes said, "it is of feet. The taste of the feet of the woman who trampled on these grapes. Some of them must have been having their monthly sickness at that time."

"Come, now," Magallayns said, "you're only saying that because the puta you were keeping in San Lucar had her sickness the day before we departed. You're still mad about missing that last fling."

Magallayns turned to me.

"You know, he was so desperate he even smuggled that woman aboard. Naturally the merinos found her and threw her out. That's why he had to go ahead on that fast caravel with Captain Mendoza."

"Who are they?" I asked, glancing at three crewmates of ours in the corner.

"They're the three irés on the *Concepción*. The only ones in the whole Armada."

"Irés?"

"From Eire or Irlande. The redhaired one is Guillérmo de Lole, the one with flaxen hair is Guillén Irés, from Galvey, and the boy is Juanillo Irés. Also from Galvey. They're all grumetes on the *Concepción*."

He turned to them.

"Well, hombres," he called, "how do you like the wine?"

"Poteen it is not," said Guillérmo de Lole, "but it'll do."

"In the absence of mead," said Guillén Irés.

"Nothing like the whisky from Bushmills, I'd say," put in Juanillo Irés.

"Mãe de Deus, what dedicated drinkers," laughed Magallayns. "Do all irés drink as you do?"

"We're only tippling here," said Guillérmo de Lole. You want to see some real drinking, you should come to my hometown. I'm from Loughrea, by the way. That's a small town east of Galway. It's beside a loch."

"Hear, hear. A toast!" proposed Magallayns.

"To Loughrea..." His pronunciation was uncertain.

"To Lole!" Fernándes said, as we clinked winecups.

"Those Spaniagh clarks in Séville couldn't spell worth a damn. They misspelled my hometown. They couldn't get my name right, either. It's William. William O'Connor."

"And the others?"

"My name," said Guillén Irés, "is Kevin. Kevin Cavanagh, from Galway. That's where the best Irish sailors come from."

"I'm from Galway, too," said Juanillo Irés. "Name's Sean. Sean McDougal."

"Your country is well known for its monks," said Magallayns, "like your São Borondão. Are any of you monks?"

"You mean St. Brendan," O'Connor said. "No, we're none of us monks. We're merely sailors."

"São Borondão was a sailor, too, was he not?"

"St. Brendan and his curragh, aye. Let me tell you, that leather curragh of his was probably as seaworthy a craft as any of these naos or caravel redondas."

"Ha! Don't tell that to Captain Mendoza. Speaking of him, Antão here was supposed to run an errand for Capitán Don Luis. We must be going now. Bom día."

"Good day, mate."

On the street, Magallayns pulled me aside.

"See that house? Antão says that's where they stayed. Mendoza is there now."

"Yes, of course," I said, "he would be."

"Cartagena and Quesada are there, too."

"I understand they're all good friends."

"There are others also. De Guerra, de Coca, and Estêvão Gomes."

"Gomes?"

"Yes. He's with them. They're all in there. You must tell Dom Fernão. Go."

My master merely nodded when I told him.

"Estéban Gómez is distantly related to me, but he bears me a grudge. He wanted to be Captain-General, you know."

"He was the first mariner to have an audience with the new King," Barbosa said. "He proposed sailing to the Spice Islands through a western route. Cristóbal Colón's original idea, if you'll recall. He didn't capture the romantic young King's imagination, though. He didn't look the part."

My master laughed.

"I looked the part," he said. "Even Ruy Faleiro looked the part. We had that secret globe, the Schöner globe, and an exotic Malay slave. How could we fail?"

"The King not only appointed you Captain-General, he also made you a Knight of Santiago. All Gomes got was a royal pilot's license. His appointment as Pilot-Major of this Armada must have seemed a consuelo de bobo to him. Why did he take it, think you?"

"I don't know," Dom Fernão said, "unless he's like the tiburón. He'll circle around me showing only the fin of his disdain. Then, at the first sign of weakness, he'll rush in and tear me apart."

We had been in Santa Cruz for two days when, on September 21, 1519, a fast caravel arrived from Sevilla. She began selling her cargo on the dock: bolts of cloth, ploughshares, axes, adzes, knives, nails, fishhooks, perfumes, brandy and almonds. Her maestre supervised the commerce. Her captain slipped away and quietly went to the *Trinidad*. There he personally delivered a letter to the Captain-General.

Dom Fernão was with the escribano, accepting men from the Canaries who wanted to join the Armada; some of them had come from as far as the Ilha Graciosa in the Açores. In all, 24 men signed up in Teneriphe, one of them a French curé who became the Armada's third chaplain.

Dom Fernão went inside his cabin to read the letter. The captain of the caravel waited for him to write a reply.

A short while later, he asked me to summon Duarte Barbosa and Cristóvão Rabelo to his cabin.

"Cuñado," he began, "I have received a letter from your father. You must hear what Papá has to say."

"What about him?" Barbosa asked, casting a sidelong glance at me.

"Oh, don't mind him," Dom Fernão said. He began to read:

"*'Most esteemed, most excellent, most beloved son, husband to my daughter, whom I love even more than myself...'* "

"Bom, bom," Barbosa said. "Very good style. What does he say?"

"*'Scarce had you weighed anchor,'*" [Dom Fernão read,] " *'than certain divers Persons, friends of men now in your command, began boasting quite openly how those aforesaid Men have every Intention of usurping the command, by foul means and treacherous...'* "

"That's nothing new," Barbosa said. "Cartagena, Quesada, Mendoza...their animosity is palpable. And it's clear that Hierónimo de Guerra and Antonio de Coca are their confederates."

"Don't forget Estéban Gómez," Dom Fernão said.

"Estêvão Gomes? What's a Putragues doing with those godos? Ah, yes, the frustrated Captain-General..."

My master put Dom Diogo's letter away.

"They're all bastards," Barbosa said. "Cartagena is Bishop Fonseca's nephew, which of course means his bastard..."

"His natural son," Dom Fernão said.

"Bastard sounds better," insisted Barbosa. His glance happened to fall on Cristóvão Rabelo. "Oh, I beg your pardon. Natural son, of course. That's what I meant."

Cristóvão Rabelo said nothing. He did not resemble his father. He was said to have taken after his mother Catarina Rabelo, who I gathered had been a lady-in-waiting at Reina Leonora's court early in the century.

"As I was saying," Barbosa went on, "they're all bastards. Antonio de Coca is the Bishop's brother's natural son. Hierónimo de Guerra is Cristóbal de Haro's nephew cum natural son cum bastard. Does that make him a Marrano, too? And Mendoza and Quesada are old cronies of Cartagena. I wonder who their fathers are? They must be bastards, too."

"De Guerra isn't a Jew," Dom Fernão said. "Jewishness is passed on by the mother and I don't think his mother was Hebrew. As for your other comments, I shall pass over them. That these men would form a cabal is perhaps only to be expected. Shall I read the rest of Papa's letter?

"'Furthermore, I venture to suggest that there has been some Collusion between the consul Álvares and the Bishop of Burgos. As the Casa demanded the particulars of the Course you intended to sail, despite your insistence that it remain confidential between yourself and His Majesty, I think it possible an Encounter has been arranged. I am of the belief that a week or more out of the Cabo Verde Islands a Portuguese fleet will Intercept your armada, Board the capitana, Arrest you for an imaginary crime, and remove you to Lisbōa. The armada will then be left, under Cartagena as Captain-General, to go on its way...'"

"A simple, straightforward and diabolical plan," Barbosa said.

"Just the sort of thing Fonseca would arrange," Dom Fernão said.

"Have you written Papá in reply?"

"Yes, I sent it by the same caravel. I said I would do these men no injuries so that they should have no reason to act thus. On that account it was not I who appointed them but the overseers of the Casa, who knew them. They have been given to me, and whether they turn out to be of good account or bad, I shall labor to do the service of the Emperor. And for that we have all offered our lives and our sacred honor."

"Bravo. Very well written."

A fishing boat docked next to our ships in Santa Cruz. Its captain went to the *Trinidad* offering to sell us most of his haul of codfish. The catch had already been salted, but still had to be packed into barrels. Dom Fernão ordered the maestre to arrange the purchase, and the tonelero to supervise the packing of the fish into barrels. They went off with a work gang of marineros and grumetes, bringing the staves of wood and the metal hoops they needed. Each stave was numbered. On the quay beside the fishing boat, the men followed the numbering and assembled the wood and hoops into barrels, then began shoveling salted codfish in. On the *Trinidad*, Dom Fernão showed the fishing boat captain the deckmounted cannon, something the man had never seen at close hand before.

Later, as a few barrels were being transferred into the hold, Dom Fernão pulled Duarte Barbosa aside.

"He told me he saw a fleet of three caravels four days ago. To the southwest, which would put them northwest of the Cape Verdes. Perhaps at latitude 25°N."

"Did he get close enough to identify their flags?"

"He wasn't sure about their mainmast flags. But their main sails showed a white cross superimposed on a red cross..."

"Don't tell me... the cross of the Order of Christ."

"Precisely."

"Portuguese warships. Did he say where they were heading?"

"Southwest."

"To Brasil...but they would stop at the Cape Verdes before crossing the Ocean Sea."

"So what were they doing at that position? Unless of course they were a patrol expecting us to pass west of the Cape Verdes."

"Five of us against three of them. Should be a fine opportunity to test that extra-heavy bombard."

"And if they're only part of a larger fleet? They know we have five ships. We don't know their number."

"*Hijo de puta!*" came a shout from below. It was the tonelero, Francisco Martín of Sevilla. One of the grumetes had dropped a barrel, and salted codfish were scattered all over the hold.

I watched them assemble a new barrel. Then I slipped away. For the next few weeks we would be eating salted codfish: in soup, fried, grilled, or however the pages would prepare them. There was unfortunately no rating of cook in the Armada. Everyone did the best, or sometimes the worst, he could. I found the tavern on the waterfront by the smell of its cooking. Before we left Santa Cruz, I wanted another rich bowl of Teneriphe tripe.

⚓

8

THURSDAY, SEPTEMBER 29, was the feast of San Miguel el arcangel. Shortly before our departure, two of our shipmates appeared, dragging a third man between them. The two were the grumete João de Grijol and the sobresaliente Gonçalo Rodrigues, both Portuguese. The third man was also Portuguese, for he was swearing fluently in that language.

"Here he is, mi capitão," Rodrigues reported as they came aboard.

"Bom," Dom Fernão said. "Welcome aboard, Maestro Pero. We sail soon."

The stranger looked sullenly at the Captain-General.

"I've got a wife and two children here, Senhor Capitão-Mor."

"Don't we all? So do I. I left a son & a pregnant wife in Sevilla."

A short ceremony was held on the deck of the *Trinidad*, presided over by Dom Fernão and Padre Valderrama, and witnessed by all the officers of the Armada. The 25 new men swore the same oath the others had sworn in Triana: to obey the Captain-General in everything, and to follow the course ordered by him.

We went out of the bay with the tide, our speed increasing in the narrow cleft between the rocks. When all five ships were out in the open sea, the *Trinidad* led the way south to the other end of Teneriphe Island. In command of the *Victoria* was the pilot Basco Gallego; once again Captain Luis de Mendoza had gone ahead, this time overland.

Early the next morning we anchored off the town of Montaña Roxa. Captain Mendoza was waiting for us at the docks with the several dozen barrels of pitch he had purchased. It would be used for caulking the hulls of the ships. After two months or so of sailing, when the wood under the waterline became infested with teredos, or woodworms, a ship had to go into drydock for graving and careening. This meant scraping the hulls free of barnacles and painstakingly prising out the teredos, one by one, before they had dug too deeply into the wood. Then the hulls were caulked with pitch. It kept the ship watertight but did not seem to deter the teredos in the least.

Montaña Roxa was a quiet little town. Behind it was a hill with sheer sides of ochre and magenta, the "red mountain" which had given the town its name. Ser Antonio called it Monte Rosso. Master Andrew called it Red Anthill.

During the three days that we spent there, it became apparent that most of the prostitutes in Santa Cruz had followed Captain Mendoza overland to be with us. Some of them must have come by caravel from San Lúcar de Barrameda. I thought I saw a few I had seen in Sevilla.

We departed Montaña Roja at midnight on Sunday, October 2. A mild land breeze had sprung up, and the first-quarter moon was sinking into the sea's western horizon. When it was gone at a few minutes past midnight it was Monday, October 3, as Ser Antonio reckoned it. For the rest of us it was still Sunday, October 2, and remained so until noon twelve hours later. The nautical day began and ended at noon, and the civil day as kept by knights or patricians meant nothing to us.

The course was southwest by south on a compass bearing of 213 degrees although Pilot-Major Gomes, per the Captain-General's order, allowed for magnetic deviation and steered 225°. Our compass was a circular card, graduated to 32 points, mounted on a pin with a lodestone under the North point. The whole was enclosed in a binnacle with gimbals so it could rotate freely. The compass was on the high poop deck in front of the officer of the watch. Forward of the binnacle was a hatch through which the officer conned the helmsman below. The helmsman steered with a heavy tiller attached directly to the rudder head. It was fatiguing work; no man was kept more than an hour at the helm.

After the morning prayers on Tuesday, October 4 by the civil calendar or Monday, October 3 by the nautical, Dom Fernão pointed to the east.

"We're abeam Cape Bojador," he told Ser Antonio. "You can't see it for the rising sun's glare and also because it's over the horizon. I've seen it on previous voyages. Quite an insignificant-looking cape, really. But a century ago Cape Bojador was the ultimate southern limit."

"Why was that, commendatore?"

"It's all desert. Endless dunes of sand. Shoals that extend twenty, twenty-five leguas out to sea. To them, it must have looked very much like the end of the world. Navigators always turned back upon reaching Cape Bojador."

"But had none of them read Herodotus? In his book *The Histories* Herodotus writes that the Pharaoh Necho sent a fleet to sail around Libya. By Libya, of course, he meant the whole of Africa. The fleet rowed out from the Red Sea and returned through the Pillars of Hercules. The voyage took them three years, but they kept stopping to plant crops and harvest them. It was the only way they could provision themselves."

"Yes, that story was well known. The Infante Dom Henrique believed it. He always compared it to the Biblical story of Solomon sending ships to Ophir. Those ships, manned by Phoenicians, also took three years to return. The Infante Dom Henrique thought it meant a circumnavigation of Africa. If so, Solomon was the first to send ships around Africa, some four centuries before the Pharaoh Necho. As for the Infante Dom Henrique, he was the first to send ships past Cape Bojador. This was in 1425, I think, when they still called the Mar Océano the Mare Tenebros, the Sea of Darkness, and they were still sailing in barcas, those two-masted square riggers of 25 tuns. The shoals off Cape Bojador and the prevailing winds make it difficult to come back. Not until the caravella redonda was invented in 1441 could sailors pass Cape Bojador with confidence. Africa wasn't rounded until 1487, and then only because storms swept Bartolomeu Dias past the Cabo de Buena Esperanza. Dias would have gone on to India if his crew hadn't mutinied and forced him to turn back."

"Leaving the passage to India to be found by Vasco da Gama."

"Which he did in 1497. Actually, Dias escorted da Gama as far as Mina. From there, da Gama wasn't sure where to go. He followed the coast of East Africa, going north, almost as far as the æquinoctial line. Finally he found an Arab pilot, in Malindi, who guided him across the Indian Ocean to Calicut on the Malabar Coast. Nakhoda Ishmail, I think, was the Arab pilot's name."

"I beg your pardon, Sire," I said, "Nakhoda Ishmail was the pilot who guided Antão d'Abreu, Simon Affonso, and Francisco Serrão from Melaka to the Molukas, although they only got as far as Banda. You must mean someone else."

"Oh yes, how silly of me! I meant...let's see now, yes, Ahmad ibn Majid. That's the one. Da Gama's pilot. Obrigado, Henrique. Your memory is egregious. By the way, what does the name ibn Majid mean?"

"Lion of the Sea in Fury," I said.

"Great navigators, those Arabs. I've read a translation of their *Kitab al-Fawa'id*, a nautical compendium for use when sailing the Red Sea and the Indian Ocean. Quite a book."

"Ah, yes. I hear it's as good as the *Periplus of the Erythrean Sea*," Ser Antonio said. "And we must be grateful to them for preserving the book written by Ptolemæus. Now we know it by its Arabic title, *Almagest*."

"You mean the *Megale Suntaxis tes Astronomias*. Have you read it? All 13 books of it?"

"Well, I was most interested in the book about computing eclipses, Book VI, I think it was. And the tables for finding latitude in Book I. By the way, I notice your pilots are still using the tables of Ptolemæus. Unfortunately, he says nothing about how to find longitude."

"A difficult problem, finding longitude. A friend of mine, Ruy Faleiro, wrote a book about it. *Regimento da Altura de Leste-Oeste*. Or how do you say it; Rules for Finding Longitude. I've a copy in my cabin, somewhere in my sea chest. Remind me to lend it to you. You read Portuguese, I take it?"

"I can manage. By the by, Don Fernan, no one calls himself a navigator who does not know the winds," he said. "You of course know the seventeen winds in the Mare Nostrum?"

"The winds in the Mediterranean? I didn't even know there were seventeen. Well...I've heard that the summer wind comes from the northwest, and the winter wind from the south...then there's the wind from the east, and the wind from the west...and there's the wind from Greece. How many does that make?"

"Only five, but very good for someone who has never sailed that sea. Of course, we have our own names for those winds. Any Italian would know them, even a Genovese."

"Any Genoese?" asked Master Andrew, who had just joined us. "Ahoy, there, Francesco! You're from Genoa, aren't you? Well, tell us about the seventeen winds that blow in the Mediterranean."

"There is the etesia," said the marinero Francesco Picora, "which blows from the northwest in summer, as il commendatore said. There is the ostralada, which blows from the south during winter. And the levante, from the east...it is said that the levante brings the smell of the Cyclopedes people in Armenia."

"Cyclopedes?" queried Master Andrew. "You mean people who have wheels for feet?"

"No, they do not have wheels. But each of them has only one leg and only one arm. When he wishes to go fast, he holds his foot with his hand, so that his body forms a circle. Then he starts to roll, like a wheel."

"What other winds do you know?"

"The maistràl, which blows from the west, and the gregalada, which comes from Greece...the sirocco, from the southeast, and the libeccio, from the southwest...I cannot remember the others."

"Capital," said Master Andrew. "A marinero who hardly knows more winds than his Captain-General. Very well, thank you, Francesco."

"Here is another Francesco," said Ser Antonio, pointing to our contramaestre, "who knows even fewer winds than his Captain."

"That is true," said Francisco Albo. "We Greeks speak of only four winds, Boreas the north wind and his brothers the south, east, and west winds. But we count all four among our gods. The Greeks are the keepers of the winds, for Zeus and Poseidon imprisoned them and gave them to us. They are in a fortress of stone in one of the Aeolian isles near Sicily. Only my people know how to collect the winds into one sack, as King Aeolus did when he gave the winds to Oddyseus."

"And you, Enrique," said my master, "what do your people call the winds?"

"We speak of only two winds," I said, "the amihan and the habagat. The amihan blows from the northeast for most of the year—"

"Ah, the northeast monsoon," said Dom Fernão.

"—and the habagat blows from the southwest for the rest of the year. But we know of other winds. Traders from Cathay have told us of the wind they call the tai-fung. It is the same wind that men from Cipangu call the kamikaze. It is a storm wind that uproots trees and topples houses. We call it the bagyo. Its coming is unpredictable."

"That very wind sank d'Alboquerque's *Flor del Mar* off Sumatra in 1511," recalled Dom Fernão, "and Simon Affonso's caravel off Java in 1512."

"You were in the Marruecos in 1514, mi comendador," said the alguacil, Don Gonzálo Gómez de Espinosa. "Did you learn the names the Moros give to the winds?"

"Morocco?" laughed Dom Fernão. "No, I was too busy fighting the Sheik of Azamor's hashashin. And there was that ludicrous case my own senior officers pressed against me. The idiots actually accused me of selling captured cattle back to the enemy...but you were going to tell us the names the Moors call the winds by. Do go on, Gonzálo."

"There are many winds in the desert," said Don Gonzálo, "and always the Moors speak first of the permanent winds, the ones that live in the present tense.

"There is the aajej—in South Morocco it comes as a whirlwind. Against it, the fellahin defend themselves with knives.

"There is the africo—which at times has reached into the city of Roma.

"There is the alm—a fall wind from far away, from the Slavic lands on the far side of the Adriatic Sea.

"And there is the ariffi—the wind that scorches with numerous tongues.

"Then there are the other winds they know about, which pass them on the way to distant places.

"The bist roz is hardly felt in Morocco, but from there it leaps into Afghanistan for a hundred and seventy days, and buries villages.

"The ghibli is a hot dry wind from Tunis. It blows and rolls, and rolls and blows, and in time unhinges minds.

"The haboob comes from the Sudan. It is a dust storm that throws up bright yellow walls a thousand yards high, which are then toppled by the rain that follows.

"The harmattan blows into the Mar Océano, where it drowns itself. It is full of red dust, so that many call it a rain of blood. Others call this wind a sea of darkness. It was this wind which lent its name to the Mare Tenebros.

"There is the imbat, a refreshing sea breeze in Libya and the Marruecos.

"There is the datoo. It comes out of the pillar of Hercules, the one called Jabal Tariq. It carries the fragrance of Andalusía and the Algarve to Morocco, and reminds the Moors of the heavenly lands they could not keep.

"There is the nafhat. It is a blast out of Arabia, but it might very well have come from Hell.

"There is the mezzar ifoullousem. Coming from the southwest, it is violent and cold. The Berbers call it 'that which plucks the fowls.'

"There is the beshabar. It comes from the northeast, from out of the Caucasus mountains. It is black and dry.

"And there is the khamsin. The word means 'fifty' in Arabic, and the khamsin blows for fifty days in March, April, and May. Always a wind to contend with, the khamsin usually does little harm. Occasionally it brings the plague of darkness, if only to remind men of its power. It was the khamsin that visited the ninth plague on Egypt.

"Then, too, there are the winds the Arabs say are poison winds. There is the Samiel, from Turkey; it is a poison wind often used in battle.

"There is the Simoom, a poison wind of North Africa, and the solano, a poison wind whose dust plucks off rare petals, and causes giddiness.

"Finally, there is the wind with no name, the wind whose presence is never more than a sudden whisper. The Bedouin say it is the secret wind of the desert, the one whose name was erased by a king after that king's son died of it."

There must have been more, but at that moment the page on duty, Andrés de la Cruz, approached the Captain-General.

"Señor capitán-mayor, el piloto-mayor sends his compliments and would remind you that you wished to be informed when we reach the latitude of 27 degrees North."

"Gracias, mi hijo. What is the course?"

"Southwest, sir."

"Change course to south by west immediately."

"Right away, sir."

The page relayed the order to the pilot, who relayed it to the watch captain. The contramaestre bellowed commands to the marineros. The *Trinidad* started veering to port. I watched the compass needle as it swung from 225° through 191°. We would be passing close to Africa then, keeping the Cape Verdes far to starboard.

In a moment the other four ships had followed the flagship's maneuver. The *San Antonio*, however, was closing in. Captain Juan de Cartagena, elegantly dressed as usual, was at the forecastle. He took out a vial, undid the glass stopper, and held it under his nose. The vial held perfume, and foppish dandies always took a whiff of scent when offensive smells assailed them: the miasma in the bilge, or the body odors of sweaty marineros. When he was almost under our stern, he called out.

"Pilot-Major!"

"Yes, Captain?"

"What is the course?"

"South by west."

"Why has it been changed?"

Gomes shrugged.

"Order of the Captain-General."

A wave splashed against the bow of the *San Antonio* and sent spray flying. Some of it hit Cartagena. But it seemed he was already foaming at the mouth.

"This is not the course laid out for us at the Casa! According to this Armada's written instructions we are to proceed southwest to latitude 24°N before turning south by west! You cannot alter course without informing the other captains! Ah, but now we all know the true purpose of this voyage. It's to take us down to Africa and sell us all on the slave markets of Guyne!"

"The slave markets of Guinea!" Master Andrew whispered beside me. "That's news to me."

At this moment Dom Fernão appeared on the quarterdeck, stood beside Gomes, and addressed Cartagena:

"*Que le siguiesen y no le pidiesen mas cuenta.*"

It was said in a firm but strangely quiet tone. He had always spoken castellano with a soft Portuguese accent, but this time he had somehow used Cartagena's own aristocratic accent.

You are to follow me and ask no questions.

Cartagena turned red, quickly went below and then up again to the poop deck—and into his cabin.

⚓

9

SER ANTONIO FRANCESCO PIGAFETTA, N.H., Knight of Rhodes and Patrician of Vicenza, has persuaded me that the civil day is less confusing than the nautical day. I have agreed with him, more for his benefit than mine. In truth, I am beyond convincing. It should be obvious to anyone with a modicum of sense that the day must begin at sunrise. That is how my people have always reckoned it. But then logic is not everything, and if Ser Antonio desires that the day begin at midnight, why, then, midnight it shall be. Sailors reckon the start of the day to be at noon, when the pilot shoots the sun, but I can understand how maddening it must be for Ser Antonio. The Jews begin and end their day at sunset, when three stars may be seen in the sky at a single glance. The Mohammedans likewise begin the new day at sunset, when a white thread in one's hand may no longer be distinguished from a black thread in the other. Our contramaestre Francisco Albo, who is from Rhodes, has told me that the Greeks too begin the day at sunset.

The ancient Egyptians, Ser Antonio told me, were the first to begin the day at midnight. The Romans adopted the custom from them.

The Xanglei named their hours after the twelve animals present at the Buddha's deathbed. The ancient Chaldeans too chose twelve animals and put them in the sky as the signs of the zodiac.

In classical times, Ser Antonio told me, the Romans had names for the hours of the night. The crepusculum was the hour in which the light faded, yielding to the dark; the fax was the moment the torches were lighted; the concubium was the hour children fell asleep; the nox intempesta was the time all activity was suspended; the gallicinium was the hour the cocks crowed; the conticinium was an hour when all was silent; and the aurora was the hour when dawn broke.

In this modern age however, the white man reckons the hours of the day and the days of the week according to the seven planets that rule them. All men know the teachings of Ptolemæus, who said that the earth is the unmoving center of the universe. Nine celestial spheres revolve around our world. The seven planets each have their own spheres, and the fixed stars occupy the eighth. The last sphere, the primum mobile, is more difficult to explain. Suffice it to say that this sphere affects the three outermost planets, and causes them to wander backward and forward most erratically.

The planets, in their order of succession from the earth, are the moon, Mercury, Venus, the sun, Mars, Jupiter, and Saturn. In counting the hours of the day, the white man commences with midnight and uses the reverse order of the seven planets whereof the most distant planet, Saturn, begins the count. Each hour of the day is ruled by a planet. Each of the seven days takes its name from the planet that rules its first hour. Saturn rules the first hour of Saturday (sabado, samedi, shabbat). Jupiter rules the day called Sunday (domingo, domenica, dimanche). Lunes is the day ruled by Luna, martes by Mars, miercules by Mercury, Jueves by Jove, and viernes by Venus. The white man may be a devout Christian, but the days of his week commemorate the old gods he may not banish from the atavistic depths of his mind.

Master Andrew had his own names for the days of the week. Three of his days were named for Saturn, the sun, and the moon. The other four, Tiw's day, Woden's day, Thor's day, and Freya's day, honored strange gods I had never heard of. One of these gods, I forget which, was one-eyed, having given away an eye in exchange for a drink of water from a well. Another carried a hammer not as a carpenter's tool but as a weapon. The others...but never mind. Were any gods ever such barbarians?

Needless to say, my people have much the more sensible system. Each day of the week has its own unique qualities, and our names for them take these into account. We begin the week with the day the white man calls Monday. Our name for it is ting-bukad, "the day when buds bloom into flower." The other days, in order, are dumasun, dukot-dukot, baylu-baylo, danghus, hingot-hingot, and ligid-ligid. Such beautiful names...

On Thursday, October 6 by the civil calendar, we passed the Ilhas do Cabo Verde. We never saw them; they were too far off to starboard. To port, one could just make out the faint bluish outline of the Sierra Leóne part of the African coast. I had been to the Cape Verdes in 1512, on a stopover from Melaka to Lisbõa, and regretted the lost opportunity to revisit them. The islands were Portuguese, and now that we flew the emblem of Spain we were not welcome there. I half expected a Portuguese fleet to materialize on our western horizon and intercept us.

In the evening, after the prayers and the evening meal, Duarte Barbosa and Cristóvão Rabelo followed Dom Fernão to his cabin.

"Have you done it?" he asked them.

"Yes. I asked Cristóvão to assist. He actually did most of the work. Well, filho?"

"Thank you, Tio Duarte. We've gone very carefully over the rosters, Tio Fernão, and have made the necessary corrections. As you know, a few men were left on the beach at Sevilla, per the Casa's orders, but most of them rejoined us secretly at San Lúcar. We also enlisted a few men in San Lúcar. And we signed up twenty-five men in Teneriphe, counting the man we, ah, crimped into service."

"Go to the summaries, Cristóvão," Barbosa said.

"Yes, I was getting to that. The grand total is two hundred and sixty-four, from the Capitão-Mor down to the last cabin boy. We have also determined the numbers according to the nationalities."

He cleared his throat.

"Of Spaniards we have 153, of which 31 are vascuences."

"He means vizcaínos," Barbosa said.

"Or vascongados," Dom Fernão said, "or vascos."

"Basques, to use the French word," Cristóvão Rabelo said.

"Don't the French also call them gascons?" Barbosa asked.

"They do," Dom Fernão said. "Different regions use different names for these people. However, they call themselves the Euskaldunac. Their language is Euzkaria. And they call their land the Euskal Herria."

"Their language is so difficult it is said the Devil himself was unable to learn it, though he tried for a thousand years."

"Yes, yes. Proceed with the count if you please, Cristóvão."

"Yes, sir. There are 37 of us Portuguese, counting those who have acquired Spanish citizenship. Three come from the Ilha Graciosa in the Açores. You should hear them speak Portuguese. Such thick accents."

"I can imagine," Dom Fernão said, "do go on, please."

"From the Italian kingdoms we have 32 men. Most of them are Ligurians from Genova, Savona or Cestre, 19 in all. We have 5 Neopolitans from Napoles de Romania and Axio..."

"He means," Barbosa said, "Naples and Anzio."

"There are four Lombards, from Vicenza or Bresa."

"Brescia is near the Alps. It's different from Baresa, which is near Genova."

"We have one man from Bolonia. And three Sicilians, one from Trapana and two from Mecina."

"No Florentines?" asked Dom Fernão. "No paisano of Vespucci's?"

"No. From Francia we have 20 men, including four from Bretaña or Normandia."

"And one from Calais, isn't there? But not an Englishman."

"No. He considers himself French. To go on, we have five Alemáns. We also have five Flemings, although two of them are actually Walloons. We have five Greeks, all from Rhodes except for one man from Corfu. We have three Irishmen. And lastly, we have four men who are the sole representatives of their nations. One Englishman, one Marruecan, one Moçambican, and one Malay. The inglés is our condestable; the other three are slaves."

"What do you know about the ages of our men?"

"The youngest is 14, Juan de Zuvileta, a cabin boy on the *Victoria*. His father is Basco Gallego, the pilot of the *Victoria*. The oldest is 44, Juan Rodríguez of Sevilla, a marinero on the *Trinidad*. I think he is the only one here who is a grandfather."

"Is he the one called el sordo?"

"No. Juan Rodríguez el sordo, the deaf man, is also from Sevilla and is also a marinero. But he is on the *Concepción*. We have two other men named Juan Rodríguez. The one from Huelva was born in Mallorca; he's also a marinero on the *Concepción*. And there is João Rodrigues de Mafra, pilot of the *San Antonio*."

"Four men! That's the trouble with Iberian names. You know, a clerk at the palace once told me he found seven of us named Fernão de Magalhães in the record books. All seven fighting in the Orient in the service of the Portuguese King. Circa 1510."

"My name is more exclusive. I know of only one other Duarte Barbosa. But his real name was Odouardo."

"Are there more names like these, Cristóbal? Names common to several men?"

"Basco Gallego, pilot of the *Victoria*, is not to be confused with Vasco Gomes Gallego, a grumete on the *Trinidad*. These two men each brought his son along. Basco Gallego's son, as I mentioned, is Juan de Zuvileta, a cabin boy on his ship. As for the other one, his son is named Juan, but everybody calls him Vasquito. Father and son are both grumetes on the *Trinidad*.

"We have four men named Antonio Hernández. The first, also called Alonso, is a grumete on the *Santiago*. The second is an interpreter on the *San Antonio*. The third is a sobresaliente on the *Concepción*, originally a Portuguese named Antão Fernandes, but now a resident of Sevilla. The fourth, a marinero on the *Trinidad*, is also called el colmenero."

"A beekeeper?"

"Yes. He supplied the Armada with five hundred casks of honey, one hundred for each ship. He assures us it's all honey from bees that drank the nectar of orange blossoms. That's the best kind, fragrant and sweet. Bees that feed on almond blossoms produce a bitter honey."

"He should have brought some of that, too," Barbosa said. "For the *San Antonio*."

"I only hope," Dom Fernão said, "that none of his honey comes from bees that have fed on the blossoms of the azalea. The Ten Thousand of Xenophon ate wild honey that had come from the nectar of the azalea. It drove them mad, causing vomiting and diarrhöea. A few of them even died of it."

"Diarrhœa?" Barbosa said. "Such honey would have had its uses..."

"As for the other names," said Cristóvão Rabelo, "we have three men named Iohan Genovés. Two are on the *Trinidad*, a marinero and a cabin boy. The third is a grumete on the *San Antonio*. There are also two named Antonio Genovés, one a page here on the flagship, the other a grumete on the *Victoria*."

"Of course," said Barbosa, "Genovés isn't a real surname. Nobody can remember these men's long Italian names, but they're all from Genova."

"It's the Spanish custom," Dom Fernão said, "to discard a difficult foreign name and simply use the man's hometown. Or change it into something pronounceable. Take Averrhoës, Avicenna or Maimonides, three of Spain's most celebrated men. Who can remember their real names?"

"Weren't they ibn Rushd, ibn Sina and Moses ben Maimon?"

"Excellent. You surprise me, cuñado. Abdul-Walid Mohammed ibn Rushd, Abu-Ali al Husayn ibn Abdullah ibn Sina, and the Rabbi Moshe. But where were we? Pray continue, Cristóvão."

"Here on the *Trinidad*," said Cristóvão Rabelo, "we have another pair of namesakes. Two men named Francisco Martín; the one from Sevilla is the tonelero. The one from Huelva is a marinero.

"We also have two Juan Bautistas. Our maestre, from Genova, is Iohan Bautista de Ponceron."

"So that should properly be," said Barbosa, "Gian Battista de Punzurol."

"The other one, a gunner, is Juan Bautista de Mompeller."

"Or," Barbosa said, "Jean-Baptiste from Montpellier."

"On the *Victoria* they have two Greeks with the same name. The contramaestre is Miguel de Rodas. And one of his marineros is Miguel Sánchez de Rodas.

"There are two men named Diego García. The one from Trigueros is a marinero on the *Santiago*. The one from Palos, a page on the *San Antonio*, is the son of Cristóbal García, a marinero on the same ship."

"Another father-and-son pair," Dom Fernão said.

"Yes," Duarte Barbosa said, looking at Dom Fernão and Cristóvão Rabelo, "we've quite a number of father-and-son pairs aboard this Armada."

"We also have two Pedro Garcías, and two Juan Garcías..."

"Never mind," said Dom Fernão. "Now, in sum, of the full complement of 264 men there are 122 Spaniards and 31 Basques, making it 153 strong from all the Spains."

"And," said Cristóvão Rabelo, "37 Portuguese, 32 Italians, 20 Frenchmen, 5 Germans, 5 Flemings, 5 Greeks, 3 Irishmen..."

"And an Englishman and three slaves," said Barbosa. "Why, the Spaniards alone, not counting the Basques, make up almost half the complement."

"It is a Spanish Armada, after all," said Dom Fernão. "The wonder of it is that only half are Spaniards. The other half are all extranjeros."

"I make it 107 foreigners and maybe most of the Basques," Barbosa said, "against 122 Spaniards."

"No, it's not," Dom Fernão said. "It's only those three Spanish captains and maybe a core group of Spanish aristocrats against the rest of the crew. It's a question of how many of us rudos marinheiros will jump to their side."

"You have an advantage there, cuñado. You're known as a real seaman. These Spanish captains are inútile fops. They're not sailors at all. They can't even navigate."

"I'm the Captain-General. That's all the advantage I need."

"True, true. No one else has the power of the rope and the knife. Not even your conjunta persona."

⚓

10

"THE CAPTAIN-GENERAL SAILS," said our contramaestre, Francisco Albo, "with the caution of a Greek, threading his way between the Cape Verdes and the African coast as though they were Scylla and Charybdis."

"It's not as bad as that," Ser Antonio said. "You can't see either of them. We're sailing in the open sea with miles of freeboard."

"Nevertheless, Africa is just over the horizon," Albo insisted, "and over the horizon too, on the other side, is Buena Vista."

He meant Bõa Vista, the nearest of the Cape Verde islands. We were at 16°N latitude; the Cape Verdes stretched from 17° through 15°. For the two days it took us to sail that expanse lookouts were posted in the crow's nest of each vessel, to watch for the westernmost islands of Sal, Bõa Vista, Maio and Praia. We were too far east to spot them, but the pilots maintained that any sighting of those islands would serve as checks of our position. Besides, the western horizon was also where a Portuguese fleet might suddenly materialize.

We never saw the Cape Verdes, nor the Portuguese fleets Dom Manoel had supposedly dispatched after us. For two weeks, as we sailed parallel to its coast, we had distant glimpses of Africa, thirty or forty leagues away.

The Spanish legua, as Master Andrew had said, was three and one-fifth Saxon miles. Now Albo clarified the matter for me. Maestro Andres, he said, used the nautical mile, which was longer than the English statute mile. And he preferred fractions to decimal notation. The legua was not actually 3.20 miles; it was 3.18. A sea mile was ten sounding-lead cables of 100 fathoms each, or 6080 feet, whereas a land mile was only

5280 feet and it took 3⅔ of those to make a legua. In either case the Spanish legua was some 19,333 feet, give or take a few.

There were of course other leguas and miles. There was a legua of 4⅕ miles, a Portuguese milha equivalent to 1⅓ English miles, and several Italian millias varying between ⅗ and 1⅖ English miles. As for the foot, Albo told me, it was the length of the average Englishman's foot, there were twelve inches to one foot, and one inch was three barleycorns laid end to end. Three feet made a yard; the yard was also the distance from the English King's nose to the tip of his outstretched hand.

I did not believe any of it. I knew it was all nice talk. But when I asked Master Andrew about it, he confirmed everything. The English indeed used three barleycorns to make an inch. They measured the feet of a dozen men selected at random, divided by twelve to obtain the average, and so found their standard foot. Most irreverent of all, they actually took the measure of their King, from his red nose to his Tudor fingertip!

By October 18, still close to the African coast, we were only 8° north of the æquinoctial line, and well to the south of the normal Portuguese route to Brasil. We were south, too, of the Portuguese track to India. For both destinations, the Portuguese steered SW from the Cape Verdes and headed for the middle of the Ocean Sea. The westbound ship merely continued on this heading until it sighted Brasil. The eastbound ship sailed ⅔ of the way to Brasil before turning southeast into a course for the Cape of Good Hope. Any Portuguese seaman would know better than to stay too close to Africa once past Cape Bojador. And here we were doing exactly that.

Few of us knew much about these waters. The skies were mostly overcast, and I could often see squall lines on the horizon. Once, with the Captain-General out of earshot, I heard Estêvão Gomes tell some of the marineros, "We're too close to Africa too far south. We should have been in the middle of the Ocean Sea by now."

Another time he said, "I thought we were to go west to Maluco, but it seems we might be making for Guyne. Maybe Captain Cartagena divined the Captain-General's secret plan?"

Then a gale blew up, and soon it had become a storm. We ride it out for several hours, drenched to the skin and dizzied by the ship's rocking. Many of the men became sick. Some were convinced we would capsize; the yardarms dipped almost to the water at the height of each swing. Some wept, others said prayers. It had been worse off the Cape of Good Hope seven years earlier, but I had nearly forgotten. I, too, was terrified. Here, at least, it was not so cold. Then, I had seen sleet form on the ropes and on the deck.

Blue balls of light appeared at the tops of the masts. Ser Antonio saw them first.

"Dulce María, Queen of the Sea, we are saved," he shouted as he went down on his knees. The pages and grumetes saw the lights too, pointed them out to the others, and went down on their knees.

"The corpo sancto!"

"Sancta Elena y San Pedro!"

"El fogo de San Ansélmo!"

"St. Elmo's fire."

"The lights of Castor and Pollux!" whispered Francisco Albo.

It lasted for about 15 minutes. Ser Antonio prayed for all that time. Later, he said the lights had stayed for three hours. I had seen them as blue balls of cool fire, but some of the men later said it had been an apparition of the Virgin. After the lights, a few albatrosses appeared. They followed us for an hour, barely flapping their long wings, flying at our stern like guardian angels.

The next day the wind died down entirely. We were in a flat calm. The sun came out and it became oppressively hot. Shark fins could be seen cruising in the water around us.

"He's navigated us right into the doldrums," Estêvão Gomes said.

Some of the men baited hooks and cast lines over the side. Nothing bit. There was a strong current below and no fish inhabited these waters, at least not near the surface. While we sweltered in the sun, the current was carrying us westward.

We did not know how long we would be becalmed. Cristóvão Colom had been becalmed in these waters for eight days, during his third voyage. We seemed to be in it for at least as long.

"Do you think we shall spot the Los Islands?" Pigafetta asked the Captain-General. These were a group of small islands off the Sierra Leóne coast.

"No, they're too far south," Dom Fernão said. "The Los Islands are at 5°N latitude. We are at 8°N, and drifting west."

Almost every day, we could see the batels of the *Concepción* and the *Victoria* ferrying Captains Quesada and Mendoza to the *San Antonio*. The three Spanish captains enjoyed each others' company, but did not invite the other two captains to join them. Sometimes Cartagena had himself rowed in his batel to the *Concepción*. Invariably, we would soon see Mendoza getting into his batel from the *Victoria*, and joining them on the *Concepción*. Dom Fernão said nothing.

A week into the becalming, a strange thing happened. We had just completed the evening prayers, and now we watched the *San Antonio* move in for her evening salute. Because of the calm, she was being rowed towards us by men in her waists using ashwood sweeps. The man standing at her foredeck was not Captain Cartagena however, but the contramaestre, Diego Hernández of Sevilla. When the *San Antonio* was very close, he made the salute:

"Dios nos te salve, señor capitán, y maestre, y buena compañía."

It was a double insult. A mere deckhand, not the Captain, had made the salute, and he had addressed Dom Fernão merely as "señor capitán" instead of "señor capitán-general." Dom Fernão spoke out sharply to Hernández:

"The next time I expect to be saluted correctly, and by the Captain himself."

Cartagena appeared on the foredeck and stood beside Hernandez.

"I sent the best man on this ship to salute you," he said. "But if you like, next time I'll send a grumete."

The *San Antonio* sheared off and fell back.

"Son of a bitch," I heard Master Andrew mutter under his breath, "the man's a real bastard."

The *Concepción* approached, and Captain Gaspar de Quesada made the normal salute.

"Very well, carry on," Dom Fernão dismissed him.

The *Victoria* and the *Santiago* closed in, each in her turn, and Mendoza and Serrano performed the usual salutes. The Captain-General dismissed them in the routine manner.

The next day at sunset, the *San Antonio*'s double insult of a salute was repeated. Dom Fernao glared at Diego Hernández, then yelled at him, "Dismissed!"

The following day it happened again. This time Dom Fernão merely dismissed Hernández with a wave of his hand.

Captain Quesada in the *Concepción* made the normal salute.

Captain Mendoza in the *Victoria* made his salute, then reported: "My Captain-General, it is my duty to inform you that two men in my crew have been apprehended for the crime of sodomy. The case awaits your disposition."

"Who are they?"

"The maestre, Antón Salomón, and a grumete, Antonio Genovés."

"I shall convene a courtmartial tomorrow. Carry on."

After Captain Serrano's routine salute, Cristóvão Rabelo went to the captain's cabin and pored over the crew rosters.

"Salomón is a Sicilian," he said, "from Trapana. The grumete must be the one known only as Antonio. He's from Baresa near Genova."

"Trapani is on the west coast of Sicily," Duarte Barbosa said. "Baresa is a fishing town on the Ligurian coast." He looked at the Captain-General. "Sodomy's not to be unexpected on a voyage like this, especially during a dreary calm. Will you have them flogged?"

"We shall see. The courtmartial will be in the stateroom, of course. All five captains in a single room, and one escribano. Something could happen."

"Yes, those three could be in a position to overpower the two of you. Should we send word to Serrão?"

"No need. Francisco Serrão's brother will stand by me in any event."

We were some 5° north of the æquinoctial line that day, October 27. The captains of the other four ships were summoned to the *Trinidad* for the courtmartial, with Captain Mendoza bringing his two prisoners. The Captain-General alone, as the King's representative, held the *poder de baraco é cutello*, the power of the rope and the knife: the power to condemn any man in the crew to death.

A murmur went up among the deckhands as the two prisoners were brought up to the deck from the *Victoria*'s batel. Antón Salomón and Antonio Genovés, their hands bound behind them, were paraded down the deck and then tied by their ankles to the foremast. The grumete was a goodlooking young boy with flowing locks of chestnut hair. He was rather slim, and I could see how his girlish figure must have tempted men like Salomón, or men who preferred boys. I overheard the page Rodrigo Gutiérrez asking in a whisper, "If the sin of Sodom is when a man does it with another man, what do you call it when a woman does it with another woman?"

"The sin of Lesbos," whispered Andrés de la Cruz in reply.

"There is another word for it," Ser Antonio told them. "Tribadism."

"And what," asked Gutiérrez, "if a man does it with a woman? Without the blessing of marriage, I mean."

"Fornication," said Andrés de la Cruz.

"Swiving," said Master Andrew. "Or fucking."

The five captains and the escribano, León de Espeleta, went into the stateroom. I was already in the captain's cabin, which could be entered through the stateroom, with Duarte Barbosa, Cristóvão Rabelo and the alguacil, Don Gonzálo Gómez de Espinosa. Don Gonzálo was in armor. Cristóvão Rabelo and Barbosa were not, but both wore swords. I felt naked with only my sheath knife at my waist. The four of us kept silent, not letting even the sound of our breathing escape.

The courtmartial began.

Dom Fernão presided, and he observed all the formalities. When the time came for Captain Mendoza to produce the prisoners, we heard him step out the door and order two merinos to untie the accused and bring them inside.

Dom Fernão was brusque and to the point with the accused.

"Maestre Antón Salomón, you have been charged with committing the act of sodomy. How do you plead?"

"Guilty."

"Antonio of Genova, you have been charged with committing the act of sodomy. How do you plead?"

"Not guilty."

"Do you deny that you were apprehended en flagrante delicto?"

"He made me do it."

"Were you aware, during the commission of the act, that it was a transgression of God's law as well as man's?"

"I suppose so."

"Gentlemen of the court, do you have any questions of the accused?"

"No questions," the four captains said.

"Very well. You, maestre Salomón, and you, Antonio of Genova, we find guilty of sodomy. We shall be passing sentence shortly. Captain Mendoza, have these two transferred to the brig, if you please."

Sounds of feet shuffling about, the door opening and closing. Then, Dom Fernão's voice.

"Escribano, what is the penalty for sodomy?"

"The minimum is a flogging, sir, the number of strokes at your discretion. I believe the usual is eighteen."

"The Romans gave our Lord thirty-nine lashes. What is the maximum?"

"Death by hanging, sir."

"Gentlemen, under the circumstances, with discipline and morale running low in this Armada, I believe we should make an example of this case. I move that we condemn these two to death. What say you?"

"Yes. Death," said a voice I took to be Captain Quesada's.

"The grumete was the victim of the Sicilian," said Captain Serrano's voice. "I concur with the penalty of death for the maestre, but I plead leniency for the boy."

"I second that motion." Captain Mendoza's voice.

"And I, too." Captain Cartagena's.

"Very well. It shall be as you have suggested. Death by hanging for Salomón, forty days of hard labor for the grumete, Antonio of Genova. Escribano, kindly inform the prisoners of their sentences."

We heard León de Espeleta leaving the room.

"Discipline would not have become so lax," a voice said, "if we hadn't been becalmed for so long. Why, it's been nine days now."

Now I recognized the voice: Cartagena's.

"It's just bad luck," said another voice, Serrano's. "Even Cristóbal Colón ran into the doldrums on his third voyage. Rare is the captain who never gets becalmed."

"Bad luck, cómo achicais. Bad navigation is what it is!" Cartagena's voice had taken a strident tone. The four of us listening in the cabin tensed. "This is what comes of deviating from the course agreed on at the Casa. Since Cape Bojador we have been sailing too close to Africa!"

"That's enough, Captain," Dom Fernão's voice said.

"Enough? I'll tell you what's enough. You are deviating from the course because you plan to sell us all to the slave dealers..."

"I will not have this..."

"...on the coast of Guyne!"

"You must follow my course. Those are my orders."

"This Armada has had enough of your fool orders! I for one will no longer follow them!"

He had committed himself, and declared mutiny. The signal came: three taps on the wall. Don Gonzálo burst through the connecting door, followed by Duarte Barbosa and Cristóvão Rabelo, each one drawing his sword as he moved. I alone remained in the cabin.

"Rebel, this is mutiny!" roared Dom Fernão. Later, I learned he had grabbed Cartagena by the shirtfront as he said this.

"In the name of el rey you are my prisoner!"

"Quick, Gaspar, Luis, stab him!" Cartagena shouted. "Do as we planned!"

His hasty words gave them away, but there was no response. Quesada and Mendoza pretended not to have heard. I heard the sounds of a slight scuffle, and went out on deck the other way, not passing through the stateroom. Don Gonzálo was frogmarching the elegantly dressed Cartagena, Cristóvão Rabelo and Duarte Barbosa on either side of them, amidships. They negotiated the stairs up to the foredeck. For a moment I thought Cartagena might try and kick off his captor while on the steps. Then they were up. Don Gonzálo tied Cartagena by the ankles to the foremast. He was alone there. Antón Salomón and Antonio Genovés had been removed and were now in the batel of the *Victoria*, waiting for Captain Mendoza.

Two hours later, he was still there. The midday meal was brought to him by Don Gonzálo's black slave, the grumete Antón Moreno. Cartagena refused to eat.

We saw Captain Quesada get into his batel. A crew of rowers brought him to the *Victoria*. A little later, both Quesada and Mendoza got into the batel and were rowed to the *Trinidad*.

The two captains formally requested the Captain-General for custody of Captain Cartagena. Although Cartagena was now a prisoner, he was an hidalgo (hijo de algo or son of somebody) and should not be tied to the mast like a common seaman. Dom

Fernão considered a moment, then ordered the alguacil to release Cartagena into Captain Mendoza's custody.

Half an hour later, a fanfare of trumpets blared from the quarterdeck of the *Trinidad*. When all the ships were paying attention, the escribano León de Espeleta hailed an announcement: the contador of the Armada, Don Antonio de Coca, was hereby appointed Captain of the *San Antonio*. The maestre of the *San Antonio*, Antón Salomón, and the grumete Antonio Genovés had been tried for sodomy in a courtmartial and found guilty. Salomón was sentenced to death by hanging; Antonio Genovés to forty days of hard labor, both sentences to be carried out on land upon arrival in Brasil.

With his maestre in detention, Captain Mendoza promoted his contramaestre, Miguel de Rodas, to maestre. From among his marineros he selected Diego Gallego, from Bayona, to be the new contramaestre. Mendoza formally notified the Captain-General of these promotions on the *Victoria*. Both were confirmed without comment by the Captain-General.

De Coca was perhaps the best choice as the *San Antonio*'s new captain. His "uncle," actually his natural father, was Antonio Rodríguez de Fonseca, the Lord of Alaejos and Coca, who was Bishop Fonseca's brother. That made de Coca and Cartagena cousins. Perhaps de Coca's appointment as captain would mollify Bishop Fonseca and alleviate the shock of Cartagena's arrest.

The escribano of the *San Antonio*, Hierónimo de Guerra, who was Cristóbal de Haro's "nephew" or bastard son, now had to assume de Coca's rôle as contador or Fleet Accountant. It was his true calling, of course. He had been sent along to protect his natural father's interests and see that de Haro's investment in the Armada made a good return.

Cartagena was transferred to the *Victoria* as Captain Mendoza's prisoner. Mendoza treated him as an honored guest, putting him up in the captain's cabin and instructing his four servants to cater to Cartagena's every whim. He then wrote the Captain-General a note requesting him to send over some of Cartagena's ten personal servants to attend to their master in detention on the *Victoria*. Dom Fernão flatly denied that request.

⚓

II

SARGASSO WEEDS DRIFTED in the water with us, and large pink jellyfish. Food was beginning to rot in the barrels, and wine to turn sour. Sweat would collect on my forehead, then roll down my cheeks and gather at my throat. I wanted desperately to dive into the water for a swim, but I knew that if my skin so much as brushed the tentacles of a jellyfish its poison would kill me slowly and agonizingly.

Our trinquetes were limp. As for the other sails, there was no point in spreading them.

Aboard ship, it is the captain's sole privilege to whistle for wind. In the Armada, the Captain-General alone had the right. But Dom Fernão either did not know how to whistle, or did not care to.

On November 9, after three weeks in the doldrums, a breeze sprang up. The trinquete filled out. Soon we had the other sails set, and a man down at the helm.

The *Trinidad* led, ship's flag at the foremast, the lions and castles of Spain at the mainmast, and the Magalhães checkered bars, quinas and lions rampant at the four capstans.

Next was the *San Antonio*, with a new flag at the capstans: Cartagena's arms had been replaced by de Coca's.

The *Concepción* and the *Victoria* bobbed loyally in our wake. Bringing up the rear was the *Santiago*.

By now I knew most of the men in the Armada. On the *San Antonio*, Cartagena had been captain as well as Veedor General, or Fleet Inspector-General. He had been appointed as a replacement for Ruy Faleiro. His salary as King's Captain equalled Dom Fernão's, 50,000 mvs. per annum. His wages as captain of the almiranta and as veedor came to 6,000 mvs. a month, 2,000 less than Dom Fernão's. In July of 1519 the King had furnished Dom Fernão a copy of the royal cédula in which the Cartagena's role in the Armada was described:

"*Se quede é vaya en su lugar* [de Faleiro] *el señor Juan de Cartagena como su conjunta persona, asi como su Alteza lo manda por su carta.*"

His Majesty's well-turned phrases made it sound as if Cartagena were Dom Fernão's equal as co-Captain-General. In fact, the cédula had probably been written by one of the King's escribanos at Bishop Fonseca's prompting, then shoved under the King's nose for his signature. Dom Fernão did not consider Cartagena his equal; the ambiguity of the cédula's wording was merely a sop to Spanish pride. Cartagena had sworn, as had every man in the Armada, to obey the Captain-General *en todo*, and to follow the course ordered by him. And Dom Fernão alone had been given the poder de baraco é cutello.

Cartagena's cousin, Don Antonio de Coca, had been appointed as contador, or Fleet Accountant, at 40,000 mvs. a year. To this was added a monthly salary, for the duration of the voyage, of 5,000 mvs. As a fleet officer he should have shipped in the capitana, but chose to be with his cousin in the almiranta.

The escribano on the *San Antonio* was Hierónimo de Guerra. With de Coca taking over as Captain, de Guerra would now assume the contador's job. He was a natural for it. De Haro must have charged him to make sure their family would receive their rightful share of the profits to be made. Spices from Maluco sold for their weight in gold at the Rialto in Venice.

The captain of the *Concepción*, Gaspar de Quesada, was a bosom friend of Cartagena's. There was one marinero on the *Concepción* who was thought to bring luck to whatever ship he sailed on. This was Juan Rodríguez el sordo, a deaf man but accounted a fully competent seaman.

The captain of the *Victoria*, Don Luis de Mendoza, had been a retainer of the Archbishop of Sevilla. Mendoza was concurrently the tesorero of the Armada, the Fleet Treasurer.

The *Santiago* had no pilot, so Captain Juan Serrano also functioned as her navigator. Unlike the three Spanish captains, he was a licensed pilot and an experienced seaman. He had been in Java waters in 1511, and knew the waters of East Africa and Índia.

Æquinoctials

Only the capitana and the almiranta had chaplains. The other three ships had no priests. It did not greatly matter. Canon law forbade the celebration of Mass at sea.

A week out of the doldrums, the sailing smooth and steady, the Captain-General estimated landfall off Brasil in ten to thirteen days, two weeks at most. Now he ordered João Lopes Carvalho, the only pilot who had been to Brasil, to transfer from the *Concepción* to the *Trinidad* and act as Pilot-Major. Pilots were supposed to retain detailed memories of places and waters they had seen even only once before. Estêvão Gomes was to exchange places with Carvalho. However, he persuaded his distant cousin to send him to the *San Antonio* instead, with Andrés de San Martín being reassigned to the *Concepción*.

Carvalho was a voluble man in contrast to the sullen Gomes. Soon he was regaling the crew with stories of Brasil. Ser Antonio especially was entranced by his anecdotes.

On his first noon on the *Trinidad*, Carvalho neglected to shoot the sun. Contramaestre Francisco Albo, on duty as the officer of the watch, noticed the omission and took a sight of the sun himself, then worked out an estimate of our latitude and logged it on his slate.

The Captain-General quietly approached Albo.

"Have you pricked the card?"

"No, sir."

"Did you enter the latitude in the derrotero?"

"No, sir. But I wrote it on my slate."

"For the pilot to copy down in the derrotero later. I see. What latitude did you obtain?"

"One and two-thirds degrees North...or one degree and forty minutes North. Longitude ten degrees west, sir. A very rough estimate."

"So we'll be crossing the æquinoctial line by tomorrow. Hm...so, you know how to estimate longitude. Interesting. By the way, what meridian did you use?"

"Ferro, sir, in the Canaries. I mean Hierro."

"Yes, Hierro." Dom Fernão emphatically pronounced it the Spanish way. "And what method did you use for longitude? Lunar distances, perhaps?"

"No, sir. Too complicated. The tables for it only confuse me. Dead reckoning, sir."

"Ah, you must have a fine sense for distance."

"We Greeks have always had a fine feel for distance, sir."

"The same feel Odysseus had, or that Jason had? I see. It's in your blood, eh? Very well, prick the card and make the entries in the derrotero. You know how lazy Carvalho is. He'll do the piloting when we sight land, but you and I will have to do the routine navigating. You may also wish to record your observations in your own derrotero. Take one from the stores and keep a log."

So it was that Francisco Albo became the de facto Pilot-Major of the Armada. He had attended the Casa's Escolar de Navegación and had learned his lessons from a faculty that included such Royal Pilot-Majors as Vespucci, Juan Díaz de Solis and Sebastian Cabot.

We crossed the æquinoctial line quietly. Dom Fernão had crossed it perhaps a dozen times before, and I had crossed it a few times myself.

"I've been studying the approach to Vera Cruz," Dom Fernão told Carvalho. "In my old friend João de Lisbõa's book." For once, he was speaking in Portuguese.

"The *Livro da Marinharia*? Yes, I've been perusing it myself," Carvalho said. "To refresh my memory. From the Cape Verdes steer South to 14° North, then south-southeast and later southeast by south to 7½° North, which will bring you within sight of the Bahia da Santa Ana of Sherbro Island off Sierra Leóne. From there, let the trade winds take you southwest across the æquinoctial line to Fernão da Noronha Island."

"Yes, that's probably the shortest route," Dom Fernão said.

"A route you took care to avoid," Carvalho said. "Did you fear Portuguese warships waiting for you on that track?"

"Most assuredly."

"And so you steered us into the doldrums, which all Portuguese pilots avoid like the Black Death. A very foolish maneuver. Or, under the circumstances, a very cunning one."

"So you saw through it."

"It puzzled me at first. If I hadn't known what a fine navigator you are, I would have thought you had blundered into it. But it seemed too obvious an error. No one's wandered by mistake into the doldrums since Colom got becalmed there on his third voyage."

"But now we're at the æquinoctial line, instead of at 7½° North. What do you think is the best track?"

"Steer west-southwest for Fernão da Noronha. We should aim for landfall at 8⅓° South, off Cabo Sancto Agostinho. There's some danger in not going far enough south. If we make landfall at 5° South, off Cabo San Roque, the prevailing winds and currents might sweep us north."

"How bad would that be?"

"Disastrous. We could be swept northwest almost to the isles of the Caribs and then northeast in a great circle back to the Sargasso Sea."

"For an error of a mere three degrees of latitude?"

"Good pilots count their errors in ascertaining latitude in minutes or seconds. Only a Castilian navigator would err by more than one degree."

"Land ho!" cried the lookout from the crow's nest atop the mainmast. It was the land of Verzin, as Ser Antonio called it, or Brasil. The sun having crossed the zenith, the date was November 29 whichever calendar was consulted. Francisco Albo had shot the sun an hour earlier, at noon, and recorded our position as being at latitude 8½° South.

"A feat of navigation, mi Capitão-Mor," Carvalho said. "But we still have to be careful. The shoals here extend 20, 25 leguas from the shore."

"We shall approach no further. Order a turn to port. Set the course due south by southwest."

"Aye, aye, sir."

"Maestro Andrés, keep all the gun crews on the alert until further notice."

"Aye, aye, sir."

We followed the coast, keeping the land barely in sight at the western horizon. It had been two months since we were last on land, in Montaña Roxa, but the Captain-General would not approach any closer. He would keep us at sea for yet two more weeks. Each ship sailed behind and to the portside of the ship it was following, with the *Trinidad* in the lead. This reduced the chances of being spotted from the shore. There were no

Portuguese settlements below 20°S latitude, so our destination now was the bay at 23°S.

"I've recommended to the Captain-General," Carvalho told Ser Antonio, "that we stop in Guanabara Bay. That's what the natives call it. André Gonçalves, its discoverer, named it the Rio de Janeiro because he came upon it on January 1, 1501. He thought it was a river, not a bay. The following year it was explored by Gonçalo Coelho and Amerigo Vespucci, who also believed it to be the estuary of a river. We now know it's really a bay, so perhaps it should be renamed."

"You have been to that place, have you not?"

"We were there for two months, June and July, in 1511. I was the pilot of the Bretõa. We had gone first to the Bahia de Todos los Santos to load brasilwood..."

"The wood we call verzin?"

"The very same. A species very like the cæsalpina tree. We called it brasilwood because of its red color, like coals in a brazier."

"Where was this Bay of All the Saints?"

"At 13°S. From there we sailed south 200 leguas to 23°, to Rio de Janeiro."

"We call that wood verzin," Ser Antonio said. "Formerly we could procure it only from India. It is used in the dyeing of wool, for the red, blue and black dyes one obtains from verzin are superior and do not fade no matter how many times the garment is washed."

"When Pedro Álvares Cabral discovered this land in 1500 he called it Vera Cruz, thinking it was only an island. Now we call it Brasil, after the tree that grows so abundantly here."

"They say the natives are cannibals. Is it true?"

"Oh, yes, it is true, although the Tamoios, Guaranis and Tupis are a gentle people, all of them. They eat human flesh not because they like the taste, but because it is the custom."

"They are cannibals only where their enemies are concerned?"

"That is so. They are a very gregarious people. They live in longhouses, 70 or 100 to a house, with rush mats to separate the different families in the house. Their men live to be 125 years old, their women to be 140. Have you ever seen swine whose navels are at the back?"

"Really? No."

"You will see it, this pecari. The indios call it...ah, the tayassu."

"Well, you say you were a month in that bay. What is there to do there? What did you do?"

Carvalho laughed heartily. Juan Bautista de Mompeller laughed, too.

"But of course, Signeur Antoine," Jean-Baptiste said, "there is only one thing they could have been doing."

He laughed again. Ser Antonio frowned impatiently.

"And what would that be, Signore?"

Jean-Baptiste shrugged his shoulders.

"Cherchez la femme."

IIª Parte
No Outro Mundo

12 The December of Our Discontent 95

13 Ipanema Desperadoes 103

14 Rio Solis 113

15 Ceilidhe 120

16 Cape Curious, Point Blighted Hope 126

17 Auto-dà-Fé 134

18 Patagón, Mahalingam 144

19 Eleven Thousand Virgins 155

20 Nubeculæ 166

21 Land of Fires 175

22 Ate o Fim do Mundo 182

12

DOLPHINS FROLICKED all around us, leaping out of the water and gamboling among the five ships.

"There's a current of cold water here," Carvalho said, "from which the cape gets its name. The dolphins seek out this current, as its cold waters are more to their liking than the warm waters of the open ocean."

It was Monday, December 13. We had rounded Cabo Frio at daybreak and then spent the whole morning sailing west. A gentle rain began to fall.

At noon we turned into the narrow entrance of a huge bay. This was the Rio de Janeiro. Guarding the entrance was a marvelous hump of granite, the Pão de Açúcar or Sugar Loaf. We glided on inside the bay to its northwest side, seeking the mouth of a small river where, a decade and a half before, Coelho had built a house of stone.

"The Tamoio Indians call it the Carioca," Carvalho said, "which means The House of the White Man."

"What do they call the river?" Dom Fernão asked.

"I don't remember. We always called it simply the Rio Carioca."

"Today being the feastday of Sancta Lucía," Dom Fernão said, "we shall name this bay after her. The Baia de Sancta Lucía. Put it down in the derrotero. "But it already has a name," Carvalho said. "André Gonçalves named it the Rio de Janeiro when he found it on the first of January, 1502."

"Because he thought it was the estuary of a big river. The men have sampled the waters upon my orders, and it's all salt. This is no river. We must seize the opportunity to make the correction."

Canoes had appeared from the shores and were paddling towards us. Behind them, people were swimming for our ships.

"Calemi!" Carvalho hailed them. He exchanged a few words with a man in one of the first canoes to reach us.

"They think we're from Heaven," Carvalho told us. "It hasn't rained for two months here, but we rode down from the sky on torrents of rain and watered their fields by the grace of our glory. Now their drought is over."

And then they were clambering all over the decks. They were people of a race I had not seen before: brown, short and stocky, with long lanky black hair that came down across the forehead almost to the eyes. Their noses were as blunt as mine. They wore barkcloth skirts or loin coverings and various decorations of bright-colored feathers, seashells and bones. Each of their men had at least three holes bored in his lips or cheeks, into which he had placed green or white stones, each the size of a plum. This practice disfigured their faces in a ghastly manner, but they were warriors who placed great store in looking ferocious. I saw some who had five holes, and one who had seven. Later, Ser Antonio said he saw one who had nine.

The women were barebreasted. Carvalho had warned us about them. The men, he said, were extremely jealous of their wives. We could not take married women lightly.

"The Guarani man will stick a poisoned arrow into your side if you so much as look at his wife," Carvalho had cautioned. "Keep your eyes off their breasts."

Unmarried girls were a different matter entirely. They belonged to their brothers and were at the latter's disposal. These people had no metal and we soon found they were eager to sell their sisters for a cheap Flemish knife, or an axe, some nails, or fishhooks. The girls themselves, after providing their services, were given necklaces or bracelets of hawksbells or Venetian glass beads. This impressed the shyer girls ashore, who implored their brothers to sell them, too. Soon we had more girls than we wanted.

In the trade for food, the best bargains were had with playing cards. One man acquired a brace of chickens, eight fowl, for a single king, the rey de bastos or King of Clubs.

The Spanish deck was somewhat different from the French or the Italian. The 48 cards were divided into four suits, the bastos or Clubs, the copas or Cups, the espadas or Spades, and the oros or Gold Coins. Each suit had twelve cards; the first nine were numbered, while the sota or Jack had the value of 10, the caballo or Knight of 11, and the rey of 12.

We had a few Italian decks, which Ser Antonio called "venetas," but no one cared for them, as each pack had only 40 cards, eight fewer than the Spanish. The suits were the same, batoni, coppe, spade, and dalnari or diamonds, but there were no cards with the number 1. Instead, there were aces.

Ser Antonio said there were also Italian decks of 78, of 56, and of 52, to suit every preference, but these were not so common in Venice and we had brought none of those.

Hans Vargue showed me a German deck, 52 cards, with suitmarks of linden leaves, hawksbells, acorns, and hearts, numbered from ace to 12, then the Untermann, Obermann and Konig, the jack, knight and king. I rather favored the French pack, 52 cards with suitmarks of coeurs, piques, trefles, and carreaux. Maître Jacques explained that the piques represented the military, the clubs the peasants, the carreaux or diamonds the merchants, and the coeurs the Church and the love of learning and of scholarship.

The four kings were always called by their titles in the French nobility. Rather than being simply the Roi de Carreaux, the King of Diamonds was the Duc de Bourgogne. In the same way, the Roi de Coeurs was the Duc de Langre. The Roi de Piques, or the King of Spades, was the Duc de Reims. And the Roi de Trefles was known as the Comte de Beauvais.

The cards, in Maître Jacques's enlightening view, were a veritable mirror of his society, but such profundity was not for me. I palmed his Duc de Langre when he wasn't looking. I later succeeded in procuring a brace of fowl for it.

We set to work with a will, graving and careening our ships, boring out teredos from the hulls, caulking with pitch. We patched tattered sails. We built lean-tos on shore, and passed the nights in languorous bliss. High summer was upon us, long days and short nights, and we knew back in Spain it was winter, the sun far to the south. Here, where the sun blazed in the northern half of the sky, the seasons were reversed.

We slaughtered swine, goats, tapirs, ducks, and chickens, salting down the meat to replenish the barrels in our holds.

The Captain-General exhorted us to eat vegetables; it was the greens, he said, that kept the escorbuto away.

"Scurvy be damned," Master Andrew said. "Peas are the only greens I ever eat, and they go none too well with such meat as we have here. By our lady, what I'd give, forsooth, for that bloody roast beef and ye olde Yorkshire pudding."

The evening of our arrival, December 13, the Captain-General summoned the captains and pilots to the stateroom of the *Trinidad*.

"According to the ephemerides in my almanach," Dom Fernão told us, "there will occur tonight an occultation of Jupiter by the moon. The moon is now in its last quarter and will be in Gemini."

"What almanach is that, Dom Fernão?" asked Andrés de San Martín in Portuguese.

The Captain-General continued to speak in Spanish.

"It is the *Almanach Perpetuum* by Abraham Zacuto, late of Salamanca."

"A Jew," observed Quesada.

"Yes," Barbosa said. "He taught astronomy until recently at the university in Salamanca. One of the few not hounded out of Spain in 1492."

"Moonrise," Dom Fernão went on, "will be at 12:16 this midnight, according to the almanach. That is of course moonrise in Salamanca. Here in the Baia de Sancta Lucía, the moon will have moved further east before it rises over our horizon. The difference will be minimal, a few minutes at most, but we may have to compensate for it.

"The moment of first contact will be at 1:48 ante meridian as observed from Salamanca. The almanach also predicts that it will be at 12:44 as seen from Nuremberg. Here in Brazil the occultation will take place much later, perhaps around 3:00 or 4:00 in the morning.

"We shall all observe this eclipse of Jupiter by the moon, and note the exact time of its beginning. This will give us the opportunity to determine our longitude."

San Martín spoke up, this time in Spanish.

"Your pardon, mi comendador, but this is all quite useless if we have not ascertained local time here, as determined by the zenith position of the sun. Is it not so?"

"You are correct. That is why I asked Caraballo and Albo to use the astrolabes and shoot the sun this noon. Ser Antonio borrowed your astrolabe and took a sight also. As did I. The rest of you were too excited watching the bay come into view."

"Our purpose this time," Carvalho said, "was not to find our latitude but to pinpoint high noon. Each of us started an ampolleta flowing at what he thought was the noon hour."

"From the looks of the four ampolletas," said Mendoza, "your reckonings of local time vary by as much as five or six minutes."

"That is so," admitted Dom Fernão. "Unfortunately. And so our computations for longitude may vary too, perhaps by several degrees. Still, it should prove a most interesting exercise."

"Wouldn't it be more accurate," asked Estêvão Gomes, "to use lunar distances? We must admit, an error of several degrees is a shame for any pilot."

"Degrees of latitude," Serrano said. "Errors of a few minutes of latitude are indeed shameful. As Cristóbal Colón himself said, 'No man considers himself a navigator who cannot make landfall within ten leguas of his goal, though it be after a crossing of a thousand leguas.' That's a margin of error of less than a full degree of latitude. But here we are looking for longitude, and a higher order of calculation is called for. There is as yet no dependable method for finding longitude. Not even lunar distances, which are too complicated and unreliable. Should our reading of our longitude be in error by a few degrees, not more than three or four, that would be quite an achievement."

December 13 ended, and December 14 began, at midnight, according to Ser Antonio's civil calendar. For me, the date changed at daybreak; for most of the others, at noon. In the almanach, since Zacuto was a Jew, December 13 must have been considered to end much earlier, at sunset.

Whichever day it was, I fell asleep and missed the occultation.

Later, I gathered that moonrise had come at 12:14 by the most advanced ampolleta and 12:19 by the most retarded; the planet Jupiter appeared to dim slightly as it touched the moon's edge. A full minute passed before it disappeared behind the waning moon, at between 4:17 and 4:22. From these observations, the longitude of the Baia de Sancta Lucía was calculated to be between 36 and 42 degrees west of Salamanca.

LONGITUDE

There was no way to check the accuracy of these figures. They were simply noted in the derroteros for future scrutiny by the cosmographers of Europe.

"Piloto Andrea," I heard someone ask San Martín, "what did that eclipse portend?"

"Indeed, Don Antonio," San Martín said, "I am hard put to understand it. Zeus is the lord of the gods, while Selena is the goddess of hunting. The occultation took place in the sign of the Gemini, Castor and Pollux. It would seem that the order that governs our undertaking now might be eclipsed by the hunt for other, baser things. The sign of the Twins lends this hunt a duality, or a duplicity if you will. The hunt could go either way."

We were eating breakfast on the *Trinidad* when we saw a native woman swimming with a boy, heading towards us. From the water the woman yelled something. Carvalho answered in the same language, which apparently had to be spoken from the throat, although Carvalho's voice normally came from deep within his chest. The two swimmers came up on deck, and the woman presented the boy, who was about seven, to Carvalho. There was no mistaking the resemblance.

"I have a son!" Carvalho shouted with glee. "I am a father!"

"So you are the father of a son," said Dom Fernão, patting the boy on the head.

Carvalho, with the Captain-General's permission, soon enrolled his son as a cabin boy in the Armada. When this became known, it increased his prestige among the Guarani.

As the boy's name was unpronounceable, we called him Juanillo. Padre Valderrama suggested that he be baptized into the Christian faith. Carvalho declined.

"We should have to acquire his mother's permission, and that would mean acquiring their headman's consent, too," he said. "Perhaps we can baptize him later, without these complications. And I didn't even know I had gotten her with child when I left this place eight years ago."

Duarte Barbosa began spending nights ashore in a hut he had caused to be built by one of the carpenters, assisted by some of the grumetes. He paid three Guaranis a hatchet each for their sisters, and appropriated a barrel of wine from the ship. When he had been absent for three days without notice, the Captain-General sent me to look for him and request him to report for duty.

I got directions to his hut from one of the grumetes. When I found it I could hear the sounds of amorous endeavor from within. I waited for them to finish.

"Senhor Duarte!" I called out.

"Who's that?"

I entered. Barbosa lay on his back, his head on a woman's lap, another woman on top of him, the third woman beside him. The first woman was giving him sips of wine from a goblet. The second was slowly undulating atop him. He was fingering the third. Perhaps my timing was bad. It seemed they were not quite finished yet. But I had a task to carry out. Still, I could not help wondering what the order of rotation was.

"The Captain-General requests you to return to the ship."

He turned surly, snarled at me.

"I don't take orders from wog slaves."

"You're drunk."

"Abaxo perro! Enough of that. Don't give me any lip, you hear? Now get out of here."

Dom Fernão went livid with rage when I made my report to him. I suddenly recalled how irascible my master was. I should have invented some excuse for Barbosa. Now it was too late.

"Alguacil, take two men and go with him," ordered the Captain-General. I led Don Gonzálo and two merinos to the hut. They arrested Barbosa, led him in chains back to the *Trinidad*, and threw him in the brig. Barbosa promptly fell into a drunken sleep.

I looked at his snoring carcass for a moment, my heart seething with contempt. Here was the dandy Iberian gentleman, King's Factor at Calicut and Cochin for many years, author of the *Livro Emque dà Relação do Que Viu é Ouviu no Oriente*, a widely praised book about East Africa and the Malabar Coast, and what had he come to now?

But when he woke up the following morning, he had no recollection of his arrest. He was in fine fettle. He wanted to get out of those silly chains and get on with the voyage, find the way to Maluco and the Indies. Dom Fernão went down to talk to him. When he came up we thought his brother-in-law would be with him. We were mistaken. The Captain-General was no softie. Duarte Barbosa was to remain in gaol.

"He is overwhelmed with saudade," I heard Dom Fernão tell Ser Antonio.

"I can understand that," Pigafetta said. "The malemolencia of the girls here can drive men to the heights of ecstasy. And now poor Duarte must languish in the brig."

Antón de color negro chose that moment to speak up. "He has no jeito," he said, obviously referring to Barbosa. "He's a tough-luck malandro. Worse, he sometimes acts like a maloque."

A few days later, on December 20, the sentence pronounced at the court martial on the high seas a month earlier was carried out. At break of day all hands assembled and solemnly watched as Antón Salomón received short shrift from Padre Valderrama. Then, face masked and hands bound, he walked to the scaffold and bowed his head so the masked hangman could slip the noose around his neck. Meek as a lamb, and at that moment it suddenly seemed to me a new form of human sacrifice.

The more I pursued the thought, the more I saw it for the sacrificial rite it was. It could not have been anything else. A man was being given up to propitiate the white man's gods and ensure the success of our venture. All done up as a serving of justice, but an offering none the less.

At the signal from the Captain-General the trapdoor was released, and we watched Salomón jerk about on the rope for a good ten minutes. Some of the Guaranis and Tamoios laughed at his antics. They did not know it was a dance of death. Or perhaps, even before Salomón finally became still, they knew it only too well.

I wondered if it made a difference.

⚓

13

THE TOUCH OF DEATH seemed to have wrought a sea-change upon the Armada. Things went on as before: we worked on the hulls of the ships, we stored food in the barrels, in the lean-tos ashore we drank, caroused and enjoyed the company of women. The Indians had began building a longhouse for us the day we arrived. Their own longhouses accommodated between seventy and a hundred people; the one they were building for us was to be three times as large. They thought we would be staying for good. No one knew how to disabuse them of that notion. They were so naïve they described our batels, tied to the naos by towropes, as baby ships being suckled by the mother ships. Their own canoes, each laboriously hollowed out from the single trunk of a huge tree, did not give birth to batels.

A hunting party was organized, several of our men going with Guarani males to the island of Paranapucu further north in the Baia de Sancta Lucía or, to use the natives' name for it, the Guanabara. At the end of the day they came back in the Indians' canoes with five antas, nocturnal animals that resembled a cross between the horse and the pig. With their elongated snouts, however, the antas looked to me more like overgrown anteaters. One of the antas was a nursing sow, and they had also killed and brought back its foal.

When I saw the suckling anta I recognized it as an animal I had seen many years before. The anta was a silent wraith in the forests back home. We called it the tapir. I asked Carvalho what the locals called it. "Tapir," he said—the same word. Were our languages related? Or was it coincidence?

The young anta they now threw on the ground had tawny stripes, exactly like its Malay relative. It was the adult that was different. The Brazilian tapir grew to become an all-black animal of about 400 pounds, although males of 650 pounds were not uncommon. The Malay tapir attained only 250 pounds or so, but it had much the more exotic coat: white from shoulder to rump, with all four legs remaining black. This gave it a strange appearance, as if it were wearing a white jacket. The outline of its body thus broken up into black and white, it looked ghostly on moonlit nights. Often a tiger would not recognize it as prey.

The meat of the tapir had always been considered tabu by my people. We believed it could cause leprosy.

I had doubts about eating the meat of the Brazilian tapir they were roasting on a spit. It smelled delicious. As my hunger overcame me, I finally decided it was well worth the risk of leprosy.

Christmas Eve was a warm balmy moonless night with wispy clouds scurrying across the sky. We roasted ducks and ate around the fires, singing madrigals and old melodies. Someone started a round song, in which separate groups sing the different stanzas together. I thought the stanzas would clash, because of the changes of pitch as one progressed from one stanza to the next, but instead they merged quite beautifully:

> *A solis orbu cardine*
> *Et usque terre limitem...*

The second group repeated those lines, in the same pitch, even as the first group moved up to a higher pitch for the next:

> *Christum canamus principem*
> *Natum Maria virgine...*

The Guaranis ate with us and marveled at our songs. Afterwards, couples began to drift off into the shadows. A knot of young men and women was talking to Carvalho. Now and then one of them cast a sidelong glance at me. Finally Carvalho beckoned me over and told me, "They like you. You're different, your color is like theirs. Choose one of the girls and reward her brother."

Different, indeed. A brown man among white men. I wondered if any of them had taken a fancy to our three black men. I pointed to the girl with the most buxom hips and the best-looking breasts. Her brother came closer. I offered him a caseknife from Middle France and a playing card—the Three of Spades. He accepted the knife but turned his nose up at the card. I substituted the sota de copas or Jack of Cups. This was better, but he held out for more. I threw in some fishhooks, a few nails, a necklace of hawksbells and a cheap mirror. He looked at it, and his own face gave him a fright. He showed it to the others, who crowded around him for a look.

"They're afraid of it," Carvalho said. "They think the mirror has the power to extract their souls and form an external image of it."

The girl led me off. She had bright eyes, long glossy hair, and a supple figure that swayed as she walked. We came to a crude hut among tall trees. Tied between two posts of this hut was a hammock. She climbed into it. I needed no invitation to climb in after her.

She smelled of the sea, and as I adjusted to what had seemed an awkward position, the hammock swayed and kept time to our rhythm.

We did it again and again, most of the time in positions I had not tried before, some of them possible only in a hammock. I remembered the positions the older boys used to brag about in my hometown: the kaja, the adharottara, the viparita surata...I always wondered what they meant. I wondered if I had now gone through any of those with this girl.

When we fell off and stepped out the sky had cleared and was ablaze with stars. Orion, newly risen, stood askew upside down in the north. At the zenith and to the south were stars I did not know. I had been farther south than this, eight years before, but off the Cape of Good Hope it had been all storms, no stars to speak of.

The girl was already in the sea. I joined her and found the waters of Guanabara Bay rather warm, warmer than the air. I pointed to the mouth of the Rio Carioca, wanting to wash in fresh water. She laughed and set off at a run, towards the Pão de Açúcar. I ran after her and soon fell behind. She was fleet as a goat, or a tapir, never stumbling. I looked in despair at the granite hump of the Pão de Açúcar. I would never manage to climb it in pursuit of her. Then she skirted it and crossed the headland instead. Beyond was the open ocean.

The surf was up and we chased each other on the fine white sands. I caught her, or maybe she allowed me to, and we collapsed in a heap.

"What is this place?" I asked in a mixture of words and gestures.

"Socopenapan," she said, or something like that.

We made love again right there, and barely noticed it when the waves of the rising tide began to lap at our bodies.

In the dawn light she sharpened a stick with my sheath knife, then waded out into the water. There were herons asleep nearby, and as I built a fire I wondered if their flesh was good to eat. She came back with a fish impaled on her spear, scattering herons as she ran. I cleaned and gutted the fish, and she wrapped it in a large leaf and roasted it over the coals.

After eating we ran west to another headland. I recognized it as the point Carvalho had said was called the Punto do Arpoador, Harpooner's Point. Past its massive rocks was another stretch of beach.

"Ipanema," she said.

I understood from her strange words and gestures that the tide was not right. We lay in the shade, waiting, and indulged yet again in the pleasures of the flesh.

We foraged a little, and ate the fruit of unknown shrubs, the fallen nuts of stately trees, the seeds of wild grasses. I remembered it was Christmas Day. I hoped no one missed me.

At high tide in the early afternoon she swam out and I watched as she caught a wave and rode it in almost to the shore. Then I followed her out and tried catching a breaker myself. After a few tries I timed a big one perfectly and rode it a long way in. And then she wanted me again. She began caressing my shoulders.

I took her right there, our bodies half in and half out of the water. Every time a wave came in, it threw us up on the beach only to drag us out again. A few times we got momentarily submerged, but we held our breath and clawed for the sand without a break in our rhythm.

On the way back, running at an easy pace, she kept talking, as if the relentless pounding of her words into my head would finally drive them into my comprehension. I tried to shut them out, unable to understand anything. There was one thing I could not remain deaf to, a certain note of insistent pleading. My ear fastened on to it. I wondered if she meant what it sounded like. Did she want me to live with her, raise children, surf in the sun forever? Did she want me to stay?

When we reached the mouth of the Rio Carioca I saw that only the *Santiago* was still being careened. The four naos were back in the water, lying at anchor. I swam out to the *Trinidad*, climbed up the rope ladder, and stood on the deck, dripping. The ship was deserted. In the warm late afternoon air I dried quickly. I went down, opened my sea chest, changed my codpiece, put on my hooded shirt of coarse serge, then went to the sterncastle, below the quarterdeck. There I curled up in a corner for a catnap.

"All right, Henrique, we saw you," came Dom Fernão's voice from up in the quarterdeck, "where have you been?"

"You missed the excitement, Enrico," Ser Antonio's voice put in. "De Coca released Cartagena."

At that moment we heard the slight splash of someone leaving the water to come up the ladder. The three of us fell silent.

The girl came aboard, the girl I thought I had left at the rivermouth. I regretted not having given her anything, as it was her brother I had paid with the cheap knife and playing cards.

She looked around and apparently decided there was no one aboard. She cast about as if looking for something. She bent down and picked up a large iron nail lying right there on the deck. It was made of metal, heavier than stone, a wondrous substance completely unknown to her people until recently, when the white man gave them their first samples. I thought she would hide it in her hair. She parted her knees, and nonchalantly inserted the nail into her cunt. I knew it was capacious, having been inside it myself, but I was catatonic with amazement. Then, bent and crouched over, she waddled off to the ladder and was gone.

"Did you see that?" asked Ser Antonio.

"I did," I said.

"I saw it, but I still don't believe it," Dom Fernão said.

"Quella vecchia troia!"

"What are we going to do about Cartagena, Sire?" I asked.

"Oh, not to worry. Espinosa recaptured him fairly quickly. They're in chains now, he and de Coca. Ashore. Mendoza has once again requested me to put them into his custody."

"I see." I was getting sleepy.

"Roldán d'Argote went off," Ser Antonio said, "to climb the Corcovado."

"Really, sir?"

"He should be reaching the summit about now."

Roldán was the Flemish gunner from the Concepcion, and the Corcovado was the low mountain that dominated the view from the ships. If you looked at the mountains with a child's eye, starting from the northwest and then on to the south, they resembled the figure of a giant lying off Guanabara Bay. A rounded mountain formed his head, the next few mountains formed his body, and the Pão de Açúcar was his feet. The Corcovado was his shoulder but by itself it also looked like the misshapen outline of a hunchback. It was Gonçalves, as Carvalho had told us, who named it the Corcovado in 1502.

We could not see Roldán in the distance. Fog was coming down; the peak of the Corcovado would soon be enshrouded in mist.

"I worked out the height of that mountain," Ser Antonio said, "using trigonometry."

"And what result did you obtain?" asked Dom Fernão.

"It's approximately 2,300 feet."

"Reasonable."

"There he is now!"

Roldán had reached the top. He stood there, very small but clearly discernible. The sun had set on us but up there he was still in the last of its light. Then he spread his arms out and kept them outstretched, as if praying, or blessing us.

"He is Moses," Ser Antonio said, "watching his men fight the Amalekites."

"He reminds me of something else," Dom Fernão said. "He reminds me of Christus Redemptor."

The mists were swirling now around Roldán and still he stood on top of the Corcovado, arms spread wide. Soon he was lost in the fog.

On Monday morning, December 26, oblivious to the fact that everyone had woken up with a Christmas hangover, the Captain-General assembled all hands on the beach for a Mass before departure. After the Mass he made a formal announcement, puctuated by trumpet blasts: Dom Álvaro de Mesquita, a sobresaliente on the *Trinidad*, was hereby appointed captain of the *San Antonio*.

There were murmurs. Then a few of the Portuguese, mostly the pilots and sobresalientes, began clapping their hands. The rest of the crew followed suit. Dom Álvaro acknowledged the applause with a bow.

The *San Antonio*'s two previous captains, Cartagena and de Coca, were prisoners. De Coca was in Captain Mendoza's custody in the *Victoria*, Cartagena in Captain Quesada's in the *Concepción*. Was Dom Álvaro the best choice as the next captain of the *San Antonio*?

For the first time in the voyage, I entertained some doubts about my master's wisdom. There were two men to be reckoned with on the almiranta: Fleet Accountant Hierónimo Guerra and Pilot-Major Estêvão Gomes. Guerra was Cristóbal de Haro's bastard, as everyone knew, and Gomes was someone who thought he should have been Captain-General of this Armada. Ever since his transfer to the *San Antonio* to make way for Carvalho on the flagship, Gomes had had little better to do than join the cabal of Spanish hidalgos plotting mutiny. All of the pilot's routine work on the almiranta had been left to João Rodrigues de Mafra.

Did Dom Fernão really think Dom Álvaro could handle hombres like this? Or had nepotism blinded him to a few things? If he had to practise nepotism, I thought he could have appointed his cuñado instead. Whatever my feelings about Duarte Barbosa, I still thought he would have been a better choice. Barbosa was an old salt, a cultured writer, and a valiant fighter who could rise to the occasion when the tostones were down. Too hedonistic and headstrong for his own good, he was still in the flagship's brig. I understood Dom Fernão's dilemma. It was not possible to release a man, especially not his own brother-in-law, from gaol in order to appoint him captain of the almiranta. And so he settled for his cousin. A nobleman of course, as a captain must be. But no seaman.

The Mass was celebrated, and about a hundred Indians joined us, Tupis, Tamoios, Guaranis, kneeling and raising clasped hands, singing, bowing to the ground when the Host was elevated. It gladdened the hearts of the Christians immensely. Both the Captain-General and Padre Valderrama had told them it was a mortal sin to have intercourse with pagan women, so these women's demonstration of their devoutness seemed to reassure the most licentious of the men that theirs had been venial sins only.

The Indians could not understand why we were leaving. Did we not want to live in the boii, or longhouse, they were building for us? It was almost finished. We could move in shortly. But when we insisted we were going, they did not argue. At least, they seemed to understand the Mass was a prelude to our leavetaking. They made it a point to attend.

Padre Valderrama's homily was a lecture on temptation and sin. He talked about the fine distinctions between celebrating and avoiding occasions of sin, about listening to temptation and giving in to it, and how one could avert sin, even at the last moment, by turning to prayer.

I could not help thinking that the Hindoos had been more exact and explicit. As I recalled, in Hindoo thinking there were eight stages of sexual temptation and sin. I knew them still:

First, there was smarana, which was the thinking of doing surata. Second, kirtana—speaking of doing it, such as bragging to other men of one's anticipation of carnal pleasures. Third, there was keli: flirting and dallying with the woman of one's desires. Fourth was prekshana, peeping at the woman's kaksha, or unmentionable bodily parts. Fifth, there was guyabshana: conversing with the woman on the subject of surata. Sixth was samkalpa, the intention to indulge in surata. Seventh was adyavasaya, or firmly resolving to do it. And eighth was kriyanishpati—the actual commission of surata, when vyadhi overcame both man and woman, and his lingam became sthanu, while her yoni became zankha, and yoti was all that mattered...

Then we had breakfast. The five Germans in the Armada sat together, and began singing the drinking songs they had perfected in our two weeks in Guanabara Bay. One of them had composed a new song, and this they sang with gusto:

Oh wie brannten euch der Lieben Flammen
Als ihr jung und voller Feuer ward
Ach der Mensch haut halt das Mensch zusammen
Das ist nun einmal so seine Art.
Oh diese Weiber, Himmelherrgottsackerment!
Arg schon die Liebe, aber ärger
noch der Tripper brennt!

Master Andrew, whose native language was related to German, had heard it often enough to attempt a translation:

Oh how the flames of love burned in your gut
When you were young, when you were full of fire
Now if it comes to beating up the slut
That doesn't interfere with your desire
Oh these damn women, many a lover sings,
Love's hard enough, love's painful—
When the pecker stings!

"Post coitum tristitia," said Ser Antonio, "post vinum capitis dolor. Ebbene!"

Then it was time to go. The alguaciles and merinos searched each ship for stowaways. They found a few, all girls, and promptly tossed them overboard. The Indians were natural swimmers, unlike our tripulantes. Most of the white men could not swim. None of the three blacks could.

João Lopes Carvalho was still with us on the capitana, still acting as Pilot-Major. He was the only one who had been in these waters before, as far as latitude 35 degrees South. Also with us was the pilot Andrés de San Martín, who had exchanged places with Gomes at the latter's suggestion, and with Dom Fernão's tacit consent.

Carvalho's son Juanillo was everyone's favorite shipmate on the *Trinidad*. Everyone spoke to him when there was a chance and the seven-year-old, not at all shy, always replied wittily. His repartée was in the Guarani language and his father patiently translated everything. Juanillo would pick up the Portuguese and Spanish languages soon enough. At his age his mind was a sponge, absorbing everything.

As the contramaestre began blowing his whistle and yelling commands to the marineros and grumetes I bent down and spoke to the boy.

"Niteroi," I said.

"The place of the hidden waters," Carvalho translated.

"Socopenapan."

"Stamping ground of the herons."

"Ipanema."

"Bad fishing. Where did you pick up those words?"

"Back there. From my garota."

"Some garota he had, too," Francisco Albo put in. "Loved her xthonic beauty."

"Yes, chthonic," agreed Carvalho. "He must have fucked her brains out."

As we sailed out with the tide hundreds of girls on the beach set up a raucous wailing. They were being left behind. How it broke their hearts. How our hearts bled for them. Would any of us ever see any of them again?

I searched their faces, but at that distance they all looked alike. I could not tell which one had been mine.

⚓

14

AFTER SUNSET, the course due southwest, a sickle moon hovered to starboard in the western sky. It would become a half moon at first quarter in two days, on December 28. The half moon, a layman's term, actually meant the moon at the first quarter phase of its cycle.

Our next stop was the Río Solis at latitude 35 degrees South. Despite its name, João Días de Solis was not its discoverer. That honor belonged to the Portuguese captain Sebastião Frões who, in 1512, had found either an estuary or an estrecho at 34⅔°S; he failed to establish which.

João Días de Solis, also a Portuguese captain, murdered his wife in 1509 when he came home from a voyage and found her in bed with another man. To escape justice, he fled to Spain. He found employment there, in 1512 retracing the fourth voyage or the Alta Viaje of Cristóbal Colón. The rumor was that Solis had secretly sought the Fountain of Youth at the behest of Spain's old King, Don Fernando de Aragón.

In 1515 Solis succeeded Amerigo Vespucci as Pilot-Major of Spain. In 1516 he led a fleet of three ships to the gulf at latitude 35°S on the new continent some cartographers were beginning to call América.

Exploring the gulf, and noting that it showed every sign of being a big river, he espied a party of friendly indios. He took seven men in a batel and rowed ashore. The natives calmly waited for them, then clubbed Solis and his men to death and began eating their flesh within sight of the three ships. Unbeknownst to themselves, these cannibals had exacted poetic justice from Solis for the murder of his wife.

According to the survivors Solis had named the river La Mar Dulce, admitting that its waters became fresh upstream while maintaining the idea of its being a strait. That left the matter unresolved. The mouth of the gulf was reportedly 37 leguas wide. Perhaps it was a strait after all, fed fresh water by rivers emptying into it. My master possessed a globe that depicted a strait there, at latitude 37°S, the land to the south being part of a great Southern continent. This was the secret globe by Schöner he had appropriated from the chart room in Dom Manoel's palace, the same globe he had shown to Don Carlos Primero in 1518. It showed the land mass of América ending at latitude 35°S. Just below it was the continent of Antarctica.

The Captain-General kept us sailing even at night. According to the Marinharia the coast in these parts had "as many miles as fathoms" so we usually kept one legua away from the coast in what we hoped was three-fathom water. At night we moved out to five or six leguas in water that was supposed to be sixteen or twenty fathoms. We kept men at the bow constantly heaving the sounding leads.

Duarte Barbosa was released from the brig a day after we left Guanabara, but he kept mostly to himself and avoided his shipmates' eyes.The look he gave me, however, was one of sheer dislike.

In the fine summer weather it was a pleasure to sleep on deck, under the stars. The moon was waxing and it grew every night, reaching its first quarter on December 28.

December 30, Master Andrew told us, was the feast of Thomas à Becket.

On December 31 we were at latitude 25°S. We hoarded our wine rations to drink it all in the moonlight.

"Here's to the end of the month," Ser Antonio proposed. "Tomorrow is another month, and the year 1519 now has only three months left to it."

It was of course a very inelegant calendar that could not have its New Year fall on the beginning of a new month. The white man's year ended on March 24, and the new year began on March 25. Thus in three months' time March 24, 1519, would be followed by March 25, 1520. As for the names of their months, September, October, November and December meant simply the 7th, 8th, 9th and 10th months. But where did the names of the other months come from? I knew some were named for Roman gods and that July and August were named for emperors who had also become gods, but the whole system made no sense to me. Why couldn't they name the months for the corresponding seasons? That was how my people did it. We began the year with the month of Dagang Buwan, the Maiden Moon, although other tribes called this month Kibaganon. This was the month the swarm of stars we called the Namurokpurok rose in the east at evening, signalling the start of the planting season. The white man called this month March, and the swarm of stars the Pleïades. Our other months, in order, were Lindanginon (or Kiling), Himbabuyon, Gobay, Hidapdapon, Lubod-lubod, Kanggurulsol, Bagyu-bagyu (or Manulsol), Panglot nga Diotay, Panglot nga Dakû, Ulalong, and Dagang Kahoy (or Higlalon). Each month was named for a unique feature of its part of the year. By contrast, the white man's months had insipid names.

January 1, the Feast of the Circumcision, was celebrated only by the uncircumcised men in the Armada, which meant most of them. Only two men in the whole crew were circumcised: one was myself, for everyone born in the Islamic Sultanate of Melaka was circumcised at the age of eight days, as Ibrahim had vowed to Allah. The other one was Hierónimo de Guerra of the *San Antonio*, because his father, Cristóbal de Haro, was a secret Jew. I did not care to celebrate the Feast of the Circumcision of the Prophet Issa because I had been circumcised on a different day. As far as I could guess, de Guerra declined to celebrate it, too—for much the same reason.

On January 4 the moon was full and all night I watched the play of its light: on the water, on the dark hulk of land to starboard, on the four ships in our wake.

January 6 was the Feast of the Epiphany, celebrated by an additional prayer at sunrise. It marked the visit of the three Magi to the Holy Infant. Master Andrew, however, told me there could have been as many as twelve Magi. Three of them, he said, were buried in the German city of Köln.

On January 8, after two weeks of continuous sailing, the Captain-General decided not to sail by night and we anchored near the coast at latitude 33°S.

On January 10 Carvalho pointed to three hills in the distance and said he recognized them. They were the hills of the Cabo Sancta María. It should have been called the Cabo Tres Marías but this was considered too obvious. Every Christian was supposed to know there were three Marys.

We hove to by the hills, which were above a point of land that marked the eastern entrance to the Río Solis. Off the point was an island. Carvalho said it was inhabited by a whole city of sea lions, which was why it was called the Isla de Lobos. This time, nobody said it was too obvious. And yet I knew, as did most of the crew, that it was unoriginal. There already existed an Isla de Lobos in the Canary Islands. As for the point of land, being the easternmost edge of the rivermouth, it was simply Punta del Este.

Turning into the wide bay, we followed its coast, our course now west by north. There were six other islands in that bay; one of them was supposed to be rich in gemstones. The opposite side of the bay could not be seen; it was 40 or 45 leguas away.

"*Monte vide eu!*" cried out the Captain-General. We looked. A mountain indeed loomed on the horizon, quite low, a hill really, but conspicuous against the surrounding flatlands. Later Dom Fernão named it the Cerro las Ánimas. He did not say why. Perhaps he believed that the spirits of Juan Díaz de Solis and the seven men killed with him now inhabited that mountain.

We anchored off a beach near the Cerro las Ánimas, our bombarderos at the cannon, our merinos and sobresalientes standing by with harquebuses and crossbows.

A canoe put out from the shore and tied up at the flagship. The lone cannibal on it came aboard. The Captain-General communicated with him through Carvalho.

The Indian seemed to be offering himself as hostage. He must have thought we had come to avenge Juan Díaz de Solis.

The Captain-General had leg irons put on the wretch, then ordered the alguacil to assemble a landing party. When it was ready Dom Fernão himself led the force, one hundred strong, ashore. We looked quite fearsome, encased in armor, firing a few shots from our harquebuses, carrying crossbows and halberds. The bombarderos manned the cannon, and fired a broadside to announce the landing party. The Indians fled inland, and most of the men chased them a while. In their heavy armor they could not run as fast as the natives, but it was enough to instill fear into their hearts. I stayed at my master's side, a pavis in my left hand and a halberd in my right, my body encased in my usual clothing. I did not care for the white man's armor. My master and I had once fought on opposing sides, and I had given a good account of myself, unarmored, against men in armor. I fought better without it.

Ser Antonio looked disappointed. He said he had hoped to kill a few cannibals in hand-to-hand fighting. I thought it more likely he had wanted to shoot some with a harquebus. His fuse rope was still smoldering. I stepped on it as if by accident and stamped out the glow.

Master Andrew looked up from his cannon and winked at Pigafetta.

"Well now, Ser Antonio," he said, "are you wanting the return of those man-eating savages, then? You might suggest to the Captain-General that he tie his prisoners to the trees ashore, Cartagena and de Coca, I mean. That should bring back those anthropophagous chaps soon enough. For good measure"—and here he winked at me—"perhaps they can be guarded ashore by Duarte Barbosa."

"Oh, it's you we ought to send ashore as bait, Maestro Andrea," Pigafetta replied genially. "Those natives would never eat you. You'd be too salty for them."

On January 12 the Captain-General ordered the ship with the lightest draft, the *Santiago*, to explore the head of the bay. She was away for three days. On January 15 Captain Serrano made his report to Dom Fernão: the bay narrowed to eight leguas at the head and was given to much shoaling.

"Did you taste the water as you went?"

"Yes, at every suitable opportunity. In most places it is brackish. As you go in, it becomes fresh."

"What about the tides?"

"The flood tide is definitely weaker than the ebb."

"Are you quite certain of that?"

"Quite. It is the effect of water being fed into the gulf by several rivers. I counted three large streams, about eight smaller ones, and innumerable creeks."

"But my sources were quite definite on this point. The paso lay at 35°S."

"Ah, you know how these cartographers are. Never can trust them. They're always putting in mythic islands. Remember the Septe Citades? And Hy-brasil? But perhaps this paso is to be found further south."

"Maybe we got the latitude wrong. Let's check it again. Where's my astrolabe?"

"Come, come, filho, there's no need for that. We're at 35° all right. They simply jumped to conclusions. They thought an estuary as wide as this, wider than Rio de Janeiro, must turn out to be a strait. This is another land, another world. Things we've grown accustomed to in Europa, even in Africa, India or Asia are simply different here."

"Perhaps one of those bigger rivers is the paso. I'll have to order a more detailed search. Send the longboats upstream until the water is fresh enough to drink."

"With all due respect, comendador, I think it will be an exercise in futility. The paso simply doesn't exist. At least, not here."

"We must confirm or deny its existence. The only way is to taste each of those rivers, one by one."

"You still hope to find a salty river, don't you?"

"We'll see."

Volunteers were found to man the longboats, five men to each batel. They were issued a week's food supplies, to be supplemented by hunting or fishing. Each volunteer also drew weapons of his choice from the stores. Master Andrew of Bristol personally checked the two serpentinas on each batel.

"The cannibals can't have gone too far," he told the crews. "They're bound to be nearby, watching our every move. Should you have to fight them, use the serpentinas and harquebuses first. Their effective range is no more than a hundred yards, about the same as the crossbow's, but these savages haven't seen gunpowder before. The surprise will demoralize them."

The Captain-General gave the crews their orders:

"Captain Juan Serrano reports at least eleven rivers debouching into this gulf. The crew of the *Santiago*'s batel will investigate the three farthest, since they've been there and can find them easily enough. The other crews will examine two rivers each. At each river, row upstream as far as is practicable. Use your sounding leads and determine whether the depth increases, decreases, or remains constant. Taste the water constantly; in a strait it will be salty all throughout, while in a river it will gradually turn fresh. At your farthest point upstream, stay long enough for the changing of the tide, and observe the strength of each tide.

"Should you find other streams the *Santiago* may have missed, explore them too, and report them to me. Anyone who finds the paso will receive a bonus of one month's salary, payable in Venetian gold ducats when I am personally satisfied it is the strait we have been seeking."

"What if," asked Maestro Pero of Teneriffe, who was going in the *Santiago*'s batel, "we should find the Fountain of Youth?"

"And how would you know it was indeed the Fuente de Joven?"

"Why, its water would be very weak. Nothing should float on it, not even wood. All should sink to the bottom."

Particularly if one threw in a piece of very heavy wood, I thought, hardwood found only in my native land, like the belian wood of the Johor forest.

"Another way," said the grumete Perucho de Bermeo, "is to throw in a bacalhau. If it is indeed the Fonte do Jovem, the dried fish should come back to life and swim away."

"Well then, should you be so fortunate as to find it, take a good long drink from it," Dom Fernão replied. "That should be its own reward. And don't forget to fill a cask from it, for the rest of us here. Remember, do not approach any indios you might come across, no matter what outward signs of frendliness they manifest. They're all cannibals. And they prize white flesh, because they seldom get it. They haven't had any since Juan Díaz de Solis."

"An acquired taste, eh?" winked Master Andrew.

15

TWO DAYS LATER, the first of the batels returned. Its crew reported nothing out of the ordinary. One by one, three of the other batels returned from their sorties, none with anything significant to report. Only the *Trinidad*'s batel, Don Gonzálo Gómez de Espinosa in command, had yet to return.

"Perhaps they found the strait and are reconnoitering it," mused Dom Fernão.

Don Gonzálo and his men reappeared on January 18.

"We camped at a site where the air was good," reported the alguacil. "On the banks of a river I named the Río Chuelo. I called the place the Puerto de Sancta María del Buen Ayre."

"And the rivers?" queried Dom Fernão.

"All became sweet upstream. In each case the ebb tide was clearly stronger than the flood tide. No question, mi comendador. The paso is not to be found here."

"Very well. Carry on."

As he went off Don Gonzálo said lightly, "If I ever come back here I'll found a settlement on that site. I'll call it Buenos Ayres."

A whole week passed without event. There was no sign of the cannibals. The ships rode at anchor near the Cerro las Ánimas, but every day Don Gonzálo went off in the batel, with a crew of rowers, to explore some other river. It seemed Dom Fernão could not accept there was no paso here. His secret map indicated a strait at latitude 35 °S, and he could not understand why nothing could be found.

On Wednesday, January 25, we heard cries from the *Concepción*. Dom Fernão hailed them. A reply was hailed back:

"We've found a dead body."

Men in the *Concepción*'s batel recovered the body. They brought it ashore. In command of the batel was Captain Gaspar de Quesada.

"Who is it?" asked the Captain-General.

"It's one of my grumetes," said Quesada. "Guillérmo de Lole. From Irlande."

"When did you find him?"

"Just now."

Dom Fernao examined the body. The cirujano approached too, but it did not require Juan de Morales, el bachiller, to tell us the man had drowned. The dead man's red hair partly covered his face. Dom Fernao gently brushed back the wet strands, and I gasped with the shock of recognition. It was William O'Connor, from Loughrea.

"Death by drowning," Dom Fernão said. "His stomach is distended from swallowing much water."

He pulled the sheet over William's head. His gaze fastened on one of the grumetes.

"You. You're from Irlande too, aren't you?"

"Yes, sir," said Guillén Irés, who I recalled was Kevin of Galway, Kevin Cavanagh.

"When did you see him last?"

"This morning, sir. At breakfast."

"Five hours ago. No one noticed his absence at lunch?"

"Yes, sir. Wondered about that. He had said he was going to the ship. After lunch I went there and looked for him. One of the merinos says he thought he'd heard a splash astern a while before. Thought nothing of it, he says. The two of us, me and Juanillo here, jumped into the water and swam down to the bottom. We found him there, sir. Must have fallen off. He couldn't swim, see? Never learned how."

"Yet the two of you swim quite well?"

"We be both from Galway, sir."

Captain Gaspar de Quesada was ordered to investigate the incident and ascertain the cause of death, with the power to summon any man in the Armada for questioning. Kevin of Galway took charge of his countryman's wake and burial, with carte blanche from the Captain-General to arrange it as he saw fit.

Kevin asked the carpenters Domingo de Iranza, Martin de Griate, and Pedro de Sabtua to make a coffin. The three Basques felled a tree and began hewing. The barber of the *Concepción*, Pedro Olabarrieta, Don Antonio de Coca's erstwhile servant, helped Kevin prepare the corpse, scrubbing it up, trimming the red hair, shaving the beard. Then they dressed William in his best clothes.

They laid him out on a slab of wood, supported by four stools. A sheet of linen covered the body, leaving only the face, hands and bare feet exposed. Kevin tied the two big toes together with a cord. He drew a pair of new shoes from the Armada's stores and placed it on the ground at the dead man's feet, "for his coming journey through Purgatory." He entwined rosary beads around the folded hands, centered the crucifix on the chest. Sean was back now, and Kevin asked him to fetch William's cloak.

The men of the Armada turned out for supper at the wake. Kevin lit the candles at the dead man's head, then burned the cloak, "to ward off the fairies." Supper was an enormous pot of Kevin's stew, for which a goat and a tapir had been slaughtered. The biscuits were freshly baked, and he had scrounged in the stores for butter and cheese. Most of the butter had turned rancid in the heat of the doldrums, so there was only a bowl of it. There were three wheels of cheese, as we still had some 500 wheels of the 984 cheeses loaded in Sevilla. There was a keg of wine, and several bottles of Master Andrew's uisgebaugh.

"May William be dead a year," said Master Andrew, "before the Devil hears of it."

"I cut this meat," Dom Fernão said, "with the knife of sorrow."

"We've lost a good man," Captain Quesada said.

After supper Padre Valderrama began the rosary. The first sorrowful mystery was the Agony in the Garden but I managed to slip away. I got back while they were calling on the saints.

Kevin was leading.
    "St. Brigid—"
    "Pray for us."
    "St. Patrick—"
    "Pray for us."
    "St. Columba—"
    "Pray for us."

"St. Brendan—"

"Pray for us."

They must have called on the whole army of saints, one by one, before that. But it was ending now, and I was in time for the drinking. A keg of wine was opened, and most of the men began drinking it neat, not mixing it with water. The two Irishmen and Master Andrew disdained the wine, drinking only whiskey. Sean was going to mix a little water in his, but Kevin stopped him. "Come now," Kevin said, "you can't be seen to be watering your whisky in front of a Sasanach, can you?"

"Oh, is this whisky then?" riposted Sean. "Thought I it was that Greek rotgut Mateo de Corfu gave us, that ouzo. Have to mix water with that, turn it cloudy, don't you?"

"Sláinte," said Kevin, raising his cup.

"Sláinte," replied Sean and Master Andrew.

"À votre santé," said marinero Pierre Gascon of the *Santiago*.

"Prosit," said Ser Antonio.

"Saúde," said Dom Fernão.

"Skol," said Hans Vargue.

"Giassou," said Mateo de Gorfo.

"Ought to have a shanachie," Kevin grumbled, "a storyteller. And a minstrel playing a harp. A harp such as the angels play. Can't have a proper wake without those now, can we?"

Kevin was watching Sean. The boy had drank quite a bit, and now there was a strange look in his eye as he approached the corpse.

"William!" Sean cried, "William! I knew you were going away! Last night I dreamt I saw the banshee, but then I woke up and it was no dream!"

"Is that right, now?" Master Andrew prodded him on.

"You don't say," Kevin added.

"In my dream we were back in the River of January," Sean said in a hushed voice, so that all strained forward to listen, "and I saw a hooded figure atop the Sugar Loaf. I heard it screech, but the sound echoed around the hills. It seemed to be calling 'Gilly-yermo!' I woke up with a start and saw the figure in shadow, against the Cerro. A hood on his head—"

"By our Lady!" said Master Andrew.

"—and a noose around his neck!" He was in tears now.

"Antón Solomón's banshee!" cried Kevin.

"Aaaiiieeegggh..." shrieked Sean, in an unearthly keening. It took us all by surprise. No one had suspected Juanillo of Galvey could attain such high notes.

"Ooh, nooo..." wailed Kevin, and now madness set in. The Basques joined in the screaming at once, and then the Italians.

"You didn't watch him!" Kevin accused Sean, even as the Frenchmen added their howls to the din.

"But it was you who were bosom buddies!" protested Sean.

"If only you'd followed him to the ship," lamented Kevin through his tears, "maybe he'd still be alive this minute!"

All at once he threw a fist at Sean, knocking the younger man down. Sean was up right away, fists flying. It would have been a real brawl, but the Basques stepped in and held them apart.

We kept the deathwatch for three days. Captain Quesada concluded his investigation and reported that Guillermo's death had been, in all probability, an accidental drowning. I wondered if anyone saw it as another human offering, demanded by the gods of this place. In this wild land on the other side of the Mar Océano every place had its own pantheon of unknown spirits, and at every stop they asked of us a sacrifice. At our first stop it had been Antón Salomón; now they had taken another man.

When the coffin was finished, the dead man was laid in it. Sean had whittled a wooden shamrock, and this he placed on William's chest below the rosary's crucifix. The grave was dug. An altar was set up in front of William. The three chaplains concelebrated a requiem Mass, Padre Valderrama in the center, Padre Sánchez de Reina at his right, and Père Calmet at his left. Kevin instructed the pallbearers to carry the coffin feetfirst. When the Mass was over the eight pallbearers picked up the coffin and immediately one of the marineros kicked the stools down, as Kevin had asked him to.

After the burial they stuck a wooden cross into the mound, over the part where William's head lay. It was a cross unlike any I had seen before, vertical and horizontal beams encased in a circle, in what Sean said was the Celtic style. Then Kevin picked up a rock and placed it at the other end of the mound, over William's feet. Sean followed Kevin's example, and laid another rock on the mound. After them most of the men did, too: first the other grumetes, then the rest of the *Concepción*'s crew, and after them the men from the other ships, Petit Jean d'Anjou contributing a menhir no one else could have lifted, so that William of Loughrea was honored by a cairn rising six feet above the six feet of earth we had shoveled on him, twelve feet in all weighing down his own two feet, the big toes of which were still bound together, that he might forbear to come back and haunt us.

The necrolith looked like it might last forever, yet the words of the priests, so evanesecent by comparison, seemed to resound among the very rocks, as though their echo might outlast mere stone.

"For I am the resurrection and the life," the three had intoned, in one voice.

16

PREPARING TO DEPART the Río Solis on Candlemas, February 2, a somber Thursday, the rest of us were in the shadow of the Captain-General's disappointment. Half a year out of Sevilla, and now we would be moving into uncharted waters for the first time, in search of an elusive strait that was not where the cartographers had said it would be.

Dom Fernão still believed finding it was a matter of time. Many in the crew were convinced there was no strait at all. Verzin was unbroken land all the way down to the South Pole. Everyone knew that.

There had been enough disgruntled crewmen to call for an open convention the day after Guillérmo de Lole's burial. Spanish crews had the traditional right to call for one, in which democratic procedure was followed. Captain Luis de Mendoza, acting as spokesman, proposed that the Armada sail back to the Bahía de Santa Lucía and spend the winter there. In such an open convention the Captain-General could not issue orders, but had to resort to cajolery. Dom Fernão had persuaded the men to pursue the Armada's avowed goals by the sheer force of his personality, appealing to their nobler instincts and their pride. I rather thought it had been a close call.

João Lopes Carvalho was again on the *Concepción*, his stint as Acting Pilot-Major over. Estêvão Gomes had chosen to remain on the *San Antonio*, leaving Andrés de San Martín with us on the *Trinidad*. These arrangements seemed to be the most satisfactory for everyone concerned. Then, the day before we sailed, the *San Antonio*'s other pilot, João Rodrigues de Mafra, requested a transfer. He said he did not feel comfortable being the only Portuguese on the *San Antonio*.

Dom Fernão accepted him on the *Trinidad*. Naturally de Mafra's son Diego, a page, was transferred to the capitana as well.

The Captain-General intended to act as his own Pilot-Major now, with Francisco Albo as his amanuensis. For form's sake de Mafra was registered as the official piloto mayor, and San Martín as the astrólogo mayor.

It was the day before the full moon, and we sailed out with the tide shortly after high noon, the *Trinidad* leading the way south by west. The season seemed right for the exploration of the unknown coast south of the Río Solis: the prevailing winds were from the northwest at 15 or 20 knots, and there were few calms or variables. I looked forward to some weeks of good sailing. South into the winter. It would gradually turn cold and bleak, but for now we were under way again. Nothing else mattered.

The following day, February 3, when Captain Álvaro de Mesquita made his evening salute to the Captain-General he reported the death of a marinero.

"Sebastián de Olarte, from Bilbao, killed by another marinero."

"Who?"

"Jacóme de Mecina. He is in the brig, in chains."

"Feed him nothing but bread and water. We shall have to convene another courtmartial for him on the morrow. Bury the dead man at first light."

From the *Trinidad* I could not see much of the Basque wake being conducted on the *San Antonio*. They kept the vigil on deck around the corpse, drinking wine from their xahakoas, goatskin bags from which they squirted the wine into their mouths. These bags were smooth on the outside, as they were always fashioned hair side in. The goathair imparted a high flavor and exotic bouquet to the wine. Domingo de Barrutía had once allowed me a taste, and I thought it awful. But perhaps I was biased. I could not handle the xahakoa right and squirted more wine into my eyes and nose than into my mouth. But I could understand how wine untouched by goathair must taste flat to a Basque. Only a Basque could squirt wine from a xahakoa into his mouth with unfailing accuracy. No Basque ever spilled so much as a single drop from a xahakoa, not even in the roughest of seas. Ser Antonio once asked to borrow Domingo's xahakoa and, after getting his face wet with wine, suggested that it be filled with water for more practice. Barrutía refused. Water in his xahakoa, he said, would spoil the taste of any wine he might put in it next.

The following dawn, the full moon setting in the west, I went with my master in the batel to the *San Antonio*. By tradition, sea burials took place at first light. The three chaplains were there, and all five captains. Sebastián de Olarte had been sewn up in a heavy shroud, along with enough weights to make sure he would sink straightaway to the bottom. The chaplains said a short prayer:

"Absolve quaesumus Domine, animam famili tui Sebastián..."

The Basque pallbearers heaved the enshrouded corpse overboard. The waves swallowed it up at once. Then all the Basques began to sing:

"Ichasoa urac aundi es du ondoric agueri..."

Later I asked Domingo de Barrutía what it meant. He translated:

"The waters of the sea are vast, and the bottom cannot be seen..."

At his court-martial Jacóme de Mecina pleaded self-defense, but the circumstances were unclear and the witnesses not forthcoming. The consensus was that they feared speaking out against the wiry Sicilian. From what I could gather, Sebastián de Olarte had made some comment about the late Antón Salomón and Jacóme had resented it as a slur on all Sicilians. In the end a verdict of involuntary manslaughter was handed down and Jacóme sentenced to three months of hard labor at our next port of call.

A third man was dead. Jacóme had killed Sebastián...or had the gods of these waters made him do it, made him sacrifice a human to them?

I watched the moon wane for a week. By February 11 it was at last quarter. I had stopped looking at the land. There it was, as it had been yesterday, to starboard: blue in the distance or lost in the mists, and never a break that might show a strait.

The weather had turned. Now the sky was always overcast. On February 13 a storm whipped up. We lay at anchor in a bay, leeward of the white cliffs, the ships getting tossed about until we were all wet, cold and hungry. Once again, St. Elmo's fire appeared in the nick of time, saving us from the woes of despair and delivering us from our travails. Listening to Ser Antonio say his desperate prayers was also an education in itself.

We called that place the Bahia Blanca, really the only name for it, and were glad to be leaving it.

Now we were at latitude 38°S, and it was as cold as Lisbõa, at the same latitude north, in autumn.

Petit-Jean d'Anjou gave an exhibition on February 21, juggling six knives, because he wanted a carnival air that day, Mardi Gras. The term meant Fat Tuesday but Master Andrew called it Shrove Tuesday.

The following day, February 22, was Ash Wednesday, the first day of the Season of Lent. Padre Valderrama went around with a bowl of ashes and drew crosses on our foreheads. Every time he daubed ash on a forehead he murmured:

"*Memento, homo, quia pulvis es, et in pulverem reverteris.*"

On February 24 we opened a bay some 60 miles wide at latitude 40°40'S. It also receded northwest some 80 miles but the dipsey lead never touched bottom and the Captain-General decided it was a dead end. He called that bay the Bahia sin fondo. The southern end of that bay was a peninsula, which he named the Península Valdés.

The day after that we rounded the peninsula and found another bay, a smaller one, on the other side of it, at latitude 42°54'S. A squall struck. We had to shelter in that gulf, which the Captain-General named the Puerto de San Matías. The feast of San Matías was on the 24th, except during leap years, when the 24th became the eve, the feast moving to the 25th. The year 1519 would not end until March 24, and supposedly a leap year had to be divisible by 4, but February had 29 days this year so that was that.

The skies remained grey, and I could hardly keep track of the moon, although I knew it was going into its first quarter phase. I saw it only briefly in the evening, riding like a ghost on clouds as heavy as our seas.

The winds blew steadily and made our ships skim across the water. We sailed all night. We must have made almost a hundred leguas that day, February 25.

February 26 was the first Sunday of Lent. We were sailing surely and swiftly into the season of abstinence.

On February 27 we came into a shallow bay that had three islands off a rivermouth in it. The Captain-General called it the Cabo dos Bahías, as that was what it was: a cape overlooking two bays. We drew close to the islands, which looked strangely bare: no trees grew on them. But they were full of movement, animals sunning themselves on the rocks, great seals and flightless birds. The Captain-General called the islands the Islas del Sansón, saying any humans that might be found there would surely be giants like Samson, if the seals were any indication. He sent a landing party ashore to slaughter some of the elephant seals and patos sin alas as he called them. Ducks without wings.

"Look like auks to me," Master Andrew said. "Got wings, for all the good it does them. Ought not to be called ducks. They're pengwins for sure, now."

An offshore gale whipped up, and our five ships were blown out to sea. For two days we held tight and rode out the storm. There was no chance to be concerned about the landing party stranded on the treeless island.

When the winds abated we returned to recover the men on the island. Miraculously they were still alive, all six of them, if stinking of raw meat. They had burrowed under the still-warm carcasses of their elephant seals and so managed to keep from freezing to death. It was February 29, the extra day of the year, and we knew something extra had been granted us that day.

The sun came out for a spell at noon. Francisco Albo took a sight of it, finding our latitude to be 45°30′S.

The month of March began with the same dreary weather. From March 1 through March 6 we suffered six straight days of storms. We kept on going in circles in a bay. We could not anchor, and our hands grew stiff handling the ropes in the cold biting winds. We could not light fires either, and could eat cold food only in snatches. Our clothes were wet most of the time, and our chafed hands remained sore owing to the salt spray as waves crashed against the bow. It was difficult to sleep in the incessant tossing about of the ship, and the Captain-General must have remained sleepless the whole time. At night we had to watch each other's lights very carefully to avoid collisions. There was no getting out of that bay while the storms raged, and there was no harbor to put into; we had to ride out the storms for as long as they blew.

The Captain-General called that bay the Bahia de los Trabajos, the Bay of Travails. It was at 48°10'S according to Albo, although San Martín's reading of that latitude was only 47°46'S. I was beginning to suspect Albo's latitudes were consistently too large, sometimes by as much as half a degree. It did not greatly matter, however, not in this part of the world.

The rest of March was a gloomy period during which we had to tack about owing to headwinds. Our progress to the southwest was desultory, and we managed only 40 leguas in 3 weeks. Everyone was too listless to go to the barbers, who were not inclined themselves to practise their profession just then. Hair grew long. Beards grew heavy, except mine and some of the page boys'. The year 1519 ended on March 24 with no fanfare. New Year's Day on March 25, 1520 was Passion Sunday as they called it. It was also the Feast of the Annunciation of the Virgin Mary. For me it was merely another passionless, colorless day somewhere between latitude 48°S and 49°S.

As March ended, so did our sailing. On the 31st, the eve of Palm Sunday, we came upon a long narrow landlocked bay, stretching to the southwest, that was guarded by high cliffs on either side. The Captain-General announced that he was naming this bay the Puerto San Julián, and that we would be wintering there.

Half a mile separated the two cliffs, each a hundred feet high, at the entrance to Puerto San Julián. The Captain-General gave them their names: Cabo Curioso for the northside sentinel and Punta del Desengaño for the other one. Contramaestre Francisco Albo was sent off in the batel, with two marineros and two grumetes, to scout the bay.

Marshland, Albo soon reported, extended from Cabo Curioso and went on to form a submerged sandbar at the mouth of the bay. At low tide the bar lay at no more than a fathom, so that the water foamed over it. An island lay inside the bay. It was quickly named Isla San Julián, just as the wide bay outside the bar was Bahia San Julián. The inlet had good beaches for careening the ships, and plenty of firewood to be found on the land, as well as wood for building lean-tos. Drinking water was available from several creeks. The area below Punta Desengaño was studded with rocks. Between the marshland and the rocks, the effective navigable width was only a couple of hundred yards. The narrow entrance was like a bottleneck, creating a funnel effect, where the current ran at six knots. The tidal range, Albo reported, was twenty-three feet. Later, we were to find it was twenty feet for the neaps and a full twenty-five for the springs.

"Reminds me of the gorge you go through on the way to Bristol," Master Andrew said, "halfway up the Avon from the Severn. Highest tides in the world. Forty feet at spring tide."

The *Trinidad* anchored just outside the bar at the center of the mouth, halfway between the two cliffs, her bow facing the bay. Beside her, to port, was the *Santiago,* and astern lay the *Victoria.* The *San Antonio* and the *Concepción* were both ordered to cross the bar and anchor inside the bay. The *Concepción* anchored just past the bar, showing her stern to the flagship. The *San Antonio* went much farther in and anchored twice as far from the capitana as the *Concepción* had. Because of the strong tides and currents, every available anchor was deployed.

Puerto San Julián was at latitude 49°08'S as determined by Andres de San Martín that same noon, March 31. Francisco Albo reckoned it as 49°40'S. Ser Antonio borrowed the Captain-General's brass astrolabe to make his own shot of the sun, and computed the latitude as 49°30'S. The Captain-General was amused at the wide variations. He had quietly made his own shot of the noonday sun, and found our latitude to be 49°12'S. He did not tell the others how badly they had been off.

Longitude was another thing entirely. There would be time enough to measure it, by whatever method.

The Captain sent the escribano, León de Espeleta, escorted by the alguacil, Don Gonzálo Gómez de Espinosa, in the batel to the other ships to relay a message: the rations of wine and biscuit were to be cut, as sources of fresh water were sure to be found, as well as plenty of game and fish.

By evening a deputation of sailors from all five ships had been formed and sent to the flagship to plead before the Captain-General.

"My Captain-General," said Diego Hernandez as spokesman for the group, "we entreat thee to restore full rations and return to Spain..."

Dom Fernão listened patiently to the speech: how it was impossible to eat meals without wine, how nothing lay ahead but death by freezing. But it seemed he had anticipated all those arguments.

"Gentlemen," he replied, "I swore a holy oath to find the paso. All of you swore to follow me. I will give up my life before I renege on my oath.

"Here, we are in a safe harbor. I am cutting the wine and biscuit rations by half so we may have more of those for the long voyage ahead. Here we have plenty of fresh water to drink, fish in the waters, and game in the woods. We shall sleep around our fires at night. When spring comes we will sail again, and I promise you that the strait will surely be found. It will lead us to the world of Asia, and the wealth of the Indies, where the girls are even more beautiful than those of Sta. Lucía.

"Bear with me. The real adventure has yet to begin. Where is your courage, your vaunted Castilian valor? Are you to be deemed by future generations as wanting? Our forefathers showed the mettle of our race in their reconquest of our Iberian homeland from the Moors. Let us not be unworthy of them. Remember, Plus ultra."

Or words to that effect. I saw at once that he had touched their pride yet again. These scions of Spain would not fail their families, their nation, or their King. They left the colloquy with renewed determination, their hearts rekindled with stolen fire. In my own heart I knew their loyalty was true, but I came from a race that regarded not the heart, but the liver, as the center of feelings. And now something seemed to be gnawing at my insides. Was I chained to a rock after all, was doubt a vulture eating out my liver?

⚓

17

PALM SUNDAY ON APRIL 1, 1520 meant a very long Mass, as it had to be preceded by a ceremony called the Blessing of the Palms. The Mass was at the Isla San Julián. The men of the *Trinidad* were all armed, as the Captain-General had quietly instructed. I had only my sheath knife, but I did not think any attack would be carried out on us. Not during a Mass. The white man was too pious for that.

I did my best not to fall asleep during the ceremonies, but the sonorous Latin of the priests had a most soporific effect. Now and then a phrase would leap out, and my mind would translate it in a bored, offhand manner. *Cur eduxistis nos in desertum istud, ut occideritis omnem multitudinem fame?* Why have you brought us into this desert, that you might destroy all the multitude with famine?

Every single man at the ceremony held a leafy branch, usually a fern, in lieu of a palm frond. After the Blessing came the Procession, with Padre Valderrama carrying a thurible of incense, Père Calmette the Processional Cross, Padre Sánchez de Reina a clutch of real palm fronds, where he had gotten them I could not imagine, and acolytes Cristóvão Rabelo and Andrés de la Cruz a lighted candle each. We marched around in a wide circle, chanting "Hosanna!"

Then came the Mass proper, with my mind wandering again. A few of the Latin phrases registered in my ear: *Deus, Deus meus, respice in me: quare me dereliquisti?* O God, my God, look upon me; why hast Thou forsaken me?

And, during the Gospel: *Qui intingit mecum manum in paropside, hic me tradet.* He that dippeth his hand with Me in the dish, he shall betray Me.

Finally it was over. The Captain-General had intended to invite the four other captains for breakfast with him in the capitana, but Quesada had not attended the Mass. Neither had his prisoner, Cartagena. Mendoza had come without his prisoner, de Coca. Dom Fernão extended his invitation to Mendoza, Serrano, and Mesquita, then went ahead in his batel. When I reached the *Trinidad*, I found only Dom Álvaro de Mesquita had accepted.

The two Captains ate breakfast in silence. "Put a strong guard on duty at all times," Dom Fernao said shortly. "The *San Antonio* is our biggest ship. We can't..."

"Yes, yes," Dom Álvaro said.

When the despensero wasn't looking, I managed to filch some of the portions meant for the other captains: raisins, figs, carne de membrilla or quince preserves, of which Dom Fernão was especially fond, salt pork and beef, ship's biscuit, two rations of wine. Not bad for a Palm Sunday breakfast.

The batel was sent out from the *Trinidad* the next morning, Monday of Holy Week, April 2, with a detail of men to cut firewood. In command was the contramaestre, Francisco Albo. They were to stop at the other ships and collect woodcutters from each. We watched them row to the *Concepción*. Their boathook was fended off with a halberd, and we saw them rowing hurriedly back to the *Trinidad*.

"What happened?" asked the Captain-General.

"The man said they were for Captain Juan de Cartagena, and follow only his orders," reported Albo.

"I saw Captain Cartagena on the poopdeck," said the grumete Basco Gómez Gallego, "in his armor."

"Back on board, all of you. General quarters."

Captain Álvaro de Mesquita's coat of arms were hauled down from the *San Antonio*'s capstans. As we watched, new flags were raised in their stead: Captain Gaspar de Quesada's cognizance. Captain Juan de Cartagena's blazon now went up on the *Concepción*. That could only mean Captain Quesada had released Cartagena. And Captain Mendoza on the *Victoria* must have released de Coca. Then Quesada had obviously led a force to the *San Antonio* and overpowered Captain Mesquita. Three ships were in the hands of mutineers.

The *Trinidad* and the *Santiago* lay together just outside the bar, with two enemy ships in the narrow bay in front of us, and one behind us. We were outgunned. It remained to be seen how many in the crews of the three ships were with the mutineers. Perhaps we were outnumbered, too.

Dom Fernão huddled in his cabin with Duarte Barbosa, Don Gonzálo Gómez de Espinosa, Cristovão Rabelo, Master Andrew of Bristol, armorer Pedro Sanildes, and the sobresalientes.

"They'll wait for the slack tide before they attack," Barbosa said, "which will be at..."

"This evening," Dom Fernão said. "And with a land breeze, too."

He took a deep breath.

"Their foremost aim will be to kill me, and for that they will sacrifice the *Trinidad*. They may, however, spare the *Santiago*. We must expect cannon fire from opposing flanks, after which they'll come alongside to grapple and board."

At midmorning a batel set out from the *San Antonio*, Don Antonio de Coca in command.

"Magallanes!" de Coca called out, "we have a message for you."

He passed us a note on the tip of his boathook. A marinero took it to the Captain-General. De Coca settled to wait for a reply, his oarsmen sculling water for a few minutes before they decided the current was rather strong and it was easier to hook on to the *Trinidad*'s anchor cable.

Dom Fernão's reply was passed to de Coca, who rowed back to the *San Antonio*.

"They want him to come to them on the *San Antonio*," Duarte Barbosa told Ser Antonio. "They're willing to recognize him as just another captain, but not as Captain-General. The same things as before: why he changed course without informing them, why he didn't follow the course agreed on at the Casa. And now why he's pushing on with winter coming and no sign of that mythical strait. They say it's foolhardy to continue and urge him to give up and go home."

"Who signed their note?"

"All four of them. Cartagena, Quesada, Mendoza and de Coca."

"Well, what did he write in his reply?"

"He ordered Quesada and Mendoza to report to him on the flagship immediately. The other two are deposed captains; it's proper to ignore them."

At noon the *San Antonio*'s batel moved out, filled with as many men as it could carry, some fifteen in all. They began rowing to the *Concepción*. As they passed it they reached out with the boathook, but missed. A marinero on the *Concepción* tossed them a rope which, however, fell short. The current was now carrying the batel to the bar. They went past it, only the quick reaction of their helmsman veering them away from the rocks. They steered accurately over the foaming bar, which also meant they would pass close to the *Trinidad*.

"Help!" several of them yelled, "the current's too strong!"

One of our grumetes threw them a hawser, which their officer in command caught. We hauled them in.

Dom Fernão ordered a drink of wine for each of them. They were ordinary seamen, most of them Basque. In command was the calafate Martín de Goytisolo.

"We're being transferred to the *Concepción*," said Goytisolo, "in exchange for some merinos and fighting men. We're not mutineers, mi capitán, you must believe me. Quesada, de Guerra, Cartagena, de Coca, Elcano and the others took us by surprise last night. Captain Mesquita they locked up. Juan de Elorriaga the maestre ordered them to stop but Quesada stabbed him several times."

"Is he dead?"

"No, he was still alive when we left a few minutes ago. But he might not last another night."

Things moved fast now. The Captain-General handpicked fourteen men and ordered them to exchange distinctive articles of clothing with the men from the *San Antonio*. The alguacil, Don Gonzálo Gómez de Espinosa, went in the batel of the *Trinidad* with a merino, Alberto de Córdova, and four oarsmen to the *Victoria*. As he clambered aboard, Duarte Barbosa and the handpicked fourteen got into the other batel, pretending to be the men from the *San Antonio*.

The signal was to be a handkerchief waved from the porthole of the captain's cabin on the *Victoria*. Barbosa and his men were drifting on the current to the *Victoria*. Then I saw it, Don Gonzálo's kerchief being waved at the porthole. Barbosa drew his batel alongside the *Victoria*, his men poured aboard, they weighed anchor, hauled up the trinquete, and rowed her with the ashwood sweeps, men in their batel also towing, into position to starboard of the *Trinidad*. Cannon at the ready, peeking out of the gunports. Captain Mendoza's flags were taken down from the four capstans, and new ones hauled up: Duarte Barbosa's coat of arms. The *Santiago* too was on the move, and took up its post to port of the capitana.

Three ships now guarded the mouth of Puerto San Julián. The mutineers still had the *San Antonio* and the *Concepción*, but both were trapped in the landlocked bay with no escape but through the bottleneck. I wondered if they would try to shoot their way out.

"Cartagena's a coward," Master Andrew confided to Ser Antonio. "Were he a bull, the matador would call him 'manso.' All bluster but no valor, as when he sent Diego Hernandez to perform the captain's salute. Silly gesture. As soon as you show him a real fight, he runs away and hides in a corner. It's Quesada who'll bear watching. He has command of the *San Antonio*, with all those guns, and there's no telling what he'll do. Perhaps he'll try and cross his enemy's T."

Don Gonzálo returned, and reported at once to the Captain-General.

"It was just as you anticipated, mi capitán," he said, as soon as the door was shut. "Captain Mendoza wanted to read the note right there, but I told him the message was confidential. He allowed both of us, Alberto and myself, inside his cabin, where I gave him the note."

Don Gonzálo paused for a drink of wine.

"And of course," said Dom Fernão, "all it said was 'Report to the King's Captain-General aboard the *Trinidad* immediately'."

"Yes. He took his helmet off to read it, as you guessed he would, and laughed aloud when he saw that message. He crumpled up the note. I bowed politely, and stretched out my hand for the note. He was still laughing. Then I grasped his beard, threw his head back, and with my other hand plunged my poniard into his throat.

"He expired with no more sound than a gurgle of blood."

"Then Barbosa and his men were aboard before anyone on the *Victoria* knew their captain was dead. Quite a feat, indeed."

"It isn't over," Don Gonzálo said. "The *San Antonio* and the *Concepción* remain in their hands."

"Three against two now," said Dom Fernão, "and they can't run away. Let's wait and see what they'll do."

The afternoon passed in quiet watchfulness and then, when dusk was deepening, the officer of the watch alerted the Captain-General.

"The *San Antonio* is drifting on the current towards us," reported Juan Bautista de Punzorol. "She'll pass within ten yards, perhaps less."

"Are her guns at the ready?" asked the Captain-General. "Are there men on her deck with the grappling irons?"

"No, sir. In fact, it looks like they don't know they're drifting. Except Captain Mesquita on the forecastle. He's signalling something. The others are all belowdecks."

While the *San Antonio* was still approaching, the *Trinidad* let loose a broadside salvo. All hell broke loose on the *San Antonio*, as on an anthill that has been disturbed. A man in full armor came out on deck and yelled orders to the crew, even as arrows from our crossbowmen ricocheted off his breastplate. But all was confusion, and it seemed most of the men on the *San Antonio* were more intent on taking cover from the *Trinidad*'s arrows and gunfire. As I watched, Dom Fernão leaped into our batel, quickly followed by four men, two of whom manned the oars. A few quick strokes, and they were at the side of the *San Antonio*. The Captain-General, moving with no trace of his limp and surprisingly agile for someone in a heavy suit of armor, ran to the deck, sword drawn. The armored man on the *San Antonio*, now suddenly confronted by Dom Fernão and two merinos, could also see the *Trinidad* and its crossbowmen and harquebusmen training their sights on his ship. He abjectly threw down his sword in surrender. Then he jerked off his helmet in disgust. It was Captain Gaspar de Quesada.

The Captain-General sent the alguacil in the batel to the *Concepción*. Her guns were all manned, but they had seen Quesada surrender. Don Gonzálo steered his oarsmen right into their gunsights.

"Who does this ship stand for?" he called out.

Juan de Cartagena came out on the deck, in armor but with the helmet under his arm. He answered in sullen tones. "We stand for Don Cárlos Primero, Rei de España, and for Fernando de Magallanes as his Captain-General."

A criado on the *San Antonio*, Juan Gómez de Espinosa, revealed that he had cut the anchor cable and so caused the ship to drift to the capitana with Captain Quesada and his mutineers quite unaware of it.

"Quesada lost his nerve when he saw how the *Victoria* had been retaken," Juan said. "He was afraid the Captain-General would simply sink the *San Antonio* and kill all of us. He asked Captain Mesquita to plead with the Captain-General. Mesquita however said it was no use pleading with that man. Anyhow he released Captain Mesquita and stationed him at the forecastle. I think his plan was to have Mesquita do some pleading and distract everyone's attention. Then, when the ship had drifted past, Quesada would spread the sails and flee into the darkness.

"I decided to do something. I might have sympathized with the mutineers, but Captain Quesada attacked our maestre in cold blood. I happened to be standing near Elorriaga. He was on duty. He was the officer of the watch. When those men came aboard without asking permission from him, he challenged them.They ignored him and locked up Captain Mesquita. Elorriaga summoned them in the name of the King to release Captain Mesquita and called for the merinos to arrest them. I heard Captain Quesada say, 'Shall we allow this fool to upset our plans?' Then he stabbed him six times. I mean, not just once or twice, but six times.

"And that's why I cut the rope."

A courtmartial was convened the next day, Tuesday of Holy Week, April 3, 1520, in the stateroom of the *Trinidad*. The five pilots made up the jury. Four f the five escribanos were present to record the proceedings and make notarized copies thereof; the fifth escribano was at the bar as a defendant. On trial were Cartagena, Quesada, de Coca, escribano de Guerra, criado Luis de Molino, maestre Juan Sebastián de Elcano, some forty crewmen who had actively joined the mutiny...and Mendoza. Ancient custom entitled every man to a fair trial, and the slight inconvenience of one's death hardly sufficed to deprive him of that right. Therefore the dead body of Captain Luis de Mendoza, wearing the armor in which he had been slain, was propped up at the bar between Cartagena and Quesada. His name was included in all the charges against the defendants.

The court-martial took all of Tuesday and most of Wednesday. Evidence was presented, depositions taken, witnesses summoned, questioned, and cross-examined. Time was on the side of the prosecution; the defense must have known, by the look of the dried bloodstains on Mendoza's armor, that it had only a few days before Mendoza's corpse began to stink.

All of the defendants were found guilty of treason, and condemned to death. Mendoza was the first to be sentenced: death by decapitation and hanging. It was to be carried out at once. Gibbets were set up on the shore of Isla San Julián, facing the bay. At dawn on Holy Wednesday, April 4, as the full moon was setting behind the land, Mendoza was cried out to the gathered men of the Armada as a traitor. He was stripped of his armor. His body was put in a kneeling position with his head on the block. After a short roll of drumbeats, the hooded executioner chopped off the head with an axe. The carcass was drawn and quartered, and then hanged as separate pieces on the gibbets. There were vultures circling in the sky above; Ser Antonio watched them with a fascination that to me bordered on the macabre. It seemed he wanted to, but did not really want to, see the vultures feast on Mendoza's dismembered body. Worse, he couldn't make up his mind as to which he really wanted to see. But there was more to come.

Quesada's sentence was promulgated next: death by decapitation and hanging, exactly like Mendoza's. It was to be carried out on Black Saturday, April 7. Quesada would be allowed to go through his devotions on Maundy Thursday and Good Friday but, unlike his Redeemer, would not be alive on Easter Sunday.

There was a problem: no one would volunteer to be the executioner.

At first light on Holy Saturday Quesada was ready to die, the three priests ready to shrive him, the sharpened axe ready and gleaming. Still, no axeman could be found. The Captain-General had asked several men if they would do it, but all had begged off. Even Master Pero of Teneriffe, who had supervised the grisly task of drawing and quartering Mendoza, refused.

It was Duarte Barbosa who pointed out Luis de Molino to Dom Fernão. Molino was Quesada's townmate from Baeza; he had enrolled in the Armada as Quesada's personal secretary. He had joined the mutiny out of loyalty to his seignior, and now, like him, stood under a sentence of death. But something about the look in his eye gave Barbosa an inspiration. "Molino will do it," he whispered to Dom Fernão, "if you'll give him a pardon."

The Captain-General called Molino forward.

"Luis de Molino," he told him, "you have been found guilty of treason and your life is now forfeit. I however am offering you clemency. You shall be pardoned if you will consent to cut off Quesada's head."

"I'll do it, comendador, so help me, God," Molino said, perhaps a bit too eagerly.

He was not given time to regret this decision. Everyone assumed his station at once. Molino put on the black hood. His hands shook when he picked up the axe. Or was that because he felt it leap up the last inch, like a pin to a magnet, into his hands? That was what I saw, but it could have been the gleam of the axeblade dazzling my eye at that instant.

Quesada received shrift from Padre Valderrama, and refused the blindfold proffered by Padre Sánchez de Reina. He knelt down, paused, raised his head to look his townmate and confidential secretary full in the eye for a second. Then he laid his head on the block, with all the dignity of an officer and a hidalgo.

The Captain-General gave the signal.

Luis de Molino swung the axe down and cut through his master's neck in one clean blow.

As Quesada's head rolled on the ground his eyes opened wide and then blinked a couple of times, seemingly at Molino. I wondered if he was blessing him, confirming in his own blood Molino's act of faith.

After several minutes, when the flow of blood had slowed to a trickle and the limbs of the torso had stopped twitching reflexively, Père Calmette came forward and gently closed the eyes on Quesada's severed head. Only then did Luis de Molino whip off his hood. He seemed to be in a trance. He fell without a word, down on his knees right into the pool of blood— and wept.

Quesada's body was then drawn and quartered. The pieces were hanged on the gibbets, next to Mendoza's.

I waited until I was sure no more blood would drip. It was human sacrifice of course, even if no one else saw it as that. Another stop, another offering. The gods of this place were particularly demanding, requiring two men at the outset, more if Juan de Elorriaga succumbed to them.

Late that afternoon I sneaked out and cut a knot of wood off the gibbet from which Quesada's head was hanging. A few drops of dried blood on it added to its value. There would be time enough, in the coming winter, to whittle that wood into something, perhaps a drinking cup. It would make a perfect souvenir.

18

ÁLVARO DE MESQUITA once again assumed the captaincy of the *San Antonio*, the ship mutineers had stolen from under his nose. What moral right had he to that post? Perhaps Don Gonzálo or João Rodrigues de Mafra would have been more suitable.

Duarte Barbosa was formally announced, to the blare of trumpets, as captain of the ship he had captured in battle, the *Victoria*. With Juan Serrano as captain of the *Santiago*, that left the pilot João Lopes Carvalho, by default, in command of the *Concepción*. Now all five captains were Portuguese.

The four captains petitioned the Captain-General to spare the lives of the ordinary seamen condemned to death for mutiny. The Armada could not afford the loss of forty sailors. We would be grossly undermanned.

After some thought, the Captain-General declared he was commuting all sentences to hard labor. It was of course unwise to execute Cartagena, who was Bishop Fonseca's bastard son, or de Coca, who was the Lord of Alaejos and Coca's, or Hierónimo de Guerra, who was Cristobal de Haro's.

The convicted mutineers, hands bound behind their backs and leg irons connecting them by the left leg to one long chain, passed in review before the Captain-General. As each man came before him, the Captain-General gave him a blow with his fist. Most he hit on the jaw; de Guerra he punched on the shoulder. Cartagena and de Coca he socked in the stomach, leaving them doubled over. Elcano ducked, but got pummelled on the back of the head instead. Then all of them, hidalgos and commoners alike, were put to work as a chain gang, graving and caulking the ships. It took them more than a month, during which they were kept on half-rations of biscuit and victuals, and no wine except a cup on Sundays. One man put to work beside them was not connected by the left foot to their chain. This was Jacóme de Messina, serving sentence for the killing of Sebastián de Olarte.

Juan de Elorriaga was in a lean-to ashore on the side of the island away from the gibbets. Everyone now called it the Isla de Justicia; quite a number of the men refused to set foot on it, as they feared the ghosts of the executed captains.

Elorriaga was suffering terribly from his six stab wounds. The Captain-General, together with cirujano Juan de Morales, visited him every morning and evening. They would dress the wounds, and then feed Elorriaga gruel specially prepared in the upland country manner by the Basques.

I happened to be in the captain's cabin when the alguacil, Don Gonzálo Gomez de Espinosa, came in as ordered and reported to Dom Fernão.

"You know that I have confiscated the belongings of Quesada and Mendoza," said the Captain-General. "These will be kept in storage, to be turned over to the Crown. However, their effects include 42 gold ducats, which I am appropriating."

He cleared his throat.

"Now, your loyalty and your sense of duty as a King's officer and an hidalgo are priceless, and cannot possibly be paid for with money. However, on behalf of His Majesty, I give you this as a token of my appreciation."

He handed Don Gonzálo a small purse. The alguacil accepted it, loosened the strings, and poured out its contents onto his palm: a heap of Venetian gold ducats.

"Twelve for you," said Dom Fernão, "six for Alberto the merino, and six each for your oarsmen."

"I am speechless," said Don Gonzálo, "but muchisimas gracias, comendador. You have expressed your esteem in gold, and there can be none finer."

The days were getting shorter, the nights longer. April in these regions was no fair month; the sun stood very low in the north. Even at noon it never rose higher than twenty degrees from the horizon, so that the *Trinidad* lay all day in the shadow of Cabo

Curioso's headland. There were but four hours of daylight in this season, and this was steadily decreasing. The sun did not rise until 10 a.m. and was retarded further every day; sunset was at 2 p.m. and each time came earlier than it had the day before. I knew that by the middle of June, at the winter solstice, daylight would be down to three hours a day.

April 23 was the Feast of San Jorge, the patron saint of Ynglande.

"St. George's Day comes in the spring," Master Andrew said. "But now I must celebrate it in the autumn. Not exactly the season for slaying dragons, is it?"

On Friday, April 27, Antonio Genovés, a grumete on the *Victoria*, committed suicide by drowning. The Captain-General ordered an investigation. A fellow grumete, Bernal Mahuri, had been taunting Antonio, asking him if he missed Antón Salomón, and calling him a catamite, a ganymede, and a donna. The last was simply an Italian word for "girl," but nobody knew what the other words meant. Mahuri, a French Basque from Narbonne and one of the better-endowed men on the *Victoria*, had developed a routine of stroking his crotch and then asking Antonio Genovés if he wanted to suck it. He taunted him one time too many. Something had snapped in Antonio. Without warning, he had thrown himself over the side. The *Victoria* was anchored in six fathom and dusk had fallen: Antonio Genovés could not have lasted long in the cold water even had he known how to swim. The strong current must have quickly carried him away.

The search for the drowned body went on for three days, four hours or more each day, or for as long as the sunlight lasted. The Captain-General called off the search after that; in all likelihood Antonio Genovés had been swept out to sea.

I wondered if Antón Salomón's ghost had called out to his catamite to join him. The gods of this eerie place had demanded another sacrifice. Antonio Genovés had been their victim.

Captain Juan Serrano, growing restless, volunteered to take the caravel *Santiago* and search for the paso farther south. How long would he be gone? A month, perhaps two, Serrano said. Permission was granted.

April ended. May was a cold, gloomy month. On Thursday, May 17, forty days after Easter, we celebrated the Feast of the Ascension. Padre Valderrama said Mass and recalled the ascent of the Lord Jesus Christ into Heaven. He then spoke of Enoch, son of Jared, who had been taken up into Heaven, and of Elijah, who too had not died but had ascended to Heaven in a fiery chariot.

I thought of the others he had failed to mention: Mohammed, who ascended from Jerusalem to Heaven on a white steed; Yudhisthira, chosen by Indra to enter the abode of the gods in his mortal form...

On May 21 two men out to fetch drinking water found the body of Antonio Genovés at the mouth of a creek. The cold water had apparently slowed down the decomposition of the body, they said. Its features were still recognizable. Dom Fernão went to see it together with the chaplain, the cirujano, an escribano, and several other men. I stayed behind, having no wish to view a bloated body that had been dead for three weeks. They said prayers for the soul of Antonio Genovés, then buried him nearby.

May 27 was Pentecost Sunday. Master Andrew called it Whitsunday. It also happened to be the feastday of his countryman San Beda, or the Venerable Bede.

On June 1 two men staggered into camp. Bearded, emaciated, their eyes hollow and their cheeks sunken, we had trouble recognizing them. They were Domingo Português of Odemira and Hierónimo García of Sevilla, a marinero and a grumete from the *Santiago*.

"Shipwrecked," they said, as they ate like famished men, "Walked eleven days to get back here."

"Casualties?"

"None, except that Negro slave."

João of Moçambique, Captain Serrão's African slave.

"Drowned jumping off the *Santiago*," Domingo said, "May 22. Everyone jumped off the ship to the beach. João did not time his jump right. He should have waited for the big wave to..."

"Suppose you start again," said Dom Fernão, "from the beginning?"

"We left on April 29," said Hierónimo García, "and made slow progress. The weather was abominable, and the winds unfavorable. In four days we managed but twenty leguas. Then, on May 3, we found a river. Good shelter and good anchorage, comendador, and plenty of fish. Captain Serrano named it the Río Santa Cruz, because it was the feastday of the Holy Cross.

"We camped ashore for two weeks or more, exploring that river when the weather permitted. Its water turns fresh upstream. We measured the tides, too. Its ebbflow is definitely stronger than its floodtide. Captain Serrano is certain it is a river and not the strait we seek.

"On May 22, in good weather, we resumed the search for the paso and sailed south. Three leguas from the Río Santa Cruz, a gale suddenly blew up. A huge roller hit us and tore off the rudder. Captain Serrano however, using only the sails, managed to drive us aground on a good sandy beach. We jumped off the *Santiago* without even getting our feet wet.

"The waves were sucking the ship off the sand. Juan of Mozambique was still aboard. Captain Serrano shouted to him to jump off. The Negro jumped just as a big wave pulled the *Santiago* back into the sea. He fell into deep water. I don't think he knew how to swim. We saw him being dragged under. He must have drowned rather quickly."

"The two of us," said Domingo Português, "volunteered to walk back here for help. Sixty leguas. We walked three leguas to the Río Santa Cruz, then built a raft to cross the river. We intended to keep to the shoreline, but the coast is full of marshes. We had to strike inland. For food, we hunted conies. We saw many antas, but they are impossible to catch."

"Not antas," Hierónimo corrected him. "Antas are tapirs, like the ones in Río de Enero. Those were guanacos."

"Chamas," said Domingo.

"No, not llamas. Guanacos."

"If you say so. Whatever."

"Eleven days together," observed Master Andrew, "and now they're just like any old married couple."

"The two of you are half-starved and lack sleep," said Dom Fernão. "When you've recovered, you will lead a rescue team back to Serrano and the rest of them."

The following day, June 2, Rojer du Pict, a bombardero on the *San Antonio*, fell off his ship after dusk. They heard his cries but had difficulty finding him in the dark. In the freezing water every second mattered, and by the time they reached him it was too late. Rojer was from Monaym, or Mannheim in Alemánia. Hans Vargue took charge of the wake. We buried Rojer near the beach below Cabo Curioso.

The next day, June 3, Trinity Sunday, a rescue party was sent off to recover the shipwrecked crew.

Thursday, June 7, was the feast of Corpus Christi.

The rescuers and the crew of the *Santiago* returned on June 12, unkempt but merry. The waves had carried off the *Santiago* and then beached it again half a legua farther south, where Serrano and his crew salvaged most of the stores. They had however been unable to find the body of João de Moçambique.

The men from the *Santiago* were distributed among the four remaining ships. Captain Juan Serrano was appointed to the *Concepción*, displacing Carvalho, who was reverted to pilot. Carvalho showed no resentment. The two were blood brothers, having sworn fealty to each other in the Marruecos, where they both fought for the Portuguese King.

Pedro Perez, the tonelero of the *Concepción*, took sick on June 15, the Feast of the Sacred Heart of Jesus, and was placed beside Juan de Elorriaga in the lean-to. Perez went into a high fever with delirium tremens, and his body was wracked by violent spasms and coughing. On June 18, he died. His fellow sevillanos sang haunting Andalusían dirges at the wake. We buried him beside Rojer du Pict.

Many of us were coming down with ailments in the cold climate. The Captain-General visited the afflicted men every morning, personally attending to each one in turn. He would spoon gruel into the mouth of one, make another drink some mandolata, wipe the hot feverish face of a third.

Among the men who took ill were the calafate of the *Trinidad*, Filippo de Troa of Reco in Genova; a grumete from the *San Antonio*, Columbazo of Bologna; a Greek marinero from the *Concepción*, Mateo de Gorfo; the despensero of the *Victoria*, Affonso Gonçales; and the *Santiago*'s contramaestre, Bartolomé Prior of Sainct-Malo.

A delegation of men went to the Captain-General to propose that the fleet sail back to the Bahía de Sancta Lucía. It would be four months before we could resume our explorations, time much healthier spent in Guanabara Bay, with its moderate climate. Dom Fernao refused to entertain the thought. Not only would the men sin there with the Indian women, who were daughters of Belial; any Portuguese fleet dispatched after us would look there first.

The graving, careening, and caulking of the ships proceeded apace, even in the dead of winter. This was the second time we cleaned out the vessels. We had rushed the job the first time, at the Bahía de Sancta Lucía. Now we were more thorough. Our maestre, Juan Bautista de Punzorol, made a shocking discovery.

"My Captain-General," he said, "I regret the necessity of coming to you with bad news...the two years' worth of provisions that you asked for...they actually loaded only a year's worth...we have already consumed most of that."

Dom Fernão did not seem unduly surprised.

"Well," he said at length, "how did that happen?"

"Very complicated to explain, sir, but mostly it had to do with their system of double receipting in Sevilla. I've gone over the cargo manifests and bills of lading twice, in some cases thrice or more. We've been cheated."

"A curse on those sevillano land rats!" boomed Dom Fernão. Then he said, "It's all my fault. I should have expected this, and kept closer watch on those officials of the Casa. They've no conscience, no sense of honor. All that matters to them is their gain. They don't care if the lot of us starve to death in the middle of the trackless ocean. I'll have their heads upon our return. But for now there's nothing to be done about them. We must redouble our food-gathering efforts. We've a long way ahead of us yet."

On July 8 a native of the region appeared on the shore of the mainland opposite the Isla de Justícia. Dressed and shod in fur, carrying a short bow and a quiver of arrows, he began jumping up and down and bellowing like a bull. Ser Antonio crossed over to him in the batel. Then, his two oarsmen covering him with harquebus and crossbow, he imitated the savage's every motion and so enticed the latter to come and visit us in the *Trinidad*. The man was taller than Petit-Jean d'Anjou by a handspan. His head was shaved, except for a tuft in the center which was stiff and stood up in spikes. He was dressed in animal skins with the fur still attached. His feet, wrapped in the same material, were huge. Later, we found he stuffed grass in his crude shoes, which made his feet look bigger than they really were.

"Such big feet," Dom Fernão said. "We must call this land Patagonia, for nowhere else may such well-appendaged men be found."

We invited the Patagonian to share our noonday meal. He ate enough hardtack for six men, and drank a full pail of water.

Afterwards he led four of our men to his hunting party. There were eighteen of them. The men were tall but the women were short and squat. Their breasts reminded me of papayas. They had six young animals with them, half-grown guanacos, which they called chulengos. They would tie the chulengos to some bushes, and wait for adult guanacos to come up and play with these decoys. Then, from their hiding places, they would shoot the guanacos. Their arrows were tipped with pointed stones sharpened by having bits flaked off by another stone. They had no metal.

The nineteen Patagonians shot several guanacos for us. In a single afternoon we acquired more meat for our larders than we usually obtained in a week. They left quite happy with the gifts we had given them: knives, hatchets, axes, fishhooks, hawksbells, colored glass beads, tin mirrors, combs.

On July 12 Filippo de Troa died of his illness. He was buried the next day.

On July 14 two more Patagonians came to us. One of them sought to impress us by swallowing an arrow. It went most of the way down his throat; only the feathered haft showed in his mouth. When he drew it out again, there was no blood. They both spent the night on the *Trinidad*, and in the morning caught a guanaco for us. We sent them off with gifts of metal.

On July 15 Juan de Elorriaga finally succumbed to the six knife wounds he had received from Captain Quesada. The Basques mourned him for three days before they buried him.

July 25 was the Feast of Santiago el mayor, the patron saint of Spain.

On July 28 four other Patagonians showed up. Something looked strange about them: they were unarmed. Nor were they leading chulengos. They must have cached their possessions nearby; they could not live without their weapons and their decoys.

"More Patagonians," observed the Captain-General. "We have an Indian from Río Solis here, but no Patagonians as yet. Nuño, Francisco," he called his criados, "get some leg irons. When I give the signal, put them on the two biggest men."

Gifts were offered to the four natives, who accepted everything with alacrity. Soon they all had their hands full. Dom Fernão then offered them the leg irons. They refused, as they obviously could carry no more. The Captain-General gave them to understand, by sign language, that these they could carry on the feet. They accepted, whereupon Nuño and Francisco placed the leg irons around their shins. The alguacil, Don Gonzálo, and his merino Alberto de Córdova swiftly bound the hands of the other two. The first two walked off to leave, and found they were chained by their feet to the ship. The four Patagonians howled.

"Setebos!" they yelled—the name of their chief god.

One of the men in leg irons managed to convey that he was resigned to his fate, if captured he must be, but desired only to bid farewell to his wife. It was decided to have the two Indians with bound hands lead a group of us to their people, and the wife in question brought to the ship. Carvalho would head the group. With him were Don Gonzálo and Alberto, and the sobresaliente Diego Sánchez Barrasa.

Three of them returned the following day.

"Barrasa's dead," reported Carvalho. "We buried him."

The story came in bits and pieces from all three of them. The two Indians had led the group to their concealed cache. Choosing their moment, they suddenly wrestled themselves free, cut off their ropes, then ran away carrying the short bows and quivers of arrows they had secreted. Our men fired their harquebuses, but the Indians ran like frightened rabbits, darting from side to side, and were impossible to hit. One arrow hit Barrasa in the leg. It must have been poisoned, for he died in quick order.

Diego Sánchez Barrasa was from Sevilla, and the remaining fifteen sevillanos, plus the sobresalientes, went to his grave and kept vigil there. They made a tombstone, chiseling out the letters in Latin:

†
HIC JACET
DIEGO SANCHEZ BARRASA
MCCCCXCVII—MCCCCCXX
REQUIESCAT IN PACE

There were a few arguments about the correct ways of rendering "1497" and "1520" in Roman numerals. Someone wanted to write the year of birth as MCDXCVII. Another insisted that the year of death could be written as the simple MDXX.

I kept the vigil, too, for lack of better things to do. The number of human sacrifices the gods of this region were demanding was piling up. They had been given Captains Mendoza and Quesada, and still they had taken Antonio Genovés, Rojer du Pict, João de Moçambique, Pedro Pérez, Filippo de Troa, Juan de Elorriaga, and now Diego Sánchez Barrasa. The Captain-General should have given them Juan de Cartagena. It seemed to me that only a worthwhile victim could propitiate them.

Then it was August. On Monday, August 6, we celebrated the Feast of the Transfiguration. On August 8 Padre Pedro Sánchez de Reina was apprehended discussing plans for another mutiny with Juan de Cartagena. He had been entering the captain's cabin in the *Concepción* on a regular basis, ostensibly to hear Cartagena's daily confession.

Another courtmartial was convened. Cartagena and Sánchez de Reina were both found guilty of treason, and condemned to death. In his clemency, the Captain-General commuted their sentences to a marooning on the Isla Justícia. They would be given a supply of ship's biscuit, wine, a harquebus and a crossbow, and a few other things. Their lives would be in their own hands.

Captain Juan Serrano had been telling the Captain-General at every opportunity how much better the Río Santa Cruz would be. Our search for the paso could not resume before mid-October at the earliest; two months of winter remained.

"Think of it," said Captain Serrano. "Two more months in this gloomy place. How can you stand it?"

And so the Captain-General issued orders. We were to sail the sixty leguas to the Río Santa Cruz three or four days hence.

We departed on August 11, a year and a day out of Sevilla. Dom Fernão took the lead in the *Trinidad*. Next was the *San Antonio* under Álvaro de Mesquita, then the *Concepción* under Serrano, and lastly the *Victoria* under Duarte Barbosa.

The man-eating Indian from the Río Solis was still with us on the capitana. So were the two Patagones in leg irons. The cannibal had been nicknamed Juan Díaz, as he must have partaken of the flesh of Juan Díaz de Solis five years before. Of the two Patagones, the one called Setebos was also on the *Trinidad*. The other one, named Cheleulle, was on the *San Antonio*. Both of them wailed loudly and wept copiously as we moved out with the tide, knowing they would never see home again. They whined piteously in their guttural language to whoever was at hand, gesturing desperately, shaking their bound legs, pointing to the beach; it was obvious they wanted to exchange places with Cartagena and Sánchez de Reina.

Our last sight of Puerto San Julián was of its beach, and the two marooned men kneeling on the sand. Their clasped hands raised in supplication, tears streaming down their cheeks, they wailed and implored the Captain-General to reconsider and take them back. "Those two would love a swop," said Master Andrew, "an they had to be in them leg irons."

Glancing back, I could not help but feel a tinge of pity for the poor devils. They were merely human after all, and greatly chastened now. They could do no further harm to us. They could just as easily have been forgiven and taken back aboard as prisoners.

Then I remembered what strange gods this place had. Some instinct had told me they wanted Cartagena, and now they finally had him. They simply would not be denied.

Dom Fernão was on duty as officer of the watch, and he was intent on conning the helmsman and maneuvering the fleet out of the bay. Not once did he look back.

⚓

19

"IT'S FULL OF SHAD," Master Andrew said. And so it was. That was one difference between Puerto San Julián and Río Santa Cruz, between a bay of seawater and the mouth of a river. Salmon, resembling the herring the white man knew in his home rivers, came in their season to swim up the stream. We cast fishing nets and brought in plenty of them, most of which we salted down to be put away in the barrels. Salmon was much preferred to the lobos marinos and patos sin alas, seals and auks, but those too we salted away, as we needed all the meat we could procure. Every time someone turned away from his work to look at the water for a moment, there were schools of shad to be seen, swimming upstream.

Clouds moved in, and we kept to our shelters, or aboard ship. The weather remained gloomy for the next two weeks, the worst winter many of us had experienced in our lives. There was no such season in my native land. The majority of the crew came from the South of Europa and knew but the milder forms of winter. Only the the Germans and the Flemings had any notion of real cold.

On Sunday, August 26, Antão Fernandes, a sobresaliente on the *Concepción,* died of illness. I remembered drinking malvasia wine and eating caldo gallego with him in Teneriphe, a long time ago.

On Wednesday, August 29, the moon was at first quarter. Not in itself an event, it became one because it was visible, the clouds having cleared for the first time in weeks. That day being the Feast of the Beheading of San Juan Bautista, some of the men lit memorial fires, for that saint as well as for Captains Quesada and Mendoza, who had also been beheaded.

Captain Juan Serrano suggested that the wreckage of the *Santiago* might yet be salvaged, mostly for its wood. It lay on the beach a short distance south, a walk of perhaps two hours. The Captain-General sent Martín Pérez, the carpenter of the *Victoria*, to the wreck in the morning of August 31, at first light. Sunrise came at about nine, and Martín was expected to be back well before sunset at three. At dusk Dom Fernão sent two men with farols to look for him. They were back in an hour, carrying Martín's body in an improvised litter. The carpenter had drowned while crossing a stream. It was not wide, and a treetrunk had been laid across it as a bridge, probably by natives of the place. He must have lost his balance and been carried off by the rushing waters, the coldness of which would also have knocked him senseless. The men found him snagged among some rushes, not far from the treetrunk bridge.

Friday, September 14, was the Feast of the Exaltation of the Holy Cross. It seemed right to be celebrating it at the Río Santa Cruz. Ser Antonio seemed a bit confused.

"Haven't we already celebrated the Feast of the Holy Cross?" he asked. "Sometime in May?"

"That was different," Dom Fernão said. "That was the Feast of the Invention of the Holy Cross. On May 3. Today we celebrate the Exaltation of the Holy Cross. Both events, as you might recall from your history lessons, happened in the year of Our Lord... what year was that, Padre Pedro?"

"Anno Domini 629," said Padre Valderrama.

"The Invention or Discovery of the Holy Cross," put in Master Andrew, "celebrates the day Emperor Constantine the Great saw a vision of the Cross in the sky. Complete with the Greek letters chi and rho."

"And the Exaltation," said Francisco Albo, "marks the day his mother Helena found the relic of the Cross in Jerusalem. Bits of the wood, along with some of the nails, and the sponge used by the centurion to give Jesus a drink of vinegar. I'm not sure if she also found the crown of thorns."

"But..." said Duarte Barbosa, "didn't Constantine fight that famous battle, after seeing the vision of the Cross, in 312 AD? I seem to recall that year from my history lessons..."

"Oh, but it's 629," Padre Valderrama. "I'll consult my Missale Romanum."

He went to his cabin and returned with a book, thumbing through its pages as he walked.

"I've found it," he said. "Here, take a look."

Barbosa read the page the padre showed him.

"It does say 629 AD," he admitted. "It must be true, then. It's in the book."

Later, however, I overheard him whisper to Ser Antonio: "Constantine saw the Cross in 312 AD, I'm quite certain of that. The missal has got it wrong."

"The date in the missal," Ser Antonio said, "is the date when the Church declared it a holiday."

He had to be right, of course, but a confusion of dates seemed more typical of the white man's calendars. The civil calendar and the liturgical calendar could not seem to agree. Historical events were assigned wildly varying dates.

On Sunday, September 16, Jacóme de Messina, a marinero on the *San Antonio*, died of illness. He it was who had killed his fellow marinero, Sebastián de Olarte, some months before.

Because the skies were often overcast, I had not noticed the change in the hours. September 21 was the vernal equinox and the day and the night were of equal length, twelve hours each. From here on the days would get longer until there would be, at the summer solstice on December 21, fully twenty-one hours of light and barely three of darkness.

On Saturday, September 29, the Feast of San Miguel el arcangel, another man died of illness. This time it was Jorge Alemán, the condestable de bombarderos on the *Victoria*. His hometown was Estric, which Barbosa thought must have meant Eichstadt. I had wondered why he was known simply as Jorge Alemán, George the German, and so I asked Hans Vargue what his late countryman's real name was.

"Jurgen Uhlmann," he grunted.

The fourth of our dead for this place, after Antão Fernandes, Martín Pérez, and Jacóme de Messina. We buried Jorge beside Jacóme, the two priests present.

I longed for summer, and its long hours of daylight, and warmer air, and good sailing weather, so that we could leave the Río Santa Cruz, and be on our way. Some of the men were now saying we should sail east from here, recross the Mar Océano, round the Cabo de Buena Esperanza, and sail to Maluco on the proven Português track. This meant they doubted the paso would ever be found. At least they were no longer suggesting we return to Spain.

They had a point. A whole year had passed, whereas Portuguese ships sailed from Lisbõa to the Spice Islands, via Africa and Índia, in a matter of months. But we were so near now. My master was sure the paso was nearby, and then a few days' sailing would take us to the Molukas. In the globe he had shown Don Cárlos Primero, Cipangu lay only a few hundred leguas from Nueva España. He did not fear the Great South Sea. He looked forward to it. So did I.

Estêvão Gomes was the most vocal about going via the Cape of Good Hope. "There is no paso here," he would say, "the only thing left to us is to sail east and reach the Moluccas after passing Africa, Índia, and Taprobane."

Taprobane was the white man's old name for the island of Serendib, or Siri Lanka, but after it was renamed Ceylon, Taprobane had somehow come to be misapplied to the island of Sumatra. Most Europeans, including men like Ser Antonio Pigafetta, were not aware of the mistake. The use of the wrong name for my native island always irked me, and now it rendered me implacably opposed to Gomes's proposal. Fortunately, it was never necessary for me to speak out.

"But we have gone so far south now," someone would always object. "Would not sailing back cost us double the distance?"

"Sailing double the distance is preferable to finding a paso here. Even if we find one, it would be so far south as to be useless. We are now at a latitude of fifty degrees south of the æquinoctial line and have found nothing. The Cabo de Buena Esperanza is the only way. It is thirty-seven degrees south of the æquinoctial line, just as Sevilla is thirty-seven degrees north. It shows the correct symmetry."

"Now I don't hold with that," said Master Andrew. "I'm from Bristol myself, and yon town lies at two-and-fifty degrees north. By your logic, something should turn up at two-and-fifty south."

"I doubt it, Maestro Andrés," Gomes replied. "Many of the others doubt it, too."

And so they did. A minority of the crew, but troublesome out of all proportion to their number.

A delegation of officers and men, led by Gomes, laid the proposal before the Captain-General on October 13, the Feast of Sainct Edouard, Kyng of Ynglande.

"Which Edward?" Master Andrew asked Padre Valderrama.

"The one who died in 1066."

"Edward the Confessor, then," Master Andrew said. "Wore a hairshirt, performed miracles. Acclaimed as a living saint by his subjects."

"Miracles?" Ser Antonio asked. "What sort?"

"Oh, restoring eyesight to the blind, for the most part, including men who'd had their eyes put out by invading Vikings. Once, he healed the Lady Godiva's neck sores...what they call scrofula in Latin. His most famous cure involved a crippled Irish beggar. Carried him on his shoulders down the aisle of Westminster, all the way to the altar."

"And the Irishman became able to walk?"

"Yes, of course. For the first time. He'd been crippled since birth."

"Amazing. What other miracles did he do?"

"Called the judgment of God down on Earl Godwin in 1053. Edward's brother, Prince Alfred, had been murdered twelve years before. He'd always suspected Godwin of some role in it. The Earl offered to swallow a small roll of bread to prove his innocence. The King accepted the offer, and said a blessing over the roll. If Godwin had been lying, he would choke to death on the bread."

"And did he?

But Estêvão Gomes had begun his speech, and everyone faced forward to listen.

"...has gone on too long, comendador. We are all suffering from the extreme cold, men are dying like flies, and finding that mythical paso seems most unlikely. And very soon we will have no more food.

"There is only one way to save this voyage in order that we may attain our destination and then return honorably to Spain. And that is to sail east..."

"Yes, I have heard that argument," Dom Fernão said. "But here, if we find the paso, we have but one more sea to cross. Sailing east means crossing two oceans, the Mar Océano, and then the Indian Ocean. Not to mention the almost certain risk of encountering Portuguese warships in the waters off Zamatra.

"I have sworn to find the paso, and we shall find it. As for food, we must catch and preserve as much meat and fish as we can before we set sail again. And yet, I say to you, I mean to reach the Islas de Maluco even if I am reduced to eating the leather chafings of the yardarms.

"We are now at the latitude of 50 degrees south of the æquinoctial line. What hardship is that? Five hundred years ago, the Northmen in their frail longships were not afraid to sail as far as 65, 70, even 75 degrees north. For our part, we shall sail on only as far as 57 degrees south. If by then we still have not found the paso, I promise you we shall turn back."

He looked Gomes in the eye, then nodded to the whole group.

"That is all."

"What did he say?" asked some of the men as they left. One man held up a hand with all fingers outstretched, to signal "5," then that hand plus two fingers of the other hand, to signal "7." Ser Antonio misread this and asked, "Seventy-five degrees? South of the æquinoctial line, toward the South Pole?"

"Sacre bleu," said Pedro Arnaot of Horrai, a grumete from the *Santiago*, now reassigned to the *San Antonio*, "we shall freeze to death in La Terre Antarctique!"

Master Andrew was among the few who agreed with the Captain-General.

"We set out to find a strait, I say we should keep on till we find it. Seven-and-fifty degrees south latitude, the man says. The same latitude north would correspond to somewhere in Scotland. Or a point just north of Ireland. When I made my first sea voyage, with John Cabot, the real sailing began when we turned west off Dursey Head in Ireland, at two-and-fifty degrees north latitude. And didn't St. Brendan sail in a coracle from Ireland and go north into the sea of crystal columns?"

"Aye, that he did," nodded Guillén Ires. "Those crystal columns must have been icebergs."

"An interesting story," said Ser Antonio, drawing closer. "When did St. Brendan make this voyage?"

"About a thousand years ago."

"Have you ever seen a coracle, Sir Antone?" Master Andrew asked.

"No, I haven't. Is it as big as a caravel?"

"Heavens, no. It's about as big as a gondola, such as you have in Venezia."

"But the gondola is good only for navigating the canali of Venezia. One would not dream of sailing a gondola in the open sea."

"Well, the Irish do. The coracle is made of leather, and is even less manœuvreable than a gondola. It's little more than a floating tub. Even with sails on it, it's helpless before any good wind. You can't point it higher than 90 degrees to the wind. But the Irish think nothing of sailing it to Ultima Thule. Craziest sailors you'll ever find."

"Only the Irish," said Kevin, "know how to sail the curragh. It's not merely an inland-water boat. It's a true seagoing vessel."

"And they have the imrama of St. Brendan's voyage to prove it," conceded Master Andrew. "That's the Irish for you. They've all got the gift of blarney."

Ser Antonio turned to Master Andrew.

"By the way, Maestro Andres, what did happen to your Earl Godwin when he ate that roll of bread?"

"Well, 'e couldn't swaller it. Stuck in his throat. Groped for water, but collapsed before his hand got to the cup. Choked to death right there, he did."

According to the almanach, a solar eclipse would occur on Wednesday, October 11. Dom Fernão was not sure if it would be visible to us at latitude 50°S.

It came at about eleven o'clock that noon, a partial eclipse that left a thin sliver of the sun uncovered. The strange thing was that the outer edge of the sun's rim remained uncovered, too.

"It's what they call an annular eclipse," Dom Fernão told us, "where the moon is so far away from us it appears to be smaller than usual. Thus its disk cannot entirely cover the sun. First time I've seen one."

Again, it was an opportunity to determine longitude. The pilots and captains brought out their instruments and carefully measured the particulars of the eclipse.

I paid even less attention to this eclipse than to the previous one, that eclipse of Jupiter by the moon. The sky darkened somewhat and the temperature dropped, but it was not a real eclipse, not a total disappearance of the sun with the world going dark as night and chickens going up in the trees to roost. This one was a mere disappointment. We had been at this place for two months, since August 13, and all I wanted was to get going again.

On October 18, the Feast of St. Luke the Evangelist, we departed the Río Santa Cruz. The moon was at first quarter. We left at first light, sailing out with the tide. Low tide was at about 6:00 a.m. Sunrise had come earlier, at around 5:00, as it was nearly a month past the vernal æquinox in the Southern hemisphere; it was springtime, and soon it would be summer. We weighed anchor just as the sun was breaking over the horizon, then drifted out as soon as the tidal bore began to pick up.

The *Trinidad* was in the van of the fleet, as nautical tradition dictated. Next was the *San Antonio*, Captain Álvaro de Mesquita in command, with the grizzled veteran Estêvão Gomes as his pilot. Then the *Concepción*, under Captain Juan Serrano, with his blood brother João Lopes Carvalho, another veteran captain, as pilot. Last was the *Victoria*, commanded by Captain Duarte Barbosa, with the old reliable Basco Gallego, as pilot. The Armada's hierarchy was now all in the family: Dom Fernão as Captain-General, the other three Captains his brother-in-law and two of his cousins, and the pilots all old comrades of his, with the exception of Gomes. Estêvão was however a distant cousin of his, too.

Aboard the capitana, the official flag pilot was João Rodrigues de Mafra, with Andrés de San Martín as astrólogo mayor, or chief celestial navigator. The real pilot was of course our contramaestre, Francisco Albo. De Mafra's son Diego, a page on the San Antonio, had transferred to the *Trinidad* along with his father. Three of them to exchange places with Gomes, but nobody thought it unequal.

San Martín and the de Mafras were not the only transferees from the *San Antonio*. Also coming aboard the *Trinidad* were the sobresaliente Antón de Escovar, from Talavera; the grumete Juanes de Segura, from Segura in Guipuzcoa, and two of

Cartagena's own criados, Rodrigo Nieto from Orense in Galicia, and Pedro de Valpuesta from Burgos.

Don Antón spoke for the four of them. The *San Antonio*, he confided to Dom Fernão, was full of men who regarded the Captain-General as a Portuguese and a foreigner. They wanted to stand by the King's Captain-General and remain true to the holy oath they had sworn in Sevilla.

With the transfer of San Martín and de Mafra padre é filho, there now remained only two Lusitanians on the *San Antonio*: Captain Mesquita and Pilot Gomes.

For the next three days we sailed south, following the coast. This was a vast land indeed, and it seemed to have no end. Indeed, many thought it went on to the South Pole. Amérika and Antarctica were parts of one unbroken land mass, the former ending and the latter beginning where soil became less evident than ice.

On October 20 we passed a prominent cape with cliffs over a hundred feet high. Beside it was the mouth of a river. A stream smaller than the Río Santa Cruz, its estuary did not dent the coast enough to resemble a bay. The Captain-General did not slow down to investigate it. We were making good time, and he airily named it the Cabo Buen Tiempo. The rivermouth reminded him of one he had seen in Galicia, so he named that the Río Gallegos.

The next day, October 21, another cape loomed in the distance. As we drew near, it seemed to be slightly higher than the Cabo Buen Tiempo, and much higher than the hundred-foot cliffs of Cabo Curioso and Punta Desengaño at Puerto San Julián. Ser Antonio performed some rough trigonometry, and announced it was 135 feet high.

"Since it is the Feast of St. Ursula and the Eleven Thousand Virgins," the Captain-General announced, "I hereby name this cape the Cabo de Once Mil Virgenes. Andrés," he addressed the page on duty, "can you tell me who Santa Ursula was?"

"She was a princess, mi capitán," Andrés said, "from Inglatierra..."

"She was from Cornwall," interjected Master Andrew, "in Wales, not England."

"Never mind, Maestro Andrés," said Dom Fernão, "let this other Andrés tell it in his own way."

He nodded to the page.

"She went on a pilgrimage to Roma," continued Andrés de la Cruz, "where her saintliness attracted other young women to come and follow her. She insisted that only virgins could come with her. By the time she began the long march home eleven thousand virgins were following her. As they were passing through the Alemán city of Cologne, Huns led by Atilla happened to attack the city. The barbarians massacred everyone they could find, including Ursula and her eleven thousand virgins."

"How very tragic. And in what year did this happen?" asked Dom Fernão.

"Oh, a long time ago," said Andrés. "I really can't say what year."

"I happen to know that," said Ser Antonio. "It was in 238 A.D."

"And I'm quite sure it was in 283," said Master Andrew.

"I have it on best authority," said Padre Valderrama, that it was in 451 A.D."

As usual, the white man's calendar had got it all messed up. There were three dates for this single historical event, and each date was supposed to be correct. Another of the white man's mysteries.

I wondered if the number of virgins had been multiplied somewhere in the telling. Eleven thousand was simply a huge number, quite impossible, to my mind, under the circumstances. However, I had never been to Rome, and could not tell if that city could produce that many virgins on short notice.

I could not help thinking, though, how wonderful it would be if the Cabo de Once Mil Virgenes could live up to its name and provide us, by a miracle, eleven thousand virgins. Not counting the two priests, the prisoners, and a few pious individuals, the Armada now had about 250 men who would gladly avail themselves of such a bounty. In simple arithmetic, 11,000 divided by 250 yielded 44. Each man would have forty-four virgins to deflower. A daunting task, but not at all likely to be shirked.

I shrugged off my foolish thoughts. Useless dreams, but they had left me giddy, itchy, and quite crazed. I remembered that Indra, the highest of the Hindoo gods, had once been plagued with a similar obsession. It led him to commit an indiscretion. To punish him, Gautama caused Indra's body to display a thousand female organs. A millenium passed before Gautama relented and commuted the yonis into eyes. I still retained some reverence for the stories of the Ramayana, and I wondered now if my skin was in danger of breaking out in a thousand coños. Doubtless that was the cause of the itchiness. I dared not scratch.

Finding the paso had now become imperative. It was the only thing that would save my sanity.

20

FOLLOWING THE CONTOUR of the cape, we sailed SE by S, then S, then SW by S: the cape curved in a gentle arc. We found that it ended in a sharp point. And then a surprise: behind it, a bay extended to the west. Now we could see that five leguas to the southwest was another cape, which the Captain-General named the Cabo de Espíritu Sancto. The two capes stood at the entrance to the bay, the inner end of which was 20 leguas west. Beyond were snowcapped mountains.

We were sailing smoothly, with a fair wind on the quarter, and it seemed a pity to have to stop for this bay. The Captain-General however gave the order to veer to starboard and steer due west, straight into the bay. It was now noon, and Albo took a shot of the sun. He gave our latitude as 52°31′S. Then he did a few more computations on his slate, and soon announced our longitude: 52°31′W.

"What meridian are you using?" asked the Captain-General.

"Hierro, sir."

"Excellent."

The symmetry of latitude and longitude seemed to have a magical effect on the crew. But then, it was only coincidence, due entirely to Albo's choice of Hierro in the Canaries for his prime meridian. The common practice was to use the meridian of the homeport, and so we should have used Sevilla. On the other hand, our Portuguese pilots were all accustomed to drawing their starting lines on their charts through Lisbõa; that might have been our prime meridian had any of them been flag pilot.

"First time I've seen snowcaps in years," said Master Andrew. "They've a strange beauty about them, and that gives me a feeling about this place. Perhaps we'll find something now. Even the numbers seem to be right."

He had done a few computations himself, using the meridian of Bristol; his result had been a longitude of 68°W. This would imply that Hierro was about 16½° west of Bristol. I thought of checking this out on the map, but decided not to; I was afraid Master Andrew's figure might be too far off.

Later I found that Dom Fernão's reading of the latitude was 52°20'S. He had shot the sun himself, and done his own computations from the declination tables. Had he compensated for Albo's usual error, latitudes too far south, he would probably have arrived at the same figure.

My master had no figure for our present longitude. He had a fastidious regard for numbers, and would not log in the derrotero any figure not obtained through a systematic method. He possessed no exact method for finding longitude. Albo's kind of guesswork, plucking numbers out of thin air, must have made Dom Fernão shudder.

The Captain-General summoned the captains, pilots, and escribanos of the other ships to the capitana. When they had rowed over in their batels and assembled in the stateroom, he announced that we would stop here, in the Bahia de Once Mil Virgenes, for several days while we examined every mile of the coast for any breaks.

"It would be a waste of time, Dom Fernão," declared Estêvão Gomes. "Don't you see that the background of this bay is all snowcapped mountains? That is clear evidence of solid land. There cannot be a paso through such high mountains. It's simply impossible."

"You're probably right," admitted the Captain-General, "but that's beside the point. It is our duty to reconnoiter and map this unknown coast, if only for geographical knowledge. Nothing further need be said on the matter.

"Captain Serrano, you will lead in the *Concepción*. Captain Mesquita, you will escort Serrano. Keep the *San Antonio* in deeper water, at Serrano's portside. The *Trinidad* and the *Victoria* will take soundings of this bay and look for good holding ground. We shall all rendezvous five days hence, right here in the shadow of this headland. Any questions?"

There were none.

We were in the middle of Bahia Virgenes, some ten leguas west of Cabo Virgenes, and another ten leguas from the bay's westernmost reach. When the *Concepción* and the *San Antonio* were some seven leguas west of us, and getting close to the bay's west edge, a northeast gale suddenly whipped up. We hurriedly hoisted our batel up onto the deck. We normally towed the batel astern, but in strong winds and rough seas it would never do to have it bobbing behind us on a tether. It would ram us, perhaps with enough force to gash a hole in our side. Or its rope would break and we would lose it. We lashed it down on the main deck while the other men trimmed sail. All this with a minimum of orders; we were an experienced crew by now.

The *Trinidad* and the *Victoria* jilled about in the bay, spooming before the waves, going in circles. We were used to these storms now, and knew we would have to ride it out for half a day or so. It had begun late in the afternoon, so we expected to have to weather it until midnight. None of us was going to become seasick.

It was the *Concepción* and the *Victoria* we were most concerned about. The storm had caught them near land, where they had no room to turn about and head for the middle of the wide bay. They could be dashed against the sheer cliffs, and we feared the worst. Ser Antonio prayed the rosary aloud while the storm raged, and most of the men prayed with him. This time they were not praying for our own deliverance, but for the safety of the other two ships.

The winds abated an hour before midnight. A short distance away were the lights of the *Victoria*. Captain Barbosa had kept her in formation with the *Trinidad* even as we went around in circles riding out the storm.

Tired as he was, the Captain-General could not go to sleep. I had to stay awake myself, ready to jump to his commands, but I felt Captain Serrano would handle the *Concepción* with consummate skill. He had already lost the *Santiago* from right under his feet, and if I understood anything about the white man's pride, he would sail the *Concepción* to hell before he would allow himself to lose a second ship. I was more worried about the *San Antonio* and Captain Mesquita. He merely had to follow Captain Serrano's lead, but that could not be very easy to do with a northeast gale pushing one's ship toward the rocks. If he had any sense, he would have left the *San Antonio* in the hands of pilot Gomes and contramaestre Diego Hernandez. Many of the marineros on the *San Antonio* were Basques who had sailed in whaling ships all around the Bay of Biscay. Some were said to have sailed as far as the coast of the Newe Founde Lande. They always denied it, in order to keep the fishing to themselves.

I had confidence in the stout-hearted men of the *Concepción* and the *San Antonio*. I kept dropping off to sleep. My master, kind soul that he was, did not once prod me awake. I would snap awake every now and then, and see him still peering out in the dark, looking for something. The sky had cleared, and the stars had come out. The constellations at this latitude were unknown to us, and it seemed the Captain-General was drafting a chart of these Southern stars in his head. Then I saw the old ppalu from the far islands of the southwest steering his prahu by the fair winds of the habagat, and I knew I had nodded off to sleep and was dreaming again.

The whole of the following day, October 22, our two ships sailed close inland, searching for the wreckage of the other two. I thought we should have sailed across the bay, to the point in the west where the *Concepción* and the *San Antonio* had been when the gale hit us. The Captain-General preferred a methodical study of the northside's every legua. It was slow going, as this was the lee shore. By nightfall we were only halfway to that point. We anchored for the night. I had to stand the watch of the modorra. By the time we were relieved by the watch of la diane, I could hardly keep my eyes open. I tumbled into a corner, dropped into dreamless sleep.

"La vela!" shouted the lookout in the crow's nest. I got up, suddenly alert. Everyone was running to the side for a look. The lookout shouted again: "Dos velas!"

Two sails, for two ships. It had to be them.

They bore down on us, the *Concepción* and the *San Antonio*, neither looking the worse for wear. They had come through the storm unscathed. As they grew bigger we could see they were flying all their flags, and in addition had strung up decorative banners. Two puffs of smoke escaped from them, one from each vessel, and a second later the twin booms of their cannon reached our ears.

"Are they saluting us?" Ser Antonio asked.

A fanfare of trumpets blared from the *Concepción*, quickly echoed by a blast from the *San Antonio*.

"Yes," said the Captain-General. "And they're also announcing good news. They must have found something."

"When the gale blew up," recounted Captain Serrano, "both our ships were too deeply embayed to head back and beat against the wind. The only hope seemed to lie in beaching ourselves, if a suitable stretch of sand could be found. Then I saw that the wind and the current combined were taking us into a break in the cliffs, half a legua in width. We had scarcely enough time to steer for the middle of the channel. As you know, the flow is always much faster where there is a passage like a funnel, and we were swept through at breakneck speed."

He paused for a sip of sherry.

"The garganta extends for a legua and a half, then opens up into a large bay. I have named that bay the Bahia *Victoria* to honor my devotion to Santa María de la *Victoria*."

"A very good name," said the Captain-General. "As for the garganta, I'd prefer to call it an angostura."

"To the west," continued Captain Serrano, "may be seen another garganta, er, angostura, which leads further into another bay. I thought we should report back to you before exploring the waters past the second narrows. Besides, we feared for your safety. We were sheltered from the winds in that bay. But Carvalho wanted to see the next bay, the one past the segunda angostura. Mesquita seconded this motion."

"After all," said Dom Álvaro de Mesquita, "it was only the second day. Our orders were to rendezvous in five days."

"Quite so," said Dom Fernão.

"And so," resumed Captain Serrano, "we entered that bay. It was low tide when we were going through the second narrows, and the highwater marks visible on the cliff walls were forty feet up. The bay, which I called the Paso Ancho, has a few islands near the entrance, and stretches to the south for twenty or twenty-five leguas. At its southern end the mountains begin. There seem at least three ways to proceed from the far end, one to the east, another to the southeast, and still another to the southwest. Only further exploration can determine which way might be best.

"The water everywhere we tasted it was brine, and the tides were of equal strength at ebb and at flood.

"My Captain-General, I firmly believe we have found the paso, just as you said we would. I propose a toast."

He raised his drinking horn.

"¡Viva el rey de Castilla, por mar y por tierra!"

"¡Viva!" resounded everyone, in chorus.

"¡Viva el capitán-mayor de la Armada de Maluco, Don Fernando de Magallanes, caballero comendador del Orden de Santiago de la Espada!"

"¡Viva!"

The Captain-General stood up.

"I swore a holy oath to find the paso for our Emperor. If we have succeeded thus far, it is only because the Almighty God, through the intercession of the Blessed Virgin Mary and all the saints, has seen fit to answer our prayers.

"In this hour of triumph, let us not forget those fellow voyagers of ours whose souls have gone to their rest. Let us remember them always in our prayers, our dear companions who gave their lives in the service of the fatherland.

"We may have found the paso, but now begins the true voyage of discovery. In the coming weeks, a high order of seamanship will be called for, and we shall all have to show what manner of men we are. Let us seek the continued guidance of Our Lord Jesus Christ and all the saints, especially Sanct Iago, patron saint of the knightly order whose habit it is my honor to wear, and patron saint of the Spanish nation. ¡Viva España!"

"¡Viva!"

"¡Viva Don Cárlos!"

"¡Viva!"

The other captains rose to propose more toasts, and after them the noblemen. When Master Andrew got his turn, he made a wry face:

"To friends, ships, and women. May all of them be fast."

Hierónimo de Guerra and Estêvão Gomes drank to the calls along with everybody, but did not themselves propose any toasts. I happened to be close by, and I overheard them.

"We didn't see a way clear through to the other side, did we?" de Guerra asked.

"No," said Gomes. "They think it's the paso. I'm sure it's really a trap for the unwary. No way out. A labyrinth."

Westerly winds plagued us for the next few days. Unable to enter the narrows, we jilled about in the Bahia de Once Mil Virgenes. This was preferable to lying at anchor; the winds here seemed erratic, and could whip up without warning into gales strong enough to make a ship drag its anchors. Besides, the bay as a whole was not good holding ground; too few places afforded safe anchorage. Much of it was deep water, beyond the 200-fathom reach of our sounding leads. The normal sounding lead had a rope of 600 feet, and we had spliced pairs of them together into 1200-foot dipseys, and still most of the bay was bottomless.

October 26 showed us a full moon through fast-moving clouds. Unknown stars shone down on us. What stars we could recognize told us we were 53 degrees south of the æquinoctial line: Scorpius lay on its side just above the mountains in the north, its tail grazing the snowcaps. The moon, a day past third quarter, was due to rise an hour past midnight.

Two faint clouds floated near the zenith, one larger than the other. They moved with the stars; two hours later, they had not changed their shapes.

The other men had seen those clouds, too.

"Most peculiar," Master Andrew said, but Dom Fernão and Ser Antonio, having been the first to see them, felt no need to belabor the obvious.

"They do not move," Ser Antonio said.

"They are rather faint," said Dom Fernão. "They must be very far away."

"A strange portent," said Andrés de San Martín. "They are not true clouds, but the ghosts of clouds."

The rest of October, 27 through 31, merged one into another, five days that seemed as one long day. The men's general attitude to Dom Fernão, I noticed, was slowly changing. Where once he was regarded as a ruthless slavedriver, now he was seen as cautious and considerate, deferring our entry into the strait until the wind was right and we had salted away enough food. Where once he had been a hopeless dreamer vainly searching for a mythical strait, now he was a visionary with the gift of foresight. Those who had secretly hated him were deferential now, and he graciously nodded at the new respect accorded him. He prayed more often now, down on his knees while alone in his cabin; he fervently believed only his devotion to the saints had brought him thus far. While I had sought a silly miracle at Cabo Virgenes, and prayed for a spate of virgins, my master had endured hardships and pursued a vision. Now it was in sight. His was the true miracle, a gift from Heaven. There was nothing the saints would not grant him.

The Captain-General had taken to calling the strange clouds the Nubecula Mayor and the Nubecula Minor. He named the constellations they occupied, too. The bigger cloud was in the constellation Dorado, the smaller in Tucana. A dorado was a fish to be found only in these waters; a tucana bird native to these lands.

"I've taken measurements of those clouds, Don Fernan," Ser Antonio said, walking up to stand beside the Captain-General on the quarterdeck.

"Oh, have you, now? Most interesting. And what measurements are these?"

"The bigger cloud—"

"Nubecula Mayor."

"—has an angular diameter of seven degrees. In other words, it covers an area some 200 times larger than the moon does. It remains visible in full moonlight. Its position in the sky may be described thus: right ascension, five hours and twenty-six minutes; declination, sixty-nine degrees."

"But we are south of the æquinoctial line."

"Oh, I beg your pardon. I meant minus sixty-nine degrees. I forgot about the negative sign."

"Right ascension 5 hours, 26 minutes. Declination -69°. Yes, that seems about right. Pray continue."

"Angular diameter of the Nubecula Minor, 4°. Right ascension, zero hours, 50 minutes. Declination -73°. It's only a fourth of the size of the bigger cloud, and its magnitude is correspondingly much less; it disappears in the light of the full moon.

"The two nubeculae are distant from each other by an angular difference of 23° in the sky. They form with the South celestial pole an æquilateral triangle."

"Excellent. We shall make a navigator of you yet. Now, if Andrés de San Martín could only tell us what these omens portend."

Finally the wind turned, and we were ready to go west. October had ended, and it was now November 1, the Feast of All Saints. After the morning prayers, the Captain-General announced that he was naming the strait the Estrecho de Todos los Santos.

The four ships fired ceremonial broadsides, then swept in single file into the Primera Garganta, the *Trinidad* leading the way. I only hoped Estêvão Gomes would not be proven right, that this Strait of All the Saints would not turn out to be a hopeless maze. Or that it would not double back and debouch farther south into the same ocean we had come from, the Mar Océano. As we picked up speed in the narrows, Master Andrew shook his fist at the ship immediately following and railed at it, albeit the *San Antonio* was upwind of us and none of the men aboard it could have heard him.

"O ye of little faith!" he shouted into the wind. "Wherefore didst thou doubt?"

21

♒

THE BAHIA VICTORIA was more like a lake than a bay, completely enclosed by land except for two outlets: the Primera Angostura to the east, and the Segunda Angostura to the west.

The lookout reported something black on the southside shore, and farther inland, a village of huts. The Captain-General ordered the ships to lie to and anchor, then sent the alguacil with two merinos and several marineros to investigate. All drew arms from the stores. Don Gonzálo and the two merinos donned armor. Ser Antonio volunteered to go with them and, when granted permission, put on his own armor.

Here between the two angosturas the land was much like the coast of Patagonia: grassy plains with flowery bushes, interspersed with forests. Of the two main kinds of trees, one was the arbol de haya, or beech tree as Master Andrew called it. The other was of an unknown kind. Using sign language, I asked the Patagonian what he called it. "Tepu," he said. I did not know if that was the tree's name or merely his word for "tree." It hardly mattered. It was springtime in these latitudes, and the flowers were in full bloom.

"How very like Ireland," said Master Andrew, "as I saw it from the deck of the *Mathew* so many years ago. I was one of the pages, a mere lad of fourteen, on my first sea voyage."

"Did you say the *Mathew*, Maestro Andrés?" asked Dom Fernão. "Do I apprehend correctly? Was that not Juan Gaboto's ship?"

"Aye, John Cabot's ship, the very same. I was indeed on that voyage."

"Have you heard of that voyage, then, comendador?" asked Andrés de la Cruz.

"A voyage to look for the Northwest Passage. The first from Inglatierra to cross the Mar Océano and reach land, unless you credit the legends of the Northmen having reached that land five hundred years ago. They called those lands Vinland and Markland. But you must relate your voyage to us, Maestro Andrés."

"Ach, it was so long ago, and me a stripling of fourteen, as I've told ye. But you, Signor Punzurol, must have heard of John Cabot. He was a Venetian, like our companion Ser Antonio Pigafetta."

"Actually, Pigafetta's from Vicenza," Punzorol said.

"The Chiabotto family was from Genoa. They moved to Venice in the 1460s. John Cabot was a citizen of Venice when he came to Bristol in 1495, with his wife and sons Lewis, Sebastian, and Sanctius. He had passed his 40th year by then; he was 44 when we sailed."

"That's nearly the same age as Juan Rodríguez de Sevilla, our oldest marinero," Cristóvão Rabelo said.

"In what year did you sail, Maestro Andrés?" asked Andrés de la Cruz.

"In 1497. John Cabot had in 1496 acquired a letter-patent from King Henry the Seventh to sail under his banners and ensignes to seeke, discovere, and finde newe landes, and to rule such lands as the King's lieutenant. He offered to sail on his own proper charges, meaning he paid for everything himself. The King merely granted him a license to earn what he could out of whatever lands he might find."

"A stingy monarch," said Dom Fernão. "But at least he granted the patent. Dom Manoel of Portugal wouldn't promote me, much less grant me a carta de doacão. Thank God for Don Carlos Primero. He spent nearly 9 million maravedis on this Armada."

"The exact figure, Sire," I said, "as Don Cristobal de Haro told you, was 8,751,125 maravedis."

"You've quite a memory, Enrique. But you were telling us about that voyage, Maestro Andrés?"

"Yes. John Cabot had no money, but Cristopher de Haro was in England, and had regaled the King with stories of the fabled Northwest Passage to the Indies. It was de Haro who financed the voyage."

"Didn't Cabot ask for three ships?"

"De Haro had the money for only one."

"One lone ship. A perilous undertaking. Very brave of Cabot."

"We departed Bristowe with the northeast trades on May 20, 1497, and sailed west to Ireland. Rounding Fastnet, we turned northwest to close in on Dursey Head, Ireland's westernmost point. John Cabot wanted to set his latitude by it. I've since found out that Inishark and the Skelligs are even farther west, but only by a few miles.

"We took the latitude as one-and-fifty and half a degree North, and shaped the course straight west. The old-fashioned latitude sailing."

"A reliable method," Dom Fernão said. "Keep your latitude at 51½°N, and never mind the longitude. And if strong winds blow you off course a few leguas, all you need do is find your latitude again."

"Precisely. We enjoyed fine sailing on our chosen latitude for a month, until we reached land. Of course, in those days, everyone still thought it was the Indies Columbus had reached five years before. John Cabot himself was sure we were approaching the east coast of Northern Cathay.

"It was June 24, the Feast of St. John the Baptist, wherefore Cabot named that island St. John. The latitude was one-and-fifty degrees and two-thirds, almost exactly the latitude of Dursey Head in Ireland."

"A very fine piece of latitude sailing," Dom Fernão said. "So you reached land at 51⅔°N? You must be the only man on this Armada who has been 51 degrees from the æquinoctial line in both directions, north and south. Quite an honor to have you with us."

"My dear Captain-General, the honor is mine. Northern Cathay was a disappointment. We did not see any Cathayans. I had hoped to see those slit-eyed, yellow-skinned men. We saw no people at all. But they were there. They hid themselves from us. We saw their fishnets in shallow water, and their traps for rabbits and small game. Today we know better, and I don't think they were slit-eyed, yellow-skinned Cathayans..."

"Perhaps," said Juan Bautista de Mompeller, "they were Esquimaux?"

"They were Skrellings, I'm sure," said Master Andrew. He paused for a sip of wine.

"Decent Spanish clarée, this. Better than metheglyn. Or hippocras."

He then resumed his narrative:

"John Cabot planted England's royal flag there, King Harry's arms. Henry VII. The tides were slack, not at all like the tides that assault the Avonmouth. Where I hail from, we have the highest tides in the world. Twenty-one feet at neap tide and a full forty feet at spring tide. There at the Newe Founde Lande, the tides were two feet at the neaps and five or six at the springs."

"You did not find the Northwest Passage. Do you think it exists?"

"Oh, aye, but too far north to be of much use. You would have to sail through seas full of pack ice."

The capitana's batel returned, the men not having fired a shot.

"A dead whale," reported Don Gonzálo, "with vultures feeding on it. We walked a legua inland, to the village. It turned out to be a cemetery. Those barrows are biers for their dead."

"A most disquieting place," Ser Antonio said. "This is a land whose men do not show themselves, but only their dead."

"Each hut rests on posts," Don Gonzálo said, "so that it is five feet off the ground. Each has a roof of thatch. The dead man we looked at must have been a giant. He would have stood more than six feet tall. Perhaps six and a half."

"The whole body was sewn up in a shroud," related Ser Antonio, "which fitted tightly, like a second skin. Over it he wore a headdress of bird feathers, and a necklace of shells and bear teeth. His weapons were laid out beside him: a knife of flint, a spear with a blackened tip, a club studded with bear teeth."

"I haven't seen any bears around here," Dom Fernão said. "That must have been shark teeth. And the blackened tip meant the spear had been hardened by fire."

"Beside him was a pouch, made of...what skin was that, Gonzálo?"

"Albatross. The shroud was of the same material."

"Quite so. In the pouch was a piece of flint, and a rock. It could not have been an ordinary rock, so I looked closely at it. It was a piece of ore. Embedded in it was a vein of iron."

"Interesting. What do you think was it used for?"

"It was a device for making fire. He would strike the flint against the exposed surface of iron, and obtain a spark. I wanted to take the pouch, but I felt I could not desecrate that man's grave."

"Here," said Don Gonzálo, handing him something.

Ser Antonio stared incredulously at him for a moment, then took the pouch.

"You're an avatar of Prometheus," he said. "Stealing fire from the dead."

If the dead lay in a village of huts, then the living could not be far behind. We had yet to see any of the inhabitants of these shores. Night fell, and we anchored for the night, throwing out ropes from the starboard side and making the ship fast to stout beech trees on the north shore. The other ships followed our example.

At dusk Ser Antonio started a fire with his flint and iron, and we crowded around it to warm our hands. We could make out a fire on the opposite shore, two leguas away, then another, and still another...there were fires at several places on the south land. Around them the natives of the place must have been sitting around their fires, keeping warm and cooking food, exactly as we were doing.

I asked the Patagonian, who was still in leg irons, about the people of these parts.

"Tehuelche," he said, pointing to the north. "Ona," pointing to the east, "Ha-ush."

Then he mimed the rowing of a canoe, pointed west, and said, "Alacalaf."

He gestured again, indicating people who moved around.

"Yaghan," he said.

I took those to be the names of various tribes.

In the morning we looked for them, but never saw a soul. That night, as we tied up again, we saw more of their fires. We had made progress of several leguas that day, and so these could not have been the same Indians, but others of their ilk further down the strait. The fires were all on the land to the south; there were none to the north, which would be the extreme end of América, if this was indeed a strait separating two lands.

"It's a land without mosquitoes," Master Andrew pointed out. "Too much wind for them here."

"It's a land of fires," Dom Fernão said.

That became his name for that land: the tierra del fuegos. Spanish grammar being what it was, it became a proper name by the use of the singular: the Tierra del Fuego.

Then we were past the Segunda Angostura and in the Paso Ancho. This broad reach stretched north and south some 20 leguas; we were at the north end. It was 5 leguas wide, and on either side were grassy plains. In front of us was an island, and beyond it, to the southwest, two islets almost completely covered by penguins and sea lions. Past those, at its furthest south, the Paso Ancho was abruptly brought up short by tall mountains, blue in the distance, streaked white at their upper halves with patterns of snow. These mountains reared up to the clouds and surmounted them. There were four peaks that stood out; they were evenly spaced, like the teeth of a saw. Ser Antonio estimated them to be the height of the Pico de Teide in Teneriphe—twelve thousand feet if worth an inch.

The mountains were a natural barrier. One doubted if there was a way through them. The eye could not accept this as anything but a dead end. Only the strong current indicated otherwise.

The scenery, to both port and starboard, of grassy fields with patches of flowers looked very beautiful—like Ireland, as Master Andrew had said. I had never seen Ireland, but I felt sure it looked much prettier than this. The land of monks and leprechauns was an island, after all. To me this place had the look of a very strange land. It surrounded an inland sea, with only one way out, the way we came in, and forbidding mountains at the other end. It was like a lake, not a large one, but small enough for the land surrounding it to be visible on all sides. We were completely enclosed, and I had an impression of how it would look at night: the darkness closing in, and the land too; blackness swallowing us up, isolating us in the sphere of our firelights, and in the morning only a puddle of water left, the ships floating in a tub, a bottomless pool, with the land around us so close we could reach out and touch the sheer walls of rock.

The fleet anchored just past the big island, on the lee side, and the Captain-General summoned the other captains to the capitana.

He was naming the island the Isla Beatriz, after his wife, he told them. The two islets, mere chunks of rock upon which penguins and sea lions were sunning themselves, he would call Santa Marta and Santa Magdalena. Duarte Barbosa could not hide a grin.

"My little sister's got an island named after her," he said. "Why don't you name it after the saint whose feastday it is? That's what you usually do."

"I can't very well name it after San Vitalis or Generál Agricola," Dom Fernão said.

Then he issued orders: the *Concepción* and the *San Antonio* were to sail east, into the big bay stretching that way. He personally doubted it would lead anywhere, and so from there they were to go southeast, where there seemed to be a seno, or a sound that might offer passage.

The *Trinidad* and the *Victoria* would sail southwest to investigate the other seno. Both pairs of ships were to rendezvous at the south end of the Paso Ancho, near the mountains, in a week.

"I wonder if sending the longboats might not be a better idea," mused our pilot, Francisco Albo.

"Too tiring," said Ser Antonio. "We don't know how far these senos lead. The rowers' arms would drop off from exhaustion."

"Those Irishmen should have brought a curragh. They claim they can sail anywhere in that vessel."

"We could build a coracle and have you command it, Albo," Master Andrew said. "What would you name it?"

"I'd name it for the city my ancestors came from," Albo said. "Delphi, from where all Greeks who went west began their travel."

"Delphi?" Master Andrew repeated. "Splendid. You can call it the Delphic Coracle, then."

⚓

22

AT THE SOUTHWEST END of the Paso Ancho was a high cape and, beyond it, a narrow sound turning sharply to starboard, to the northwest.

"Something tells me this is the right way," Master Andrew said. "Northwest. The *Concepción* and the *San Antonio* won't find anything to the east or south. The Captain-General ought to name this sound after me. El Seno Inglés. That's got a nice ring to it." The mountains began here, and the seno was a deep cleft in the sierra. After the serene, gentle pampas surrounding the Paso Ancho, the vertiginous and stark mountains, groping for heaven, laden with patterns of snow on their upper slopes and thickly forested with huge trees on their lower halves, put us in thrall to the awe of entering a mysterious place. Clouds swirled around these windswept crags, and after I had stared up at them for some time, I saw clearly that the peaks surmounted no less than three regions of clouds.

Ten leguas into the seno we came to a little bay, almost completely landlocked, with two narrow rivers feeding into it. The waters at both rivermouths were full of sardines, so the Captain-General named the bay the Río de Sardinas. The Captain-General decided to camp there, the best anchorage we had seen so far in the estrecho. We set out to catch large hauls of sardines, to be preserved in the food barrels.

The Captain-General ordered the alguacil, Don Gonzálo, to scout the paso in the batel, with a crew of five. Dom Fernão had not given this sound a name, but in my mind I thought of it as the Paso Inglés. A deep furrow in the midst of craggy mountains, it seemed to have as much character as Master Andrew.

Now a night suddenly clear, after a week of clouds spooming, scudding, or swirling overhead. November 4 was my birthday by the white man's calendar. The year before, I had forgotten my 27th birthday as we sweated in the doldrums somewhere in the middle of the Mar Oceáno. Now I was turning 28, and this time I had a sky full of stars, plus two ghostly clouds, to remember it by.

Don Gonzálo and his batel crew returned in three days, firing their serpentinas and waving flags.
"We've seen it!" they yelled.
Or, to be precise, Roldán d'Argote had seen it. Don Gonzálo had rowed the batel some 20 leguas northwest, following the paso. Never narrower than half a legua anywhere, he reported, its steep rock walls made it seem narrower. They had seen several waterfalls emptying directly into the paso...
"I climbed a mountain," Roldán said, "and caught a glimpse of the Mar del Sur. No more than twenty leguas away. A cape overlooks the exit...where the surf pounds against the rocks it is full of spray...like smoke. I could almost hear the breaking of the waves..."
"I shall name that cape the Cabo Deseado," said Dom Fernão, "for I have long desired it..."
Roldán looked away, as if acutely embarrassed. I shot a glance at my master. There were tears in his eyes. The first time I had ever seen him weep, and I had known him for nine years. I looked away, too.

Ten days in the Río de Sardinas. November 11 now. With the Mar del Sur sighted, it was time to rejoin the other ships. The *Trinidad* and the *Victoria* lifted anchor and sailed back to the Paso Ancho.
We found the *Concepción* sailing in circles around the agreed rendezvous point.
"Where's the *San Antonio*?" was the Captain-General's first question.
"I don't know," replied Captain Juan Serrano.
They had found nothing in the first bay they entered, the one leading east. It was a dead end.

"I named it the Bahia Inútil," Serrano said. "A calm bay, untroubled by strong currents, but completely enclosed. From there we wandered to the next bay, or sound, which I called the Seno Almirantazgo. The currents were tricky. Encountering fog I ordered the farol lit, so Mesquita could follow my light. But when it cleared, the *San Antonio* was nowhere to be seen."

A strange world indeed, where only the dead members of the population showed themselves, and the living were seen but as distant fires at night; where the currents and winds baffled even the old salts among us; where canals and senos either led nowhere or doubled back on themselves; where clouds flew by night in a sky that no wind could touch; where a ship could disappear into the fog and vanish without a trace.

There were whispers now among the men.

"It sailed off the edge of this world, and fell into another world," went one.

"Inveigled into a whirlpool somewhere in this maze of waterways," went another.

"It's the eleventh of November," Master Andrew said. "Strange things always happen on Martinmas."

Why couldn't they see it? This place had strange gods, unlike any other deities in any other place. Surely they would demand human sacrifice? We had not lost a man since Jorge Alemán in the Río Santa Cruz, but we had lost an entire ship. The ways of the gods were not to be fathomed. Where everything baffled us, their ways would be the most befuddling of all.

The Captain-General lost no time in ordering Duarte Barbosa to sail back in the *Victoria* to look for the missing ship...or its wreckage. The *Concepción* he also sent back, to the place where Captain Serrano had last seen the *San Antonio,* in the Seno Almirantazgo.

The *Concepción* returned in eight days, from Admiralty Sound. Serrano had not turned left from Paso Inglés into Paso Ancho and then right again into Seno Almirantazgo. Instead he had gone straight, through a narrow channel he called the Seno Magdalena.

"No trace of the *San Antonio,*" he reported.

The *Victoria* returned after twelve days. Captain Barbosa had not found anything, either. He had sailed all the way to the Mar Océano, a little past the Cabo de Once Mil Virgenes, and left two messages for Captain Mesquita. Each was in the form of a letter placed in an earthen pot and buried at the foot of a cross erected at the top of the more prominent headlands. One was at the Cabo Virgenes. The other was atop a hill just past the Segunda Angostura, at the entrance to Paso Ancho.

Andrés de San Martín offered to consult his cards for an explanation of the *San Antonio*'s fate. We all went into the stateroom. San Martín brought out a pack of cards I had not seen before.

"Gitano cards?" asked Dom Fernão.

"Yes, gypsy cards," said San Martín. "Tarot cards, actually, as they're called. I learned how to read them from the Çingane in Triana."

"The Zingani say the knowledge embodied in these cards," Ser Antonio said, "came from the ancient Egyptians. It was handed down to the Chaldeans, the Israelites, the Greeks, and so to them."

"Don't forget," Duarte Barbosa said, "the Manicheans and the Albigensians."

Andrés de San Martín selected one card, then asked the Captain-General to shuffle the cards. "You are the Querent, Capitão-Mor," he said. "You must allow some spirit-essence from your body to flow through these cards."

"Never mind," Dom Fernão said, declining to shuffle the deck. "Just tell us what happened to the *San Antonio*."

"Oh, all right then," San Martín said. He shrugged, picked up the deck of unused cards as if to shuffle, put it down again.

"Estêvão Gomes has overpowered Captain Álvaro de Mesquita. Mesquita is locked up in the captain's cabin, manacled and in leg irons. Gomes has made Hierónimo de Guerra the new captain. They have turned the *San Antonio* around and are returning to Spain."

"Are they making a stop in Puerto San Julián to pick up Cartagena?"

"Hard to tell. The prevailing winds and currents would not favor a stop there...no, I find no indications to that effect...I think they are sailing straight back across the Mar Océano. They have barely enough provisions for such a voyage. Not stopping to pick up Cartagena. Not even stopping by the Río de Janeiro."

I had been right all along; male names would not do for ships. I should have told someone, anyone, but none of the modern, sixteenth-century men on this Armada would have credited my superstitious feelings. Still, ships with masculine names always brought bad luck. First the *Santiago,* now the *San Antonio.* Now only three ships, the ones with feminine names, were left.

I could sense that my master was secretly glad to be rid of Estêvão Gomes and Hierónimo de Guerra, even at the cost of the Armada's largest ship. Of the cabal that had formed the core of the mutinous group, only two remained. Antonio de Coca was still a prisoner on the *Victoria.* Juan Sebastián de Elcano had been reinstated as maestre of the *Victoria.*

De Coca was no sailor, but Elcano was an experienced mariner who had once captained a 400-tun warship. There was no need to deprive the *Victoria* of Elcano's services. Dom Fernão did not fear the Basque maestre. He could deal with him. The *Victoria* had been built in Guipuzcoa, the only ship in the fleet made in the Basque Pays, and Elcano had a proprietary attitude towards her. The Captain-General thought it best to leave him that much.

Full moon on November 24. The clouds were very faint, the bigger one barely visible, the smaller one obliterated by the moon's glare. Last chance to catch fish, albacore, bonito, and missioglioni as Ser Antonio called them, and penguins, all to be salted down. Last chance to forage for wild celery. Dom Fernão firmly believed eating greens was the one sure way to prevent the escurbuto, and he ordered everyone to eat as much of the celery as they could. He insisted we eat the bitter ones, as these were the most effective. "Bloody umbelliferous parsley," grumbled Master Andrew, barely managing to get it down.

Out of the Río de Sardinas, out of the enclosed bay, into the middle of the Paso Inglés. Sunday, November 25, the day after the full moon, which meant high tide was in the morning, shortly before 7:00, and low tide past noon, a little before 1:00. To avoid the strongest tidal flows—the currents were confusing enough—we went out with the tide, at 9:00.

The *Trinidad* led, Dom Fernão on duty as officer of the watch, with Don Gonzálo Gómez de Espinosa acting as pilot. Next was the *Concepción,* Captain Juan Serrano commanding. Bringing up the rear was the *Victoria,* Duarte Barbosa her captain.

Passing an island he called the Isleo, in the middle of the Paso Inglés, Dom Fernão suddenly ordered the *Trinidad* to lie at anchor, then sent a crew ashore in the batel. They were to erect a cross on a prominent hill commanding a fine view of the seno. The hill, he told them, was to be named the Monte de Cristo. He had written another letter for Captain Mesquita. He placed it in an earthen pot, and this he charged them to bury at the foot of the cross.

On the move again. Past the Isleo we veered slightly to port to follow the seno. Veering the other way, to starboard, would have led us into another passage, but Don Gonzálo said it was a canal fed by an inner bay that was itself fed ice by glaciers. The Captain-General called it the Canal Jerónimo.

"Observe how the water from the canal is of a slightly different coloring from the water of the paso," Don Gonzálo said, pointing to the line where the waters met.

And indeed it was. The water from the Canal Jerónimo was lighter, greenish, while the water of the paso was blue. As we came nearer, we saw that the paso was only slightly wider than the canal. Where the waters met the tides crossed and confounded the currents. Men in the waists ready with the ashwood sweeps. Don Gonzálo and a crew of five all prepared to man the batel and tow the ship if necessary.

Then we were in the Paso Tortuoso. Dom Fernão kept a leadsman at the bow to take soundings, no matter that Don Gonzálo's batel crew had found no bottom here. The rushing waters had divided the seno down the middle, with water flowing in opposite directions on the left and right sides. We stayed in the northern half of the paso. The water across the dividing line, near the south bank, flowed backward nearly as fast as we were borne forward.

The scenery changed again. Sides of the mountains ribbed granite. In the clefts, shrubs. No more trees. Snowcaps on the mountains somehow heavier.

A bay surrounded by high cliffs, a waterfall tumbling directly into the sea. The most spectacular of the falls we had seen in this Strait.

"Plenty of swallows," Master Andrew said. "I'm sure el comendador will name this Swallow Bay."

Another day, another seno. Now the Paso Largo.

"There's the mountain Roldán climbed," said Don Gonzálo, pointing to it, to starboard.

"This is as far as you went?" asked Dom Fernão.

"Yes. Not too far off now from the Mar del Sur. Notice how the heavier swells roll in all the way from the open sea?"

"The last part is often the hardest. Relieve the leadsman on the bow. A bonus to whoever finds bottom."

"I believe there is not a more beautiful or a better strait in the world than this one," Ser Antonio murmured as he wrote. I glanced over his shoulder and read:

"Credo nõ sia aL mondo el piu bello et meglior streto como equesto."

How simply he put it! But its beauty came from its very strangeness, and no words could do it justice...for one had to see it for himself, and there was no use describing snow at the mountaintops melting down through three layers of wild clouds to come rushing as rivers that ended in waterfalls jumping straight into the sea, or ducks that swam as no other ducks in the known world swam, using their wings as paddles, or islets completely covered with penguins and elephant seals that seem to have grown out of the rock, or unseen giants wearing the scantiest of clothing against the bitter cold and seemingly huddled in holes by day, like frogs, only to come alive by night in an exaltation of fires.

This was the Strait, the one that was not supposed to exist. Except in my master's mind. And in maps no one had seen. It was as if he had willed this strait into being by sheer force of will. One passed through it as through a dream, and of the last few leguas I could remember only fragmented images...

...the hidden rock off an island my master named the Isla Tamar...submerged at 2½ fathom, found by the sounding lead in the nick of time...the sound of ocean surf breaking on rocks on the other side of the land....the winds gathering resentment at being forced into the narrow cleft of the paso.

...the sense of coming into something awesome, the expectation of things unknown, as waves possessed by a secret power surged in from the great sea to break on both sides of the paso.

...Cabo Deseado, then a shoal of four rocks just outside the strait, inevitably named the Evangelistas...more rocks further on, half-hidden in the misty spray...eleven of them? thirteen?...Everyone agreed they were the Doce Apóstoles.

...the ceremonial broadside upon entering the Mar del Sur...the rightness, after so difficult a passage, of attaining so placid an ocean...the Captain-General dressed up in the Knight of Santiago's habit, the chaplain beside him...the prayers. The speech.

"How calm and peaceful! From here on, this be its name: the Mar Pacifico."

Ser Antonio writing again.

"*Mercore a 28 de nouembre 1520 Ne disbucasemo da questo strecto ingolfandone neL mare pacifico.*"

"Wednesday, November 28, 1520, we debouched from that strait and engulfed ourselves in the Pacific Sea."

How simply, how limpidly he could write. How matter of fact. As if this ocean had always been known by that name. And never by any other.

I spat into it, and called its name.

The Mar del Sur.

Ang Kamaguyhang Laut.

IIIª Parte
O Mar Pacifico

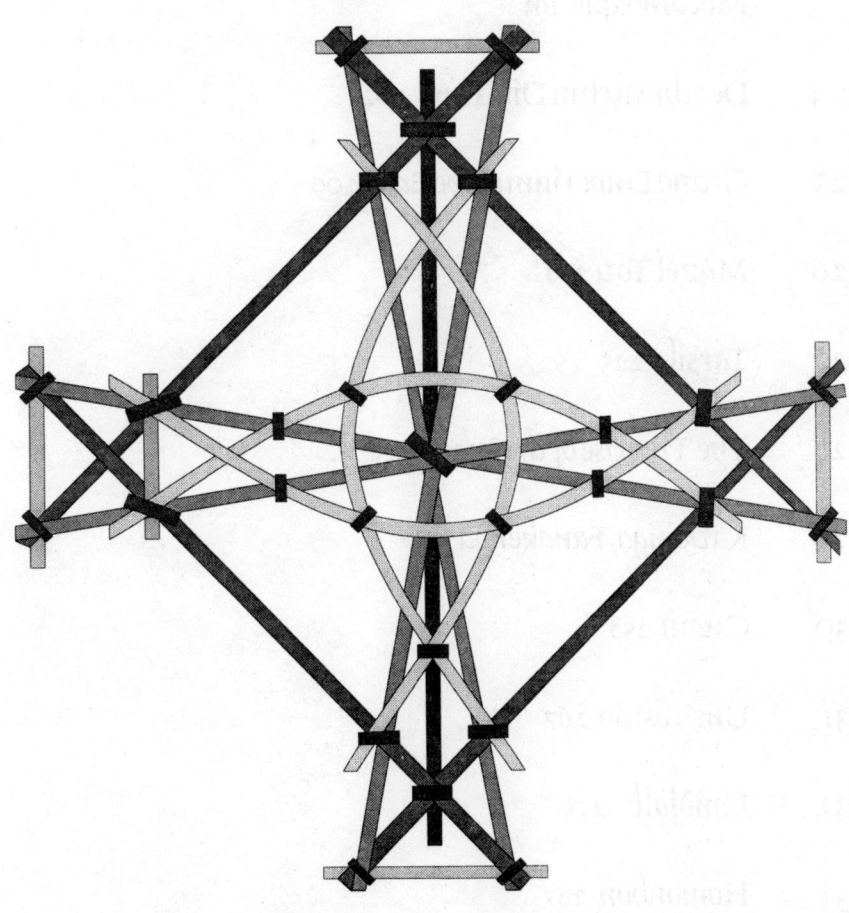

23 How Lovely from my Bergantym, Quilóa, Sofála, Moçambique 193

24 Deathwatch in Diu Time 202

25 Grand Emporium of the East 209

26 Mazel Tov 219

27 Tarsila 225

28 The Treatise of the Sphere 236

29 Kaveinga, Fanakenga 247

30 Guam 258

31 Um Tostão 267

32 Landfall 275

33 Homonhon 287

23

COURSE: NORTHWEST, away from the land, away from the cold. Out into the open ocean, reveling in sea room after the close confines of the Strait, up into warmer latitudes. Wind on the quarter, sails stiff with speed.

Only three ships now, and some 185 men out of the 264 men in five ships when the Armada was crossing the Mar Océano. We had lost some 65 men with the desertion of the *San Antonio*. Sixteen other men had died, and the two marooned men were now presumably dead—eighteen in all. On the other hand we had picked up three men, Indians, and a boy, Carvalho's son.

"Landscape like the fjords of Norway," Master Andrew said.

The Strait's exit was at 52°S. By noon of the next day, November 29, we were at 51°. It was still cold, and so the Captain-General changed course again, to north.

"It's like Ultima Thule," Master Andrew said.

November 30 was the Feast of St. Andrew.

"Must be my birthday," Master Andrew said. "I was born around this time of year, hence my name."

"Felicidades," Dom Fernão said.

On December 1, the beginning of the Season of Advent, we saw a good landmark, a headland with three peaks atop it, at 48°S. We changed course to N by E to close in on it.

"Very tall," said Ser Antonio, as we came to within two leguas of the cape, "At least 1,300 feet."

The Captain-General named it the Cabo Tres Montes, shot the sun himself, and determined our latitude to be 47°S. As usual, Francisco Albo's latitude placed us too far south.

The cape became our reference point, our point of departure. We lay at anchor in its shadow, making ready to strike out across the ocean, and waiting for more favorable winds. Men in the batels went aft to inspect each ship's rudder. The Captain-General wanted a Mass said, but Padre Valderrama assured him it was against canon law to celebrate Mass on shipboard; he could say Mass only on land. There was no good landing place on the coast, so the Captain-General led us through the doctrina cristiana instead, the pages leading the singing of the Salve Regina, the Te Deum, and all the church hymns they could remember.

On December 2 we lifted anchor, spread sail, and steered northwest. I watched the compass needle swing clockwise from true North and settle at 23°, which meant we were heading 337°.

"What's the variation here?" Dom Fernão asked Albo.

"Two points, to the northeast," was the reply.

"Twenty-two and a half degrees? Unusually large. I'd have guessed fifteen, maybe seventeen. Are you quite sure?"

"Quite, sir. That is, if we consider the South celestial pole to be 27° below Delta Crucis, the star that forms the foot of the Southern Cross. I've dropped the half-degree and rounded off the correction to 22°. Of course, we can check our accuracy when we reach the æquinoctial line and Polaris once again becomes visible. I'm more familiar with that star, sir."

"Yes, of course. So am I. But the compass variation may decrease, too, as we go north. Hm... northeasting the compass box by two whole points. Very strange."

"Everything's strange in this part of the world, comendador," Master Andrew said.

"So I've noticed."

"Look here, Francisco," Ser Antonio said, "do you mean that when our compass read 22°, our actual course was 0°? Due north?"

"Precisely. Zero degrees. Or 360."

"And now our bearing is 337°. What is our actual course?"

"Subtract 22° from 337. We're heading 315°. Due northwest."

"Rub that needle some more on the lodestone," ordered Dom Fernão.

The Pacific Sea was aptly named. Its moods grew more mellow each day, its gentle swells and susurrant breezes lulling me into a peaceful lassitude, even as the air grew warmer and our latitude smaller. The last sight of land soon dropped below the horizon astern.

Three or four weeks' sail, and then I would be home.

We continued northwest until the following day, December 3, at noon of which we were at latitude 46°30'S. Albo estimated our longitude to be 5°1'W. How accurate was it, and what was his margin of error? My guesses were: not very, and large.

Day turned into night, but things seemed different to me: as if night were a permanent region of this ocean, and we had only to sail into it; as if we could find day again by sailing back, or that daylight would be ours sooner could we go forward faster. "I've been on the other side of this ocean," Dom Fernão remarked. "In 1512. Such a long time ago."

A lifetime ago, I thought.

"A lifetime ago," my master said.

He was like that.

He could read my thoughts.

He had read Cartagena's, Quesada's, and Mendoza's, and now he kept watch on Elcano's. He did not bother with mine, except idly; I was among the very few who had been on the other side of this ocean, too.

"You were in Malacca, weren't you, commendatore?" asked Ser Antonio.

"Yes, twice. I was there for a few days in 1509. Then I took part in the conquest of it in 1511. I was there until 1513, eighteen months in all."

"And made a voyage from there to the Spice Islands, didn't you?" asked Master Andrew.

"No, I didn't. It was Francisco Serrão who reached Ternate."

"You must tell us about your time in the East, comendador. Seven years, wasn't it?"

"Oh, there isn't much to tell. I left Portugal in 1505 as a sobresaliente in d'Almeida's fleet. I was stationed in East Africa, first in Quilóa, then Sofála, then Moçambique. In all three posts I commanded a bergantym. I was transferred to the Malabar Coast in 1507, in Cochin, later in Goa, with Cananor and Diu in between. That was when I learned how to handle a caravel. Then Malacca...

"From Malacca I sailed my caravel into the eastern waters. I made many exercises in celestial navigation. Through my observations I became convinced that the Spice Islands lay in the Spanish zone, slightly west of the Demarcation Line. None of the Portuguese would believe me, not in Malacca, not in Goa. They sent me home early in 1513."

"What about the battles you fought in, the fortunes you made?" asked Ser Antonio. "You've hardly told us anything!"

"Well..." Dom Fernão's voice trailed off. He yawned. I felt sleepy, and went off into my corner to lie down. I knew all about Dom Fernão's exploits in the East, and could probably have told his story as well as he could. But of course Ser Antonio wanted to hear it from the horse's mouth. My eyes were growing heavy. I let go, and fell into the deep abyss of sleep.

...strange dreams were beguiling me and I struggled to come out of sleep stand on my feet and be master of my own movements but try as I might I could not break free. The dream had enslaved me. I had to do its bidding.

How dreary this life has become, being a clerk at the Mina House! This is the department of the palace that deals with trade in the Indies, and I no longer want to listen to stories of adventure in exotic places. I want to go on these voyages myself.

I volunteer for a post in Captain-General Francisco d'Almeida's armada, the largest armada Portugal has ever assembled, some 2,000 men in 22 ships. It dwarfs even Vasco da Gama's armada of three years ago, which had consisted of only 14 ships.

To my surprise, the King gives me his permission. Perhaps Dom Manoel wants only to be rid of me.

Also granted permission are my elder brother, Diogo da Sousa, and my best friend, Francisco Serrão, who like myself is twenty-five. As noblemen, albeit of the lower grades, all three of us are accepted as sobresalientes on d'Almeida's flagship, the *São Miguel*.

I say goodbye to Catarina Rabelo, a lady-in-waiting at Donha Leonora's court, and baby Xpoual. Not quite three years old, he bears only the slightest resemblance to me. He does not have my swarthy skin and my full lips, the legacy of my Moorish blood, acquired when some ancestor, during the Reconquista, took for his own a Moorish woman whose husband he had slain in battle. Xpoual takes after his mother: her auburn hair, fair skin, and delicate features. Only his eyes and his ears are mine.

Marriage has never entered my head; I am a second son, and have not the wherewithal for a proper marriage. Catarina understands this.

After a High Mass we go aboard the *São Miguel* to wait for the ebb tide that will carry us out of the harbor and into the Mar Océano.

Not everyone knows that Diogo and I are brothers. My name is de Magalhães, his da Sousa; he has been given our grandmother's name so he can inherit her estate. Many think it is Franciso and I who are brothers. Francisco is in fact a second-degree cousin of ours. He went to school with us. Diogo is my elder by two years, but Francisco and I are the same age and so are very close, having always done the same things together from earliest childhood.

We depart on March 25, 1505, a day some people still consider New Year's Day. Every detail my senses note seems to have acquired an extra dimension of clarity: the rooftops of Lisbōa, the color and smell of the Tagus, the way its waters swirl and mingle with those of the sea, the softness of the fluffy clouds in the blue sky, the proud bearing of our Armada.

Twelve of our vessels are warships, caravels and naos, belonging to the Crown. These fly the red Crusader's Cross of the Knights of Christ. The other ten are merchantmen, naos laden with cargoes they hope to exchange for spices in the Orient. These merchant ships are owned by banking houses, some of them foreign. On the three largest naos, the *São Jerónimo*, the *São Rafael*, and the *São Leonardo*, I recognize the family emblems of the Fuggers, the Welsers, and the Marchionis.

We pass the Madeiras in four days, and the Canaries within the week, stopping at neither. Our first stop is to be the Cape Verdes, which we make on April 14, three weeks out of Lisbōa. There the Captain-General opens his sealed orders: the merchantmen are to sail to the Angedive Islands, where they will wait for us. The warships are to seize three ports in East Africa, and three ports in Índia's Malabar Coast, before joining the merchantmen in the Angedives and pushing on for the Spice Islands. Along the way, we are supposed to seize Malacca.

A week after leaving the Cape Verdes, we are becalmed in the doldrums. Pilot-Major Pero Anes says there is nothing to do but wait until we drift out of it. But on April 25 Captain Pero Fogaza reports that his nao, the *Bela*, has sprung a serious leak. His men are furiously working the pumps. The Captain-General orders us to man the batel, and as we are rowing to the *Bela*, it begins to sink before our eyes. The other ships have followed our example and sent their own batels, and we save all the *Bela*'s men and most of her supplies.

In another two months we are rounding the Cape of Good Hope. Bartolomeu Dias had tacked laboriously down the African coast, but Vasco da Gama had shown it was better to boldly sweep out 300 leguas to the western half of the Mar Océano, almost to Brasil, and catch the westerlies south of the æquinoctial line in a wide swing back to Africa. Pilot Anes follows this track, "a volta do mar Sargasso," the Sargasso loop. He also knows it is best to sail south hundreds of miles past the last land before turning back and going round to the other side of Africa. The Cape is at 35°S, but Pilot Anes keeps us relentlessly on course, into the howling winds and the freezing cold seas, all the way to 40°S, which latitude we attain on June 20.

On July 2, still south of Madagascar, a storm whips up. We lose one nao, commanded by Captain Gaspar Correa. It goes down with all hands. In those tempestuous seas it is impossible to attempt a rescue. There is only one consolation for the poor devils in that nao: death must have been quick, even for those who knew how to swim. They could not have lasted long in the icy water.

Then we are in the Moçambique Channel between Africa and Madagascar. We have a fair following wind now, and Captain-General d'Almeida decides to forego the usual stop at the Ilha de Moçambique.

On July 14 we anchor off the uninhabited Ilhas Primeiras past Madagascar, our first rest ashore since the Cape Verdes.

We leave on July 18, and reach Quilóa at 8°S on July 22. It is a small island close to the coast. The Arabs have occupied it for more than seven hundred years and made it the entrepôt of all trade in this region, drawing in ships from the Indies, Arabia, and Persia. The houses in Quilóa, built of stone in the Moorish fashion, are three or four stories high. Towering over these are the minarets of two mosques. Quilóa is the most splendid of any city on the whole East African coast, and, loath as we are to admit it, Quilóa owes its glory entirely to the Arabs. They call it Kilwa Kisiwani; a noble island city, not at all to be confused with its namesakes across the channel, on the mainland. Both Kilwa Kivinje, northwest of the island, and Kilwa Masoko to the southwest, are squalid Bantu villages.

The Sheik of Quilóa, who claims Persian descent, swore fealty to Dom Manoel during da Gama's first visit, in 1498. However, he must have resented the heavy tribute da Gama exacted from him during the latter's second stopover, in 1502. Now he ignores our fleet. No one puts out in a boat to our flagship, and the city does not hoist the quinas of Portugal on the flag da Gama had given the Sheik.

The Captain-General arranges a meeting with Sheik Ibrahim. The latter is supposed to be a Portuguese vassal, and his cooperation would be useful. The Sheik sends a messenger with his regrets. He cannot come. He had been on his way, but a black cat had crossed his path.

The Sheik is toying with us.

We attack Quilóa's walls on July 24. The Captain-General's son, Dom Lourenço, leads the invasion. Sheik Ibrahim manages to flee inland, and Dom Lourenço installs Ibrahim's rival, Mohammed, as the new Sheik.

We construct a fort in twenty days, calling it the Castela do Santiago. Captain Pero Fogaza, he whose nao had sunk from under his feet off the Sierra Leone, is named Captain of the garrison. Two priests and half a thousand men are assigned to him, among them Diogo da Sousa, Francisco Serrão, and myself. Then Captain-General Francisco d'Almeida and the rest of his force sail off to take the island of Mombassa, some 200 leguas to the north. We later hear they captured it on August 15.

Captain Pero Fogaza picks out Diogo da Sousa to be an escribano on his staff, while Francisco Serrão and I are given commands of bergantyms. We patrol the coast up and down in these oar-driven craft, putting an end to Quilóa's main commerce, which is trafficking in slavery. Quilóa does not sell ordinary slaves. The slave traders of Quilóa, most of whom are Arabs, kidnap only children from the inland villages. The boys are castrated, to be sold as eunuchs, and the girls infibulated, to be sold as sealed virgins. They are exported to the countries of the Arabs, Mussulmen, and Turks, where they fetch extremely high prices. Eunuchs are always valued as courtiers and as harem guards. As for sealed virgins, it is the first time I have heard of them. Girls too young to have had their first flow of monthly blood are subjected to a surgical operation in which their female organs are mutilated. The lips of the vagina are sewn together, leaving but a tiny aperture for the passage of urine. Eventually the lips become melded into a solid wall of flesh, and on such a girl's wedding night (they are always sold as brides), her husband is obliged to cut her open with a knife before he can penetrate her. A most vicious and barbaric practise. It behooves us as Christians to do our duty and eradicate it.

Mohammed, our puppet Sheik, is unable to avert tribal troubles in Quilóa. Civil war breaks out in December. Captain Fogaza sends for reinforcements, and they arrive from Lisbõa on Christmas Day. They are led by Captain Nuño Vaz Pereira, Knight of Christ.

The revolt quelled, Pereira commandeers my services. He has orders to go to another Portuguese port in East Africa. This is Sofála at 20°S, 300 leguas or more from Quilóa. Sofála is said to be the Biblical land of Ophir, the source of so much gold for Solomon that his court disdained to use silver.

My bergantym makes good time, for in this season the current favors my oarsmen, while the southwest monsoon merely hinders Captain Pereira's caravel. We arrive on January 1. According to the new style, it is the first day of 1506, but all of us belong to the old school that celebrates New Year's Day on March 25.

After a month in Sofála, during which I see gold being extracted once again from the abandoned shafts widely supposed to be King Solomon's mines, we sail for the small narrow Ilha de Moçambique at 15°S, to meet an incoming armada under Captain-General Affonso d'Alboquerque. One of his captains is João Serrão, Francisco's elder brother. Captain Fogaza has a letter from Captain-General d'Almeida authorizing him to requisition one of the dismantled caravels loaded in d'Alboquerque's naos. D'Alboquerque cannot hide his dislike for d'Almeida, but he does not countermand the order. His dislike for me, due entirely to my association with d'Almeida, is obvious, too.

The caravel is put together under Captain João Serrão's supervision. Captain Pereira takes command of it, turning over his old caravel to another captain, and returns to Sofála. Captain-General d'Alboquerque sails off for Índia with his armada, but not before appropriating my services. I am ordered to remain in Moçambique, with my bergantym and crew.Captain Duarte de Mello is to be my new superior.

I spend the next year and a half at Moçambique, endlessly patrolling the coast in my bergantym. The Ilha de Moçambique is the chief of three small islets in the mouth of the Río Meghincate. A coral island half a legua long and a couple of hundred yards across, it is full of casuarinas, willow trees that cannot grow except where they can hear the sound of the surf: a pleasant enough spot to live in. Captain João Serrão contrives to have his brother and mine transferred to Moçambique. Diogo da Sousa and Francisco Serrão duly arrive in the middle of 1506. And so the four of us are together in a strange land, as much a family as we had ever been in Portugal. But there are times I miss Xpoual, and nights I pine for Catarina. Sometimes, at odd moments, I suddenly remember small cruelties I did her. All at once I find myself overcome by remorse...the twinge of pain in the chest, the tear in the eye.

My brother, due to inherit grandmother da Sousa's estate, does not seek a fortune in foreign lands. In July of 1507, when the winds turn, he takes passage on the *Santa Marta de Lagos,* as a guest of Captain Antão da Saldanha, and returns to Portugal.

As for me, I have yet to find my fortune. In Africa I see only the lack of opportunity. I seek the wealth of the Indies, and it is clear I will not find it here. When in October of 1507 Captain Nuño Vaz Pereira puts in at Moçambique and asks for volunteers to accompany him to Índia, Francisco Serrão and I immediately come forward. The most enduring symbol of Africa, in my mind, is the infibulated, sealed virgin. But I want wide open chances.

24

...ON THE VERGE OF WAKEFULNESS, I stopped tossing and turning.Sleep was my escape, I no longer thought of escape as such, I identified completely with my master now. Here was a man to go around the world, someone I would follow to the ends of the earth, and I had made his dreams my own.The ship sailed smoothly, rocking me gently, too early to wake up, too dark and too cold...

First nao I have sailed in, the *São Simon*. How well she catches the wind, how responsive to the helm! We put in at Cochin, latitude 10°N on India's Malabar Coast. We are back in the northern hemisphere. I can see the Transmontana, the pole star, again.

In Cochin the *São Simon* is handed down to a junior captain. Captain Nuño Vaz Pereira is given a new caravel, the *Santo Espirito*. Francisco Serrão and I are sobresalientes under him, but he orders us to assume the duties of the different officers at various times, in rotation.We act in turn as contramaestre, tonelero, calafate, maestre, alguacil, and piloto. My forte being navigation, I often act as pilot; Francisco's being commerce, he is often the maestre.

Cochin is the first capital of Portuguese Índia. It is not the richest trading post on the Malabar Coast. That honor belongs to Kozhikode, or Calicut. The name "Calicut" means "cockcrow" and refers to its beginnings, when the god Kali granted to its first rajah the area in which the crowing of a a single cock could be heard.

Calicut is where Vasco da Gama was first guided to by the renowned Arab pilot, Ahmad ibn Majid. But da Gama insulted the Zamorin of Calicut by giving him six basins of worthless trinkets, glass beads and such, as gifts. Then he managed to violate Hindu taboos, insulting the people. Two years later, in 1500, when Pedro Álvares Cabral arrived, he was given a rude welcome. Cabral replied by burning a ship laden with pilgrims returning from Mecca. Da Gama himself, on his second visit in 1502, bombarded Calicut and left it in ruins. And so d'Almeida left Calicut alone. He took Cochin, to Calicut's south, and Cananor, to its north. Calicut is now surrounded. D'Almeida chose Cochin for his capital, and in a mere two years it has surpassed Cananor and now rivals Calicut. Dom Francisco blockaded the whole of the Malabar Coast and seized control of the spice trade from the Arabs in Índia. It is only a matter of time before we capture Calicut. And after that, another well-placed trading center, Goa...

The Zamorin of Calicut is not without cunning. He knows that Venice considers Portugal an upstart trying to supplant it as Europe's entrepôt of the spice trade. The Zamorin therefore procured an alliance with the Republic. In addition, he strengthened his ties with his neighbors to the north, the Rajah of Goa, the King of Cambaya, and the Governor of Diu. Cambaya has a fleet of dhows full of fighting men and equipped with cannon; this fleet's homeport is Diu, on the southernmost point of the Kithiawar Peninsula, in the land of the Gujarats.

Captain Pereira puts two and two together: if the Cambayans have cannon, they will have imported artillerymen to handle those. Their bombarderos must be Mamluk Turks...or Venetians. This is for us to find out—the sooner the better.

Francisco Serrão and I are eager pupils for Captain Pereira's most advanced lessons: how to handle a caravel in a naval battle. Against the dhows and zambucos of the Arabs, we learn, it is best to use artillery and remain outside the range of their archers. The zambuco is propelled by oars. The different kinds of dhows all use square sails and always require a following wind. The caravel, with lateen sails fore and aft, can tack into the wind. This means it is important not to get becalmed behind a headland or in narrow waters, where a zambuco can row to us, grapple, and board. Against a dhow, the caravel's most disconcerting tactic is to break away by sailing into the wind, which always baffles the enemy. Then the caravel loops back and uses its guns at a distance.

The fine points of handling a caravel are a revelation to me. I am proficient at commanding a bergantym, and have fought some skirmishes with blockade runners off the East African coast. But the bergantym relies on its oarsmen, and rowers tire easily.

Captain Pereira teaches us how to keep to windward, to fire first at the enemy's rudder and foremast, which will leave him immobile, then to sink him by blowing the roped timbers of his hull apart with the heaviest cannon balls.

If the wind fails, and the enemy gains on the caravel by rowing hard, one must wait until the last moment. Then a broadside of small-bore pellets to cut down the warriors on the deck...

The year 1507 passes. It rains much of the time in Cochin. I am surprised to learn that one marketplace there is called Jew Town. And when I see a Cochin Jew in that marketplace, I am even more surprised. He looks like an ordinary native of Cochin: a black Dravidian. It is the first time I have seen a Jew who is black.

The Jew speaks Farsi, Arabic, and Malayalam, and Francisco Serrão translates from these into Portuguese. The Jew tells us his family moved here seventeen centuries ago. He promises to introduce us to a friend of his who is Christian.

We meet the Christian the next day, a man as Dravidian as the Jew himself. This black Christian says his family came here eight hundred years ago. We ask him certain questions regarding his faith and his rites. We also ask him to recite the Pater Noster. From his answers, and the way he says the prayer, we guess him to be a Nestorian.

The heretic asks if we plan to go to Meliapur, on the other side of Índia, on the east coast. There is a shrine to the Apostle Tomás there.

The one who doubted, who had to feel all five wounds of the Christ?

Yes, that one. He came here in the year 3812.

Later, we manage to calculate it. By the Jewish year 3812, he had meant 52 A.D.

The year 1507 ends, and 1508 begins. Dom Francisco d'Almeida now styles himself the Viceroy of the Estado da Índia. His son Dom Lourenço is now our senior Captain.

On patrol off the northwest Indian coast, Dom Lourenço, leading a fleet of caravels, encounters a force of Indian ships.

He calls a council of war, and his captains advise discretion. The Indian ships duck into Dabul.

Dom Francisco has his son court-martialed for cowardice. Dom Lourenço is acquitted, but Dom Francisco demotes the captains who advised caution. Being called a coward rankles Dom Lourenço. Now anyone who wants to pick a fight with him has only to whisper the word "Dabul."

In March of 1508 a fleet of thirteen Egyptian ships, many of them manned by Venetian gunners, sail down from the Red Sea to break the Portuguese blockade. A hundred dhows and zambucos join them. The fight begins with two days of cannonading, the Venetians surprising the Portuguese with their accurate fire. Bested, most of the Portuguese ships turn south and flee. Dom Lourenço d'Almeida leads his remaining ships into battle at close quarters to grapple and board the enemy ships. He is killed, along with 140 others. An equal number are wounded. Sixteen men are captured and taken to Diu.

The *Santo Espirito* is being careened, and we have been unable to take part in the battle. Dom Francisco d'Almeida, deeply embittered by the death of his son, vows revenge.

In April the rains of the southwest monsoon arrive, and we know that for the next four months the stormy winds will keep all ships in harbor, Portuguese or otherwise. Upon Captain Pereira's recommendation, Dom Francisco detaches me from the *Santo Espirito* and reverts me to the command of a bergantym. I am to foray into enemy harbors and destroy their ships in port. I lead a few raids in my bergantym, my oarsmen grimly rowing in the rain, and burn a few dhows. Sometimes I march my men into the town and we burn some buildings as well. We take whatever loot we can.

In September, when the northeast monsoon blows the rains away, I return to the *Santo Espirito*. Dom Francisco has received reports from his paid informers. Ships from Calicut have slipped away and sailed to the Moluccas. They will shortly be returning across the Arabian Sea to deliver their cargoes to Aden. We are to intercept them off the Maldive Islands. We sail from Cochin in October.

In the Laccadive Sea we run into a storm, and seek refuge in Ceylon.

Resuming the voyage, we find nothing at the Maldives. We go back the way we came, but bypass Cochin. Viceroy d'Almeida is in Cananor, and we report to him there.

Dom Francisco is assembling revenge for his son Lourenço's death. He has put together a fleet of nineteen ships, naos, caravels, and bergantyms. He is drafting every Portuguese who can hold a sword, and he now has a force of 1,300. The Rajahs of Cochin and Cananor are soon persuaded to add 200 men each.

Viceroy d'Almeida himself is Captain-General. Captain Nuño Vaz Pereira is second-in-command.

The armada leaves Cananor on December 12, and sails north for Diu. The Red Sea armada is still there, say the dispatches, waiting for favorable winds before going home via Aden. The strong southwest wind favors us.

We pass by Dabul, which reminds Dom Francisco of how he had called his son a coward. He orders the town put to the sword, and personally leads the first wave, scaling the walls, setting every building on fire, and indulging in a massacre. In his vindictiveness he does not spare the women and children. Francisco Serrão later remarks that d'Almeida must have considered Dabul a Christmas present to himself. The destruction is so great the city loses its name; when rebuilt, it will be renamed Damão.

We reach Diu late in January of 1509. Properly speaking, Diu is the island very close to the tip of the Kithiawar peninsula. It is about 2 leguas long and half a legua wide. The mainland settlement, considered a village of Diu, is called Goghola. Farther off, 3 leguas to sea, is a smaller island with fortifications built upon it, Simbor. A whole fleet is anchored between Diu and Goghola, while more ships are scattered between Diu and Simbor. There are so many ships it is hard to tell which are the islands and which the vessels. All of them, however, are only auxiliaries to the Red Sea armada sent by the Soldan of Egypt, under the command of the Turkish admiral Emir Husayn, whose retinue of bodyguards is an army of Mamluks in chain mail.

The battle takes place on February 2. The whole morning is devoted to artillery, with the enemy getting much the worse of it. In the afternoon we close in. The capitana and the almiranta make for opposite sides of Emir Husayn's flagship, then grapple and board from port and starboard. Clad in armor, Captain

Pereira and I leap into the Egyptian vessel together. The deck is swarming with Mamluk Turks.

Later I am told we fought for five hours. In the fifth hour, as he saw the last of his Mamluks being mowed down, Emir Husayn escaped in a yawl. The quinas of Portugal were raised on the mainmast, and among the mass of fallen men was the body of Captain Nuño Vaz Pereira, Knight of Christ. Beside him I lay wounded, unconscious and near death myself.

For a week they are uncertain which way I will go: into blissful death, or back into the miserable land of the living. But my travails in this world are not yet over. I recover, and spend the next five weeks recuperating. Francisco Serrão acts as my nurse, and Viceroy d'Almeida himself comes every day to personally dress my wounds and coax some soup into my mouth. He administers to all his wounded men the same way. He must feel the need to prove he has a tender side. He has already shown his hard side. Francisco Serraõ tells me the Viceroy set apart all the captured Venetian gunners, whom he considered responsible for the death of Dom Lourenço, his beloved son. He tortured them, then placed them at the mouths of their own cannon and blew them to pieces.

I become well enough to return to Cochin in March. With my prize money I buy an Arab steed, a chestnut stallion. Sixteen hands, beautiful fetlocks. Francisco Serrão buys a bay mare of fifteen hands. Mares endure better, he tells me; in a hard ride, his horse will outlast mine. Our animals being Arab, we saddle them with infidel names. My mount is Tariq. Francisco's filly is Ayesha.

We control the trade in Arabian horses now. The capture of Diu has led to the blockade of Calicut, Goa and Hormuz. Horses are Hormuz's chief export, and the great market for them is Goa. Viceroy d'Almeida is building up a corps of cavalry, for he wants to ingratiate himself with the King. He knows Dom Manoel's great dream is to steal Mohammed's tomb in Medina and ransom it for the sepulcher of Jesus Christ in Jerusalem. With Hormuz blockaded, the Persian Gulf is almost ours. Aden will soon fall, and then we can send a force of perhaps 400 cavalrymen to land near Medina, ride inland, and overwhelm the defenders of the Mosque of the Prophet, where Mohammed's bones lie. I mean to be in that number. The whole scheme is rather wild, even for a dream, but these days everything sounds believable.

25

IN JULY OF 1509 there arrives in Cochin a flotilla of three caravels under Captain-General Diogo Lopes de Sequeira, Knight of Christ. He had once been a judge, then comptroller to the Crown Prince. Now he is Dom Manoel's Inspector-General, with authority to oversee the viceregal government in the East.

The Viceroy has not been informed of de Sequeira's mission. This means Dom Francisco's position is delicate, for he has never been close to the King, while de Sequeira is present as the King's personal representative. De Sequeira reportedly stopped in East Africa to arbitrate disputes between captains in the different garrisons there. When it transpires that his orders are to proceed to Malacca on a scouting expedition, d'Almeida divines the King's machinations as a plot to divide the viceregal authority into three parts, with one governor each. These three provinces will come from the carving up of Portuguese Asia into East Africa and the Malabar Coast, and the addition of Malacca. Dom Francisco knows it is inevitable. He will be ordered to conquer Malacca, only to have to hand it over to someone else. Someone like Affonso d'Alboquerque. Or this newly arrived fop of a courtier.

The Viceroy's attitude to Captain-General de Sequeira is one of exquisite correctness. To de Sequeira's three caravels he adds a fourth, and a taforeia, a large slow nao with square sails, designed to carry horses. It can only mean that a cavalry contingent will be assigned to de Sequeira. Captain João García da Sousa is given the command of the taforeia. As is only to be expected, Francisco Serrão and I are posted to da Sousa's crew as cavalry officers. We load 75 horses into the taforeia, among them my stallion Tariq and Francisco Serrão's mare Ayesha.

The additional caravel, with a full complement of fighting men, has Captain Jerónimo Teixeira in command. There is no mixing of crews. The men who came from Lisbõa with de Sequeira remain in their three caravels. The fourth caravel and the taforeia are manned by Portuguese veterans from Cochin. We refer to ourselves as "Cochin men" and to the newcomers as "Lisbõa men."

We leave Cochin on August 18, 1509, with five Indian pilots, one for each vessel, for no Portuguese ship has as yet gone beyond Ceylon. The caravels trim their sails to adjust to the slower taforeia. We round the tip of Índia, then turn southeast to pass between Ceylon and the Maldives. This is as far east as I ever sailed in the *Santo Espirito*.

For two weeks we sail due east. When the Nicobar Islands come into view, the Indian pilots steer southeast on a course for the Strait of Malacca. After another week we make landfall on the Golden Khersonesus, as Ptolemæus called the Malay Peninsula.

At the entrance to the Strait we stop at Pedir, in Sumatra, to exchange greetings with its Rajah and to erect a padrão, a stone monument, with his permission.

Then on into the Strait and on September 11, 1509, trumpets blaring and all flags flying, we enter the harbor of the Sultanate of Malacca.

Malacca's face is brown, a front of castellated ramparts the color of mud, with gleaming brass cannon eyeing us balefully. It looks impregnable, but the city itself is not enclosed by walls. It spreads for many leguas all along the shore and the riverbanks.

Malacca lies on both sides of the Malacca River, the estuary of which serves as the harbor. A bridge spans the river some 400 yards from the rivermouth. Malacca is at the Strait's narrowest part; the island of Rupat off the coast of Sumatra is only twelve leguas across. It is one of the few stretches of land along both the Malayan and Sumatran coasts not choked with mangroves. Behind the fortress, and scattered all over the city, are palm trees the like of which I have not seen before. Our Indian pilot says they are sago palms, and the natives of Malacca obtain their bread from the hearts of those palms. These people are unique. They prefer sago to rice. Is there no rice in Malacca, then? No, it does not grow there, he says, but Malacca buys plenty of rice from other regions. One can tell who is a true native of Malacca, and who has come there from somewhere else. The native disdains rice and eats only sago with his meat or fish.

The highest buildings are the mosques, with their minarets and domes. There are plain brick houses, thatched-roofed bamboo houses, and houses with ornate green roofs of tiles that resemble the scales of the Indian alligator. The Indian pilot, however, says these are meant to look like dragon scales, for the green roofs are those of Cathayan houses.

Lording it over everything is the Sultan's palace, on top of the hill, an acropolis unto itself. It reminds me of the Moorish palaces that still stand in Portugal and Hespanha. The largest building in the city, its roofs are covered with tiles presented a hundred years ago by an emissary of the Cathayan emperor to the first Sultan of Malacca. It must be even more impressive inside.

The Indian pilot tells me that eighty-four languages can be heard on the streets of Malacca.

I believe it.

Malacca is the wealthiest city I have ever seen, its harbor crowded with more vessels of more kinds than Lisbõa's. We have heard that Malacca's markets trade more goods than those of Alexandria, Venezia or Antwerp, and now we can see it was no idle boast.

We nudge our way into the harbor, the quinas of Portugal on our mainmasts, and the blood-red cross of the Knights of Christ on our sails. Each ship fires a broadside. Our trumpets blow recheats.

A prahu approaches the capitana. Its sides are draped with Persian rugs. Men aboard it are pounding out a rhythm on drums, gongs and cymbals. The rowers time their oarstrokes to this rhythm. While a party of port officials comes aboard, a smaller prahu rows in circles around the capitana with musicians playing a rhythm, different from the bigger ship's, on their drums and little gongs.

We know what de Sequeira will be telling the Malays. We have come to trade, he will say, and he has gifts and greetings for Mahmud, Sultan of Malacca, from Dom Manoel, Rei do

Portugal. He will also be seeking a license to trade ambergris, copper, and Venetian glass for spices, dyes, and medicines.

That evening Francisco Serrão, who learned the Malayalam language in Cochin, goes ashore to hide in some courtesan's room and listen to what the people are saying.

The following morning, the Captain-General goes to call on the Sultan. His party is made up entirely of Lisbõa men.

We remain alert on the ships, ready to fight or to sail off on short notice. The Captain-General and his party return late that night, riding on elephants and escorted by Malays bearing torches. Our anxieties have been unfounded. Sultan Mohammed had given them a feast.

On the morrow a delegation from the Sultan, led by his bendahara or Chief Vizier, come to the capitana to work out the details of a trading agreement. The Sultan has graciously given permission for the men of the armada to come ashore, and many of us are given leave. The horses on the taforeia, weary of three weeks at sea, are taken to stables inland.

Francisco Serrão and I, along with most of our cavalry detachment, exercise our horses on the grounds near the stables. Then we go off on foot to see the Sultanate of Malacca, Grand Emporium of the East.

Malacca was founded only a century ago. It has grown immensely wealthy in that short time by taking advantage of its position as guardian of the Strait of Malacca. The Strait connects two oceans, the Indian Ocean and the Eastern Ocean. In the olden days the Arabs would sail to Cathay while the Cathayans would sail to Arabia. Either way, they had to accomplish the voyage in two stages, heeding the monsoon winds. In the season of the northeast monsoon, in January or February, the Cathayans would start from Canton and head for the Strait. The Strait was the halfway point, where they stopped to wait for the wind to change. When the southwest monsoon came, the second stage became possible, and the Cathayan junks would be blown by those winds from the Strait to Índia or Arabia.

The Arabs sailed the same voyage in reverse. They would wait until late March or April before leaving Aden for the Strait. When the wind changed, their dhows would be pushed from the Strait to Cathay.

The founding of Malacca simplified matters for these traders. Arabs and Cathayans now needed to sail only as far as Malacca, where they could trade with each other. No longer was there any need for the Arabs to sail all the way to Cathay, nor for the Cathayans to go as far as Arabia. Their voyages were shorter, the profits on their investments realized in less time.

The middlemen of Malacca knew that the Arabs and Cathayans seldom arrived at the same time. They took it upon themselves to buy the goods of the Arabs, in order to sell it at a profit to the Cathayans, whose goods they would buy while waiting for the next Arab dhow.

In time the traders learned to put up their own shops in Malacca, but the natives kept control by charging fees, taxes, and rentals, and by issuing licenses.

Malacca bustles with trade. Guajarati, Bengali, or Tamil merchants sell linen, calico, muslin, dungari, Kashmir wool, cotton, and many other fabrics. Cathayans sell silk, porcelain, brassware. Cinghalese from Ceylon sell rubies and sapphires. Javanese and Sumatrans sell rice, vegetables, chickens, fish, meat, and fruit. The Arabs have acquired a monopoly on spices; they are the only ones who sell cloves, pepper, nutmeg and mace, ginger, and rhubarb.

Everyone is armed. Most men wear a scimitar or a kris, and even the most elegant jeweler has at least a dagger tucked into his cummerbund.

Francisco Serrão reports that the Sultan has exchanged letters with the Zamorin of Calicut, who advised him of our fleet's arrival. They have been expecting us.

The Sultan's bendahara informs the Captain-General that a pier with a warehouse on it will be reserved for us, and we are to unload our merchandise there. This is done the following day.

How vulnerable we are! Our horses and our goods are on land, and if most of our men can be lured ashore as well, either to transact business or to indulge in sensual pleasures, our ships can be captured.

Francisco Serrão smells a plot. The Sultan, he hears, has brought in fighting men and war elephants from other towns. A fleet of prahus supposedly lie hidden in a cove up the Malacca River. He reports all this to Captain García da Sousa that evening. García da Sousa asks him what he thinks it means.

"They'll find a way to get us all ashore," Serrão says. "Then the prahus will overpower the few men left on the caravels. We'll all be stranded here, and they can massacre us at their leisure."

"What do you think, Fernão?"

"I think he's right, sir," I say. "If the Sultan succeeds, he will become the first Moro leader to defeat a Christian force in a long time. His prestige among the infidels will be as great as that of Tariq ibn Ziyad's in 711 Anno Domini."

Captain García da Sousa goes to the capitana to relay his apprehensions to Captain-General Lopes de Sequeira. He is back in a short time. Dom Diogo has dismissed his fears as imaginary.

In the morning of September 14 port officials inform the Captain-General that a large load of pepper is at the market, ready to be sold to us at a low price. When I was a boy, pepper sold for its weight in gold in Lisbõa. The price has dropped only slightly since then, and a few sacks would still be worth a fortune for us. The Captain-General orders all the maestres, with such assistants as they might require, to go ashore in the batels and handle the purchase and the transfer to the ships of the pepper.

I happen to be on the capitana when a delegation led by a datu comes aboard. They tell the Captain-General that a Cinghalese jeweler has just received a consignment of gems, and wants to barter with us for copper. A party of fidalgos, Lisbõa men all, goes ashore to see the stones. Now every last batel is separated from its mothership. Prahus have been idly moving about the harbor, and quite a number, most with vendors hawking food, are around us. Some of the vendors have clambered up to the decks of the caravels, where they cry out their wares. On the deck of the flagship, the Captain-General is playing chess with the datu. The Malays in the datu's retinue stand around, watching the game.

One batel returns to the capitana with sacks of pepper. Francisco Serrão is on the pier. I catch his eye, and he signals. I do not understand it, except that something is imminent. His eyes are wary.

On the chessboard, the Captain-General's attack is going nowhere. The datu has defended well, and the position is locked. Neither side sure of where to try and break through.

One of the Malays behind the Captain-General seems to be itching to draw his kris. Francisco Serrão has moved to a clear spot on the wharf, away from the bustle of sailors mixing with the locals. He signals me again. The Sultan's palace, he points. He mimes something. I shake my head. He mimes it again, something about firing a cannon, and caps it by drawing his finger across his throat. Then I understand. A cannon fired from the palace is to signal the start. The prahus will then attack the caravels, men ashore are to be massacred, the datu is to take the Captain-General prisoner.

De Sequeira picks up a bishop and captures a pawn. Now the bishop is *en prise*. He has sacrificed it in order to break through the datu's pawn phalanx. The datu hunches forward and ponders. I approach, and speak in a calm voice to the Captain-General. I point to the sacks as I speak, so that I seem be saying something about the pepper. In an offhand manner I apprise him of the danger signs I have noted, and tell him the Sultan's cannon blast is to signal mayhem.

For once, Dom Diogo is equal to the occasion. He pretends to be annoyed. He does not lift his eyes from the game. In a bored voice, he summons his contramaestre and orders battle stations, pointing at the pepper sacks as he speaks.

The datu picks up a pawn, and takes the bishop.

A booming sound: cannonfire from the palace!

Dom Diogo jumps up, overturning the chessboard while whipping out his sword, and neatly checkmates the datu. The crewmen on the deck exhibit reflexes as good as the Captain-General's and quickly dispatch the Malays, although three or four manage to jump overboard. I yell for the rowers and leap into the batel. We reach the pier in time to save Francisco Serrão and several others. The other batels make it back to their motherships with full loads, but too many men have gone ashore.

Cut the anchor cables, hoist the sails, move out. The only thing to do. Then come about and bombard the prahus with the cannon.

We sink quite a number.

About forty men have managed to make it back in the batels. We lose some sixty men, killed on the pier or taken prisoner. As best as can be estimated, it is thirty of each: thirty captured, thirty dead by treachery.

The Captain-General orders two of our pilots, a Gujarat and a Hindu, to go under a flag of truce and negotiate for the ransom of the captured men. No officials come forward. Men on the pier belligerently motion the pilots away. The Captain-General sees the futility of it, and orders the armada's departure.

At sea, our taforeia gradually falls behind. The flagship is making full sail, the other caravels are keeping up with it, and the Captain-General cannot be bothered to adjust his speed for the slowest ship. Captain García da Sousa had explicitly warned him of the dangers, de Sequeira had disregarded it, and now he is being surly towards García da Sousa. We have lost all of our horses and the unballasted taforeia, riding high in the water, is proving most difficult to steer.

The next morning, September 15, with the four caravels now far ahead on the horizon, the lookout espies a four-masted junk with batwing sails bearing down on us from astern. It is a pirate ship. Armed men stand ready on its deck, their hair and dress marking them as Cathayans. Our bombarderos fire at their foremast and rudder, but still they approach, come alongside, grapple, board.

We put up a better fight than they are used to.

We beat them off.

The pirates jump back into their junk, leaving several of their number dead on our deck, and begin hacking away at the lashings. Before they have cut free, something totally unexpected happens.

"After them!" yells Francisco Serrão.

He leaps across and follows the retreating pirates into the junk. Several of our men, their fighting bravado rekindled by Francisco Serraõ's impulsive spark, jump across, too. The Cathayans have never seen anything like this before. But the junk is moving away, and it soon becomes clear that Francisco and the men with him are outnumbered. They have their backs to the mainmast now, and the Cathayans are moving in for the kill. Captain García da Sousa orders the taforeia to come close. But we are pitching in heavy seas, and the ship does not respond to the helm.

There is not a moment to lose. I call for men, and we push the batel overboard. Rowing in such rough waters is madness, but no bergantym under my command has ever been rowed as madly as this. Reaching the junk, we join the fight and cut down the fiercest of the pirates. Then the rest of them throw down their swords in surrender.

The junk is carrying much plunder: bolts of silk, bahars of nutmeg and cloves, sacks of pepper, large crocks of food. Captain García da Sousa deems it a seaworthier craft than ours, and decides to exchange ships. We dump the dead bodies of several pirates overboard, transfer our supplies and gear to the junk, then throw the surviving pirates into the unwieldy taforeia. They have no food, but land is not too far off.

The junk is faster than the caravels. The next day we regain them on the horizon. We follow their farols that night, and by noon of the following day we have caught up with them.

Captain-General de Sequeira shows no emotion, not even surprise, at seeing us again. He assigns a prize crew of 28 of us, our contramaestre in command, to man the junk. The rest of us he distributes among the caravels. Captain García da Sousa is put in the Cochin caravel. Francisco Serrão, wounded in the arm, is taken aboard the capitana, the only ship with a cirujano. I accompany him to act as his nurse.

The junk holds its own beside the caravels for three days, then drops its rudder. Our bombarderos had hit it after all, and weakened it. The Captain-General decides to tow it to the nearest island and transfer its cargo. Before we can reach the island a gale whips up, and the junk rolls about and tugs upon its towline to the capitana. The Captain-General brings the capitana alongside and takes the prize crew off the junk. It is too dangerous to attempt to save the junk's cargo. Shortly after it is abandoned, it sinks.

The gale intensifies into a storm, and one of the Lisbõa caravels goes down with all hands. The Cochin caravel rides out the storm, but comes through badly. Captain Jerónimo Teixeira manages to beach it on the island, where we burn it after transferring its men and supplies.

Only two caravels remain of our fleet. We reach Travancore on the Malabar Coast, north of Quilon, but south of Cochin. They tell us that Dom Francisco d'Almeida has been relieved and has sailed home. Dom Affonso d'Alboquerque has succeeded him as Viceroy.

Captain-General Diogo Lopes de Sequeira has no desire to report his débâcle in Malacca to d'Alboquerque in Cochin. Now he decides to sail direct to Lisbõa. He will report personally to Dom Manoel. He has enough spices, silk, and gems from Malacca to impress the court. There is still time to concoct a good story and whitewash his fiasco. He takes everything, leaving nothing for us. All of us Cochin men are left to make our way back to Cochin on foot.

26
♒

I HOVERED NEAR THE SURFACE of sleep, but was powerless to come awake. My mind was embellishing my dreams. It was weaving the stories I had heard over the years, from my master as well as his comrades, into ornate patterns...

Francisco Serrão and I are highly praised by our Captain, João García da Sousa, in the latter's report to Dom Affonso d'Alboquerque. The new Viceroy rewards our meritorious services by promoting both of us, in December of 1509, to the rank of capitão mor é guerra, and giving each of us the command of a caravel.

I still grieve for my fine Arab horse, but my loss suddenly seems puny when I hear how badly Dom Francisco d'Almeida took the loss of his viceregal position. Dom Francisco immediately boarded the first ship for Portugal and remained there until it sailed, a full month later. Not once did he go ashore in all that time.

The pride in being promoted to Captain quickly wears off. There is as yet no caravel for me to command. I have been in the East for more than four years now. Time I went home. I acquire permission to sail on a westbound caravel commanded by Captain Sebastião da Sousa.

We are waiting for the onset of the southwest monsoon in late December when Viceroy d'Alboquerque suddenly cancels all leave. The Zamorin of Calicut has marched inland to fight a strong band of dacoits, and it is thus an opportune time to surprise Calicut with a lightning attack. D'Alboquerque requisitions the services of all available men and ships.

We land at Calicut on January 3. Although the premier center of trade on the Malabar Coast until recently, Calicut has no harbor. It is only a beach. We fight our way into the town, meeting but token resistance, and plunder the palace. The nayres of Calicut, mounted warriors, choose this moment to counterattack. Their timing is perfect. A massacre ensues. Hundreds of our men are killed, including seventy Knights of Christ. I am in a unit that closes around the Viceroy as we fight our way back to the beach. I have been wounded, but not as badly as he. Dom Affonso is half-dead by the time we pull him up into the flagship. He remains in a coma for three days.

In mid-January my voyage home with Captain Sebastião da Sousa is finally approved. This time a caravel commanded by Captain Francisco de Sa will sail with us. I attempt to persuade Francisco Serrão to come home with me. Francisco says the East has gotten into his blood. He has no wish to return to Portugal.

A caravel commanded by Captain Diogo Coutinho had gone ahead the day before. Captains da Sousa and de Sa determine to catch up with it, and choose a shorter route. The normal route is southwest, in order to avoid the Laccadive, Malicoy, and Amindiv islands west of Cochin. These atolls and shoals are at 10°N, as is Cochin, and one can pass them safely by going down to 9°N or, even better, to 8°N. These passages are called, appropriately enough, the Nine Degree Channel and the Eight Degree Channel. The two Captains however now steer northwest, as their charts show no shoals past 12°N. I have my doubts. From what several Indian pilots have told me, the Laccadive shoals may extend as far as 14°N. As a passenger, however, I am not expected to offer my opinion. The southwest monsoon is blowing, and following the normal route would mean bucking a headwind, very slow sailing.

A few days out of Cochin, at night, we run aground. Shoals. Both our ships are wrecked beyond repair. The only thing to do is to row back to Cochin in the two batels and procure a caravel to rescue the others. As a fidalgo I am entitled to a place in my ship's batel. However a blood brother of mine, Martín Gaddis, who had fought beside me at Quilóa, is not a fidalgo. He has no place in the batel. When this becomes apparent, I give up my own place at once, being loath to abandon an irmão sangue.

Being a Captain, I am the ranking officer on the atoll. I make certain the rations are divided equitably, assure the men that help is forthcoming, and keep them from pilfering the cargo.

We are on that atoll for three weeks before the rescue party arrives, a caravel commanded by Captain Antão Pacheco. These are the Shoals of Padua, they tell us. Had you never heard of them?

Back in Cochin, I find that my fellow Captains, Serrão, García da Sousa and Teixeira, have sailed in an armada under Captain-General d'Alboquerque. They are off to attack Hormuz. With most of my familiars away, I come to know other people, men I had heretofore taken no notice of. There is Duarte Barbosa, the King's Scrivener in Cochin. A man of commerce, he is also a keen observer. He is writing a book about East Africa and the Malabar Coast, to be called *Livro Emque dà Relação do Que Viu é Ouviu no Oriente*. A sonorous title. He fears it does not sound sufficiently scholarly. I assure him it does.

Barbosa introduces me to his colleagues, the two Royal Factors of the Estado da Índia, Dom Antão Real and Dom Lourenço Moreno. They are the Crown's trade representatives, and as such, arbitrate all matters of trade between Índia and Europa. For this reason they are cultivated by the foreign banking houses that have invested in Dom Manoel's armadas. The Fuggers and the Welsers of Antwerp depend on Real; Moreno actively protects the interests of the Marchionis of Florence.

Real and Moreno, as Barbosa confides to me, think the present system of trade too cumbersome. The Arabs control the trade in spices, having made the rulers of the Spice Islands their allies. Those Malays sell their spices only to their fellow Malays from Malacca, who in turn sell only to the Arabs. The Arabs ship the spices to Índia, to sell to us at a huge profit. It would be simpler and more profitable if we could send our own ships to the Spice Islands, take on a load of spices, and sail directly back to Lisbõa. Eliminate the middleman, Real and Moreno say.

For this they will need men who can navigate the entire distance back and forth, men to command ships into unknown waters. They look meaningfully at me, as if wondering if I am that sort of man.

They have pricked my interest. They are men of influence, men who can procure the backing of the banking houses. There would be funds enough for ships to sail the route to the Spice Islands if these men were behind it. It had better be done soon, if at all. Real and Moreno both feel Cochin to be living on borrowed time. Everyone knows d'Alboquerque intends to transfer the capital of the Estado da Índia to Goa. When this has been accomplished d'Alboquerque will naturally revamp the bureaucracy and put his own men in the important posts. Certain to be replaced are the King's Factors and the King's Scrivener.

It remains but for Goa to be conquered. And that is only a matter of time.

Glossing over his unsuccessful attempt to conquer Hormuz, Viceroy d'Alboquerque forms another armada, this time of 23 ships, and sails off to attack Goa. Hormuz did not matter, the momentum is all that matters, he has to attack a city, any city, while the morale of his fighting men remains high. He takes Goa on February 17. He does not hold it for long. The Rajah of Goa regroups his forces, counterattacks, and wins back his city. D'Alboquerque's armada limps back to Cochin.

News comes of the supplanted Viceroy, d'Almeida. After a month in Moçambique to wait for favorable winds, he had resumed his voyage home in March. Off South Africa the winds petered out. He happened to be off a small village. With nothing better to do, he led a landing party to the village. The whole party had been unceremoniously murdered by a band of Hottentots.

Around this time, in the middle of 1510, Duarte Barbosa persuades me to engage in a scheme that will double my money. All I have is ten gold coins, each with a value of ten cruzados—100 cruzados in all. The cruzado is more or less at parity with the Venetian ducat, 7 cruzados currently being worth 6 ducats, so that the money is equivalent to some 35,000 Spanish maravedis: a paltry sum for one who has spent five years in the East. Of course I have lost many times that amount, in Malacca, on the Shoals of Padua where my consignment of Malabar pepper melted into the sea...

A Jewish merchant named Pero Anes Abraldes is returning to Lisbõa, and Duarte arranges for my gold coins to be delivered to my brother, Diogo da Sousa, in Portugal. If Abraldes buys a load of pepper in Cochin with the 100 cruzados he can sell the pepper in Lisbõa for anywhere between 500 and 4,000 cruzados. The price fluctuates wildly, but a huge profit is assured regardless. He therefore agrees to pay my brother interest of 100% on the money after a year. Of course, it isn't as simple as that.

In Portugal, 10% interest per annum is the legal maximum rate. To circumvent the laws against usury, a system of two receipts is used. In the first receipt, Abraldes acknowledges having borrowed 100 cruzados from Captain de Magalhães and agrees to repay it with 10% interest within a year's time.

In the second receipt, Captain de Magalhães undertakes to insure Abraldes's load of pepper for a premium of 100 cruzados.

The final result is that my money will be transferred to Portugal and incidentally get doubled at the same time. The risk is that Abraldes might refuse to pay, and since the 100% interest involved is illegal, there might be no way to fight him in court.

Ordinarily I would not indulge in such an undertaking, but Duarte sways me by telling me everyone does it all the time. Then, too, I quite resent my enormous losses, and the Crown's failure to recompense me. I had counted on Dom Francisco d'Almeida to give the King a favorable report of my service in the East, but now that he is dead, who can I turn to?

The ten gold coins are the sum of my earthly goods. I have only Duarte's assurance that Abraldes is trustworthy. Abraldes and I sign the receipts with Duarte Barbosa and Dom Lourenço Moreno as witnesses. Only later do any of us remember that Abraldes had neglected to follow Jewish custom and seal the bargain with an oath. Duarte does not know exactly what Hebrew words Jews exchange, only that those oaths, uttered while each party clasps the other's hand, are more binding than any piece of paper. But perhaps Jews do not always follow that form when dealing with Gentiles.

Viceroy d'Alboquerque's second attempt to conquer Goa, in November of 1510, is successful. To punish it for the shame he suffered in losing it after his first attempt, he savages its entire population. By his express orders, the city's Arabs are set aside from the ordinary population of Marathi Indians, and the most barbaric forms of torture reserved for them. The men have their right hands cut off, and the women their ears and noses, before being killed. The children are killed along with the parents, even babes-in-arms. The Indians are massacred straightaway, without prior mutilation. Only young Indian women are spared, at the warrior's discretion, so that the comeliest of them might be used as handmaidens.

I take part in the conquest of Goa the Golden, but not in the slaughter. The atrocities so repel me that I take no part in the plunder of the city. The sacking and killing are done at the same time, and go on for six days. Later I hear that six Saracens were killed for every single fighting man in the Portuguese force. The loot is enormous, but I have no stomach for any of it. I am a warrior, not a butcher, not a scavenger of other people's gold.

Viceroy d'Alboquerque makes Goa his new capital, leaving Cochin to wither on the vine. Goa is an island, the Ilha da Goa, between the estuaries of two rivers, the Mandovi and the Zuari. The rivers form a natural moat around the Ilha da Goa, which make it look a much juicier grape than Cochin.

As soon as the transfer is complete, everyone, including the Sultan of Malacca, knows more conquests are in the offing. Sultan Mohammed has spies in Goa. He must know by now, as well as we do, that Malacca is next on the list.

⚓

27

DAYLIGHT BLINDED ME. I turned away, realized I was hungry. I woke up. I was a slave on a ship that would bring me home. I was a Malayu, not a Faranghi. They called me Henrique, but that was not my name. None of my shipmates knew what my true name was, and I felt secure in this. Would I ever tell them? I thought not. My name was my own. Curses only worked against one's true name, and my secret was safe.

After the Cabo Tres Montes dropped below the horizon on December 4, we continued heading NW. The following day strong winds forced us to turn some 70 degrees to starboard, so that we were going NE. Headwinds retarded our progress for the next two weeks. We fought the wind and crept north. For the next few days, December 6 through 12, we made only six or seven leguas daily. The coast ran northwest here, and on December 13 we came within two or three leguas of a point the Captain-General called the Punta Galera.

Pilot Albo shot the sun at noon and found our latitude to be 40°S. He ventured a reading of our longitude, saying it was 56½°W. The last time he had guessed at our longitude, ten days before, it had been 58°W. Had we been blown a good way east?

In the morning of December 14 we passed an offshore island at latitude 38°S. The Captain-General called it the Isla Mocha.

It marked the turning point.

From then on we were in balmy climes; we had reached the fair southeast winds. We made our second attempt to leave sight of land and strike out into the open sea. This time we were successful. By noon of December 16 the mountains of Tierra Firma were hazy blue outlines on the horizon, astern and slightly to starboard. By evening, in the last of the sunlight, they had dropped out of sight entirely.

As the sun sank below the sea, the Armada went through the evening prayers. The two other ships ran close to the flagship, the *Concepción* first, then the *Victoria*, as their captains saluted the Captain-General by the light of the first-quarter moon.

"Tell us about your native city, Enrico," Ser Antonio said after supper. "You were there when the first Portuguese arrived. What did you think of them?"

"It's been conquered," I said. "I don't want to talk about it."

"Oh, everybody's kingdom has been conquered at one time or another," Master Andrew said. "England by the Normans in 1066. Visigoth Spain by the Moors more than eight hundred years ago. It took the Spaniards and Portuguese all this time to get their land back. Now, we've heard stories of Malacca from Portuguese men who helped conquer it—"

"And from a Venetian," said Ser Antonio, "who visited it before any Portuguese did: Ludovico Varthema."

"But we haven't heard the story of Malacca from one of its own natives," said Master Andrew.

"Is it a very old city?" asked Ser Antonio. "Tell us how it was founded."

"Not very old," I said.

They waited. I paused to take a deep breath.

"Melaka," I told them, "was founded in the year 803 of the Hejira..."

"Haven't you been baptized as a Christian?" Master Andrew said. "Give us Christian years, then. None of those infidel years, if you please, or it's cortén la cabeza for you."

"A thousand apologies. I am accustomed to the Muslim calendar we always used in Melaka. It was after all an Islamic Sultanate."

"Very well," said Ser Antonio. "Pray continue."

"Melaka was founded in...1401. By a Palembang prince. He was descended from the Shailendra Dynasty of the old Sri Vijayâ. His name was Sri Parameswara, but he was known as Sri Harimau."

"Sri Harimau?" asked Ser Antonio.

"Yes, not Sri Singa which means Lord Tiger in Sanskrit, but Sri Harimau. By using the Malayu word for 'tiger,' the other meaning is emphasized. 'Sri Harimau' may also be translated as 'King of Terror'."

"Lord Tiger the Terror, then," said Master Andrew.

"His megat title was 'parameswara' which translates as 'Prince Consort' and meant he was his wife's inferior in rank. Sri Harimau, seeking a dynastic alliance with the enemy, had married a Maja Pahít princess. The Maja Pahít had conquered the Sri Vijayâ a generation before, although there remained parts that still resisted them. By marrying the enemy princess, the prince increased the area he ruled in Palembang. The whole of his territory, however, was a vassal kingdom. The Rama of Sukothai was his suzerain.

"When he did not pay the satrap's yearly tribute to his suzerain, Sri Parameswara was attacked by Khamheng, the third Rama. He fled, taking to his balanghais and prahus. Among his followers was my ancestor, a Palembang warrior in the prince's court. Sri Parameswara sailed across the Malayu Strait to Temasik, where his wife had relatives. She was kin to the Rajah of Temasik, a Maja Pahít noble. Temasik is an island at the tip of the Malayu Peninsula.

"Sri Parameswara murdered his host the Rajah, and seized the throne. The Rama's forces, enraged by the news of this treachery, attacked Temasik. Once more Sri Parameswara fled, this time to Muhar. He found a stretch of shore not choked by mangroves and landed there, between two rivers. The big river was of course the Muhar. The small one he called the Melaka River because of the melaka trees that grew along it. Sri Parameswara went hunting on a hill near the Melaka River. One of his hounds cornered a white pelandok, a mousedeer. The deer fought back and kicked the dog.

"Sri Parameswara was impressed that even the pelandok in that place fought so valiantly. He decided to found his city there, and built a rough palace on top of the hill. After he had fended off another attack by the Siamese, his town was secure."

"Such treachery," Master Andrew said. "Makes one wonder why it didn't fall to the Portuguese by treachery. Had to fight long and hard for it, didn't they?"

"A most interesting story, anyway," Ser Antonio said. "Be glad Don Fernan took you and brought you into the true faith, Enrico. Now your soul has a chance of finding eternal salvation."

They were off to their respective beds. Ser Antonio, being a Patrician of Vicenza, had a berth in the sterncastle. Master Andrew, as a fleet officer, had a bunk in the forecastle.

I went to my old corner, wrapping my woolen gown tighter around me as I lay down on the planking. The story went on in my mind. My father had told it to me many times; as I listened to it again in my mind, it was as if I was hearing his voice.

Melaka's first settlers, finding that rice would not grow in the salty marshes, ate sago instead. Later, when Melaka had grown rich on trade, a thousand and one varieties of rice were sold in its markets, but anyone descended from Sri Parameswara's original band preferred sago.

Melaka was the best port along the Malayu Strait, better than Pasai or Jambi, although in the olden days the honor had belonged to Palembang, then the capital of the Sri Vijayâ, and before that, to Kedah, and before that, to Samudra. The mausim wind called the amihan, which blew from the northeast from October through March, blew in the chuan, the huge three-masted ships of the Xanglei, from Khanfu. Those ships, with large eyes painted on their bows, looked like strange animals gliding into the mouth of the Melaka.

The amihan also brought, along with the Xanglei, the Siamese, the Javanese, and the Bugis.

They came for the goods of the Malayu: beeswax, camphor, sandalwood, cardamom, rhinoceros horn, and bezoar or stones taken from the stomachs of monkeys. They prized our hardwoods: our ebony, our gharuwood, our chengal wood, and our belian wood, the wood so heavy it would not float. In time we learned to refer to these varieties by their Xanglei names: *chien, su, ch'en, chan, sheng.*

For these they traded their own goods: earthenware bowls, lacquerware, celadonware, porcelain vessels; sponges, parasols, metal needles, knives, and fishhooks; skeins of Ho-ch'ih silk; sugar, wheat, and rice wine; gold, silver, and iron.

The Xanglei sailed down the Strait a few days before the habagat, the southwest mausim, or monsoon, set in. They would wait off Temasik, and be in position to be blown home when the habagat came.

The habagat also blew in the merchants from the Gulf of Khambhat. They were Arabs, Saracens, Kaffirs, Farsis, Mamluks, Turks, Gujarati, Bangali, and many others. They sailed in large merchantmen they called qurqur. These ships were laden with woollens, copperware, scarlet-in-grain, and opium; rose-water, patchouli, kumkum or black kohl, red henna, brown summaq, green malachite, and a liquid for brightening female eyes, collyrium; spikenard, myrrh, frankincense, teryak oil from poppy flowers, and liquid storax or almasiga; raisins, figs, and thirty kinds of dates; indigo, putchuk, catechin, tapestries, rugs, calico cloth from Calicut, mosulin from Mosul, bokhram from Bukhara, demesq from Damascus, dungari from the Chola coast, fine wool from Kashmir, and two dozen other kinds of cloth; books in Farsi, using Arabic script, done in vellum, parchment, or paper, beautiful tomes with colorful illustrations and gold lettering; and finally, goods for which buyers competed madly, no matter the prices being demanded: swords, scimitars, daggers, and firearms, for the Malayu nobleman always wore a kris, and the commoner a badik or a sundang, but both of them felt naked without a Damascus blade. The habagat then, having blown the Xanglei home, in May or June blew in the men from the west, from Khambhat, Kojikode, Cholamandal, Kalikati, Srihalam, Sawankhalok, Sisatchanalai, Sukothai, Martaban, Chenla, or Kling.

Melaka would be ready for them. Each year men from Melaka loaded eight large ships, viray or balanghai, with Khambhat cloth and banteng, white Bangali cattle, and sailed for Bandan and the Molukas. It took them three days to reach Bandan, where they bartered the coarse cloth for nutmeg and mace. Then they would sail for two weeks from Bandan to the Molukas, where they bartered the cattle for five or six thousand bahars of cloves. In Melaka, these spices would be sold to the Arabs, Farsis, and Indians. Those people also bought our tin, camphor from Burnei, sandalwood from Timor, huge pearls, mother-of-pearl, and seed pearls from the Sulu Sea, civet cats, batik, Javanese krises, and bird-plumes. By October the amihan would blow them back the way they came, the same wind that later, in January or February, would blow in the Xangleis in their demon-eyed chuans all the way from Khanfu.

Spices accounted for the bulk of the town's trade: pepper, nutmeg, mace, cloves, camphor, sapanwood, agallochium, not to mention civet cats, hogs' stones, porcupine quills, and rhinoceros horn...the Xanglei used all of these in their medicines. They believed, for example, that the horn of the rhinoceros, taken as a potion, restored virility. We Malayus, knowing the horn was not made of a bony substance, but of densely compacted hair, appreciated its power to detect poison. Anyone who feared death by poisoning had a drinking cup made of rhinoceros horn. In such a cup, a tainted drink announced itself by bubbling up a froth of foam...

Gold from the mines of Pahang, on the east coast of the Malayu Peninsula, crossed the mountains to Melaka on the west coast. The gold would flow up the Pahang River to its tributary, the Serting River, and then to its tributary, the Jempol River. Where it narrowed to a little brook was a spot, opposite Bukit Penarik, where the Jempol came to within two arrow flights of the Muhar River, at those heights itself a humble creek. A penyarikan was established there, a dragway where rivercraft could be dragged from one stream to the other. And the gold, unloaded at the Jempol's edge and carried by porters to the Muhar while the empty ship was hauled across the penyarikan, would float down the Muhar to Melaka.

The volume of trade in another metal, from Perak, was even bigger. "Perak" meant "silver" but the metal it sent to Melaka was tin; only the Xanglei knew the difference. Tin was much in demand, for it had its own uses.

By the year 805 of the Hejira, Melaka's reputation as a trading center had attracted the notice of the Son of Heaven himself. Yung Lo, also known as Chu Ti, of the Ming Dynasty, had recently ascended the Celestial Throne. He sent to Melaka an envoy named Yin Ch'ing. Official recognition of Sri Parameswara's reign at Melaka thus dated from 805, although he had actually begun his reign in 803.

In 807 Sri Parameswara was visited by a Xanglei fleet of sixty large warships commanded by Admiral Cheng Ho, a Moslem eunuch, who presented to the Rajah an official decree from the Emperor Yung Lo. In it, Sri Parameswara had been appointed King of the District.

In 812 AH, by another Imperial decree, Melaka was changed from a District into a Kingdom.

In 814 Sri Parameswara sailed with Cheng Ho and paid a visit to the Emperor of the Han.

In 818 Melaka was visited by men of the Sayyid family from Hadhramaut in South Arabia. They were descended from Fatima, the Prophet's daughter, and stayed in the palace as the King's personal guests. Soon after, Sri Parameswara converted to Islam and took a new name, becoming the Sultan Iskander Shah. He would take only a name that had been borne by the greatest of men, and none had been greater in his estimation than Iskander the Macedonian, or Alexander the Great. The Sultan envisioned his kingdom as the center of a dar-ul-Islam, and so the Kingdom of Melaka became Melaka Darussalam, the Islamic Sultanate of Melaka. The length of Sultan Iskander Shah's reign in Melaka was twenty-three years, and he reigned from 803 through 829.

Sultan Iskander Shah was succeeded by Sri Maharajah, an apostate who forsook Islam and returned to the ways of the Buddha. Mahayana Buddhism flourished in his reign, as did the worship of Brahma, Indra, and Vishnu. Islam was tolerated, as were the animistic religions of the lower classes. Hinayana Buddhism and its emphasis on the worship of Shiva's phallus was discouraged. The practice of Tantra yoga was outlawed. Sri Maharajah ruled Melaka for eleven years, and his reign lasted from 829 through 840.

The Bendahara or Chief Vizier then sat on the throne as regent. This was Seri Amar Diraya, the Rajah of Rokan, who plotted to place his nephew, Seriwa Rajah, on the throne. Seriwa Rajah, however, died of poisoning in 845.

Sri Maharajah's second son, Deva, who was Seriwa Rajah's grandson, came of age in 847. As Rajah of Melaka, he retained his grandfather Seri Amar Diraya as Bendahara. Deva's wife, a Maja Pahít princess, outranked him, obliging him to adopt the title of parameswara. Sri Parameswara Deva Shah reigned for 17 months, from 847 through 849.

Sri Maharajah's eldest son Kasim, whose Muslim mother was a Tamil commoner, returned from his pilgrimage to Mecca. He led a coup, and both his brother Deva Shah and the Bendahara Seri Amar Diraya were killed.

Kasim took the name Muzaffar Shah and reverted the title of Rajah to Sultan. His Bendahara was Tun Ali, who served for twelve years, until 861, when the wind happened to slam a door shut; Tun Ali, thinking it was the Sultan, displeased with him, who had slammed it, went home and committed suicide. He was succeeded by Tun Perak, who acquired Minjam for his Sultan, and Selangor, and Batu Pahat, and command of the Lenik River as well. And in Sultan Muzaffar Shah's reign successful campaigns were waged against Kampar, Indragiri, and Rokan, so that the Sultanate won control of both sides of the Strait. This ensured the protection of the flow of gold from the lands of the Minangkabaw. Late in his reign, the pirate lairs of Temasik and Bentan were taken as well.

The length of Sultan Muzaffar Shah's reign was thirteen years, and he reigned from 849 through 863.

And Muzaffar Shah slept with his fathers, and his son Mansur reigned in his stead. Sultan Mansur Shah sent auliyas, mashayikh, faqihs, 'ulamas and imams to Java, Burnei, Sulu, and other nearby lands, so that during his reign many areas converted to Islam.

In Mansur Shah's reign Tun Perak built up a force of fighting men and many times led it into battle, winning new lands for his Sultan. On the peninsula, Kedah and Perak were won for the Sultanate, and Bruas, Bernam, Johor, Pahang, and Tringganu; and in Sumatra, Rupat and Siak and Jambi and Bengkalis; and the Karimun Islands at the southern end of the Strait.

Mansur Shah took to wife many princesses from Java, Champa, Siam, and the lands of the Han. The most celebrated was the Princess Hong Lim Po, the Han Emperor's daughter, who arrived with 500 ladies-in-waiting. The Sultan allowed them to reside on a hill just outside the town. At the foot of that hill was a well from which Admiral Cheng Ho had once drank. That well never dried up, not even during the worst droughts; its water had magical powers.

Sultan Mansur Shah ruled Melaka for nineteen years, and he reigned from 863 through 882.

And Mansur slept with his fathers, and his son Al'a'ud-Din reigned in his stead. Sultan Al'a'ud-Din Riayat Shah's Bendahara was Tun Putéh, the White Lord, a man unusually fair of skin for a Malayu.

Al'a'ud-Din Shah often walked the streets at night. Once, espying two men committing a robbery, he himself apprehended them. The next day he reprimanded his temenggung for having been remiss in the performance of such duties. The temenggung, mortally insulted, must have had a hand in the fatal poisoning of the Sultan.

Al'a'ud-Din Shah reigned eleven years, from 882 through 893. He ascended the throne at 15 and died at 26, and it was during his reign that the Kingdom achieved its greatest extent.

And Al'a'ud-Din slept wih his fathers, and his son Mahmud reigned in his stead. Sultan Mahmud Shah's Bendahara was Tun Matahir. Mahmud Shah once more freed Melaka from Siamese suzerainty. He ruled for twenty-three years, from 893 through 917, or 1488 through 1511, and during his reign was called the greatest Sultan Melaka had ever known.

I was born in Melaka five years into Sultan Mahmud Shah's reign, early in 899. My family however had not forgotten the ancestor who had come with Melaka's original settlers, the noble from Palembang who had fought for the Sri Vijayâ against the invading Maja Pahít. He had always considered Melaka a place of refuge. His son felt the same way, and his son's son after that. My father too thought of Melaka as a temporary abode, a place where he had to bide his time before regaining the family's rightful inheritance in Palembang. And so I always thought of myself as an exile from Sumatra, someone merely carrying the sojourn in Melaka into the fifth generation.

Melaka attracted traders, and by my time some four thousand merchants from many places had settled there, so that eighty-four languages could be heard on its streets. There were Minangkabaw from Sumatra and people from Moluka, Bugis, Jawà, Madura...people from Sulawesi...from Sunda...from Sulu...in the marshy district of Minjam were even people from Lu-Süng, a whole colony of them, a hundred families strong.

Melaka was also home to Arabs from the different caliphates; to Mamluk and Seljuk Turks, Farsis, Armeniyans, Baluchis, Telugus, Sindhis, Bhils, Gujarati, Bangali, Marwari, Tamils, Sikhs, Sinhalese, Yahudi, Annamese, Mien, Ru-kius, Nippon men, Xangleis...Baba and Nanya, and also Hoy-hoy, or Xangleis who were Moslem. A few were converts. Most Hoy-hoy, however, came from towns in Kithai which had been Moslem for centuries.

I was thirteen years old, in 912, when I saw a Faranghi for the first time. He came as a passenger in an Arab qurqur, and was dressed as a rich merchant. But something looked different about him. The 'ustaz who was teaching me to read the Koran told me the Faranghi was a traveller, like ibn Battuta, a man who wanted to see the world. This Faranghi was a Veneziano, like that other Faranghi of more than two centuries before, the one who had been an ambassador for Kubilai Khan...Ser Marco Polo. The Faranghi's name was Ludovico Varthema. I had taken him for a Persian; he spoke Farsi quite well. I remembered him for his inordinate interest in the cocoanut palm. The rich and varied markets of Melaka seemed not to fascinate him so much as the uses we Malayus had for the cocoanut. We could obtain meat from it, and sweet water, and wine, and from its leaves roof thatching, wrappings, brooms; and from its coir we could weave rope, sennit, that did not rot in seawater...our old men were delighted to show Varthema how the cocoanut served us. None of them told him only poor men made so much use of the cocoanut. We had all grown wealthy in Melaka, and when not drunk on cocoanut tubâ, which was proscribed in that Moslem town, we might wear silk clothing and feast on roast peacock, which were not.

I was sixteen when we learned a flotilla of five Faranghi ships was on its way to Melaka, the first Faranghi force ever to visit us. This was in 915, or 1509. They were spotted at Pedir in North Sumatra, where they stopped for two days. The Rajah of Pedir followed his instructions and treated them cordially, even exchanging blood vows with their laksamana. It was a great feat for the town of Pedir, marking the first time Atjin men had acted in a friendly manner to strangers. The men of Pedir were free to follow the Faranghis a day later, as long as they reached Melaka by night and hid their prahus in a cove up the Melaka River. Many of them took the opportunity to do so.

We were still waiting for the Sultan of Johor's warriors on their war elephants when the five Faranghi ships entered the harbor, firing their lantakas, blowing their trumpets, and flying the signs we had been told to watch for: the red cross on their sails and the five bezants on their flags.

After the usual ceremonies they were induced to come ashore and help themselves to the tempting bargains we had prepared for them. One of their ships, as we had been told, carried seventy war horses. They were persuaded to bring these animals to stables we had kept empty for their arrival.

However, a few of the Faranghis must have smelled something. When the blast of the lantaka from the palace signalled the start of fighting, the white men on the ships reacted very quickly. They managed to fetch some of their men from the piers, then put all five of their ships out to sea. We had killed about thirty Faranghis and captured thirty others, and we thought the ships were fleeing in fear. But they turned around, headed back, and began firing their lantakas at our prahus.

They sent two of their Hindu pilots, flying a white flag, to ransom the men we had captured. We refused to talk. The five ships sailed off, leaving us their captured comrades, their dead, and their seventy-five superb Arabian horses. We had bested them, at cost of the lives of forty of our own men. Among Moslem cities, our reputation could only be enhanced for having repelled a force of Christians. But one question haunted us now. When would they return?

28

WHAT WAS IDEAL WEATHER for me, at latitude 37°S, was too hot for the Indians from América. They grew more miserable each day as the temperature became more civilized. When it was balmy enough to resume bathing, the Indians became listless.

I bathed with seawater pulled up in a bucket. It left a strange smell, but I still smelled much better than everyone else. None of them bathed, of course. The risk of getting colds was too great. Some of them told me I was shortening my life. One of these days, they said, the sudden pouring of seawater on my body would have a fatal effect. I would fall down dead from the shock.

On December 16, shortly after dropping the last land below the eastern horizon, the two Indian captives took sick. Two days later the one we called Juan Díaz died. The other one, the one we called Setebos, died the next day. I suspected that his countryman on the *San Antonio*, the one we called Cheleulle, was moribund, too. Our cirujano, el bachiller Morales, shook his head in disbelief. It was as if those men, he said, had simply willed themselves to die.

"The sight of land kept them alive," Ser Antonio said. "We've been in this Pacific Sea since November 28 but we've stayed within sight of land for more than two weeks. Only now, when we started to sail across the ocean, did they lose heart."

We unshackled those poor unfortunates from their leg irons, wrapped up their bodies in heavy cloth, and buried them at sea, at latitude 33°S. Ser Antonio watched both burials closely. Later, he claimed the bodies had turned over and sunk face down, looking at Hell; the Christians we committed to the waves had all remained face up, staring at Heaven.

The course was northwest. Then, on December 21, at latitude 30°S, we moved into a current that bore us west. Our speed picked up measurably. Land could not be far off. All the maps and charts extant showed the lands of the Indies to extend south as far as latitude 35°S, where they came close to América. That was why, on the east coast of América, the Captain-General had insisted on a careful search of the littoral at 35°S. It had seemed logical for a strait to exist there, with the Indies close at hand on the other side.

We had passed latitude 35°S several days ago, and the Armada had struck out on a northwest course at that point. It would not be long now.

On Sunday, December 23, while giving the evening salute to the Captain-General, Duarte Barbosa reported the death of a man due to illness. It was the sobresaliente Alonso Português of Evora. The following morning he was buried at sea.

The moon was full on December 24.

Christmas Day at latitude 29°S was merely another good sailing day. All were issued an extra cup of wine. The Captain-General rowed over to the two other ships to greet their crews. He also visited several men in sick bay on the *Victoria*: the grumetes Domingo Português of Coimbra and Rodrigo Gallego of La Coruña; the alguacil Diego Peralta of Navarra, and the blacksmith Gonçalo Rodrígues.

Surely land could not be far off. Having left the coastal waters of América on December 16, two or three weeks would suffice to cross the Mar Pacífico. We could expect landfall in the second week of January.

Domingo Português died on December 26 and was buried at latitude 28°S.

Our course varied between WNW and NW by W. A fair wind on the quarter, nothing to do but cast fishing lines and try to hook a fish or two. Dorado, albacore, and bonito, large fish that preyed on flying fish, were our best prospects. The way to catch them was to attach a lead weight, a piece of wood, a hook, and a bit of rag to a fishing line, in that order. The wood floated on the water, keeping the rag a foot above. As it fluttered in the wind, it looked like a flying fish. The bonito or dorado would leap up to eat it, and find itself hooked.

When these fish were not to be found, the only alternative was to catch a shark. They were always around us, following our ships like dogs, most of them two yards or so in length. Catching them required some skill and agility.

Domingo de Urrutia, the lone Basque on the *Trinidad*, averred that only the Euskaldunac really knew how to catch and cook sharks. After he had caught one, many of us were quite flabbergasted to learn that the male shark was equipped with two virile members.

"When having communication with the female," asked Ser Antonio, "does it use both?"

No one could say.

Domingo de Urrutia made a soup of both penises and presented the steaming bowl to Ser Antonio. The latter grimaced when he saw what was in it, but the aroma of Basque cooking quite overcame his aversions, and he ate with relish.

On Tuesday, January 1, Diego Peralta died of his illness. We buried him there, at latitude 24°S.

According to the official way of reckoning, January 1 was the first day of 1521. Tradition died hard, however, and the real New Year's Day would not be celebrated until the vernal æquinox, on March 25.

The course was WNW, the latitude 24°S, and Albo made a guess at our longitude, noting it down as 80° or 82°W of Fierro.

On Friday, January 4, Gonzalo Rodríguez, a blacksmith on the *Victoria*, died of illness.

Men were dying off in the *Victoria*, our smallest ship, and the first to run short on supplies of food. Even worse than their starvation diet was the scourge of the escorbuto. The only cure was fresh green vegetables, certain to be available on the first land we would find on this ocean. How many days away was it?

The entire voyage was now coming down to a single question: how wide was this Mar Pacífico? Nobody knew, and we would soon be the first to find out. In the answer lay the key to other important questions. What was the circumference of the world? How many miles or leguas was one degree at the æquinoctial line? The best minds in the world had grappled with these profound questions.

"Aristotle in his time," said Ser Antonio, "estimated the world's circumference to be 400,000 stadia.. Archimedes, for his part, estimated it to be 300,000 stadia, and the world's diameter to be 96,000 stadia. And there was Eratosthenes. He computed the circumference to be 252,000 stadia, and the diameter to be 80,700 stadia."

"How many miles was a stadium?" asked Master Andrew.

"Heaven knows. But he gave the distance from Alexandria to Syene as 5,000 stadia. Today that distance, from Alexandria to Aswan, is about 500 miles. I once had the exact figures, and I calculated the mile to be some 10⅖ stadia. According to Eratosthenes then, the circumference of the world is about 24,500 miles."

"A bit overlarge," Master Andrew said. "Why, if the world were that big, it would take us months rather than weeks to cross this Pacific Sea. But I wonder...what value did he use for pi?"

"Why, the quotient of 22 divided by 7, of course."

"Not the square root of 10?"

"Marinus of Tyre," Ser Antonio said, "in 100 A.D. gave 225° as the breadth of Eurasia, while Ptolemæus in 150 A.D. gave it as 177°. Fra Mauro, in 1459, suggested that Eurasia was only 125°, from the west coast of Portugal to the east coast of Cathay."

"Cristóbal Colón," said Dom Fernão, "knew all that."

"Ah yes, Colombo," said Ser Antonio. "His favorite book was the *Historia rerum ubique gestarum,* by Æneas Sylvius Piccolomini, who later became Pope Pius II. Another was a book by Flavius Josephus, *De Antiquitatibus*. In it, he read that Solomon's gold came from 'Ophir, now called the Land of Gold, in India.' From a kingdom on the Sea of Tarshish Solomon obtained silver, 'elephants, peacocks, and apes.' Still another book he read was the collection of geographic tracts by Pierre d'Ailly, *Imago Mundi.*"

"Wasn't it d'Ailly," asked Dom Fernão, "who first said one could go to the East by sailing west?"

"No, it was an Italian, Paolo dal Pozzo Toscanelli, a Florentine. In a letter he wrote to the King of Portugal in 1474, he said that Quinsay, the capital of Mangi Province in Cathay, was about 1600 leguas due west of Lisbôa. Cristoforo Colombo acquired a copy of that letter by writing to Toscanelli himself in 1481."

"Colón died thinking he had found the Indies," Dom Fernão said. "But what he found was a new continent. How did his estimates come to be so wide of the mark?"

"Well, he began with Marinus of Tyre's figure for the breadth of Asia, 225 degrees of longitude, as it was the largest estimate," said Ser Antonio. "He added 28° for the discoveries of Ser Marco Polo. Since Cipangu would be reached first, he put in 30° for the distance from the east coast of Cathay to the east coast of Cipangu. Polo's book, published in 1485, had given this distance as some 500 leguas. Colombo would start from the westernmost of the Canarias, and so he credited 9° to the difference in longitude between Europa and the island of Hierro. It added up to 292° of longitude. A complete circle around the world is 360°, and that meant there remained but 68° across the Mar Océano from Hierro to Cipangu. Colombo thought one degree of longitude was 56⅔ Roman miles at the æquinoctial line. He planned to sail west at latitude 28°N, where the degree would be shorter—perhaps only 47 Roman miles. That left him with an estimated distance of a thousand leguas from Hierro to Cipangu, the easternmost of the Indies."

"His seamanship was excellent," said Dom Fernão, "but his geodesy left much to be desired. You know what impressed me most about him? His signature."

Ser Antonio took the watch captain's slate and chalk and wrote a facsimile:

.S.
.S. A. S.
. X . M . Y.
:χρoFERENS.

"Yes," said Dom Fernão. "That's it exactly. Has anyone ever seen a more mysterious signature?"

"What does it mean?" Master Andrew asked.

"I've no idea," Dom Fernão admitted.

"Nonsense," said Ser Antonio, "I happen to know that those letters stand for *Servus Sum Altissimi Salvatoris, Christoû Mariae Yîov*—"

"Servant am I of the most high Saviour," translated Master Andrew, "Christ the Son of Mary."

"And the way he wrote his given name," said Ser Antonio, "in Græco-Roman characters, served to emphasize its original meaning: xp̄oFERENS, the Christ-bearer. In other words, he bore Christ in his heart always."

"He bore Christ in his heart," Dom Fernão said, "across the seas to the lands of the heathen. He saw that as his sacred mission. Gentlemen, I say to you: that mission, and the torch of zeal he carried, have been passed on to us."

"Amen," Ser Antonio said, making the sign of the cross.

"Amen," Master Andrew said, crossing himself.

"Ebarasai!" I said, unable to stifle a sneeze.

"I didn't tell them," Master Andrew told me later, "but I have my own mystical signature." He took the watch captain's slate and wrote:

```
S A T O R
A R E P O
T E N E T
O P E R A
R O T A S
```

"Observe," he said proudly, "how it reads the same backwards and forwards, horizontally or vertically. It's my talisman. These words are magical. They can go forward or backward in time, to the past or to the future. They can be read in a mirror. They're an enigma. As St. Paul said, *Videmus nunc per speculum in aenigmate.*"

"Now we see through a glass darkly?" asked Andrés de la Cruz.

"No, it translates as 'Now we see through a mirror by means of an enigma.' St. Paul always did have a penchant for metaphor."

I understood none of it. I was lightheaded from lack of food. At this point in the voyage we were soaking the chafing covers of the masts in seawater, then boiling them into soup. The original covers were made of leather. Those had worn out, and been replaced by guanaco skins. It took three days of soaking before the skins became soft enough to cook. Everyone got a little piece of it in his soup. Chewing on it gave the tongue a taste of meat, if one had enough imagination—or enough teeth.

Many of us had scurvy, which made the act of chewing a painful ordeal. Even those with strong teeth had to chew the tough skin for a long time before they could attempt to swallow it.

Ser Antonio was offering 12 ducats for each fat rat a grumete could cook.

The water in the casks had grown so bad we were cooking rice in seawater.

I knew why land could not be found: this ocean was much wider than anyone had thought, than my master had estimated. Perhaps Eratosthenes had been correct, and the circumference of the world was really 7700 leguas. Months of sailing, not weeks. As Master Andrew had guessed.

The Captain-General, at Ser Antonio's importuning, was telling Master Andrew and the pages about the conquest of Melaka.

"We had spread the rumor that we were invading Aden. We left Goa in March of 1511, then sailed north as if on course for Aden. Out of sight of land, we turned around and headed south. There were storms en route, and the voyage too much longer than anticipated. Four months. We reached Malacca on the first of July. We bombarded the town and besieged it. Still, it was three weeks before we broke through..."

The drone of his raspy voice was lulling me to sleep, and I lay in the corner, barely listening. I had been there too, on the other side, among the besieged. After nearly ten years, the invasion of Melaka still seemed to me like a bad dream. My mind went back to the year 1511 A.D. Properly speaking, that was the year 917 A.H. But I would always remember it now by the white man's reckoning.

Fast asleep, I had fallen into the dream; I was wide awake...my dream had taken me nearly ten years back into the past and everything there was as real as it had ever been...

Forty days into the siege...the Faranghis are slackening. They break through on the twenty-fourth day...only to be driven out again by evening. That must have shown them how we could hold our own. Any day now they will call off hostilities and retire to their ships.

The next day they bring in a converted junk, a contraption so silly we want to laugh. We have heard of war machines before, such as the vimanas in the Ramayana, but this one must be part of some huge joke.

At high tide they row the junk up the Melaka River, its cannon fire rousing us out of sleep. The junk, with walls of heavy teak, is a floating box. We attempt to set it on fire. They manage to douse it everytime with river water. The junk continues up the river, stopping at the bridge to disgorge armored warriors who deal out death. When outnumbered they return in slow stages to the junk, fending off arrows, challenges, feints. A ridiculous way to fight.

In two days it is all over. They have stormed the Istana Besar, the Sultan's palace.

Sullen in defeat, chained and imprisoned in the market courtyard along with hundreds of my fellow defenders, I stand indifferent to my fate. At best, death; at worst, slavery and a life of torture. I am eighteen and my city is no more; what place in the world for me now?

Two Faranghis pick me out and lay claim to me. The one who signs the papers has dark piercing eyes, thick curly whiskers and beard, and lips fuller than usual for the white man. He is also swarthy. He has been here long enough to have turned as dark as one of my own people: a monster, as all Faranghis are.

They take me to a priest and baptize me into their faith. Then they bring me to the house they have commandeered from a Xanglei towkay. I do all the menial tasks for them, washing strange clothes, polishing armor, putting away the dishes. Most of the towkay's crockery is intact, blue-and-white porcelain bowls and jars, celadon platters. The Xanglei, a Hoy-hoy named Bo Ang, made sure only of his gold dishes when he fled. He was killed a short distance away, his body looted and left lying on the street for hours before a burial detail reached him.

The Faranghi who chose me is a nobleman in his country, a captain, and a navigator. An illogical combination, for captains are above the bother of navigating, and navigators do not rise to command. His name is Fernão, and I must use the honorific "Dom" when addressing him. His fellow captain, Francisco, a lower class of nobleman, acts truer to their type: Francisco knows nothing of navigation.

I choose to count my blessings: invoking the privileges of his high rank, my master has refused to release me to the workpress gangs. I do not have to join the fifteen hundred men upon whose slave labor a fortress is being constructed. The Faranghis are building it with headstones from Muslim graves in the cemetery. They are also looting those graves, taking gold and jewels from our dead.

I understand implicitly that Dom Fernão will dispense with my services should I prove incapable of learning his language. Under those circumstances, I accomplish in three weeks a basic competence in Português. I learn too that these white men detest being called Faranghis, the name by which they have been known to us since the days of Temujin. The Franks, they tell me, are another nation in another land.

Along with the language I learn to think like the white man. Or perhaps it happens the other way around, and I acquire the knack for their language only when I begin thinking like them. After that, reading and writing Português become enhancements to my accomplishment.

My master at first assumes I am illiterate, as are some of my people and most of his. Yet he expresses no surprise upon finding I read Jawi Malayu, Arabic, and a little Farsi.

We spend less time in the house than aboard ship. They are constantly on patrol in the Strait, two caravels sailing in formation. Always I have to go along as body servant, an unwilling sailor.

One day Francisco sails to the Spice Islands as the captain of the third caravel in a flotilla of three caravels and a dhow. In command is Captain-General Antão d'Abreu, in the caravel *Catarina*. The second caravel, the *Sabaia*, is under Captain Simon Affonso. It is the first voyage of white men to the Molukas. Not knowing the way, they rely on the dhow to lead them there. Its commander is the veteran Gujarat navigator, Nahoda Ismail. Dom Fernão, left behind, cannot hide his disappointment.

Only the dhow and one caravel return. The other two caravels were lost in a storm off Jawà, they report. The Spice Islands were not attained, the wily Gujarat guiding them only as far as

Banda before the monsoon winds changed.

A passing balanghay duly delivers a letter from Francisco. He is alive after all. He had ridden out the storm and, in doing so, become separated from the others. Then the caravel caught fire because of a careless cook. Francisco has been through wondrous adventures, escaping from his burning caravel, lying in ambush with his men, capturing a Xanglei junk and sailing it to Amboina, helping the Rajah there crush a rebellion, joining up with the Datu of Terrenate's thousand men in ten prahus to wage war on the Datu of Tidore. In the Molukas Francisco averted war, effected a truce, married the Datu of Tidore's daughter, and became the Grand Vizier of Terrenate. He has turned the two datus into puppets. He urges Dom Fernão to sail there and make his fortune.

Dom Fernão receives orders to sail his caravel to Terrenate and join Francisco. They are to build a fortress there; Datu Abuleysi has given his permission. Datu Al-Manzor, for his part, wants his own white man to invest as Grand Vizier of Tidore. My master, however, has other ideas.

We sail southeast down the Strait, past the island of Temasik at the tip of the peninsula. From there the course is southeast, past Sumatra and Jawà, east to the Banda Islands, and on to Terrenate in the Molukas.

Off Temasik, Dom Fernão gradually veers the wrong way, to port, until we are headed northeast.

In nine days we reach a group of islands. We spend a week coasting around. There are thousands of islands. Dom Fernão is ecstatic. He has heard of these islands from a Taga-ilog, one of the few who remain in Melaka. Before the siege there had been a colony of them, some five hundred strong, mostly from the island of Lü-sung.

One of the older men in the crew, an enslaved Melakan like myself, but originally from Bugis, tells me he has been to some of these islands. Boatloads of Malayus settled here, he says, people of the Sri-Vijayâ fleeing from their Maja Pahít enemies.

Back in Melaka, Dom Fernão attempts to communicate his elation at finding a rich, new, uncharted archipelago to his superiors. He also writes to Francisco in Terrenate.

The reaction is not what he might have hoped for. His

superior, Dom Fernão Petre Andrade, orders him to sail to Goa and report to the Viceroy, Dom Affonso d'Alboquerque. Francisco Serrão writes back only to complain his old comrade has deserted him.

In Goa Dom Fernão is deprived of his command, and repatriated. We sail for the land of the white man as passengers in a caravel. The captain, Jorge Lopes, treats my master as an honored guest. There are stops at Melindi and Quilmana, a harrowing time going around the cold stormy Cabo da Bõa Hesperança, and more stops at the Cabo Verdes and the Açores. Then landfall, and soon we are in the harbor of Lisbõa.

Seven years pass. I remain loyal to my master all this time, living in different places. A dog's life. I should have jumped overboard under cover of darkness and swum for the shore long ago, when we were off an island where lived people from the old empire of the Sri Vijayâ. All the old Bugis man's fault, really. He had told me those waters were full of sharks.

29
♒

TWO WEEKS OF SAILING into nothing. Many were sick, gums swollen, teeth falling out, joints aching and limbs acutely painful to move.

Why was land taking so long to appear? Never before had any of us voyaged a full month without landfall. Cristóbal Colón, on his first voyage, had taken 33 days to cross the Ocean Sea. We had last seen land on December 16. It was now January 17.

On Friday, January 18, Rodrigo Gallego of La Coruña, a grumete on the *Victoria*, died of illness. We buried him at sea, in the middle of nowhere.

The course was NW by N, and we kept to that for the next two days, until latitude 15°S.

"Sumbit Pradit is at this latitude," Ser Antonio said. "Perhaps we'll find it soon."

What was our longitude now? Albo had a wild, probably useless, guess. If the cosmographers had been right, we should have reached land by now, 33 days after leaving sight of América, land at the longitude of Cipangu. The lands of the dark men of the South.

Ser Antonio announced a reward of ten ducats for the first sighting of land.

The 33rd day with no land had come and gone. Where the Indies, where land at all? Nothing but ocean, blue water, infinite waves.

January 21 and 22. Deflected SW for two days. Headwinds.

January 23. Moon at second quarter—full moon.

January 24. The feast day of St. Paul. Thirty-nine days now without landfall. Hungry all the time. Hardtack fallen to powder, full of maggots. Yellow where the rats urinated on them. Living on rice cooked in seawater. Cooking rice in salt water, some of the men mutter, is what's making us sick. I don't think so, but I hold my tongue.

In all the casks the water stinks.

Bright morning. Course W by N. Fair following wind.

Ahead, slightly to port, low puffy cloud just above the horizon. Bit of green on its base.

Beautiful color, green. My mind foggy. My head full of cocoanut beetles. Green cloud bottom looks nice. Must be reflection of shallow water...shallow water. As in an atoll—a lagoon, and therefore an island. Still below the horizon.

Had the lookout seen it?

Young Vasquito was up there in the gavia. Now and then he glanced at the cloud. Had he noticed the green? But soon the land under it would come up over the horizon.

"Tierra la!" came the cry. Vasquito had finally seen it. Everyone rushed up for a look.

The Captain-General took over from the officer of the watch, and ordered a slight turn to port to close in on the island.

High noon. The page on duty reversed the ampolleta. Francisco Albo took a meridional sighting of the sun with his astrolabe. His latitude: $16\frac{1}{3}°$S.

All hands came alert except the few men in sick bay. Nobody had to be told what to do. Two marineros were at the bow with the sounding leads. Others made ready to cast all four anchors. A team lowered the batel into the water to be towed by the ship while the alguacil, his merinos, and the rowers prepared to board it.

When the Captain-General ordered the sails struck, marineros were waiting for the command. The two other ships followed the capitana's example immediately. The papahigo was furled first, then the cebadera, then the mesana. We sailed with only the trinquete to within half a legua of the island, then lowered that, too. Men waited in the waists with the ashwood sweeps. The current was strong, and we continued to drift closer. The island was lush with cocoanut palms, but had no houses or boats; no sign of human habitation.

"No bottom!" cried the leadsman on the larboard side.

"No bottom!" replied his partner on the starboard side.

"Are they using the double-length ropes?" asked Ser Antonio of the contramaestre.

"Yes, of course," answered Ginés de Mafra.

Dom Fernão said nothing. He knew the 200-fathom sounding leads were fully played out. That meant 1200 feet, yet no anchorage could be found.

Then we were drifting past it.

"Send off the batel!" Ser Antonio yelled.

Dom Fernão continued to peer into the waters. It was obvious that the strong current and the fair wind would make it impossible for the naos to turn back and recover any batels that rowed off to the island. We could not even circle the island to look for anchorage on the other side.

"Woe is me," said Ser Antonio.

"Mãe de Deus," swore Dom Fernão. "What sheer walls. Must be the top of a sunken volcano."

The Captain-General entered the island in the derrotero as the Isla de San Pablo, and shot the sun to ascertain the latitude. He determined it to be almost exactly 15°S, perhaps less. With some extrapolation, it was probably between 14°50'S and 14°40'S. Francisco Albo, as usual, had overestimated the latitude and put us too far to the south.

Ginés de Mafra reminded Ser Antonio he owed Vasquito Gomez Gallego ten ducats. Ser Antonio said he would not pay for land unattained. Ginés gently told him that was not what he had promised. He had promised to reward the first man to sight land. It wasn't Vasquito's fault if the island had no anchorage.

"All right, I'll pay him later," Ser Antonio said.

"Now," de Mafra said.

Ser Antonio glared at him.

"Oh, give the boy his money," Dom Fernão said.

De Mafra motioned Vasquito forward. The grumete stood there and held out his hand while the Venetian counted ten gold ducats into it.

The next day, January 25, Captain Duarte Barbosa reported the death of a marinero, Miguel Benesciano of Bresa in Lombardia. Ser Antonio said a prayer for his paisano's soul.

The course was generally NW, but we were gradually curving to WNW, then to W by N.

The island of San Pablo, for most of us, seemed typical of this unknown region: a magic island that mocked us and allowed us to come close, but seemingly floated on a bottomless sea, so that no anchorage could be found. For some, however, it banished the unspoken fear that this was an endless ocean which led nowhere.

The days passed: dreary, hungry days. One night as January was ending, the Captain-General stood the watch of la modorra. The other men on watch stayed on the foredeck, leaving the two of us on the quarterdeck. The waning moon rose late that night. We stood astern to watch it.

"I always find the play of its light on the waves fascinating," he said.

I grunted.

"Nine years ago, when we made that voyage from Malacca to the northeast islands, we began under a waning moon. The old Malay pilot said he was waiting for the new moon, when its light would not distract us. Why was that?"

"So he could see the te lapa, Sire."

"What is that?"

"Underwater streaks of light. Others call it the te mata, others the ulo'a e tahi. It is all the same. Streaks or flashes of light, deep in the water..."

"Aren't you speaking of surface phosphorescence? When the water takes on a luminous quality?"

"No, Sire, that's quite different. These streaks dart out from the direction of an island still below the horizon. They are best seen some thirty or forty leguas out. They look like underwater lightning, some five or six fathoms below the surface. The te lapa no longer appears when the island is close enough to show on the horizon."

"A singular phenomenon. No Portuguese mariner has ever mentioned it. Point it out to me should you happen to see it."

"Yes, Sire. As for that old pilot, he wasn't really a Malay. He was an orang laut from one of those small islands far off to the southeast, Savai'i, I think it was. He liked cloudy skies, too. The te lapa becomes easier to see then, even if it means one can no longer see the stars."

"The two of you often played with that toy of his—that contraption of bamboo sticks. What was that?"

"His mattang, a device for teaching the different patterns that ocean waves make. He was a ppalu, like his father before him, and his father's father before that. The secrets of sailing the oceans and finding small islands at the end of long voyages were handed down from father to son."

"He feared for his life, and for his son's life. He had seen what you Faranghis had done to Melaka. His son had been enslaved there. The Portuguese have a special respect for pilots, but nobody knew the young man was a ppalu. If that son would die in Melaka, the secrets of the ppalu's family would die with him. That was why he decided to teach me some of those secrets."

"Wasn't he saying something about me, too?"

"Yes. He said you too were a navigator, of the sort who trusted his instruments more than his own senses. As such, you could not hope to be as great a navigator as those of his own family. Only when you learned to navigate the oceans by your senses could you become a true navigator."

"And what exactly did he mean by that?"

"Many things. The ppalu knows all the stars in the sky by sight. He knows the different seas and the feel of each one, the currents and the set of waves for a given sea. He feels the push of an ocean swell through his scrotum."

"Through the scrotum? I've never heard of anything so absurd."

"No, Sire, it's true. A navigator's got to have balls."

I wanted to tell him more: that a ppalu navigated by the stars, and knew the names and positions of some 150 of them. That he knew the star courses from a given island, usually his own, to any number of other islands, would set his course by a star newly risen on the horizon, would keep this star on his foremast, and when it had risen too high, would steer by the next star that rose from the same point of the horizon. That the star he steered by was the kaveinga, and the ppalu knew which stars succeeded each other as kaveinga.

The fanakenga on the other hand, I wanted to tell him, was a star on the zenith. The ppalu knew the fanakengas of his seas, knew which stars stood exactly on the zenith of which islands.

And I should have told him how the ppalu knew the patterns of the waves, how they were broken when they flowed around a small island, with some waves reflected back while other waves were deflected at angles around the island to continue in a changed pattern on the other side. The ppalu would have learned all that from studying the mattang, the web of interlocking bamboo sticks on which all the basic patterns of waves could be shown.

I might have told him that the ppalu could feel the swell of a sea, the faint pulse that came, if it came at all, perhaps once every ten minutes. Called the hoa hua dele tai, it was useful only when a ship was travelling in the same direction. Then the ppalu could maintain course by keeping the swell dead astern. It was a slight push that lifted up the stern without rolling the ship. Its rhythm was fairly even, but could be no more felt than the upstream push of a flood tide on a riverboat. To make sure he felt it, the ppalu would go to the bow of his vessel and crouch down in the hull. He had to be as close to the waves as he could. Even then, he knew the best way to feel the swell was through his testicles.

I wondered if my master knew the winds and their ways as the ppalu did.

I wondered if he knew the birds of the sea, and how far each kind ventured from land. Perhaps he knew that birds, upon leaving an island, always flew into the wind. He must have known that birds flying with the wind were going home, and that such birds showed the way to the next land.

Perhaps he also knew that if there were several islands near each other, birds flew among all the islands of that group. By observing the patterns of bird flights, one could steer for the center of the group. Only when landfall had been made would it be time to steer for a specific island in that group.

Did he know, as the ppalu did, how clouds piled up over an island, and how this gave them shapes different from those of clouds over empty water? Did he know that such clouds did not move, and that a cloud on the horizon, a thick mass that remained in the same place, often meant an island two days away?

He probably knew the green of shallow water when reflected from the base of a low cloud.

He knew, I was sure, the smell of land from a great distance out.

But what I most wanted to tell him was that the ppalu rarely ever used maps. The few the ppalu had, usually inherited from an older ppalu, were made of shells stuck on oddly-shaped sticks.

And once in every generation, I wanted to tell Dom Fernão, a family of navigators might produce a ppalu who could dip his hand into the water and tell which sea it was. The legends accorded this skill to one family only, the members of the Taitu clan, who were called feelers of the sea.

We had seen our first island in the Pacific on January 24. After that, a whole week passed. This was a limitless ocean, indeed. We endured the first three days of February in increasing despair.Then, sometime in the dreary, hungry evening of February 3, I suddenly saw it.

The te lapa.

Underwater. Streaks of light darting out from a single source. From somewhere far to the west. In front of us.Beyond the horizon. The moon was on the wane, not due to rise until the wee hours, and no more than a crescent by then. I could see the te lapa clearly enough, but the streaks were so faint as to make the uninitiated think his eyes were playing tricks on him. Under the clear, starry sky, the light of even a diminished moon would blot out the te lapa. But we were headed for it. There was no need to change course.

In the morning we raised our second island. It was Monday, February 4.

We approached it as previously, men heaving the sounding leads at the bow, batel ready to cast off. It was an atoll of coral reefs encircling a lagoon, and as we came close we could see shark fins cavorting around in the lagoon. I knew the lagoon would be full of fish. So, apparently, did the sharks. They would naturally congregate in the lagoon to feed.

This island looked quite uninhabited, too. There were trees festooned with cocoanuts, and the first thing I would do would be to climb a tree, throw down some cocoanuts, and split them open for their milk. Already I could taste that ambrosia on my parched tongue.

But the leadsmen were frantically sounding, and still they kept saying, "No bottom!"

Soon we were past it, once again unable to stop at an island because it simply did not have an anchorage.The Captain-General called it the Isla de Tiburónes.Pilot Albo noted its latitude as 10°40'S and its longitude as 132°45' west of Ferro.

Dom Fernão checked the latitude and found it to be exactly 10°S. There was no way to check Albo's figure for longitude. At least Albo's errors were getting smaller.

On Wednesday, February 6, Nicolas Genovés, a marinero on the *Victoria*, died of illness. On Saturday, February 9, another death: Juan Flamenco of Enveres, a page on the *Concepción*, one of those transferred from the wrecked *Santiago*.

On we sailed. Hungry all the time. Course NW. February 12 was Mardi Gras, or Shrove Tuesday. On February 13, Ash Wednesday, we finally reached the æquinoctial line. Albo's noontime shot of the sun showed our latitude to be 0°. He may have been slightly off as usual, but it did not matter. Albo guessed our longitude to be 146°W.

On February 15 we were at 1¾°N, and Albo reckoned the longitude to be 148°W. That night Ser Antonio finally saw Polaris again, for the first time in more than a year. The moon was a day past first quarter, bright enough to obliterate some of the fainter stars, but not his beloved Transmontana.

February 17 was the first Sunday of Lent.

The days passed. We were fortunate if we could catch a rat to eat. The chafing gear for our masts and yardarms, made of guanaco skins from Patagonia, were soaking in seawater. It took them three days to become soft enough to boil in soup. Into the kettle we would add scrapings of wood from the bottoms of our food barrels. This wood retained some of the flavor of whatever the barrel had contained.

"This soup tastes good," said Francisco Albo. "Like taramosalata. Now, if only it would be followed by a double serving of kefalaki..."

He pinched his nostrils with thumb and forefinger as he took a drink of vile water. Having swallowed, he looked at the dregs in his cup.

"Stale retsina," he said, spitting over the side, "mixed with horse piss."

The Molukas islands, our destination, were on the æquinoctial line. Presumably we could reach them now by old-fashioned latitude sailing, keeping straight west. But the Captain-General stayed with the fair winds and steered WNW. By February 21 we were at 8°N. The moon was full on February 22. We were making sixty or seventy leguas a day.

February 24 was the second Sunday of Lent. The course was WNW and we were at 12½°N.

"Cape Gaticara is at this latitude," Ser Antonio said. "Twelve degrees north of the æquinoctial line. Perhaps we'll come across it soon."

By the next day, February 25, we were at 13°N. From then on, the course was due west.

The Captain-General was going in for old-fashioned latitude sailing, after all.

On February 28 Basco Gallego, the pilot of the *Victoria*, died shortly after dictating his last will and testament to escribano Sancho de Heredia of the *Concepción*, who had come over to the *Victoria* for that purpose. I did not know why Basco did not entrust that task to his own ship's escribano, Martín Mendez. Basco Gallego's namesake on the *Trinidad*, the grumete Vasco Gomez Gallego, was still very much alive, and so was the latter's son Vasquito.

Why were so many men dying on the *Victoria*? We wondered about it. Pages, grumetes, marineros, a bombardero...and now the pilot. I wondered when the malaise would reach the *Victoria*'s captain.

February ended, now it was March, and still the course was due west on latitude 13°N. Dom Fernão knew the Spice Islands began at 4°N. What destination was he aiming for?

Master Andrew had fallen victim to the escorbuto. Now he lay in bed in great misery. Every morning he was nursed, along with the other sick men, by the Captain-General himself.

"We should reach land soon," Dom Fernão assured him. "It's been nearly a month since we passed the Isla de Tiburónes. The next island can't be more than a few days away."

"Give my love to my wife when you get back to Sevilla, comendador," Master Andrew said. "Tell Ana Estrada she's the only woman I ever loved."

"Don't talk rot, old fellow," Dom Fernão said. "You'll tell her yourself, of course. When we get back."

But he grew worse day by day.

"When we reach the longitude of eighty-and-a-hundred degrees from Europa," he whispered one morning as the Captain-General and the cirujano made the rounds, "we shall be in tomorrow."

"He's delirious," el bachiller Morales said.

"No, I mean that," insisted Master Andrew. "We shall be a day ahead of Europa. Going west can only mean a gain of a day, can't it? Crossing the antipodean line and all that."

He closed his eyes, breathed a sigh. He was asleep.

"What does he mean?" asked Ser Antonio.

"Something to do with the gain of a day," replied Dom Fernão, "at longitude 180°."

"Is that east," Ser Antonio asked, "of one's prime meridian, or west of it?"

"Both," said Dom Fernão. "Since 180° West is exactly the same as 180° East."

My master rose to go. Master Andrew's eyes opened. He looked earnestly at Dom Fernão.

"I had hoped to die in battle, you know," he said. "No other way to get to Valhalla."

"That is only in the myths of the Northmen, my dear Andres," said Ser Antonio. "Pagan superstition. We are Christians. We know better."

"Oh, but I am a Northman," said Master Andrew. "On my mother's side. Were I to die in battle a Valkyrie would pick me up from among the fallen and take me on her winged horse to Valhalla. There I would feast with warriors on pork and mead for eternity. What could be better?"

Ser Antonio knelt beside him.

"Let us say a prayer together."

Master Andrew rolled his eyes and fell asleep.

By March 5 it was obvious only fresh food and drink would save our condestable de bombarderos, if an island could be encountered in time. That evening I saw the te lapa again. Two sources this time, indicating two islands. I did not tell anyone. Those islands might have no anchorage either.

I fell asleep dreaming of a great feast, for which dozens of pigs had been slaughtered and were now being roasted on bamboo spits. They were nearly done. The skins of the pigs had turned red, and one showed a small crack from the intense heat. Melted fat oozed out through this crack and fell on the coals. I could hear the hiss it made, and smell the aroma it released. But I was chained to a post. I was a captive, somehow. I was not to participate in that feast.

"Tierra la!" cried the lookout in the midmorning of March 6. We were at latitude 13°N. The longitude was 163°W of Ferro, according to Francisco Albo. Ser Antonio had it as 146°W of the Line of Demarcation. Even accounting for the difference between Ferro and the Line, those figures did not agree. But at this point I hardly cared.

"Praise be to God," said Ser Antonio. "It's been ninety-nine days since we debouched into this ocean."

"Should be thousands of islands here," said the Captain-General. But as we drew closer we could see there were only three. Two of them lay close together. The bigger one looked to be ten leguas long, and the smaller about two leguas. North of them, some distance off, lay the third island, also two leguas long.

We would go past them and then look for anchorage on the leeward side.

In mid-afternoon we passed between the two islands, then turned south to follow the coast of the big island. There was no break in the reef. Down the coast we sailed, looking intently at the land. A legua, another legua, and soon we had sailed seven leguas and were in a channel between that island and an islet offshore, to its west. We had sailed almost the entire length of the island, and could see that another rocky islet lay ahead, off the island's southern end.

Then we saw it.

The break in the reef. A bay, with many prahus clustered by the shore. A village of thatched huts.

Naked people.

30

THE *TRINIDAD* TURNED into the bay, towing her batel. Prahus put out from the shore to meet us. Each prahu had one lateen sail, one outrigger, and four men.

"I shall call this the Isla de Velas Latinas," the Captain-General declared. It was Wednesday, March 6, 1521, and we had finally reached an island we could put into, after an ocean crossing three times the magnitude of Cristovão Colom's.

Francisco Albo had done some calculations, and logged the longitude of the island as 163° west of Ferro. Ser Antonio put it down as 146°W of the Demarcation Line.

According to Ser Antonio, the linea de ripartitione was supposed to be 30°W from the meridian of Ferro, which itself was 3°E of Santo Antão in the Cape Verde Islands. Albo disputed this. He put Santo Antão as 7°E of Ferro in the Canaries. The 370 leguas from the Cape Verdes to the Line he regarded as equivalent to only 21° of longitude. Still, it was not sufficient to explain Albo's 163°W or Ser Antonio's 146°W. I could not account for their difference, and I was left more confused than ever.

A thought occurred to me: how far were we from longitude 180° if the prime meridian were that of our starting point, Sevilla? As far as I could guess, Sevilla was about 20°E of Ferro. If we had passed that antipodal line, and if Master Andrew were right, we should have gained a day. Perhaps it was already Thursday, March 7, 1521, and none of us knew it.

The prahus were much closer now. Their hulls were painted in different colors, some in white, some in black, many in red. Their lateen sails were of plaited palm leaves. Their paddles ended in sharp points, for use as harpoons.

"Those boats resemble dolphins," Ser Antonio said, "the way they leap in the water from wave to wave."

I watched one prahu tack into the wind. As it began turning into the next leg of its zigzag, the man at the prow luffed the sail and passed it to the two men in the middle, who passed it to the helmsman, who had stowed the broad paddle he was using as a rudder. The helmsman attached the sail to the other end of their boat, so that when the wind caught it they were now going rear end first, on a course at an angle to the previous one. The first man took out his own paddle and began steering with it: what had been the bow was now the stern. These boats could sail with either end forward. Those men could reverse roles very smoothly, so that tacking into the wind was done faster than by turning the boat hard left or hard right. All those prahus sailed in that fashion, those men disdaining to use their paddles for rowing, for they were adept at making the wind work for them. Then several of them were crowding around the *Trinidad*.

I looked back, and saw the *Concepción* and the *Victoria* keeping well back, at the entrance to the bay.

The natives were agile, and were soon clambering up the side onto the deck.

They wore nothing but bark breechclouts and palmleaf hats. They were tall, as tall as white men, and had well-formed bodies. Some wore short beards, others were beardless. All had long hair, usually reaching down to the waist. Their teeth were red from habitually chewing betel.

Their lances were tipped with sharp points that we later found to be of fishbone, and they carried clubs in which rows of shark teeth had been embedded. They had no metal. They were a primitive people indeed, and I was still far from home. These people had never yet had intercourse with a culture that possessed metal, not even with the Xanglei.

They swarmed all over the deck like children who had found a new playground. Much to our surprise, they began taking our things: buckets, rope coils, block and tackle equipment, an old shoe, nails, trenchers, oakum. Their concept of ownership seemingly was of the most primitive type: what anyone could pick up was his. Our men motioned them off. They shoved their way forward.

One of them happened to push our maestre, Juan Bautista de Punzorol. Giddy from starvation and incipient scurvy, Punzorol fell down heavily. They laughed at how weak we were, and went on picking up everything in sight. Marineros rushed to confront them, but were no match for them.

Dom Fernão signalled to two men at the ready on the quarterdeck. The crossbowman let loose, and an arrow buried itself to the haft in the leading native's chest, its point sticking out of his back. He let out a hideous cry, then pulled the arrow out with his hand. I marvelled at his strength. No ordinary man could have pulled it out like that. Then the man expired on deck.

A blast from the harquesbusman. Another native down. The crossbowman again, but the natives, yelling and screaming in terror, were jumping over the side and swimming to their boats.

The halberdiers moved in. One native was taken prisoner.

As the rabble paddled off, we saw that they had the *Trinidad*'s batel in tow.

"What thieves they be," said my master. "They cut the batel's tow rope and stole it from right under our noses!"

I detected a note of admiration in his voice.

"I was going to call this the Isla de Velas Latinas," he said, but now I think I'll call it the Isla de Ladrones."

We jilled about in the bay all night, with the watches doubled. The Captain-General summoned a council, and they began planning an assault on the town on the morrow.

I attempted to talk to the prisoner, but his answers consisted of grunts and words I could not understand. For the fourth time in the voyage, I was utterly useless as an interpreter.

Master Andrew lay in sick bay, elated at having reached land. If he was disappointed at our failure to procure any fresh food, he did not show it.

"Nail the bloody chaps...smite them with fire and brimstone..." he told Dom Fernão, but speaking had become a painful effort and he fell back, exhausted.

At dawn that day, March 7, 1521, a crescent moon rose in the east: so thin it could hardly be seen, the waning moon a mere day from death and rebirth.

With only two batels available, we could not form a landing party as numerous as the first one, the one at the Río Solis. The Captain-General, fully armored, led the force of forty men, twenty in each batel. I was at his side, wearing breastplate armor. At his other side was Ser Antonio, in full armor.

As our batels pushed off, the bombarderos opened fire and began raining artillery on the town. Hans Vargue of the *Concepción* directed the operations, having gone to the capitana to take Master Andrew's place as condestable de bombarderos. We had begun the voyage with fourteen bombarderos. Rojer du Pict had drowned in the Puerto San Julián; Jorge Alemán had died of illness in the Río Santa Cruz; Maître Jacques and Juan Jorge had been in the *San Antonio* when that ship disappeared in the Strait of All Saints. That left ten, and with Master Andrew very sick, there were only nine of them to man the cannon, three to each ship—just enough. All of them were assisted by marineros or grumetes who had shown the aptitude for these weapons.

We found the village deserted. It was the first time we had been on land since the Río Sardinas in the Strait of All Saints, exactly one hundred days before. Walking on land again was a strange sensation.

There was blood on the ground. The bombarderos had found their marks, but the natives had carried away their dead or wounded as they fled. We raided their huts. Every house had a pile of rootcrops I recognized as gabi, or taro, and kamoti, ubi, small beans, squash, and bananas. Many also had earthen pots in which cooked meat or fish was stored. And every hut had livestock, chickens and pigs as well as small dogs. Most of us were so hungry we wolfed down food as soon as we found it. The Captain-General quickly restored order. All food was to be taken to the batels. We would all eat together, on shipboard.

Houses that had been ransacked were put to the torch. Soon the whole town was in flames. We quickly transferred food and earthen jars of drinking water to the batels. The sobresaliente Antón de Escovár, the marinero Juanes de Segura, and the criados Rodrigo Nieto and Pedro de Valpuesta, late of the *San Antonio* all four of them, had located the *Trinidad*'s stolen batel. It was dragged to the shore to be loaded with food as well.

Eight men had been left to guard the batels, four to each boat, and so these batels were ready to return to the ships as soon as the food supplies had been loaded.

As the first two batels began moving out, the natives emerged from hiding and ran whooping to their prahus in pursuit of us. Several of them were cut down by our crossbows and harquebuses, but still they kept coming.

The *Trinidad*'s batel was still hugging the shore, and we turned to face our adversaries. Dom Fernão and Ser Antonio each cut down a native with their swords. The others began running away. A native emerged from behind a bush and rushed the Captain-General. Antón de Escovár displayed the reflexes of a cat. He fended off the thrust in the nick of time. Then the two of them were at it like gladiators in a coliseum. Don Antón's swordsmanship was not only a fine display of valor, it was also an exercise in gracia worthy of a Spanish hidalgo. The native fought very well. Don Antón feinted, and the native reacted. A spot was left unguarded for an instant; Don Antón had anticipated this opening. He made a clean thrust, and the duel was suddenly over.

We rowed out in our recovered batel, laden with water jars and food, and returned to the *Trinidad*.

As we moved out of the bay, dozens of lateen-sailed prahus sped out after us. Some of them sailed around our ships in circles, the men in them shaking their fists at us and calling out imprecations we could not understand.

Dom Fernão ordered us to hold our fire. There was nothing those ladrones could do, and my master felt no need to kill any more of them. Our sails were picking up the wind now, and soon the outriggered canoes were far behind us.

I attended to our prisoner. He motioned for the leg irons to be taken off. We were too far for him to swim back, so I unshackled him. He seemed grateful for that, and once more I applied myself to the task of talking to him. My worth as interpreter had yet to be proven. I had been unable to understand the language spoken in the Río de Janeiro, but at least there Carvalho had taken over as interpreter. I had been just as ineffectual with the languages used in the Río Solis and in Patagonia. Now, for the fourth time, I had to admit failure. The islander's language was gibberish to my ears.

Ser Antonio spoke to him in slow, measured words combined with much gesturing. His words were counterpointed by the shrieks of a pig and several pullets. Down in the bilge the men were slaughtering those animals. Soon we would be feasting on pork and chicken.

"Umatak," the man said. We took that to be the name of his island.

"Guam," he said. Eventually, by sign language, he made himself understood. Umatak was the name of his village, the town we had raided. Guam was the island's name.

"Rota," he said, pointing to the island next to Guam.

"Tinian," indicating the third island, far off to the north, barely visible in the distance.

Ser Antonio spoke to him again, in measured words and eloquent gestures. I myself, watching him, was much impressed. Only the Italians could gesture so gracefully.

The captive began talking, this time with the sureness of gesture Ser Antonio had given him.

In his land they worshipped no gods save those of the sea, the sun, the trees, and the winds. Their men worked the fields, while their women wove baskets and sails. Their women wore barkcloth around the waist, and had hair that reached down to the ground. They put cocoanut oil on their hair and on their bodies. Their houses were of wood, their roofs of banana leaves. The floors were of the same wood they used for their walls. The houses had windows. Palmleaf mats were strewn on their floors, and they rolled out more of these mats for sleeping on.

What did they call themselves? gestured Ser Antonio.

"Chamorro," the man said, pointing to his stomach.

"Omatu," he said, pointing again to himself. Soon we understood. His name was Omatu, and he belonged to the race of the Chamorros.

Dom Fernão took the first bowl of chicken broth and brought it to the sick bay to personally spoonfeed Master Andrew. Ser Antonio and Hans Vargue came along, each with his own bowl of soup, from which they fed the other sick men. The page Juan Gutiérrez de Villasevil was there, as was the pilot Juan Rodríguez de Mafra. One never knew who would be stricken with the escorbuto next.

"The guns all fired well, Meister Andreas," Hans Vargue told Master Andrew. "No duds at all. We hit most of our targets on the first attempt. We missed three or four times but even these served their purpose. We corrected our aim by them."

"No duds?" whispered Master Andrew, too weak to even raise his head. "Not bad, eh?"

I knew enough to know that, under the nonchalant words, Maestro Hance was paying tribute to Master Andrew's supervisory work as condestable. Under Master Andrew the guns had been periodically cleaned and regularly tested. Their calibrations had been fine-tuned. The powder and fuse ropes had been kept dry through the humidity of the tropics, a long winter in Patagonia, and many storms.

The bombarderos too had been honed into effective teams, very sharp in such matters as adjusting the elevation, finding the range, and correcting for the wind. And now, in battle, both the cannon and the bombarderos had performed as they were supposed to.

This was only the second time the cannon had been used in battle. The first time had been against the cannibals of the Río Solis. Master Andrew must have been greatly disappointed at being unable to direct the firing this time, but his services had proven their worth. Considering the number of shots fired, a few duds would have been normal. No duds was extraordinary.

My master and the others were going, and I turned to follow them.

"Henry..." came the faint whisper. I turned back to Master Andrew. He held something in his hand.

"Here, keep it," he said. "I wanted to give it to Don Fernan, but he doesn't need it. He's made landfall in this uncharted ocean. He knows how to navigate."

"What is it?"

"A solarstein...I mean piedra del sol. A sunstone. My mother gave it to me when I ran away from home to sail with John Cabot. Said it was handed down in her family from a Viking ancestor. The Vikings used that stone to find the sun. Works best when the sky is overcast. It's translucent. Turn it this way and that until it turns opaque."

He winked a puffy eye at me.

"Now I want you to learn a poem and recite it with me."

I listened, read his lips, and recited after him all at the same time. My memory was good, but we went over it three times before he was satisfied:

> Nu scylun hergan hefænricaes uard, metudæs maecti end his modgidanc,
> uerc uuldurfadur, sue he uundra gihuaes, eci dryctin, or astelidae;
> he ærist scop aelda barnum heben til hrofe, haleg scepen.
> Tha middungeard moncynnæs uard, eci dryctin, æfter tiadæ firum foldu,
> frea allmectig.

"A comfort to speak ye olde Englishe once more," he said.
"What does it mean?"
"Oh, it's an old poem," he said, "by a peasant named Cædmon. The Venerable Bede calls him the first English poet."
He closed his eyes, fell asleep. All that talk had drained him.

The next island could not be far off. Friday, March 8, was a day of lazy sailing, nibbling all the while on the food we had taken from Umatak. It had been years since I last tasted gabi and kamoti, and their piquant flavors awakened memories of home, emphasized how near my native land was now.

On Saturday, March 9, 1521, Master Andrew of Bristol died of his illness. We spent the rest of the day and the whole night mourning him. There was no moon at all; it was one night past new moon. Just before sunrise on March 10, when we were due to bury him at sea, Hans Vargue requested the Captain-General for permission to fire the cannon in salute to Master Andrew.

Dom Fernão hesitated. It was a breach of protocol, as the Englishman had not belonged to the nobility, whether in his native country or in his adopted one.

"He cared well for his cannon," Dom Fernão said after a moment. "It is only fitting that they be fired one last time for him."

He turned to face Hans Vargue.

"A broadside from each ship."

At break of day on March 10, 1521, the fourth Sunday of Lent, we consigned Master Andrew of Bristol to his Maker at latitude

13° North, some two hundred leguas west of Guam. As Juan Bautista de Mompeller and Guillermo Tañegui heaved the canvas-shrouded body overboard, the *Trinidad* fired a broadside in salute. The splash of the corpse as it hit the water was louder than anticipated; the *Concepción* had fired her guns at that instant. The canvas, white against the blue of the sea, seemed to hover on the surface in defiance of the laws of buoyancy. Then the blast of the *Victoria*'s cannon, and Master Andrew went on his way, merging with the waves before the eye could see that he was gone.

31

A SEASON OF FAIR WINDS and clear skies. Moon coming out at evening, very thin. Course west by south, fair wind giving us five or six knots. Old-fashioned latitude sailing, keeping to 13°N. Easier to sail west by south rather than west, because of the northeast wind. We could coast down to 10°N if need be, make our way back to 13°N when the wind slackened.

March 12 was the day of the vernal æquinox, as best as Andrés de San Martín could determine. The hours of daylight were equal to the hours of night, and from then on the days would become longer until the summer solstice on June 12.

On March 13 clouds rode the winds overhead, so that the sky was overcast. I took out Master Andrew's sunstone. Fitting my palm nicely, it was a translucent disc, made of whitish stone, and cut to show the grain to best advantage. I turned it this way and that, noting how it remained translucent. Suddenly it turned opaque, and I realized it was receiving the sun's light full in the face.

Soon the clouds drifted off. The sunstone still worked, turning opaque when it faced the sun. The wondrous thing was that it seemed to work much better in an overcast.

On Friday, March 15, we began to see signs of imminent land. There were a few birds far off, flying westward. Bits of leaves and twigs floated by on the water. That evening, as soon as it was dark enough, streaks of te lapa appeared. The moon was now at first quarter, and it hung right in front of us, so that the te lapa was somewhat hard to see. But not for someone on the lookout for it. We were about to reach land in the East by having gone west.My master would be vindicated.

How different it had been in the measly years! Between his loss of a command in 1513 and his appointment as a King's Captain-General in 1518 he had aged considerably more than the five years that had elapsed on the calendar. Those years had affected me, too, yet I remembered them mostly as a blur...

Shortly after our arrival in Lisbōa in 1513, Dom Fernão reports to the palace, where he is still a member of the royal household...
He finds his old listing as junior squire unchanged. In all the time he has been away, it has not been updated. He has been forgotten completely. Had he stayed, he would have been promoted in due time to gentleman-in-waiting, and then to cavaleiro fidalgo. Time spent close to the center of power in the royal court assures promotion better than time spent fighting for the King in distant lands.

By now he is too old to be still a squire. It is disgraceful.

We take passage on a caravel and sail north to the port of Viana do Castelo in Minho. Then we hire horses and ride to his brother Diogo da Sousa in the old donjon keep, the Torre de Magalhanes, in the town of Ponte de Barca. Dom Diogo lives there with his wife and two children, and Isabel, his unmarried youngest sister.

While living in that drafty castle, I accompany my master to Ponte de Lima. There we find that Pero Anes Abraldes has died. His inheritor, his father Abraham, is away in Galicia.

The two brothers go to see their cousin João de Magalhanes, the Lord of Ponte de Barca, at Paço Vedro. Dom João's wife, Ysabel da Sousa, is a distant relative of theirs. The talk is of inconsequential matters; everyone has heard that Dom Fernão was repatriated by Viceroy d' Alboquerque for cause, but no one is so tactless as to mention anything of this.

My master and I go over the mountains to Sabrosa to see his sister Tereza, who is married to Dom João da Sylva Tellez, Lord of the Casa Pereira da Sabrosa. While in Sabrosa, Dom Fernão also visits the vineyard he owns there. He accepts a cask of vinho verde from the tenant.

Back in Ponte de Lima, he hires a lawyer, his kinsman Duarte da Sousa. They outline their strategy: they will move to sequester any spices in the Casa da Índia accruing to the account of the Abraldes estate.

Returning to Ponte de Barca, we find a royal order promoting Dom Fernão to the rank of gentleman-in-waiting. It is a sop, nothing more.

We go to call on the family's feudal lord, the Archbishop of Braga. Perhaps His Eminence can put in a word to the King about promoting Dom Fernão to cavaleiro fidalgo. The Archbishop is not there; he is in Lisbõa. Moreover, we soon learn it is the Archbishop of Lisbõa who actually holds the reins of power, despite the Archbishop of Braga's being the Primate of Portugal. The Archbishop of Lisbõa is Dom Manoel's son Alonso, who had become a cardinal at the age of seven.

The short hot summer of 1513 descends on Minho Province. Captain João Serrão arrives from Cananor, glad to be home after seven years, his third voyage to the East. He was in Vasco da Gama's armada in 1502, and in d'Alboquerque's in 1506. Now he presents a letter to the King from Duarte Barbosa. In it, Barbosa complains about Goa being made the capital of the Estado da Índia to the detriment of Cochin and Cananor.

It is a mistake to criticize Viceroy d'Alboquerque, even indirectly. Later that year Captain Serrão quietly slips across the border to Spain, where he finds employment as a piloto de Su Alta.

My master goes to see influential people who might help advance his career: his old Captain-General Diogo Lopes de Sequeira, under whom he first sailed to Malacca, and the Royal Factors he first met in Cochin, Dom Antão Real and Dom Lourenço Moreno.

No one can help him.

He hires a scrivener to draw up a formal document petitioning His Majesty for preferment and elevation to the rank of cavaleiro fidalgo. To be granted an audience, he follows the old ritual of begging to kiss his sovereign's hand. The audience is duly granted, and the document formally presented. All decorum is observed. Dom Manoel likes having men beg the favor of kissing his hand. His answer to the petition will of course take some time. After a few weeks, it becomes apparent that no reply is forthcoming.

Talk of war charges the air. The Sheik of Azamor in the Marruecos, a Berber named Mulei Ziyam, has not paid his yearly tribute.

Now he taunts the King of Portugal to come and collect it. Dom Fernão, *faute de mieux*, volunteers for the campaign. He is accepted as a cavalryman in the Ponte de Barca contingent. His brother Diogo buys him a horse. Portugal assembles a huge armada of 400 ships for an army of 2,000 horse and 20,000 foot. In command is Jayme, Duke of Bragança, Dom Manoel's nephew.

We sail from Lisbõa on August 13, 1513. The Pilot-Major of the armada, João de Lisbõa, makes Dom Fernão his assistant. We take two weeks to sail to Morocco. Once there, João de Lisbõa presents my master to the Proconsul of Africa, Count João de Meneses, who will act as General-in-Chief of the army. Meneses will direct the war as field marshall for the Portuguese forces, which include a detachment of Spanish volunteers and German mercenaries; Dom Jayme is of course but a figurehead.

My master fights valiantly. In one battle, his horse is killed under him. In another, while storming the enemy walls in March 1514, he is wounded in the knee. This wound leaves him with a permanent limp.

Horseless and lame, he is appointed, while still recuperating, to the post of Quadrilheiro-Mor. There are only two such quadrilheiros for the whole army, and they have charge of the prisoners and the booty. The plunder by this time has come up to some 200,000 head of cattle and 3,000 camels and horses. There are several hundred prisoners of war. Opportunities abound. As a matter of policy livestock is sold to the desert tribes as soon as possible; prisoners are ransomed or sold as slaves. A quadrilheiro who knows how to doctor the records can keep a large share of the money for himself. Dom Fernão's appointment as Quadrilheiro-Mor is no accident: Conde Meneses has sized him up as a man of rare honesty.

Meneses falls ill and dies suddenly in May of 1514. Just when Dom Fernão has found himself a new patron, death cheats him of that lord's favor, as death snatched Viceroy d'Almeida away.

The new General-in-Chief, Dom Pedro da Sousa, accuses him of selling 400 horses back to the enemy. The charge is so ludicrous that Dom Fernão packs up and sails for Lisbõa in a huff.

In Lisbõa he is reimbursed for the loss of his horse. He does not mention the silly charge to anyone.

In September of 1514 his lawyer procures a court order for the sequestration of spices the Casa da Índia might owe the Abraldes estate.

Dom Fernão seeks an audience with the King, hoping to interest him in a venture to sail to Ternate and join Francisco Serrão. Cristobal de Haro, he knows, is eager to finance such a voyage. Dom Pedro da Sousa, however, has written to Dom Manoel from Morocco. The King dismisses the subject of sailing to the East, reprimands Dom Fernão for deserting the army, and orders him to report back to Dom Pedro to face the charges.

Back to Morocco we sail. Dom Fernão resumes his post. No one seems interested in conducting a trial. There is a war on. Dom Fernão confronts his superior officers and demands to be put on trial.

The first charge is that of having enriched himself in office; the second, that of selling horses to the enemy. Both are dropped for lack of evidence. The verdict: acquittal. The judge's written decision, however, describes the charges as "not proved." Somehow, it attempts to imply that Dom Fernão was actually guilty, but managed to eradicate the evidence. The unfairness of it, laying a stigma on a person who had been honest all along, makes a deep impression on me.

Dom Fernão secures a formal discharge from the army. We return to Lisbõa, where he resumes the post of gentleman-in-waiting. Again he applies for an audience with the King. He is pointedly ignored.

How best to plead his case before Dom Manoel?

The traditional right to make supplication before the King is accorded to all, but not everyone can gain a private audience. And so every now and then the King condescends to give a public audience, when even the humblest of his subjects has the chance to lay a petition at his feet. That is exactly what always happens. Peasants from distant villages all push into the hall: churls, villeins, serfs—come one, come all. They are a sight to behold. These uncouth yokels comport themselves very seriously, unaware of how comic they appear to the old hands at the court. On such occasions the hall always fills up with nobles, courtiers, and servants of the royal household, all ready to enjoy the show.

After a few peasants have approached the King, Dom Fernão suddenly shows up at the entrance. A hush falls over the hall. He starts limping forward. Murmurs fill the air. Dom Manoel frowns. Dom Fernão kneels before the King, and humbly requests that his moradía, his monthly allowance, be increased by one tostão.

That is the difference between a gentleman-in-waiting's allowance and a cavaleiro fidalgo's. The tostão is a silver coin worth a trifle, but behind that negligible difference is a great increase in rank. From gentleman-in-waiting to cavaleiro fidalgo is as big a step up the ladder as from priest to bishop. Asking for the increase is the accepted euphemism by which one asks for the promotion.

"No," Dom Manoel says. "The request cannot be granted."

"M-may I then," stammers Dom Fernão, still on bended knee, "serve Your Majesty as before, and command a caravel to the Spiceries?"

"No, that is not possible. In fact, I have no opening anywhere for your services."

"May I sail with your license on a private ship?"

"No. No!"

It is the repetition that stings. He gets to his feet, and cries out:

"Do I have Your Majesty's permission to seek service under another seigneur?"

The King rises from his throne and stands in front of the supplicant. He is taller, and the dais gives him the advantage of another three steps. I note with wonder how long Dom Manoel's arms are: they reach almost to his knees, like those of the jungle animal we call the orang utan.

"I don't care where you go! Now get out of here!"

Dom Fernão bows.

"Your Majesty, I beg one last boon. May I kiss your hand before I go?"

Dom Manoel instinctively pulls back his hand, then turns his back and walks away. As Dom Fernão retreats down the aisle, someone calls out:

"Walking like a lame duck never helps!"

Laughter resounds throughout the hall.

His humiliation complete, there is nothing left for him in Portugal...but that had been so long ago, on the other side of the world. Now, as dawn broke, I waited for the call to come from the grumete up in the gavia. It was Saturday, March 16, 1521. Dom Fernão kept gazing at the horizon ahead, even before the sun was up.

Now and then I would look, too. As the sky grew lighter I could see that the clouds in the distance were piled up the way they would be over an island. My master must have seen it, too.

"Land ho!" said the grumete Blas de Toledo up in the crow's nest.

We watched it grow bigger.

The whole crew went through the ritual of morning prayers with unusual fervor. After a quick breakfast the Captain-General went to visit the sick: the pilot Juan Rodrigues de Mafra, the sobresaliente Martín Barrena, the merino Juan de Aroche, the page Gutiérrez de Villasevil. The first three responded to his ministrations. But when he got to Villasevil there was no response; the young page had expired during the night. We bundled him up for burial at sea.

Dom Fernão continued grimly with his duties. He boarded the batel and visited the sick aboard the *Concepción*: the sobresaliente Juan Villalon, and the prisoner Don Antonio de Coca. From there he went to the *Victoria* to visit the pilot Baltazar de Genovés, and the grumete Ochot de Randia.

An endless sea. Wave after wave rolled by my eye, each wave lasting but a second. Year after year rushed through my mind, each as fleeting as a single wave, each worth but the wink of an eye...

December of 1514...my master files action in court versus the Abraldes estate.

June 1515...case decided in his favor.

July 1515..executes a power of attorney...authorizes Duarte da Sousa to collect payment from the heirs and assigns of the late Pero Anes Abraldes.

News from Spain...three Portuguese pilots petitioning the King, Don Fernando, for command of an armada to search for the Strait of Anian... João Dias de Solis, Ruy Golez and Estêvão Gomes...Solis a fugitive from justice...murdered his wife in Portugal, a crime of passion...Solis wins the appointment, is named Captain-General...the fleet of three caravels sails that October.

November...200 cruzados paid in Ponte de Lima to Duarte da Sousa...Dom Fernão has finally doubled his money...took him three years and a lawsuit.

Early in 1516...meets Ruy de Faleiro for the first time. As Faleiro has a baccalaureate degree from the Universidade do Coimbra, Duarte Barbosa introduces him as "el bachiller"...a cosmographer, celestial navigator, author of *Regimento da Altura de Leste-Oeste*. He gives Dom Fernão a copy of his book. They sit down and talk for hours, drinking vinho de verde.

João de Lisbõa comes to Porto, tells of his secret voyage the previous year...captain of the second caravel under Captain-General Sebastião Frões, looking for the Strait of Anian...down the coast of Brasil at 35°S was a cape...the Cabo Santa María. A headland at the mouth of a wide river...or at the entrance to a strait. Further exploration needed, but João thought the paso might be found there...sailed home ahead of Frões, who stopped in the Caribs to repair his capitana.

Summer, 1516...we learn de Solis has been killed and eaten by cannibals in the bay past the Cabo Santa María.

Cristóbal de Haro has fled Portugal, returned to his native town of Burgos in Spain. De Haro sent goods on every Portuguese armada and received spices and jewels as return cargo...bribed the factors to smuggle in his consignments from Índia and avoid paying customs duties...Dom Manoel sent an armada to attack and sink a fleet de Haro had dispatched to Índia.

The year 1517 mostly a hazy time...Duarte Barbosa arranging myriad details for Dom Fernão's move to Spain. Duarte's father, Dom Diogo, sits on the Casa's board and is a Knight of Santiago...

October 1517...Dom Fernão finally makes the move, boards a ship for Sevilla. With him are his cousin Álvaro de Mesquita, his nephew Cristóvão Rabelo, the pilots João Rodrigues de Mafra and Basco Gallego, and his slaves.

⚓

32

A NEW LIFE...from now on he is Don Fernando de Magallánes. He speaks the Castillian tongue well enough. I have to learn this new language, a bother, but not so hard for someone with a memory like mine.

A new wife...Dom Fernão is formally engaged to Beatriz de Barbosa é Caldeira, Duarte's sister...the wedding is set for December 6, 1517, the dowry at 600,000 maravedis. The penniless years are over.

A new King, too. Don Fernando Quinto died last year, leaving the crown to his grandson, a Hapsburg prince...Spain has waited a year and more for Charles of Ghent to come from Flanders. The boy King, whom the Spanish call Don Cárlos Primero, arrived at last in September 1517...the second-rate navigators on his ship missed Spain's chief ports and landed him on Villa Viciosa, a fishing village in Asturias.

A legacy of complicated arrangements, the Spanish monarchy. Ysabel and Fernando ruled different kingdoms, uniting those with their marriage; Ysabel at her death in 1504 was succeeded as Queen of León and Castilla by their daughter Juana...Fernando, still King of Aragon, continued as King of Spain as well.

Juana married the Austrian prince, Philip the Fair, and their union produced Charles du Gänd, or Charles of Ghent. When Felipe el hermoso was poisoned to death Juana went mad...refused to bury him...ordered the coffin opened, whereupon she kissed his feet...a Carthusian monk had assured her that fervent prayer would resurrect Felipe.

She went on a tour of her realm, with a full royal entourage and Felipe in his coffin on a horsedrawn cart, seeking a place where he might be inspired to return to life...a jealous wife: no other woman, not even a nun, could go near her husband...she continued to talk to him, entreating him to delay no further, to come back to life soon...

With Doña Juana unfit to rule, Don Fernando made his grandson his successor. Now Don Cárlos alone rules, but on paper he is merely King of Aragon...only by a joint monarchy with his mother may he be styled King of a united Yspaña...as soon as Juana la Loca was persuaded to bury her husband, Bishop Fonseca ensconced her in a castle in Medina del Campo...Felipe was buried in Granada, as he had specified...now Don Cárlos rules as both halves of the monarchy...

November 1517...Dom Fernão goes to the Casa, sees three officials...only one shows any interest. Juan de Aranda says he has the commission to enter into agreements and contracts with those who would discover new lands...doubts if the King will sponsor two Portuguese...Aranda proposes to send them on a private venture, in return for a fifth of the profits...Dom Fernão is uncertain of how much authority Aranda has...as soon as Faleiro arrives in Sevilla the two of them will go and see the King...Aranda says no, he has written the Grand Chancellor, Chièvres, regarding them, and they should await the reply first.

December 6, 1517...my master's wedding to Beatriz at the Cathedral...the best man is Ruy de Faleiro... the newly married couple moves into rooms in the Alcázar.

January 20, 1518...off to Valladolid to see the new King...as yet no reply from Chièvres, but nothing to be gained by passive waiting...the Faleiros, Ruy and his brother Francisco, are travelling with us on funds lent them by Aranda...we join the cavalcade of the Duquesa de Arcos...safety in numbers, for brigands infest the highways and mountain passes.

A joyous time, mild winter of clear skies and crisp air, the entire party singing as the wagons roll along...my master and his lovely bride cantering side by side on their horses...I ride an old bony nag, easier to handle than a water buffalo or an elephant. We pass through beautiful country, great rolling plains, walled towns built around old alcázars or churches with tall spires, farmhouses with windmills, brooks hidden by copses of trees. The Sierra de Guadarrama, Álmaden, Córdoba, Toledo,

Segovia...a kingdom without a capital. The Spanish pride themselves a nation of warriors; their monarch must comport himself like a tribal chieftain on the move...their great cause the wars of religion. Ysabel and Fernando held court wherever they happened to be, wandering around their domains like Moses leading the Israelites in the desert. The new King, a romantic at heart, will continue the tradition. Today, Valladolid. Tomorrow, Zaragoza. Then Cerdaña. Ruysellon. Barcelona. Granada. Then perhaps some mean town like Madrid...

In Medina del Campo, we find Juan de Aranda waiting for us...he wants $\frac{1}{5}$ of the profits in return for the services he will provide, promoting the sailing venture and acquiring financial backing...Faleiro offers $\frac{1}{10}$. They haggle...all very acrimonious. Finally they agree on $\frac{1}{8}$, but only if the King declines to sponsor their voyage, and then only if Aranda invests 2,000 ducats in the venture...they shake hands on that understanding. Aranda leaves for Valladolid ahead of us...we push on through Simancas. The cavalcade's pace is very slow, but having started out with the Duquesa's party we must complete the journey together with her...in mid-February we reach Valladolid. Aranda arrives, too...insists on committing their agreement to writing... on February 23 the contract is duly notarized.

"Know all ye who shall see this public testament that we, Rui Faller, citizen of Cunilla in the Kingdom of Portugal, and Fernando de Magallánes, citizen of the city of Puerto in the same Kingdom, consent, make manifest, and declare that...it has been agreed between us...and you, Juan de Aranda, citizen of the city of Búrgos and Factor for the King our Lord in the Casa de Contratación de las Índias of the city of Sevilla...that of all gain and income pertaining to us from the discovery of lands and islands (which if God wills we are to find...in the demarcations of our Master the King, Don Cárlos) you shall have the eighth part. And we shall give this to you from all the income and gain accruing to us therefrom, whether in money, allotment, or rent, or by virtue of our office, or in anything else whatsoever, of whatever quantity and quality, without any shortage, and without deducting or excepting anything whatever of our possessions."

Is it too late? The King, we hear, has given Estêvão Gomes a royal commission.

The King sees Gomes. We hear about it soon after: unsatisfactory...Gomes perceived as a pirate asking to go to the Spice Islands and poach in Portuguese territory...the King, betrothed to Donha Isabel, Dom Manoel's sister, has no wish to impose on the domains of his future brother-in-law...

Bishop Fonseca notifies Aranda: capitán Fernando de Magallánes and el bachiller Rui Falero to be evaluated by the Royal Council prior to being granted an audience with the King.

Aranda takes them before the Council.

Behold, two very elated men. Over dinner they recount the interview to Beatriz and Francisco. Ruy Faleiro is a good mimic.

"Ladies and gentlemen, it is my honor to present the Royal Council...Bishop Fonseca and three Flemings. His Excellency Guillaume du Croix, Lord of Chièvres, the Grand Chancellor. His Eminence, Cardinal Adrian Florensz of Utrecht, the Archbishop of Brugge. Both men are very close to the King. They were his tutors. The honorable, or is it dishonorable, Jean le Sauvaige, the Treasurer, known as 'der Niederlander'..."

Aranda extolled Faleiro's eminence as cosmographer, displayed Ruy's book...outlined Don Fernando's campaigns in the East and in the Marruecos. Emphasized that Magallánes left Portugal with Don Manuel's consent, and Don Manuel's permission to enter the service of another lord. Dom Fernão asked to clarify why the Spice Islands lie in Spain's side of the Tordesillas demarcation line...Cardinal Adrian quite assured that both of them were devout men. Not the sort to violate a Papal Bull...not the kind of men who would poach. Rather both were dreamers, men who understood Spain's destiny as a bringer of light to the Terra Poniente, the Far West...

March 22, 1518...the great day. We are ushered into the royal presence...the thin young King, too young to grow a beard, strokes a falcon perched on his wrist...greets Dom Fernão as one warrior to another...interested in the tactics used against the enemy in the Marruecos...Don Cárlos attempts to speak Spanish...soon reverts to French...still, the interpreter is not needed. Dom Fernão can understand the King well enough.

Dom Fernão admires the King's peregrine falcon. In Morocco he once took a hawk from a sheik he had killed in battle...bad-tempered, like its owner. He himself always hunted with a gyrfalcon...no bird is nobler than the eagle, but only kings may hunt with eagles...has His Majesty thought of acquiring an eagle?

Cardinal Adrian coughs politely. Chièvres and Sauvaige look expectantly at the petitioners. Bishop Fonseca nods at my master. Dom Fernão begins...how they have determined, from Ruy de Faleiro's studies and from his own navigational observations in Malacca and the Java Seas, that the Spice Islands lie in the Spanish zone...he shows their exhibits: Faleiro's book...Francisco Serrão's letters...the *Itinerario* of Varthema, written in Italian, with its description of Ternate and Tidore...the sphere made by Pedro Reynal, depicting Maluco in the Spanish half of the world...another sphere, by Martín of Bohemia, the one "borrowed" from Dom Manoel's chartroom in Lisbõa, with a blank space where the Strait of Anian is supposed to be...the mappamundo made by Martin Waldseemüller in 1516, showing the short distance from Terra Incognita to Çipangu and Iaua Maior...saving the best for last, his final exhibit is a live specimen of a creature from the Orient...me.

I recite a stirring speech in the Malay language, actually bits of my race's tarsila...what I could remember. To my ears I sound exactly like my father:

"*Sa tungâ gayud sa kalibutan ang bukid sa Meru, nagabarug sa kataás nga napulo'g walo ka libu ka parasang, nakasaghid na ganì sa buwan...*"

The strange words and my histrionics seem to have a magical effect on them. I continue:

"*Near Meru the people of our race founded their first kingdom, the Kingdom of Funan, in the year Vikrama 35 of the true calendars...*"

Dom Fernão's eyes alive with fervor, the boy King's lower lip drooling, Chièvres and Sauvaige looking on, Fonseca smirking, Cardinal Adrian smiling beatifically—

March 28, 1518...the cédula and the capitulación are promulgated. Both dated March 22...both now formal royal documents. In the cédula, *Doña Juana y Don Cárlos, por la gracia de Dios reyes de Castilla*...addressing *el bachiller Rui Falero and capitán Fernando de Magalhayns, hidalgos, natives of the kingdom of Portogal...* say that *inasmuch as we have ordered five ships to be armed, manned, provisioned and supplied with whatever is necessary...*

"It is our will and pleasure to hereby appoint you our captains of the said armada, and we give you the power and the authority to exercise said office from the time you set sail...until by the grace of our Lord you return to these kingdoms. You may and shall hold office as our captains on sea as well as on land...in everything and in all cases attached and pertinent to said office.

"We command...whomsoever the contents of this letter may concern in any way...that they regard, accept, and consider you as our captains of the said armada, and as such to obey and fulfill your commands under the penalty or penalties which you shall impose on our behalf and which we hereby impose and consider imposed...and grant you power and authority to execute those on their persons and properties.

[All are] to observe...the honors, favors, graces, privileges, exemptions and liberties, preeminences, prerogatives, and immunities that are due you as our captains...

"In case disputes or differences arise while you are on the said armada, be it on sea or on land, you may properly weigh, decide, and do what should be done, without question or doubt, that justice might be served. To decide and pass sentence on the said cases and for everything else contained in this letter of ours and all that are attached and pertinent to the said captainship, we bestow on you the power and authority to mete out justice, with all the implications and consequences attached to said office, as well as the obligations and responsibilities thereunto appertaining."

Signed by both Their Majesties, and endorsed by Johanes le Sauvaige, and Fonseca, archbishop and bishop. Registered with a notary named Juan de Samana. Sealed with Chièvres's mark, "Guilhermo, chancellor."

As for the capitulación, it is nothing short of astonishing...still essentially as it was drafted by the petitioners...reworded into elegant legal language by the King's escribano...signed by the King without further ado.

After charging Magallánes, *hidalgo from the kingdom of Portugal,* and Falero, *from the same kingdom,* to go and *discover islands and continents...within our boundaries, it promises that for the duration of ten years, no license will be granted anyone else to go and discover lands following the same course you will take.*

A very generous King, indeed:

"...it is our will and desire that in all the lands and islands you discover, whatever advantages or benefits would be derived from rentals or taxes after reducing costs and expenses, the twentieth part will accrue to you.

"You will have the title of gobernadores or adelantados of said lands and islands. This will pass on to your children and legal heirs forever...

"We likewise consent, and give license and authority, that from now on, every year, you may take or send to those lands...the equivalent of the amount of one thousand ducats in principal taxes due us, to spend for things which you think you can sell there...and to purchase what...you would want to take back to these kingdoms...leaving us the twentieth part of their amount as taxes...

"...it is our will and desire...that of those islands, after first choosing six for us, from the rest you may pick two from which you may have the fifteenth part of all profits and interests in rentals and taxes, after deducting costs...

"It is our desire and will, considering the expenses you will incur and the work you will put in during the trip, to grant you one-fifth of all the proceeds...of the first armada, after costs for outfitting the armada are deducted...

"And because it is our desire and will that you be protected...we grant that if in the said pursuit any of you should die, your aforementioned interests will be safeguarded by the survivors as completely as they would be protected if both of you were living..."

The usual seals and flourishes at the bottom, *fecha en Valladolid a XXIJ dias del mes de marzo, año de mjll quinientos & XVIIJ años.* An illegible scrawl above the words *yo el rey.* Below that, *por orden dEl Rey: Francisco de los Cobos.* Three more signatures, the escribano's and the two captains'....

The grandeur of it all quite overwhelms me: no competition for 10 years...$\frac{1}{20}$ of the revenue from all lands discovered...$\frac{1}{15}$ of the revenue from two islands of their choice...⅕ of the profits from the first Armada...privileged tax concessions...the right to invest 1,000 ducats per annum in future voyages...the title of adelantado. They will be joint viceroys, no less, and the title will be hereditary...and in perpetuity. The only thing lacking is the promise of some vainglorious title...Grand Admiral of the Mar del Sur ...or First Circumnavigator of the World...or Viceroy of the Terra Poniente...

The smell of perfidy...where does the stink come from? No, impossible. Bishop Fonseca is indeed a powerful man who knows how to arrange matters and manipulate people, including his monarch...but would he undermine this venture? scheme to gain the wealth of the Indies for himself?

April 1518...Fonseca convinces the King it is embarrassing that a Spanish Armada should be commanded by two Portuguese...an affront to the national pride. A third Captain-General is needed, a true son of Spain...Juan de Cartagena's name is floated. The King won't sign. Did he smell what I smelled?

We join the King's entourage. Aranda del Duero, Zaragoza, Barçelona...the Armada's departure is set for August 25...

Ruy Faleiro a thorn in the side...fumbles the simplest tasks, makes irrational demands...insists he be sole custodian of the royal flag during the voyage.

Dom Fernão, exasperated, is receptive when Fonseca whispers in his ear. Write to the King, suggests the Bishop, and request the relief of your co-Captain-General...a possible replacement is Cartagena. Masterful intrigue...Fonseca had played on Ruy's vanity and encouraged him to claim sole rights to the flag...manœuvered Dom Fernão into doing the dirty job himself.

Faleiro is quietly dropped. He resigns his shares in the capitulación. The Bishop has promised to have him named sole Captain-General of the next Armada...an elaborate fiction by Fonseca. No such second Armada is planned...but the Bishop is at leisure to help himself to Faleiro's shares...

The sudden resignation sparks rumors...Faleiro had consulted astrological charts and found they predicted dire fates for the men of the Armada...Fonseca abets the rumors. How simple it was to get Faleiro out of the way...how easy to hide behind plausible tales...

In May the date of departure is extended to December, as more time is needed to prepare the ships and hire crew members...we take leave of the royal court...back in Sevilla by June.

Dom Fernão arranges the purchase of five secondhand ships, a caravel and four naos, all requiring extensive restoration...shipwrights put to work under João Serrão...Duarte Barbosa sent to buy cannon in Bilbao, harquebuses and crossbows in Flanders...other men off to Cadiz to purchase ship's stores...

In July of 1518 the King dubs Dom Fernão a Knight Commander of the Order of Santiago de la Espada...a signal honor, one that Ysabel and Fernando never conferred on Cristovão Colom. Clearly, the King regards Dom Fernão as a favorite. Fonseca had recommended the knighthood...only because he saw that the King wanted to bestow it on the lame soldier.

The Bishop continues to intrigue...not against Dom Fernão, but against the men around him. Faleiro has been disposed of... Aranda is next, then Dom Diogo Barbosa...more delays...the Armada now to depart in May 1519...

Aranda's contract with Magallánes and Faleiro is cancelled...as it stood, Aranda would have had a legal claim to an eighth of the proceeds accruing to Dom Fernão under the terms of the royal capitulación...Aranda is accused of venality, of attempting to enrich himself in office...Aranda censured, an investigation launched...in October, Aranda is suspended. Now his share, too, will be swallowed up by Fonseca...

The Bishop approaches my master, reminds him how helpful he has been...he it was who arranged the audience with the King...who persuaded the King to confer the knighthood...doesn't el comendador think a share of the profits would be appropriate? Oh, say, *cincuenta por ciento*...a secret agreement, of course...the contract all drawn up, merely awaiting his signature...

The threat is implicit. If Dom Fernão won't sign, the Bishop will make things difficult for him...

"No."

Dom Diogo approves of his son-in-law's decision. Fonseca's attempt at extortion is odious, but only to be expected...the

Bishop has done it before, with João Dias de Solis in 1512...conferring on de Solis a Knighthood in the Order of Santiago, promising to make him Adelantado of any lands discovered...in return for half the gains...that voyage however was cancelled by the King, Don Fernando, for political reasons...

Life does indeed become more difficult...the absurd order limiting the number of Portuguese seamen to seven...the inclusion of the Spanish captains and their numerous servants...later that October, the silly incident...when the sight of my master's flags, with their quarterings of the quinas, gives agents provocateurs an opportunity to stoke the ire of the waterfront rabble...Sevilla never sleeps, has no trouble gathering a mob at 3 in the morning...but after that, after Dom Fernão complains about it to the King, everything becomes water under the bridge. The rest of the preparations go smoothly...

The Armada's crew complement still incomplete...not enough Spanish seamen can be found, although recruiting parties have gone as far afield as Galicia and the Basque provinces...Sevilla is full of mariners, but they know a voyage of this magnitude will be full of hardships...that many will not return. Only seventeen sevillanos sign up, most of them non-sailors from good families...as escribanos, sobresalientes, and pages. Dom Fernão asks the King to rescind the order limiting the number of Portuguese to seven...the King raises the maximum to twenty-four, twelve to be nominated by himself and twelve to be nominated by the Captain-General...Dom Fernão immediately hires thirty more Portuguese, bringing the total number of Lusitanians to thirty-seven...daring the Casa to protest. Bishop Fonseca, who knows when he has been beaten, says nothing.

Beatriz gives birth in November, and my master's cup overflows...the infant is named Rodrigo...the winter passes.

In April Dom Fernão receives a letter from the King.

"...my voluntad es que derechamente sigais el viage a las dhas islas por la forma e maña que lo he dicho e mandado a vos el dcho fernando de magallãins, porende yo vos mando."

It seems a mere formality, but of course the Spanish mind delights in belaboring all the legal nuances:

"...I order you, the said Fernando de Magallãins, to pursue a direct course to the above-mentioned islands, exactly as I have told and commanded you."

Much latitude, however, has been left him:

"...& despues De fecho esto se podra buscar lo demas que convenga conforme A lo q̃ lleuais mãdado & los unos nj los otros non fagadĩs njn fagan ende Al por alguna maña, so pena, dep dimỹ de biens e las p sonas a la nr̃a merced fecha en Barçelona a diez e nueve dias del mes de abril año de mjll quinientos & diez e nueve años.

Yo El Rey.

por mandado dEl Rey
Franco de los covos

pa q̃ los del armada sigan el pareçer y determynaçiõ de magallanes pa q̃ antĩs y pm̃o q̃ a otra pte vayã a la espeçierja.

Clearly, the King wants the spices loaded on the ships first, after which the Captain-General may do as he fancies:

"...& afterwards you may seek other suitable things, in accordance with your orders. & none of you shall act contrary to this our will, in any manner, under penalty of loss of property and life. Barçelona, date the nineteenth of April, year one thousand five hundred & nineteen.

I the King

by command of the King
Francisco de los Covos

[endorsed: in order that those sailing in the armada may heed the counsels and decisions of Magallanes, and that first and foremost, before other things, they sail to the spicerics]

An island was rising over the horizon. It was March 16, 1521, and we were at latitude 12°N, longitude unknown. By dead reckoning, we had sailed 4,000 leguas across the Mar Pacífico. In whose half of the world were we now? The question no longer seemed a matter of great concern. It remained only to be seen if these were the islands Dom Fernão was aiming for, the archipelago north of the Spice Islands and slightly west of their longitude.

I was sure they were. He had found them again, this time coming from the east. He had found them first in 1512, coming from the west, and kept them a secret, as that voyage had been unauthorized. Now he would discover them officially, as Captain-General of a royal Armada.

I was going home, and suddenly I dreaded it. I was a brown European now. I would see the old lands with the white man's eyes. A short spell among people of a culture I had left behind, no more. Then I would look forward to the return trip. I knew my master would manumit me after the voyage. After that, I would seek naturalization as a Spanish citizen. ¡Viva Yspaña!

33

AT HIGH NOON ON THAT DAY, March 16, the island was still very far away. Its mountains, visible from a great distance, had made it seem closer than it was. Now we saw that it stretched far to the north. Beyond was more land, hazy in the distance; impossible to tell if part of that island or of another. As we watched, the southern tip of that island gradually emerged as a separate island, cut off by a narrow channel. Farther south was a stretch of water, then eleven or twelve leguas beyond it another large island: beyond that strait, I felt sure, would be more islands.

Francisco Albo shot the sun: we were at latitude 12°N.

As the afternoon wore on we watched the big island gradually change color, from blue to green. We saw there was a small island at the entrance to the strait, a heavily wooded one three and a half leguas long. And then, as we came nearer, a small islet, just outside the strait, began to stand out prominently.

Five or six leguas from the large, mountainous island, at 11½°N, the Captain-General veered hard left, from west by south to due south, to make for the small but conspicuous islet. He was following the strategy he had learned in his years as a Portuguese conquistador: use the smallest island available. In East Africa, Kilwa Kisiwani and the Ilha do Moçambique; in Índia, Diu and Goa. All had been small islands.

The Captain-General did not intend to land on that islet. He merely wanted to anchor in its lee.

We took most of the afternoon to sail parallel to the large island for about fifteen leguas. As far as we could see, it had no good harbors. The small islet, the lone sentinel in front of the strait, grew more inviting as we neared. Its nearest neighbor, the wooded island just inside the strait, lay two and half leguas behind.

Men at the bow heaved down the sounding leads. The *Trinidad* led as we turned to follow the western coast of the islet, now falling into the shadows of dusk. A thin trail of smoke rose from it, from someone's fire. The sun dipped behind the mountains. A bright half-moon, a day past first quarter, hung in the cloudless sky. We lay at anchor, doubled the guard, and went to sleep beside our favorite weapons. Dom Fernão measured the elevation of the Pole Star and determined our latitude to be 10¾°N.

That night the islet showed a few lights. They must have seen us that afternoon. They were watching us.

In the morning we sailed east to the heavily wooded island at the strait's entrance, a mere 2½ leguas away. The island looked to be 3½ leguas in length. We reached it in two hours, casting anchor at midmorning. It was Sunday, March 17. I wondered if the Captain-General would cause a stone padrão to be set up.

Ashore we erected two tents, to which we moved all the sick men. Our last animal from Guam, a sow, was slaughtered. We climbed cocoanut trees and brought down young nuts. We foraged for vegetables and fruit. Omatu, the Chamorro from Guam, knew exactly which things were good to eat, and which were poisonous. He went around pointing to plants he recognized.

We made a soup of starchy roots, green leaves, and bits of pork. Omatu found a breadfruit tree. We roasted several of the "kulo," then scooped out the starchy insides and mixed them with cocoanut water to make a gruel. Easy to swallow, it was ideal for the men with swollen gums, better for them than the soup.

With the water from Guam already turning stale, we followed two creeks inland, all the way to their sources. The fresh water from those springs tasted heavenly.

I immersed myself in the creek. No more than a yard of water, very shallow, but as I lay down on the rocky bottom with only my head above the surface, it felt good to be bathing again. Several of the men followed my example. We splashed about and rolled around. One of them, Juan Hernández of Triana, picked up a handful of sand. It was coarse, laden with pebbles and stones, all rounded and smooth.

"Gold!" he said.

It was gold indeed, two or three bits mixed with the sand and pebbles.

Now everyone scooped up a handful from the creek's bottom and began panning for gold with bare hands. A few men found pieces the size of rice grains.

"The water washes it down from the mountain, you know," said Pedro García de Herrero of Ciudad Real, the blacksmith of the *Victoria*.

"Is that so?" prodded Ser Antonio.

"Yes. The gold is carried by the water, and deposited in stretches along the river, at random. Often, many bends will have nothing, and only one bend will have anything. It's a matter of finding that bend."

"There is never very much of it," said Gonzálo Hernández of Santa María del Puerto, the blacksmith of the *Concepción*. "In one whole day of panning and washing sand, you might glean a thimbleful of gold. But it grows back. That is the wonderful part. You come back in a week or so, and the mountain has deposited more gold in the bend."

"You can usually find more," said Pedro García, "when the weather is good, and the moon is waning."

"Are we certain this is not some kind of pyrite, fool's gold?" asked Juan Hernández.

"How can you tell?" asked Ser Antonio.

"Pure gold is quite soft," said Pedro García. "Any pyrite would be very hard. If that bit is gold, you should be able to pound it flat."

"Yes, that's what they say about gold," said Juan Hernández. "If this is a pyrite, what happens?"

"Nothing happens," said Gonzálo Hernández. "It would be so hard you couldn't do anything to it."

The assertion was put to the test at once. A few grains placed on a flat rock by the bank were vigorously pounded with a large smooth rock. The grains proved to be quite malleable. A cheer went up.

"The saints themselves have led us to this place," Ser Antonio declared. "Good drinking water, and good signs. Signs of gold. I shall call this place the acquada da li buona segnalli."

And so everyone called the island by that name: the aguada de las buenas señas, the watering-place of the good signs.

Padre Valderrama set up an altar and celebrated low Mass. Canon law forbade Mass at sea, and this was the first opportunity since our camp at the Río de Sardinas, three and a half months ago. The date was March 17, he reminded us, the fifth Sunday of Lent, dedicated to St. Lazarus. For more than a hundred days we had seemed to be sailing into empty waters, into an ocean of lost souls. But now an archipelago had come up from the sea, like Lazarus risen from the dead. Behold, a miracle!

Finding these pristine islands had made a poet out of our chaplain. In fact, the image he had conjured would surely appeal to my master. Dom Fernão would probably name the whole group the Islas de San Lázaro. I only wondered how he would see himself. Would he feel he had indeed wrought a miracle, raised these islands from the sea by the power of his will?

He would, too. That was what frightened me. He had been praying daily to his favorite saints, most especially to the Blessed Virgin Mary, who was the Queen of the Sea. By now he was quite convinced they had interceded for him. They had kept him safe, delivered him from his enemies, and guided him to this land. His gods were looking with favor upon him, their loyal and ardent disciple. Whatsoever he set out to do, they would increase the cunning of his right hand, grant him success. He only had to pray for it. His prayers and devotions, if fervent enough, would accomplish miracles.

There was a word in his own language for this: hagiography. It was regarded, among certain Catholics, as a virtue. I wondered if it was ever considered an affliction.

His agenda was crystallizing before my eyes now. Our avowed destination, the Spice Islands, lay on the æquinoctial line. He had steered for latitude 13°N, nine or ten degrees too far north. He knew an archipelago lay at that latitude, and he wanted to discover them officially. He would claim the taxes from two islands of his choice, and a twentieth part of the revenue from thousands of islands. After assuming the title of Viceroy of this archipelago, he would sail south to the Molukas, take on a rich cargo of spices, and be entitled to a fifth of the profits thereof.

When the Mass was ended the Captain-General announced that he expected every man to have his hair cut and his beard trimmed. We looked at each other: we indeed looked like a pack of wild animals, each man's glassy eyes peering out from a tangle of hirsuteness.

The Captain-General continued: he had intended to name this archipelago the Valle Sin Peligro.

I had guessed wrong.

Then, he added, Padre Valderrama's homily had caused him to change his mind. Now he would name it the Islas de San Lázaro. So I had guessed right, after all. But then, he had not yet heard about the gold.

Albo reckoned the Aguada de las Buenas Señas to be at $9\frac{2}{3}°N$. Later, Dom Fernão determined it to be almost exactly at 10°N. As usual, Albo's latitude had us a bit too far south. The island's longitude was 161° west of the Demarcation Line, according to Ser Antonio. I did not trust his guesswork. Longitude was something impossible to ascertain, and the Captain-General himself had not guessed at it. Lacking a precise figure for our longitude, I did not know where we were. The Captain-General did not know where we were. Omatu did not know where we were.

We needed men to tell us where we were; natives of this region who would affirm we were indeed where the Captain-General must have guessed we were. What was his guess? He was not telling us. The word would have to come from men who lived here.

A single boat appeared from out of the sea the next morning, Monday, March 18. It rode the waves straight toward our camp, the men in it paddling in an easy rhythm. The prahu, which had outriggers on either side, passed between our ships lying at anchor and glided up to the beach.

There were nine of them. Fearless men on the face of it, clearly outnumbered but going straight into a gathering of unknown men who had come in strange ships.

Or was this merely an advance party? Was a whole fleet lurking out of sight, ready to move in should these nine fail to return very soon?

They wore breechclouts of what looked like cotton cloth, and kerchieves wrapped around their heads. All had long hair reaching down to the waist. Some wore gold armlets. No one wore anklets. Among all the tribes of my race, it was the custom that no one below the rank of datù could wear anklets. I wondered if these people respected that custom.

Their leader had stylized dolphins painted in blue on his arms. Each man had a dagger tucked into his waist. Each carried a wooden shield in his left hand, and a weapon in his right, of which they had quite a fearsome assortment: spears, blowpipes, clubs studded with shark teeth, and short swords with single-edged blades. These swords looked more like large knives, and did not have wavy blades; had I seen a Malay kris, I would have embraced its possessor as a long lost brother-in-arms.

The sight of their weapons and shields made an impression on us. For the first time in the voyage we had met a native people who possessed metal.

As they jumped out into shallow water and waded ashore, we saw that their daggers and bolos had hilts inlaid with gold.

"Dari mana tuan?" I hailed them. I was standing beside the Captain-General, and flanking us were Ser Antonio, the alguacil Don Gonzálo, the escribano León de Espeleta, and Padre Valderrama. The rest of our men watched warily from the tents and from behind the trees. Those aboard the ships stood ready on the decks, crossbows and harquebuses at their feet, out of sight.

The nine men stopped in a body some two yards in front of us.

Their leader said something.

I could not understand his words.

"Where do you come from?" I asked again, "Are your intentions peaceful?" but none of them responded.

"Dirì sila ma-aram magyakan hin waray," one of them said, or something like that.

I did not know what to make of those words. For the fifth time, I had proved useless as an interpreter.

Ser Antonio questioned them in sign language, and they replied in that wise.

They had seen us coming from the direction of the sunrise, and watched our lights the night we anchored off their islet. They pointed to it and told us its name.

"Sulu-an."

What was the name of the island we were now on?

"Homonhon," said one of them, the first to understand the question.

And that large mountainous island?

"Samar."

And that one over there? And those others?

"Dinagat," they replied.

"Gibuson."

"Kabugan."

"Silani."

"Kabali-an," pointing to each.

None of those names meant anything to us. We still could not establish our position with any certainty.

The Captain-General asked if they had any food.

From their prahu they fetched raw fish, two cocoanuts, a bamboo culm of palm wine, and two bunches of bananas, each of a different variety.

Listening to them, I realized I understood some of their words: *saging, isda, arak*, for "banana," "fish," "wine." Their language was related to mine, but very distantly; the grammar was different, most of the words were strange, and the few familiar verbs I could pick out seemed to have been declined in curious ways. It made their speech sound like a garbled version of what should have been: our tongues were farther apart than those of the Portuguese and the Italian, or the German and the English.

At an order from their leader, four of them paddled off in their boat to fetch their fellows who were out fishing in another boat. The other five, including the leader, remained. The Captain-General invited these five to partake of the midday meal with us.

Francisco Albo took out his astrolabe and determined that this island, Homonhon, lay at 10°N latitude.

After the meal the Captain-General invited the five men to come aboard the flagship. We all boarded the batel and rowed to the *Trinidad*. The Captain-General gave them gifts of red caps, mirrors, combs, hawksbells, ivory figurines, and bocasine. Then he showed them the ship's cannon. At his order, Hans Vargue directed the firing of a broadside. The deafening noise frightened the natives out of their wits; they would have jumped overboard had we not restrained them.

The four men returned in the prahu later that afternoon. There was no sign of the others they had gone to fetch. The whole party of nine then took their departure. They promised to return in four days, and said they would bring rice and cocoanuts. I recognized the words they used for those: *humay, lubi.*

On Tuesday, March 19, we began the graving and careening of the ships. The parts of the hulls below the waterline were encrusted with barnacles. Doubtless the wood was infested with teredos which would have to be painstakingly dug out one by one.

Some of the men went to the creeks and panned for gold, bringing washbasins and a few quills that had served as pens. They would swirl handfuls of sand in the basins until the heavier gold separated from the sand, then put away the gold grains in the quills. The gold was not as plentiful as they had hoped; they returned with only one quill, half full.

"A waste of time," said Gonzálo Hernández. "The moon is still waxing."

"No matter what moon it is," said Pedro García de Herrero, "the way they pan doesn't help. They don't know the correct way of swirling." He made a rotary motion with his hand. "It's all in the wrist."

"I don't think," Juan Hernández said, "that they know how to find the one good bend in the river."

On Thursday, March 21, Ochot de Randio died of illness. A grumete on the *Victoria*, he was a Basque from Bilbao. His fellow Basques dug a grave for him inland.

On Friday, March 22, the men from Sulu-an returned. There were two prahus this time, and a total of eighteen men. They disembarked from their craft bearing gifts for us: bunches of green cocoanuts; a basket of oranges, small but sweet; jars of arak; a rooster.

With them was an older man, his long hair flecked with gray. The man who had been their acknowledged leader four days earlier seemed to defer to this older man. He presented the latter to the Captain-General, saying this man was the datù—another word I recognized.

Their datù was dressed like them, but his breechclout was bordered with a strip of silk which had tassels, also of silk. His purong, as they called the kerchief worn around the head, was likewise bordered with a silk strip and silk tassels. He had tattooes on his arms, legs, chest, and back. Two gold earrings dangled from his earlobes, one each on left and right. They were fashioned from gold that had been beaten into very thin sheets, and then folded like paper into curious shapes. They weighed next to nothing, but were very beautiful. Two gold armlets encircled his upper arms, two gold anklets shone from his ankles, and a gold ring adorned the big toe of his left foot.

The anklets reassured me. This man was indeed a datù.

He introduced himself to the Captain-General: he was Inaroyan. Then he pointed to his men and told us their names: Limbas, Bukad, Lagong, Kalipay, Badau, Kabiling, and other names I could not remember.

They started a new fire from the ashes of one of our fires. They slaughtered the cock and prepared it for roasting. Some of them foraged for edible plants and roots, others went to the shore to catch crabs. Ser Antonio examined their boat and the fishnets in it.

"Their fishnets are like rizali," he reported.

"What are those?" asked Dom Fernão.

"You know, rizzagno. An inverted cone. There is a barrel hoop attached to the circumference as selvage. The net opens when they throw it into the water. As it sinks to the bottom, it closes and covers the fish."

While their men attended to the fires together with our own cooks, the Captain-General invited the datù aboard the flagship. He showed him our stores of trade goods, our armory, our navigational instruments, and fired a broadside in his honor. Then he gave the datù and his retinue gifts of red caps, mirrors, hawksbells, combs, fishhooks, and strings of Venetian glass beads which they immediately wound several times around their necks.

Their word for gold was "bulawan." It bore no resemblance to the Malayu word "mas," but apparently had its root in the word "buwan," or "moon." They believed the moon to be a goddess. When she wept for a lost lover, her teardrops fell into the streams and hardened into nuggets of gold.

We returned to shore for the midday meal.

"Why, they eat with the right hand only, like the Moros," said Dom Fernão.

"Their island is named Sulu-an, Sire," I said. "It means 'place where there are men from Sulu.' I have heard of Sulu before. I'm not sure where it is, but the people there are Muslims."

"Why don't Muslims eat with the left hand, commendatore?" asked Ser Antonio.

"An indelicate question. I'll tell you later."

Each mouthful was followed by a sip of arak. The wine was new, as I could tell from its fine taste. Dom Fernão had tasted palm wine before, in Melaka, but none of the others had.

Ser Antonio swished his arak around in his cup.

"Strong bouquet," he said, "without, however, being displeasing."

He took a sip, swirled the liquid in his mouth, swallowed.

"Full-bodied," he said. "It has its own unique taste, no hint of cocoanut at all. Faint notes of clove, and of apple. Long, pleasant finish, with a bit of a sting. Clean aftertaste."

"Don't drink it too fast," Dom Fernão told him. "It has a kick like a mule's. It has been known to make men run amok."

After the meal Datù Inaroyan became voluble. He stood up and addressed the Captain-General in a formal manner, his men repeating certain words of his speech as a chorus. Then he began to dance.

I was slightly drunk from the palm wine, and the afternoon heat was making me sleepier. I felt as if I were dreaming even while wide awake. But between the datu's dancing and the chanting of his men, I found I could understand the tale.

"In the beginning was the sea...

(*"Dagat!"* chorused the men, *"dagat!"*)

"...and the sky."

(*"Langit!"*)

"Between them flew a bird. The bird grew tired. It could not alight. The bird set the sea against the sky. The water rose up to fight the sky, but the sky dropped islands on the sea. Burdened by those islands, the sea fell back.

"The bird alighted, and built a nest. The sea breeze married the land breeze, and they brought forth the bamboo. When the bamboo was fully grown it split open, and out of it came forth man, si Kalak, and woman, si Kabay.

"Brother and sister, they married under the rainbow. They had a son, si Bo, and a daughter, Lubluban. And Lubluban married a man named Pandagu-an, and their son was Anor-anor, who invented the fishnet.

"Anor-anor caught a shark with his net. When the shark died, Anor-anor's father Pandagu-an wept. The sea god sent the flies to ask why Pandagu-an was weeping. The flies would not go. The sea god then sent the weevils. When the weevils returned, they said Pandagu-an wept for the shark that died. The sea god told this to the sky god, who threw down a thunderbolt. Pandagu-an was killed.

"Pandagu-an went to Hell. Lubluban married again, becoming wife to Manakuyron.

"After some time, Pandagu-an was given his life back by the gods of the underworld. Pandagu-an went home.

"Pandagu-an missed Lubluban, and sent Anor-anor to look for her. Anor-anor found her at a feast, where Manakuyron and his clan were roasting a stolen pig. Lubluban refused to go home with Anor-anor, as she did not believe Pandagu-an had returned. The dead, she said, do not come back to life. If Pandagu-an had indeed come home, he could simply go back to Hell.

"Anor-anor went home without Lubluban. Pandagu-an returned to Hell."

The datù and his men bade us farewell. We watched them sail east to Sulu-an, the last of the sunlight casting a golden haze over them. Night fell without warning. I waited for them to show a light, but it seemed that the dark had swallowed them up. They were nowhere to be seen by the time the moon's rim began edging over the horizon. Soon the full moon was afloat on the waves, a goddess in the bloom of youth, a huge gold nugget the sky had panned from the sea.

⚓

IVª Parte
O Mundo Velho

34   *Masawa* 301

35   *Takubon* 312

36   *Sugbu* 323

37   *Gold* 336

38   *Glory* 345

39   *Gore* 356

40   *Mat-an* 366

41   *Demônio* 377

42   *Amihan* 386

43   *Habagat* 392

34

MARCH 23, A SATURDAY, was spent careening our vessels. March 24 was Palm Sunday. We celebrated Mass, this time with plenty of palm fronds. March 25, a day devoted to the Virgin Mary, was a rainy day. The work on the ships was completed by noon. We departed late in the afternoon.

The only thing we left behind was the wooden cross set up in front of Padre Valderrama's altar, and Ochot de Randio's mortal remains. As the marineros unfurled the sails, Ser Antonio told us he had almost drowned. He had fallen off the poopdeck, made slippery by the rain, that morning. Most of us were ashore, and there was no one to hear his cries for help. He of course, like most white men, did not know how to swim. Fortunately, his hand happened to brush against a clew line. He grabbed it, and hauled himself back aboard. Now he understood the ill fortune that had befallen the others: Guillérmo de Lole, Rojer du Pict, Martín Pérez, João de Moçambique, even Antón Genovés.

We followed the strait, keeping to the middle: WSW, then SW, then S. The islands looked ghostly in the rain. I glanced over Ser Antonio's shoulder as he wrote down their names: Cenalo, Hiunanghan, Ibusson, Abarien.

March 26 was Tuesday of Holy Week. While we were at sea, two of the sick men died after long illnesses. The first was the pilot João Rodrigues de Mafra. The other was Don Antonio de Coca, who had began the voyage as contador, become captain of the *San Antonio*, been taken prisoner after a fracas in the Rio de Janeiro, and briefly enjoyed a rebel's freedom during the mutiny in Puerto San Julián. His had been a distinguished career. Now the gods of the vast Mar Pacífico had claimed him.

The ringleaders of the mutinous captain's cabal formed in the doldrums of the Sargasso Sea were all gone but for Juan Sebastián de Elcano.

We buried them at sea the following morning, March 27, at daybreak: first de Mafra, then de Coca. Both of them sank face up, their dead eyes upon Heaven.

We sailed S by W until the strait opened up into an inland sea, then turned W, and then NW. That night we jilled about. Light from a fire appeared on an island to the northwest. In the morning of Maundy Thursday, March 28, we sailed to that small and narrow island. Behind it, to the north, the big island of Silani was visible some ten leguas away. We had come about 25 leguas from Homonhon.

The island was less than a legua and a half in length from north to south and perhaps a mile across, from east to west, at its widest part. It was shaped somewhat like a bell, thin at its northern top and bulbous at its southern bottom. Francisco Albo determined our latitude as 9°40'N. Our longitude was 162° west of the Demarcation Line. Albo had discarded Ferro as his prime meridian, in deference to Ser Antonio's request.

A boat emerged from somewhere along the shore. There were eight men in it. Their vessel had outriggers on both sides, as had the prahus of the Sulu-an men, but was slightly larger and longer: a baloto.

They came alongside some twenty yards off the capitana and kept position there, lazily sculling the water with their paddles.

"Dari mana tuan?" I hailed them.

"Sa among pulau!" came the reply. "Kamo, dari mana?"

From the lands of the Faranghis, I yelled. *Across the Kamaguyhang Laut*. At last we had reached a people who knew my language. My worth as an interpreter would pay off now.

Is that right, they said.

What is this island called?

Masawa.

Come closer.

No, we'll stay here.

We come in peace, I said. *Look, here is a gift for you.*

The Captain-General put a red cap on a piece of wood, and sent it floating down the current to them. They paddled their baloto backwards a bit to intercept it, and retrieved it with no trouble. The man who had done the talking took off his purong and put the cap on his head.

"Salámat tinggal," he said, as they took their leave.

"A momentous event," Ser Antonio said. "We have reached the East by sailing west."

"Was he," asked Dom Fernão, "a native speaker of your language?"

"No, Sire. He spoke it with a few peculiarities, like a language he has acquired by study."

"So that was not his own language he was speaking?" asked Ser Antonio.

"No, but it was the language of Malacca," Dom Fernão told him. "It's the lingua franca around here."

"Ah," said Ser Antonio, "like the trade French spoken around the Mediterranean."

"Or the trade Farsi in the Near East," said Duarte Barbosa.

"Trade Malaccan," said Ser Antonio.

"We call it the pasar Malayu," I told him.

They returned in two hours, this time in two bigger boats, the kind called "balanghay," large enough to have huts on the decks.

They stopped at the same distance the baloto had kept. I realized they were staying just outside bowshot range. The man who had spoken from the baloto earlier now emerged from under an awning. As he stood on the deck, not in the hull, the anklets he wore were now visible. The man was a datù.

I speak in the name of Rajah Kulámbò, he called out across the water. *What is the purpose of your coming here? What do you seek? And how may we be of service to you?*

His accent was different from mine. But he spoke the language quite well, with enough elegance and formality to show he was no mere fisherman.

We come in peace, I said. *We have spent four moons sailing across the Kamaguyhang Laut, and have no more food. We would fain procure food from your island; we will pay for everything we take. Come, come aboard and see our ship.*

A prahu was pushed off the Rajah's balanghay and into the water. Five men jumped into it, apparently at Rajah Kulámbo's behest, and came across to the *Trinidad*.

The first thing I noticed was their weaponry. Each of the five wore a sword, a Malay kris.

The Captain-General greeted the men by pressing his palms together in front of his chest and nodding—something he must have learned in Índia. The men responded with the same gestures. He gave them gifts. They reciprocated with gifts sent by Rajah Kulámbò: a bar of gold and a basket of fresh ginger.

The Captain-General accepted the ginger, but refused the gold. He knew that any sign of gold lust would drive its price up.

The oldest of the five natives gave him a puzzled look. Were these white men really not interested in gold? Perhaps, like the Xanglei, they preferred silver? To his credit, he did not say anything.

They could not stay too long, they said. I understood it as a matter of courtesy, a formal visit of ten minutes, no more. As they prepared to return to the balanghay the Captain-General told them they would lead, and we would follow.

We weighed anchor, and they took us to a bay in the middle of the island. There were huts on the shore, but not very many; a small village.

In the morning of Good Friday, March 29, Fernão Portoguês, one of the Captain-General's criados, died of illness. We still had several men stricken with the same affliction, their gums horribly swollen so they could not eat. Only gruel and cocoanut milk would help them.

The Captain-General sent me in the batel to see the Rajah.

Kulámbò received me in one of the huts. He was sitting on a mat, eating rice and fish off a blue and white plate. It had to have come from the Xanglei, porcelain fired in the Sung or the Ming dynasty.

He invited me to eat with him. A plate was set before me, and more rice and fish brought in on green celadon platters.

Rajah Kulámbò cut a handsome figure, the best-built man we had seen since reaching Homonhon. His long glossy hair reached down to his shoulders. The rippling of the muscles on his lightly-oiled body showed through the tatooes on his chest, arms, neck, back, and legs. Wrapped around his head was a purong of yellow silk, and his garment, which covered him from the waist to the knees, was of cotton embroidered with silk. The dagger at his waist, in a scabbard of carved wood, had a haft of gold.Gold gleamed all over his person:earrings, bracelets, armlets, anklets, rings on the second and fourth fingers of his left hand, and on the fourth finger of his right hand. Each ring crowned with a jewel, one with a ruby, another with an emerald, and the third with a diamond. I looked at his feet, expecting to see gold rings there, too, but his toes were strangely bare. His teeth were red from chewing betel, which made a fine contrast with the three gold spots affixed on every tooth. He exuded a mild perfume of something I should have recognized but could not. Later I found it was almasiga and binyugin; Ser Antonio called it storax and benzoin.

I extended my master's greetings to him, and told him we needed food. He graciously reciprocated with greetings of his own, and said he understood our plight.

Shortly thereafter, he was riding with me in the batel to the capitana, eight of his men carrying two large tuna and three large porcelain jars, covered with banana leaves, full of raw rice.

The Captain-General welcomed him aboard, and accepted the food with many thanks. Then he gave the Rajah a purple and yellow Turkish coat and a red cap, and helped him put those on. The Rajah's men were given fishhooks, knives, and mirrors.

The Captain-General told the Rajah he desired to be the latter's blood brother.

I translated this.

"Bu-ót di-áy siya makig-igsù-on kanakò sa kasing-kasing?"

Dom Fernão picked out the key word and repeated it before I could translate the Rajah's words:

"Si. Kasi-kasi."

The Captain-General ordered a carpet spread on the deck, and cushions scattered on it.

I fetched the Captain-General's own cup, the silver one bearing his coat of arms, and his last bottle of vino de Jerez, a pale fino.

The two of them sat down on the cushions. The Rajah's men, legs drawn up and crossed, sat on the carpet. None of the white men cared to sit down in that manner, like tailors, and so they all remained standing. Dom Fernão pulled back his sleeve, and with his dagger swiftly made a small cut on his lower left arm. Blood dripped from the wound and I, sitting in front of him, caught the drops in the cup.

I turned to Rajah Kulámbò. He pulled out his own dagger, the one with the gold haft. I expected a to see a blade of shiny steel, but it turned out to be flint. He pulled back the sleeve of his silken Turkish coat, wounded his left arm, and dripped blood into the cup. I swirled the cup a little, watching both bloods tinge into the pale gold of the wine, and handed it to Dom Fernão. He swirled it some more, until the wine and both their bloods were thoroughly mixed. He took a sip, then passed it to Rajah Kulámbò. The Rajah sniffed the bouquet. He sipped, and almost gagged on the liquid. He managed to control himself; he swallowed. He smiled.

The men cheered.

We showed them our trade goods: cloth of various colors, linen, coral trinkets. We fired the cannon, which impressed them. None of them were frightened by the loud blasts as the men from Sulu-an had been.

Rajah Kulámbò said he knew what lantaka were, but never before had one been fired so close to him.

A demonstration was arranged, and men in armor passed in review before the delegation on deck, wielding their swords, halberds, crossbows, harquebuses, cuirasses, bucklers.

Dom Fernão singled out the tallest man in full armor, who turned out to be Petit-Jean d'Anjou, and ordered him to stage a mock battle against three of the other men. They attacked him with swords and daggers, their thrusts bouncing harmlessly off his armor. Rajah Kulámbò was duly impressed, or pretended to be. I had the impression he had seen armor before, if not exactly of the type Petit-Jean wore.

"One such man," Dom Fernão told Rajah Kulámbò, "is worth one hundred of your men."

"Usá ka gatús?" asked the Rajah.

"Usá ratús," I affirmed. Our languages were not that dissimilar. When it came to numbers, the words were almost identical.

"Tinú-od gayúd," he replied to Dom Fernão.

"He says that's a fact," I translated.

The Captain-General led him into the sterncastle, where he showed him the navigational instruments. He spread out a map, and told the Rajah how we had spent months crossing the Pacific. The Rajah was truly amazed. The Kamaguyhang

Laud stretched to the ends of the world, he said, and was impossible to cross.

As they were leaving, the Captain-General asked if two of our men could be sent ashore, that they might be shown something of the Rajah's island. Kulámbò was amenable to that.

Late that afternoon the Captain-General sent Ser Antonio Francesco Pigafetta to the Rajah. I accompanied him as interpreter.

Rajah Kulámbò greeted us formally, as soon as we stepped down from the batel and onto the beach, by raising his hands to the sky, facing the setting sun, then turning towards us. We returned the gesture. Then all his men greeted us in that manner.

We dismissed our crew of rowers, agreeing to light a bonfire when we wanted them to fetch us. They rowed back to the *Trinidad*.

Rajah Kulámbò took Ser Antonio by the hand, and led us to a beached balanghay under a bamboo shed. We sat at the stern, surrounded by his men, all of them armed. Every single man had a sword and a dagger, and most of them also had spears, clubs, and blowpipes. A plate of roast pork was brought in, and a jar of palm wine. We ate as we conversed, dipping the meat in a sauce of vinegar and pounded ginger. Half of my conversation was in sign language, for only one man was fluent in the pasar Malayu. He was Rajah Awi, Rajah Kulámbo's brother. Rajah Kulámbò admitted he could understand my language much better than he could speak it; he spoke it haltingly.

Every mouthful had to be followed by a drink, and one had to drain the cup. Rajah Kulámbò shared his cup with Ser Antonio, keeping it covered the rest of the time. Rajah Awi shared his cup with me. The others had their own cups.

Rajah Kulámbò took the first drink. Palms together, he raised his hands to the sky. He then brought them down to his chest, palms still together, and bowed slightly, or nodded, to Ser Antonio. With his right hand he lifted the cup to his lips, thrust out the clenched fist of his left hand at Ser Antonio, as if to strike him, then drained the cup, his fist in Ser Antonio's face.

Rajah Kulámbò passed the cup to Ser Antonio, who imitated the Rajah's actions exactly. This elicited a hearty laugh from the company.

Wine left in a cup was poured into another jar. This jar received the dregs of Ser Antonio's first drink, and then of mine. After that, it became a matter of honor not to leave anything in the cup.

Ser Antonio presented more gifts to Rajah Kulámbò: a roll of cloth, handleless drinking cups of Venetian glass, and glass mirrors in gilt frames, much finer than the ordinary mirrors made of shiny plate metal.

I noticed that Ser Antonio was not eating. He had taken a mouthful of pork to precede his first drink, but had chewed only small bits after that. The two rajahs kept exhorting him to eat more. He would smile and nod at them, then nibble at a titbit.

"Mamma mìa," he whispered to me, "it's Good Friday and here we are eating meat!"

I grunted. My mouth was full.

He had brought along his writing paper, quill, and inkpot. Now he busied himself. He would point to something and ask the locals its name in their language, then write down what he heard. Whenever he read back to them a word he had written, they laughed appreciatively.

He was acquiring a glossary, his third on this voyage. He had written down the words of the Guarani in the Río de Janeiro, and the words of the patagónes from Puerto San Julián. Every culture was best appreciated in its own unique language, as I who spoke several could attest, and it gladdened my heart to see Ser Antonio reach out to all men, no matter their roots, as his brothers.

I asked Rajah Kulámbò what they called themselves, and what their language was.

He said they were Bisayâ, and their language was Binisayâ.

Now I knew I was among remnants of the old Sri-Vijayâ.

I ascertained from the two rajahs that Masawa was merely an island they went to when they wanted to see each other. That explained the absence of females. Masawa was an island where these rajahs and their men found respite when they wished to escape from their womenfolk. Here they could all be boys again. Here they indulged in the male pleasures of hunting and drinking.

Unfortunately, Masawa could not produce enough food for the Armada. The Captain-General wanted all his barrels filled, so that the ships would have food supplies good for half a year at least, a full year if possible. Masawa simply did not have that much. A month's food for the Armada would strip the island bare. A week's supply was as much as it could spare.

Sri Kulámbò was the Rajah of Butuan, a city on the northern part of a large island called Mindanaw. Sri Awi was the Rajah of Kalaghan. His territory adjoined his brother's.

Very few people lived permanently on Masawa. All of them had been impressed into Rajah Kulámbo's service. They cultivated the fields for him, planted rice, balanghoy, ubi, gabi, bananas, and other crops. He came here to harvest the fruit of their labors, for he was their harì and they were his subjects and that was how it should be.

Rajah Kulámbò wanted to know more about me. I said I was from Melaka.

He had heard of it. Wasn't that the town invaded by the Parangis?

Yes. How far is it from here?

I don't know for sure. I haven't yet gone to that place. Perhaps in Sugbu there is somebody who has already gone there. He will be able to know.

I found it taxing to follow his train of thought in my native language. After eight years of disuse, the way things had to be phrased in it now sounded awkward to me.

Supper was announced. A celadon platter of stewed pork, immersed in its own gravy, was brought in. A second platter held a steaming heap of fluffy rice. We had been eating pork, but that had been as sumsuman, something to go with the drinking. Now we were eating it with rice, as a meal. Both pork and rice were piping hot. After every swallow, the mouth demanded to be cooled off with palm wine.

"Today may be Good Friday," I said to Ser Antonio. "But you can eat now and confess later."

He could not answer; his mouth was full and his hands were digging into his plate for more. I was dead drunk now, and the hour was late. We were taken to a hut. It was built on posts, and looked a mile high. We climbed up to it by a ladder that seemed to lead to the stars. Halfway up I nearly fell off.

Torches were lighted. These were of banana leaves rolled into cones, and filled with the sap of the animi tree. The wicks were of cocoanut husk fiber.

A young man entered, and Rajah Kulámbò introduced his eldest son to us. The boy's name was Mimpat.

He had not yet supped. Food was brought in for him. The four of us sat facing one another on the polished bamboo floor. Mimpat would not eat until we joined him. The platters before him had rice and fish cut into pieces, in a sauce made from sambag, a sour fruit.

I had eaten so much pork that the very taste of it had become cloying. The wondrous thing was, now that I was sated with pork, my tongue had become extremely glad of the taste of fish.

The more of the fish we ate, the better it tasted. It went very well with the side dish of a seaweed they called gusô, a food so exotic Ser Antonio did not eat of it.

Rajah Kulámbò excused himself, as he was very sleepy. He must have been as drunk as I was, but there was no sign of it. I was so drunk I urinated right there on the bamboo floor, but my water went through the slats so there was no mess. Mimpat rolled out mats of plaited palm leaves and pillows of dried banana leaves. I fell asleep as soon as my head touched the pillow.

Before we could accept Rajah Kulámbo's invitation to breakfast, the batel arrived to fetch us. It was March 30, Black Saturday, and Ser Antonio had yet to do his devotions and say his prayers. Rajah Kulámbò asked if he might send his son and his brother with us so they could see our ship. Ser Antonio said we would be happy to take them. Accordingly, Rajah Awi, Mimpat, and two other men went in the batel with us.

The Captain-General gave them a tour of the ship, and plied them with gifts.

They stayed for the midday meal.

Rajah Awi seemed much impressed with what he saw. His talk during the meal was full of bombast, as if to impress us in turn.

In Butuan and Kalaghan, he said, one merely had to sift the earth to turn up nuggets of gold as large as eggs. All the dishes in his house, he said, were made of gold. He washed his face every morning in a golden washbowl, the condiments box for his betel-and-lime was of gold, the balanghay-prow motif on the roof of his house was of gold...We didn't believe him? Why, he would send these two men back to his house to fetch some of his gold plates. They should be back in four days...

The Captain-General forestalled him. It was not necessary for those men to fetch those dishes. Besides, we were more interested in spices than in gold.

Ser Antonio, to change the subject, asked if they were of the same race as I was.

My tribe was originally from Sumatra, I said.

Yes, replied Rajah Awi, they too belonged to tribes that had come from Sumatra.

They were descended from the tribe of Katu, Mimpat said.

I said I came from the tribe of Piliang.

Ser Antonio asked what those tribes were.

The race of the Malayus, Mimpat told him, came from the four sons of a king. The first, Katu, married a woman. The second, Piliang, married a tiger. The third, Bodi, married a dog. And the fourth, Tjemago, married a cat. Out of these unions came the four branches of the Malayus.

"The orang laut," Mimpat said, "are descended from the brother who married the cat."

"And the Maja Pahít," I said, "from the brother who married the dog."

35

WE KEPT THE EASTER VIGIL, staying up all night. The last-quarter moon rose at midnight and reached the zenith at sunrise the next day. Against the blue of the sky, it looked exactly like a half-wheel of Basque cheese.

Early that morning, March 31, we celebrated Easter Sunday Mass on Masawa. Padre Valderrama, the pages, and I were the first ashore. They began setting up an altar. I informed Rajah Kulámbò we were not going to eat with him, but were going to observe a religious ceremony. He was somewhat put out, as he had begun preparing a feast for us. Withal, he sent the two pigs he had slaughtered to the ships. He had men ready to shave those pigs and roast them, but he now decided to leave those jobs to our cooks.

Fifty of our men came from the ships to hear Mass. All were dressed in doublets and their finest clothes. The Captain-General wore his white habit with the blood-red cross of the Knights of Santiago. Six of the men carried harquebuses. Upon landing, they fired a volley.

Rajah Kulámbò and Rajah Awi met the Captain-General at the beach. He embraced them both. They took him by the hand, and conducted him to the place Padre Valderrama had prepared. Before the Mass began, he took out a small bottle and sprinkled both of them with musk water.

The two rajahs stayed beside the Captain-General throughout the Mass, standing when he stood, kneeling when he knelt. Many of the natives stayed on the sidelines, watching. At the consecration, when the Host was lifted, the six harquebusmen fired a volley from their muskets, and were answered by a blast from the ships.

After the Mass some of the Basques performed a beautiful sword dance, with Juan Sebastián Elcano as captain of the dance.

A cross was carried in, five nails protruding from it and a crown at its top. The Captain-General gave a fine speech about that cross, which I forgot as soon as I had translated it. We retired to the ships for the midday meal. The two rajahs graciously escorted the Captain-General to the batel. They seemed to be wondering why the men of the armada, at the end of their curious ceremony, did not have a feast right there. Rajah Awi conjectured that these white men's way of cooking pork might be much better than roasting. Perhaps their cooking was so good they did not want to share it. That had to be why they would go off to eat without inviting any others to join them in their meal. Kulámbò nudged his brother and told him to be quiet. Perhaps their customs, he said, were different.

I did not translate any of that. Kulámbò had guessed correctly. A white man found it normal to eat in the presence of others without offering to share his food. The brown man would never do that. Inviting everyone present to eat with him was the well-mannered thing to do, albeit in many cases the invitation was not meant to be accepted. But the white man's way, not extending an invitation at all, seemed to the rajahs a lack of fineness.

After eating on shipboard, we returned to shore, still in our doublets, to plant the cross on the highest mountain there.

We were all perspiring heavily by the time we attained the summit. The view was breathtaking. To the west-southwest, three islands could be seen. Rajah Awi said gold could be found on those islands. "Pieces this big," he said, curling his thumb and index finger into a circle big enough for a lentil or a chick pea.

"Not as big as this?" asked Francisco Albo, curling his hand so that it held an imaginary egg.

"No. That big only in Kalaghan. In those islands"— he pointed at them to the WSW— "only this big."

The Captain-General asked the rajahs where the best place to get food was.

Rajah Kulámbò said there were three choices: Silani, which was the nearest, Sugbu, and Kalaghan. He pointed out their respective directions to the Captain-General, and offered to give him pilots who knew the way.

Which was the best of the three? asked Dom Fernão.

"Sugbu," said the Rajah.

"Ah, Çubu," repeated my master. In the Rajah's pronunciation the hard *g* in the middle of the placename had been quite distinct, but the white man's phonetics had no provision for anything like it. Perhaps the white man's ear could not correctly hear a sound as strange as that.

I wondered why Rajah Kulámbò gave his brother's place, Kalaghan, as last choice, and why he did not nominate his own place, Butuan, at all.

The Captain-General asked Rajah Kulámbò if he had any enemies, for we would vanquish them if he but gave the word.

Rajah Kulámbò admitted there were two islands hostile to him, but it was not the season for going there.

The cross was erected, and all recited the Pater Noster and the Ave María.

The descent took us through their cultivated fields. Back in the balanghay under the bamboo shed, they served us green cocoanuts, each with a small part lopped off to expose a drinking hole. We were all very thirsty, and the cocoanuts were a very good physic, slaking thirst much better than water ever could.

Dom Fernão said he intended to depart on the morrow. He hoped the pilots would be ready. He would leave one of us behind as a hostage.

I wondered who it would be. Not me, I knew. He could not dispense with my services. It was probable he could dispense with Elcano's. I hoped, perhaps unrealistically, that he would dispense with Barbosa's.

On April 1, Easter Monday, Rajah Kulámbò sent a man to the capitana to ask if we could delay our departure by two days. He needed some time to harvest his rice. If the Captain-General would be kind enough to send men to help with the harvest, perhaps it could be finished sooner. He hoped the esteemed Captain-General would wait for him. As a gesture of his high regard for his blood brother, he, Kulámbò, would himself be the pilot.

Why the delay? The questions began bubbling up in my mind. If Rajah Kulámbò piloted us, with enough men to crew one balanghay, surely his brother Rajah Awi could attend to the harvesting? If Rajah Awi rounded up the people of the island, surely he would find enough men for the harvest?

The Captain-General ordered as many men as he could spare to go and help with the Rajah's rice harvest. All were commoners; noblemen and officers could not be expected to perform such labor.

The two rajahs, however, stayed in the beached balanghay under the bamboo shed. Much food and drink were spread before them. The men from the Armada were invited to join them, and by noon both rajahs had lapsed into drunken stupors. They lay down where they were and slept off the rest of the day. Many of our men became intoxicated, too.

My suspicions increased. Why had they begun drinking so early in the morning? Why had they suddenly brought up the problem of the rice harvest, only to ignore the detail of extra men sent to help them with it?

A possible explanation occurred to me. Rajah Kulámbò, after adroitly scheduling Sugbu as the fleet's next destination, wanted time to warn the Rajah of Sugbu. He must have sent a man, or several men, in a prahu to Sugbu. Our coming would be expected.

The more I thought about it, the more I became convinced such was the case. But what could I do? My fears were too nebulous to bare before my self-confident, redoubtable master. He was not the sort to let himself be lulled into complacency by the lack of overt danger signs. Twelve years ago he had been quick to smell treachery in Melaka, and his nose was as good as ever. He would take things as they came, for he trusted in the Almighty, and his faith was everything.

Some of the natives, drafted for the harvest but now idle, rowed out to the ships to barter items of food with us. "Itlog, manoy, aksuhà," they cried from their prahus, holding out their wares to us.

"What are they selling?" the sobresaliente Juan Miñez of Sevilla asked me.

"Hard-boiled eggs," I said, "and oranges."

A man came up the ladder of the *Trinidad* with a bunch of bananas and a bamboo culm of grain. He wanted to trade those for a knife. He had seen the shiny knives we had given to the

Rajah's men: cheap implements made in Brussels, but better than their own knives. The Flemings at least knew their steel blades.

Ser Antonio toyed with the native, proffering a copper quattrino for the rice and bananas. The man shook his head; he wanted a knife.

The Captain-General entered into the spirit of the fun, and offered the man a silver tostão for his goods. Again the man shook his head; he would accept only a knife.

Dom Fernão opened his purse and took out a Venetian gold ducat. In Europa, that coin would have bought several dozen of those Flemish knives. The man refused. My master showed him the biggest gold coin he had, a doppione, twice as big as the ducat. It was a collector's piece, a Franco-Italian coin minted in Milan by Louis XII, King of France, to celebrate his occupation of that city. The native did not want it. Finally a cheap Flanders knife was produced, and he bartered his wares for it with alacrity.

On April 2, a Tuesday, the harvest began. Rajah Kulámbò cut the first sheaves himself, and ceremoniously burned them up to some god, right there on the field. He went on to finish that furrow, then retired to the shade of some trees on the edge of the field. Bamboo culms of palm wine were waiting there, and he spent the rest of the day drinking.

On Wednesday, April 3, two men died of illness. The first was Juan Villalon, a sobresaliente on the *Victoria*. The other man was Baltazar Genovés, the pilot of the *Victoria*. He had been hired as the maestre of the *Santiago*, had become the maestre of the *Victoria*, and subsequently, her pilot.

On Thursday, April 4, we buried the two dead men on ground Rajah Kulámbò selected for us. The gods of the Pacific Ocean were very powerful, and even now they continued to claim human tribute. Many of our men had fallen sick in the Pacific, eleven of them having been thrown into her waters for burial, and we still had a few sick men in the clutches of those gods. Was it too late to save them? We had buried a man in Homonhon, we were burying two men in Masawa, would more men die to be buried in Sugbu?

It seemed likely. Two men on the *Victoria*, both of them originally from the *Santiago*, were still sick of the escorbuto. They were the sobresaliente Martín Barrena, a Basque from Villafranco in Guipuzcoa, and the merino Juan de Aroche, from the town of that name, a village not far from Sevilla. I accompanied the Captain-General every morning when he went to see all the men in sick bay, and these two were visibly wasting away.

At dawn on Friday, April 5, we finally departed, having spent a full week in Masawa. Rajah Kulámbò in his balanghay led the way, followed by the *Trinidad*, the *Concepción*, and the *Victoria*. He had quietly ignored the Captain-General's offer to leave a hostage in Masawa. The only men we left behind were the two we had buried there, Juan Villalon and Baltazár Genovés.

One of our marineros on the *Trinidad*, León Pancaldo of Savona, was no longer with us; he had been transferred to the *Victoria* to be her new pilot, replacing the late Baltazár Genovés.

The course was west at first, then north by west. We sailed between the islands of Silani and Bu-ol, then Kanighaw and Baybay. The three naos had to trim sails to adjust to the speed of the balanghay. Kulámbò was under full sail, but sailing northwest with a northeast wind was not easy, and his balanghay could achieve only five or six knots. By nightfall we had sailed some 20 leguas. Dead ahead was a small island, over a legua away. Rajah Kulámbò sailed on for another hour, lighting torches on his stern, until we reached that island.

We anchored off it. Rajah Kulámbò beached his boat so his crew could rest ashore. Later he invited the Captain-General to dine with him. Ser Antonio and I accompanied Dom Fernão.

The island, Rajah Kulámbò told us, was called Takubon, although there were people in these parts who called it Himuktan. It derived its name from a bird that was to be found there, the tabon bird. The word "tabon" meant "to cover"; this bird dug a shallow pit, laid its eggs there, then covered them up with sand. Rajah Kulámbò summoned a few of his men, and led a hunt for game. They returned shortly with a few large bats, the kind that fed on ripe fruit. They roasted these kabug and we ate that meat with a sauce of vinegar and pounded ginger. Ser Antonio said it tasted better than chicken.

The whole of Saturday was spent on Takubon. Saturday was the day Dom Fernão revered most, because it was the day special to Our Lady. I wondered if this reverence for the

Sabbath also honored, in a vestigial way, some all but forgotten Jewish ancestor. Most of the noble families in Portugal and Spain had bloodlines enriched or debased, depending on point of view, by distant Judaic forebears. Many had Moorish antecedents as well.

Francisco Albo shot the sun at noon, and determined the latitude of Takubon to be 10½°N.

The Captain-General kept to himself, walking along the beach, taking sights with his brass astrolabe, writing in his derrotero.

I could guess what most perplexed him now. The Pacific Sea had turned out to be very wide, about five times wider than anyone had estimated. Both Dom Fernão and Ruy Faleiro had calculated that three weeks would be enough to cross it. A week or two more would not have mattered. But from our last sight of América on December 16 to our Samar landfall on March 16 had been a full twelve weeks.

Clearly, this trans-Pacific route was too long. It also meant going all the way south to the ends of América, then negotiating a tortuous strait through windy, frigid wastelands. The Portuguese route, via Africa and Índia, was shorter and better. The King of Spain would think my master's achievement a hollow one.

It must have been a blow to Dom Fernão's pride as a cosmographer. He had made studies of longitude, and publicly concluded that the Spice Islands lay within Spain's half of the world as divided by the Treaty of Tordesillas. Now all estimates of the world's circumference would have to be revised. The length of a degree of longitude at the æquinoctial line would have to be increased. The Line of Demarcation would have to be redrawn. It ran 370 leguas west of the Cape Verdes, giving Brazil to Portugal, but where would it run on the other side of the world? Conceivably, it would place the Spice Islands, too, in Portugal's half. If that were proven to be so, this Armada might turn out to have been guilty of poaching in Portuguese territory.

There was only one thing left to confirm. Where exactly were these Islas de San Lázaro? If they belonged to the archipelago Dom Fernão had seen in 1512, we were now past the longitude of the Spice Islands. We needed men to tell us which way the Molukas lay. Such men would certainly be found in Sugbu.

These thoughts must have run through the Captain-General's mind. True, much gold was to be obtained in these isles. The taxes from two islands of his own choosing were to be his. A twentieth part of the revenue from these islands would be his as well, and there were thousands of islands here. After assuming the title of Viceroy of this archipelago, he would sail south and find the way to the Molukas, take on a rich cargo of spices, and be entitled to a fifth of the profits. But these were consuelos de bobo.

These things were plain to see. I only hoped my master would face the facts, accept the unavoidable conclusions. But, knowing him, I feared he would blot out such thoughts and choose to delude himself instead.

As for the town of Sugbu, it was useless to wonder what it might have in store for the Armada. I was by now quite convinced that Rajah Kulámbò had sent word to the Rajah of Sugbu, who was a kinsman of his.

Early on Sunday, April 7, the new moon bringing on the high tide at sunrise, we set out toward a group of three islands to the northwest. Rajah Kulámbò said it was possible to sail directly for Sugbu by going west and then turning southwest, but reefs abounded in those waters. The best way was to go northwest first, passing close to the three islands, then southwest from there. The three, he said, were the Kamuti islands. The Captain-General decided to use all his sails and reach those islands ahead of the balanghay. It was early in the morning of a sunny day, not the time to lumber along at a turtle's pace. Sailing northwest with a northeast wind was not too difficult for us, and our fleet attained a speed of ten or eleven knots before we had to slow down upon nearing the islands. We lay at anchor for an hour before the balanghay caught up.

Rajah Kulámbò was much impressed with the speed of the naos. He left his balanghay and asked to sail the rest of the way to Sugbu in the capitana. The Captain-General gladly welcomed him, and his entourage of four men, aboard.

He named the islands of the Kamuti group as he pointed to them: Ponson, and west of it Poro and Pasihan, connected to each other by a narrow strip of land, like Siamese twins. In the distance beyond, to the west, said Rajah Kulámbò, was Pulao

Kang Dayang. The Captain-General estimated the Kamuti Islands to be about seven or eight leguas from Takubon. Rajah Kulámbò said Sugbu was now only six hours away, but that the naos could reach it in five, perhaps four. This meant, said Dom Fernão, that Sugbu now lay only seventeen or eighteen leguas away.

From the Kamuti islands we sailed southwest with the wind. We soon raised the outline of Pulao Kang Dayang on our starboard horizon. Rajah Kulámbò told us that Sugbu was situated on the coast of that island, halfway between its northern and southern tips. The island was long and narrow and ran from northeast to southwest, as if the monsoon winds had forcibly shaped it into being. This archipelago was full of long narrow islands that ran northeast to southwest. Sulu-an was one, Masawa another.

After a couple of hours we saw that a small island lay very close to that long island. It was the isle of the Mat-an, or "well-endowed with eyes," and opposite it lay the town of Sugbu.

Ser Antonio asked the Rajah about Sugbu and Mat-an, and how they acquired their names.

Rajah Kulámbò said Sugbu came from the word "sugbò," which meant "burned down." The first Rajah of that town, facing an attack by pirates, had burned the whole town down and then fled inland with his people. They lost all their houses, but nothing was left for the pirates either.

"A Pyrrhic victory," said Ser Antonio.

"What?" asked Rajah Kulámbò.

"Nothing. What about Mat-an?"

The people of that island were different from those of Sugbu, the Rajah said, and were very suspicious of the people of Sugbu. They acted as if the people of Sugbu would try to cheat them, although Sugbu had been trading with Tsung Guo for centuries, and never cheated the lang-yaw. The Sanglay, in fact, were much impressed with the honesty of the Sugbu-anon people. And so the Sugbu-anon would make a game of trying to cheat the orang laut who had settled on the islet facing their town. It was all in fun, but they never succeeded in cheating them. Those people acted like they had many eyes, and could see what was behind their backs. The Sugbu-anon called them "mat-an," meaning "many-eyed," and that became the name of the island.

I was reminded of the god Indra, after the yonis all over his body had been turned into eyes. Were the orang laut of Mat-an avatars of Indra?

We entered the narrow channel separating the two islands. Low tide at noon reminded me it was the day of the new moon. The channel was at its narrowest, no wider than a medium-sized river, but Rajah Kulámbò assured us it was very deep in midstream. On both sides were houses that stood offshore on stilts, whole villages of them. Rajah Kulámbò told us their names: the town of Mantawi to starboard, and the Mat-an village of Opong to port.

The coast of the long island now curved away even as the southern tip of Mat-an became visible, and we veered west, to starboard, to follow the shore. The Captain-General ordered all flags and standards broken out, and the other ships immediately followed the capitana's example. Rajah Kulámbò instructed the Captain-General to steer for the point of land that protruded into the bay. There were several ships in that harbor, balanghays, balotos, prahus, a viray or two...soon we could see the piers that extended from the point, and the vessels docked at those piers, and then we were anchoring close by. People were coming out on those piers to gape at us. Others were paddling out to us in prahus. It was Sunday, April 7, 1521, according to the white man's calendar. If Master Andrew had been right, and we had indeed gained a day, then it should have been Monday, April 8. But it remained to be proven that we had passed the 180th meridian.

On our sails, the red Cross of *Santiago*. On each mainsail, the Holy Roman Emperor's Hapsburg eagles. At the top of each mainmast, the lions and castles of Spain, in red and gold quarterings. On the capitana's foremast, the symbol of the Holy Trinity; on the other ships, the symbols of the Immaculate Conception and Our Lady of Victory. On all four of the *Trinidad*'s capstans, the Captain-General's three bars chequy, in red and silver patterns, quartered with the quinas. Juan Serrano's coat of arms on the *Concepción*'s capstans, and Duarte Barbosa's on the *Victoria*'s.

The sun stood at high noon, and we cast no shadows as we slowly glided into the city's outstretched arms. Here was the most populated town we had seen since leaving Europa. Here was a thriving village busier than San Lúcar de Barrameda, wealthier than Santa Cruz in Teneriphe, livelier than Río de Janeiro, nobler than Umatak in Guam.

So this was the city that savored its Pyrrhic victories. This was the city that thought nothing of burning its own self, a city that knew how to leave the taste of ashes in the mouths of its enemies. So this was the city of Sugbu.

36

"¡*TIRA!*" YELLED THE CONDESTABLE de bombarderos, Hans Vargue. The three naos fired broadsides, frightening the people out of their wits, and stampeding them into a run. In the mad scramble some of them stumbled over each other and fell off the wharves, plopping into the water with heavy splashes. A few of the natives rowing toward us in sakayans jumped overboard.

The Captain-General's first emissary ashore was Cristóvão Rabelo, with myself as interpreter. Rajah Kulámbò told us that the Rajah of Sugbu was named Humabon, and his wife was Humamay.

"How many wives does he have?" I asked.

"Only four. The principal wife is Humamay."

Cristóvão Rabelo and I made an unlikely pair as we walked the short distance from the wharf to the Rajah's palace. Many of the men we passed were armed. By the look of the scabbards, their swords all had wavy blades. People along the way cowered if we looked at them, and little children fled at our approach. But they sneaked looks nevertheless, or gaped. Most of them must have been seeing a Faranghi for the first time. Cristóvão Rabelo's blond hair and beard and piercing blue eyes made him look quite the foreign devil.

"Buagaw ug buhok," I heard some of them say. Later I learned it meant "sunbleached hair." They had seen blond hair before. Some of their fishermen had hair exactly that shade. They thought Cristóvão Rabelo's hair had lost its blackness the same way, from long exposure to the sun.

The istana was the biggest building thereabouts, and most of the populace seemed to have crowded into it. All seemed curious, and eager for a look at the strange men who had come in those gaudy ships.

The space in front of Rajah Humabon had been left clear. The Rajah sat on a mat, clad only in a cotton loincloth, a yellow silk purong, a necklace of pearls, large gold earrings set with precious stones, and the anklets of a datù. He wore no armlets. His body was covered with fine tatooes, so that he seemed to be wearing a shirt. He was fat and potbellied, and even in his sitting position looked short. He was sucking an egg. On another mat beside him were two porcelain dishes and four porcelain jars, all of Xanglei provenance. The dishes contained eggs. Each of the four jars was covered with fragrant herbs, and each had four small reeds poking through the herbs. Rajah Humabon picked up a jar, put a reed into his mouth, and noisily slurped up his drink.

The man sitting to the Rajah's right was probably his bendahara. But I was more interested in the man sitting at his left, a man who wore the robe and cap of a Muslim, and shoes with pointed tips: the only man among them whose feet were shod. Everyone else, including the Rajah, was barefoot.

Salaam aleikum," I greeted the Rajah of Sugbu, with Cristóvão Rabelo echoing my words: "Shalom aleichem."

Rajah Humabon nodded.

"Aleikum salaam," replied the Muslim, coming to his feet. He was not an Arab. His features were no different from any of the other men's, except that he wore his hair pulled back and tied behind his neck, and had tried to grow a beard.

Do not be afraid, I said to the Rajah, for we have come in peace. We made much noise with our lantaka in order to honor the rajah of this kingdom.

The Rajah huddled with the two men. Then the bendahara looked up, rose to his feet, and accosted us:

"What do you want?"

Cristóvão Rabelo now spoke up.

"My fath...er, my seignior, is a Captain of the greatest King in the world. He has come to discover Maluco. But he comes here to visit you because of the good fame accorded your king by the King of Mazaua. And he comes here to buy food with his merchandise."

I translated all this, rendering the key words as "laksamana," "Sultan," and "rajah."

Rajah Humabon turned expectantly to the Muslim. The latter then spoke in what sounded like the Bisayâ language Rajah Kulámbò and his people used.

Rajah Humabon spoke up.

"Ma-ayong pag-abút," he said. "Apan, bayad lang kamo sa dinunggu-an."

I thought quickly. His language was similar to mine, but I could understand it only if I caught his drift. He was welcoming us, but he was also suggesting we pay some kind of fee. "Dinunggu-an," was a word new to me. "Dunggu" meant "to dock." Ah, he charged fees for ships that docked in his harbor.

Rajah Humabon spoke again, pointing to the Muslim.

"Bisag kini siya, nibayad man."

The Muslim nodded.

"Yes, I pay the dinunggu-an," he said. "Upon my arrival. Everyone pay the dinunggu-an here. You must pay it, too. I am trader from Siam. I arrive here four days ago. My ship leave yesterday, but I am left here to trade for gold and slaves. It come back for me in one moon."

He had spoken in the pasar Malayu. His grammar was wretched, but I was relieved. My interpretative tasks would be that much easier. In Masawa I had managed only because Rajah Kulámbò spoke a bit of the pasar Malayu himself.

"Pay the docking fees?" I stared at Rajah Humabon. "Don't you know my master is a laksamana of the greatest Sultan in the world? He does not pay tribute to anyone. If you want peace, you will have peace. But if you want war, you shall have war!"

Both the bendahara and the Siamese trader recoiled in alarm.

"Kayata, Rajah, kitâ ka?" the Siamese said. Fuck it, Rajah, do you see now?

He continued in the local language. I could catch the drift well enough.

These are the same men, he told Rajah Humabon, who destroyed Calicut, Goa, and Melaka. They are vindictive men who remember every slight. In Goa they cut off the right hands of all Arab men before killing them. They killed the women and children as well. These men eat the hearts of their enemies. But if you treat them well they will be kind to you. In the

Molukas they have not destroyed any of the towns, but have engaged in trade.

I understood most of it, but had the impression the Siamese was talking over my head. He must have thought I could not understand their language.

I put up my hand.

All that he said is true, I told the Rajah, but those men he spoke of were from the Sultan of Portugal. My laksamana's lord is much more powerful, being the Sultan of España and Caliph of all Nasirans. If you do not wish to be my laksamana's friend, his Sultan will send many many ships and men, to destroy you.

They were hanging on my every word. They understood me well enough, including the word "Nasiran," the old Arabic word for "Christian" and actually a corruption of "Nazarean." I took a deep breath and continued in a quieter tone.

We desire only to buy food, I told them, and to trade. We have brought much merchandise, fine cloth, metals, and glassware. We shall not stay very long, for we must go on to the Molukas.

Rajah Humabon listened carefully as the Siamese translated my speech. Then he said he would have to discuss it with his datus. His answer to the laksamana would come the next day. He invited us to a meal with him.

We sat down on the mat, feet drawn up like tailors. This, the normal posture for eating, made Cristóvão Rabelo very uncomfortable. His discomfiture reminded me of the first time I had to sit on a chair to eat. Food was brought in and placed on the mat: rice, roast fish, stewed pork. I tasted the eggs Rajah Humabon had been eating. Very good. They were turtle eggs. I picked up one of the jars, put a reed into my mouth, and sucked up the liquid: palm wine.

"Tubâ sa niyog nga nipà," the bendahara said, "dilì sa lubí."

That was easy enough to understand. "It's palm wine from the nipâ palm," I translated for Cristóvão Rabelo, "not from the cocoanut palm."

"Yes," he agreed, "it's better than the arak we drank in Mazaua."

It was most irregular, Rajah Humabon said, but upon the advice of both his bendahara and the Siamese trader he was inclined to waive the dinunggu-an. Ala bab Allah. He would also prepare supplies of food to be sold to us; this would take a few days. And if we wanted to trade, he could set up a place for us in the market square. Of course there were so many minor details...

Cristóvão Rabelo said the details could be worked out with our factors the next morning.

I asked the Siamese trader what his name was.

"Kulnarit Sungvornyothin," he said.

When we rose to go, Rajah Humabon looked relieved. I wondered if he knew how close to disaster he had come. At the last moment, his diplomacy had saved him. The invasion of his city, which had been imminent, had been staved off.

As we were walking away, I had a sudden insight: Sugbu had a fine harbor, at which many vessels called. Surely the men of Sugbu were much exposed to the languages of this region. Now that I thought about it, the old bendahara seemed to have understood the pasar Malayu well enough. What about Humabon himself? The more I thought about it, the more sense it made. Humabon probably understood the pasar Malayu very well. Perhaps he spoke it better than Rajah Kulámbò did. Then I remembered how the interjection Ala bab Allah, "All is in the hands of Allah," had escaped his lips.

Rajah Humabon had no need of an interpreter. It was all a sham, in order to make things cumbrous, and gain himself more time to think. And it allowed him much latitude. Embarrassments could be blamed on faulty translation.

Cristóvão Rabelo and I made a detailed report, closeted in the stateroom of the *Trinidad*, to the Captain-General and the fleet's officers. One detail alone I held back: my suspicion that Rajah Humabon knew the pasar Malayu. As interpreter, I would keep that edge to myself.

When we came out, I had to report all over again to Rajah Kulámbò and his datus, who plied me with questions. Only after digesting my report did Rajah Kulámbò and his entourage go ashore. His leavetaking was very ceremonious. Among other things, he assured his blood brother he would tell Rajah Humabon of the great courtesy of the Captain-General.

Dom Fernão was not to be outdone, and expressed hopes and sentiments worthy of the occasion. Translating everything was tedious, and I abbreviated their speeches.

The following morning, Monday, April 8, the Captain-General sent escribano León de Ezpeleta ashore to thresh out the details of our trading agreement with Rajah Humabon. I of course accompanied him as interpreter. Rajah Humabon received us in his istana, with his bendahara and the Siamese trader present.

We walked to the town square, which became the market square whenever traders came in their ships. The Sanglay, Humabon said, did their trading in this square. So did the others, although they did not come as often: the men from Annam, from Lei Kiyu, and occasionally from Persia and Arabia.

Rajah Humabon asked how many laksamanas there were in our fleet.

Only one, said Ezpeleta.

Does he desire that I pay tribute to his lord, the Sultan of Ispaniya and Caliph of all Nasirans?

No, he does not.

It is well. But if your laksamana wishes to become my friend, he should send me a drop of blood from his right arm. And then I too will send him a drop of blood from my right arm. Only thereby may we become truly friends.

He will do it.

All the laksamanas who call at my harbor exchange presents with me. It is the custom. Do you want your laksamana to commence by giving me a present, or should I give him one first?

You're the one who wants to follow your custom, I told the Rajah. You should start it.

"Ala bab Allah na," he said.

Now my ear picked up the slight twist of pronunciation, emphasized by the extra word at the end. The old Arabic interjection had, in his language, been corrupted into something like "Halá, bahalà na."

He led us back to his palace and sent us off with his gifts for the Captain-General: a necklace of gold links with a single large pearl as its pendant, the whole wrapped in a silk purong; frankincense in a lacquered Sanglay box that had ducks, lotus leaves and waterlilies painted on it; myrhh and sandalwood in a blue and white porcelain dish, the decorative motif of which was a dragon.

On Tuesday, April 9, a tent was set up in the square and the Armada's goods put on display. The three maestres were in charge: Juan Bautista de Punzorol, Juan Sebastián de Elcano, and Miguel de Rodas. Several marineros and grumetes were there, too. Also with them, to keep detailed records of all transactions, were the escribanos Sancho de Heredia and Martín Mendez, assisted by some of the pages.

Rajah Kulámbò and the Siamese trader came to the *Trinidad* as Rajah Humabon's emissaries. They informed the Captain-General that Rajah Humabon had been advised by his council of datus to sue for peace. To this end Humabon would be sending his nephew and heir, with a delegation of datus, for a ceremonial ratification of peace. Rajah Humabon also wished to inform the laksamana that supplies of food were being collected, and would soon be brought to the ships.

The Captain-General had Petit-Jean d'Anjou dress up in full armor and demonstrate a manual of arms. Petit-Jean displayed some fancy motions with the sword, the halberd, the Swiss pike, and the lance, and fired a shot from an harquebus. The Siamese trader was much impressed.

Captain Juan Serrano was on the flagship, and Duarte Barbosa grumbled to him:

"Ceremonial ratification of peace, indeed. Why doesn't he simply conquer the city? That's what we always did in East Africa and India. Malacca, too. Massacre the indios, enslave the survivors."

"Perhaps it's simpler this way. He got that Humabon fellow agreeing to waive the fees. We've been allowed to trade. They're selling us food, and their women seem interested in us. All that, and no bloodshed."

"But we should invade this city before they can bring in allies from nearby islands. We're not too strong a force, you know. Three ships and some 170 men...we should establish strongholds, and make the indios build a fortress for us. Malacca was taken that way."

"That's not the point," Serrano said. "He could attack anytime, but he doesn't want to. It's not on his mind. The only thing on his mind is religion. The people here are heathens, who are never as obdurate as Muslims. He's planning to convert them."

"Ah, yes. Turn them into vassals, loyal to our King and Christian into the bargain. Vasco da Gama tried that with Quilóa. It didn't work."

"Quilóa was Muslim."

After the midday meal the peacemaking delegation arrived. At its head was a young man I had not seen before. Flanking him were Rajah Kulámbò and the Siamese. Behind them were ten men, all of whom wore anklets: every single one of them was a datù. Dom Fernão went into his cabin, and I helped him change into his white robe with the red cross whose tips were fleurs-de-lys. He would face the delegation as a Knight of Santiago.

Rajah Kulámbò presented the elders of Sugbu and Kang Dayang to the Captain-General: Sri Tupas Kamparang, Rajah Humabon's nephew and heir apparent; Sri Ambilik, the old bendahara; Sri Sumatro Kadaru, the temenggung or chief of the manggugubat, and then eight datus from the neighboring towns. From the region of Si-alo, south of Sugbu, Sri Laton, Sri Gibukan, Sri Matikat, and Sri Kanbul. From Mantawi, Sri Magpanawan. From Kutkut, Sri Baghaling. From Lilu-an, Sri Tapan. And from Lambusan, Sri Lumay. I knew none of these datus would travel without a contingent of his own manggugubat, so there must have been a concentration of warriors in Sugbu at that very moment. I wondered if the presence of so many forces had been orchestrated.

The names did not confuse Ser Antonio, who diligently wrote them all down. All these datus were formally introduced as honorable men by the use of the old Indian honorific "Sri." In subsequent mentions, however, their names were prefaced by the Vijayan article "si." It was this personal article that befuddled Ser Antonio. In the white man's languages, articles applied only to things. There were no articles for persons. In the language of the Bisayâ, however, there was the personal article "si." It was almost impossible to form a sentence where one was not grammatically obliged to use "si" before a person's name. Ser Antonio thought most names in this region began with "Si" and wrote down the datus' names as Çimattichat, Çigibucan, Çilaton.

The Captain-General invited them all into the stateroom. The criados rushed to obey his orders. Two velvet and leather chairs, one red and the other purple, were placed side by side, with space for the despensero to stand in between and serve wine. Dom Fernão and Sri Tupas sat on these chairs. A carpet was spread on the floor, and cushions scattered on it. Rajah Kulámbò and the datus sat on these.

The bendahara and the temenggung stood behind Sri Tupas. Behind Dom Fernão were his captains, Barbosa and Serrano. In between the two chairs stood the Siamese and myself, as interpreters. Standing off the carpet, behind Rajah Kulámbò and the datus, were as many of our officers and hidalgos as could be admitted into the room.

The Captain-General commenced.

"Is it your custom," he asked the delegation, "to speak in secret or in public?"

I was not sure how to translate the word "secreto." I had to rephrase in the pasar Malayu for the Siamese.

"He's asking if it's their custom to speak in hiding or out in the open."

He translated that into Binisayâ. Tupas answered:

"In the open."

"Are you, Principe Tupas, and you, Rei Colambo, empowered to make peace?"

"We are so empowered," replied the pair.

"Therefore, by the power vested in me as Captain-General of this royal Armada, I accept your offer of peace in the name of my sovereign, Don Cárlos Primero, by the grace of God King of España, and concurrently Carolus Quint of the Holy Roman Empire.Would that this holy peace between our two noble peoples be confirmed in Heaven by the Almighty God, Lord of all creation."

I made the most exact translation I could, word for word as far as was possible. There had to be compromises, of course: I described Don Cárlos as "Sultan of España and Caliph of all Nasirans." For "God" I used the word "Allah."

The Siamese translated it all into Binisayâ for the delegation, rendering "Allah" as "gino-o."

Dom Fernão then launched into a long speech extolling the virtues of the Christian faith. Among other things, he said he had cautioned his men against indulging in communication with the women of this port. They were Gentiles, and communication with them would mean mortal sin for Christian men.

I glossed over that point in my translation. I thought it unwise to mention that sort of thing to the elders of Sugbu. I had some trouble with the word "gentillos." The concept of Gentiles was Jewish, but I could not use their word, "goyim," as these people knew nothing of the Yahud. I decided on the borrowed Malayu word "kapri," a corruption of the Arabic "kafir," or "nonbeliever."

I succeeded in conveying the Captain-General's basic message: he wanted them to convert. The uneasy peace we were inaugurating—more of a truce, really—was contingent on their wholehearted acceptance of the white man's religion.

The men of the delegation were quite swayed by the Captain-General's eloquence. Sri Tupas, as form required, politely said he had never heard such sweet words and could not hope to reply as beautifully as was called for. But he desired to receive instruction in the faith. If the laksamana would leave a man, or even two men, to teach them, those men would be well honored in this city.

The Captain-General said he could not leave any men. However, if they truly desired to become Christians, our priest would baptize them. Then, next time, he would come with priests and friars to be left here to give them religious instruction.

Sri Tupas said they all earnestly desired it, but must needs seek approval from their Rajah. On that note the meeting was concluded.

Refreshments were served. Rajah Kulámbò quietly made a sign to one of the datus, who stood up and signalled to someone ashore. A noisy party of bearers appeared on the wharf with swine, goats, fowls, and hampers of rice. Sri Tupas and Rajah Kulámbò pointed to them and asked the Captain-General to accept the rice and animals as gifts from their lord, apologetically mumbling that they wished there had been more, but that was all Rajah Humabon could collect.

The Captain-General gave Sri Tupas a white linen robe, a red cap, strings of glass beads, and a gilded glass drinking cup. The others also received gifts, all except Rajah Kulámbò, who had received similar things in Masawa.

The Captain-General sent Ser Antonio Francesco Pigafetta, N.H., Knight of Rhodes and Patrician of Vicenza, to Rajah Humabon with gifts: a purple-and-yellow silk Turkish robe, a red cap, and strings of glass beads, all on a silver platter, which I had to carry. Ser Antonio carried two gilt glass drinking cups.

We walked with the delegation and were shown into Rajah Humabon's presence. Ser Antonio was seeing him for the first time, and he was impressed with the Rajah's graciousness and affability. As soon as the Rajah signified his acceptance of the gifts, Ser Antonio went to put the robe on him. I helped him drape it on the Rajah's tattooed shoulders. Ser Antonio then put the fez on Humabon's head. After that he kissed the beads, then put them around Humabon's neck. The Rajah lifted the necklace and kissed the beads, too.

The Rajah invited us to eat and drink with him. The turtle eggs were so good I ate five before I remembered my manners. Sucking up the wine through the thin reeds seemed to enhance its flavor. Ser Antonio quite enjoyed it. Unlike the squirting of wine into the mouth from a Basque *xahakoa*, there was no danger at all of getting messy.

I advised Ser Antonio to eat just enough to be polite. Then we took our leave.

Rajah Humabon professed surprise.

"Going so soon? Are you not staying for supper?"

"Oh, but uncle," said Sri Tupas, "if it please you, let them have supper at my house instead."

"Well...all right."

All very spontaneous, but it seemed to me that Rajah Humabon's had been a courtesy invitation, not meant to be accepted. A point of protocol was involved: as Rajah, Humabon's graces were reserved for the *numero uno*, our Captain-General. Mere emissaries were properly delegated to his representative, a young man our equal in age. Tupas had stepped in at precisely the right moment, extricating Humabon from the unseemly predicament of having to entertain men not his equal in rank.

We followed Sri Tupas to his house nearby and climbed up the short bamboo ladder. Inside, there were gamelan instruments lying about: a drum, suspended gongs, small gongs, and bamboo xylophones. Unbidden, the Malay names of those things came back to me: dabakan, agong, kulintang, saronay, gabbang.

Ser Antonio glanced up at the rafters, started, then panicked.

"There's a serpent up there!" he fairly screamed.

"Nada!" I said, gripping him by the shoulders. "It's nothing. Quite harmless."

About five feet long, mottled colors: a sawá. A large snake, but small for a python. I had seen the type before. Not poisonous. It killed its prey by constricting them.

"Oh, dear me," Sri Tupas said. "Gave him a scare, did it? Awfully sorry. It's just for catching mice, you know."

"It's only a pet," I told Ser Antonio. "They keep it around so the house will be free of rats."

"Don't they have cats?"

"Of course they have cats. But serpents catch more."

"Botyok!" called out Sri Tupas.

A dark young man with thick lips and kinky hair, of the race we called the orang asli, came running up the stairs.

"Take that away," said Sri Tupas. The boy propped up a ladder, climbed it, and took the python, draping it on his neck and shoulders as he climbed down. His right hand gripping it just below its triangular head, he used his left to put the tip of its tail in his mouth. Sucking on the tail, he made his exit.

"He always sucks the tail," Sri Tupas said. "For good luck."

He clapped his hands. Four girls appeared and applied themselves to the gongs. The music changed the mood in the room in some undefinable, magical way. The girls were clad only in skirts; their breasts were exposed. They were all quite young, and they all had lovely, well-formed breasts. One of them looked much like the snake handler: a girl of the orang asli, of the Semang or Jakun tribe. Like him she had kinky hair, thick lips, and dark skin. Faces of that race all looked alike to me, but at a guess she would be the snake-handler's sister.

Ser Antonio's jaw dropped. The physical charms of these young women had taken his breath away. His eyes bulged until I thought they would pop out of their sockets. When the girls had worked up a good rhythm with the drums and gongs, Tupas clapped his hands again, and three other girls burst in, dancing to the beat, bearing platters of food. These three were stark naked. They set the food before us, then resumed dancing. Ser

Antonio stared raptly at them, quite enchanted. Tupas and I ate, drank, ogled. We urged Ser Antonio to eat, and to drink palm wine through the thin reeds.

Ser Antonio moaned. He saw the food for the first time, gulped a mouthful. He sucked up wine through a reed.

The rhythm of the gamelan was hypnotic, and all three dancers were even better-endowed than the gamelan players. Ser Antonio was writhing in ecstasy. The seven girls were all singing as they danced and played. No matter where my eyes turned, there was always the sight of swaying breasts and gyrating pudenda. The wine seemed to be a love potion that went straight to the seat of my virility. I was getting a powerful erection. The words of the song the girls were singing rang in my ears like a ritual chant, and I knew that whether or not I understood those words, their magic would be worked on me.

⚓

37

"WHEN SRI LUMAY LEFT SUMATRA," they sang, "he left behind his father Bataugong, his mother Balintawak, his elder sister Panampawahi, his brother Sri Barat, and his sister Anduki."

I could follow the sense of it well enough. The song must have been an old one, for it used words and expressions I had not heard in the ordinary speech of the people here. Similar words existed in my own language. We no longer used them ourselves; we considered them archaic.

"Sri Lumay sailed his balanghays north, past the large island of Burnei and on to Bibaton, a small island that served as his landfall. Going northeast from there, he passed Pulao-an, then sailed east to the region of Kang Dayang and Bu-ol."

The words iraga and utara I guessed to mean "north" and "northeast." Of course, timor meant "east."

"Sri Lumay settled on good land between the mouths of two rivers, the Tinagò and the Bulalaki. The place was a natural harbor, fronted by a small island. The black people, the Agtà, were already living on that land. The Agtà became the slaves of the Bisayâ.

"After only a few years they were attacked by Taga-ilog pirates, people from the island of Luwasong. Sri Lumay burned his town, and fled with his people to the mountains.

"Three times the pirates of the Taga-ilog came to ravish the settlement. Three times Sri Lumay burned the houses and fled. The town came to be known as 'kang Sri Lumay'ng sugbò,' and Sugbu it is even unto this day."

Not a bad name for a town, I thought. Sri Lumay's burnt town, or, taking a variant meaning of "sugbò," Sri Lumay's ash-heap. I had heard of towns with worse names.

"Sri Lumay became the rajah of the greater part of Pulao Kang Dayang. He built a fleet of large boats and trained all his men, under his temenggung, to engage them at sea should the pirates return. But the Taga-ilog men never came again.

"When Sri Lumay grew old, he assigned his four sons different places in his domain. The eldest, Sri Alho, ruled a region in the south extending from the Mananga River through Kamparangga, Naupas Mayana, Kabulihan and Napo as far as Busay Sibonga. Within that region may be found the towns of Karkar, Argaw, and Dalagit. That region is now called Si-alo after him.

"The second son, Sri Ukob, ruled the region of Nahalin in the north, with its towns of Lilu-an, Kutkut, and Lambusan.

"The two younger sons, Sri Bulalaki and Sri Bantug, he kept with him, to help him rule Sugbu."

The song ended. The dancers exited. Ser Antonio turned eagerly to Sri Tupas.

"Was that all?"

"No," said Tupas, "there is more."

He nodded to the girl who played the kulintang. She began to play, tapping them vigorously with two short sticks. Another girl picked up that rhythm and began beating her suspended agong with her sticks, which had heads covered with paddings of cloth. Then the drum, the dabakan, joined in, and lastly the gabbang, the large bamboo xylophone, and now we had a new rhythm, very different from the previous one.

The three naked girls reappeared, their bodies glossy with sweat, and danced to the beat. Their dancing incorporated many expressive gestures with the hands. Much stylized, these gestures all hewed to a convention, by which one could follow their meanings. As a child, watching dances based on stories from the Ramayana or the Mahabharata, I had known most of those meanings, but by now had forgotten most of them.

None of the girls sang this time. Sri Tupas alone recited the words, speaking in a sort of singsong chant.

"Peace reigned in Sugbu. The people grew cotton in Si-alo, wove it into lumpot, and brought their lumpot to Sugbu. In Sugbu they bartered their lumpot for the porcelain dishes and jars of the Sanglay."

The word lumpot was new to me, but from the context I decided it meant "cloth." It seemed to be a special word, specific to the cloth woven from their cotton. They used another word, panapton, for cloth in general.

"Sugbu thrived on trade. The soil was poor, but everyone came to the port between the two rivers, facing the small island, to trade for gold and slaves, beeswax and civet cats, lumpot and pearls.

"Two hundred years passed. Now the Rajah of Sugbu was Sri Bantug, a descendant of Sri Lumay's eldest son Sri Alho. Rajah Bantug had eight children, six sons and two daughters. The eldest was Sri Parang Bungdara, who was born with a clubfoot. When Rajah Bantug died, Sri Bungdara declined to become the new Rajah. A man not perfect of body, he said, was not meant by the gods to be King. Therefore the second son, his brother Humabon, became Rajah in his place. Sri Bungdara, born to be king but too humble to arrogate what the gods preferred to deny him, has always been called Harì Palanggà by the people.

A term of endearment: Beloved King.

"Humabon's accession did not affect the line of succession. Rajah Humabon, it was agreed, would be succeeded by Sri Bungdara's eldest son. The fact that Humabon has had no sons, only daughters, has kept matters simple."

He was also talking about himself, of course. He, Sri Tupas, was the heir apparent. He was Rajah Humabon's designated successor. He was Harì Palanggà's eldest son.

"As for the other children of Sri Bantug, the third son, Sri Agu, was sent to Butuan to be Sri Kulámbò's bendahara. Kulámbò is an uncle of mine, he being my father's cousin.

"The fourth son, Sri Sumatro Kadaru, a renowned warrior, is Sri Humabon's temenggung.

"The fifth child, a daughter, is Birorang Dondonay. She is the shahbandar, the harbormaster. She collects the fees paid by all ships coming into the harbor to trade with us.

"The sixth, Sri Dula, rules Bu-ol, and all the islets between Bu-ol and Mat-an. He lives in the southern part of Mat-an, in Kamulinaw.

"The seventh, Birorang Mandalib-on, is a babaylan, a priestess.

"And the youngest, Sri Binukot, rules the land behind Sugbu, at the foot of the mountains:Talamban,Pung-ol,Bukid Abukayan, and Sahulsol all the way to Kabgan."

The playing ended. Again, the dancers exited.

"How many children," asked Ser Antonio, "does your father, Sri Bungdara, have?"

"We are three:myself, my brother Magiyu, and our sister Batungay."

"In what year," I asked, "did Sri Lumay leave Sumatra?"

"Tu-ig Saka 1195," Tupas said.

"Would you know what year that is in the Vikrama calendar?"

"Why, yes. It would be...ah...Vikrama 1410."

"What about now? What year is it now?"

"Tu-ig Saka 1441. Or Vikrama...1656."

It was now 1521 Anno Domini, or 928 Anno Hegirae. I did a few mental calculations: Sri Lumay had fled Palembang in 673 or 674 AH. Something like 1275 AD. He had sailed north for a few weeks, then founded Sugbu. This town was nearly two and a half centuries old by now, if one gave those old legends any credence.Sugbu was older than my own late, sorely lamented native town of Melaka.

"Why did Sri Lumay leave Sumatra?" I asked. "Why did he leave behind his parents and siblings?"

Sri Tupas nodded to the dark girl, and she began yet another rhythm, which was quickly picked up by the others. I noticed that the gabbang player had transferred to the saronay, a smaller bamboo xylophone. Once more the dancers came in, regaled us with their sinuous movements.

"The Maja Pahít invaded Sri Vijayâ in 1195," Tupas said. "Our people fled to Sulawesi, Burnei, and the Molukas. Sri Lumay's parents felt they were too old to flee. Sri Lumay's sisters wanted to stay with their parents. Sri Barat wanted to stay and inherit Sri Bataugong's lands in Palembang.

"Sri Lumay fled when the habagat was blowing. He therefore sailed northeast, where he had heard there were many islands. Most were uninhabited. A few were inhabited by bands of dark people, the Agtà.

"He saw this point of land, between two rivermouths and shielded by an island in front of it. He decided to settle here."

"And what of the rest of the Sri Vijayâ?" I asked. "What happened to the Rajah?"

"The royal family held out in Palembang," he said, "but by 1202 they too had to flee. All except a rajah retained on the throne as a figurehead. They went to Temasik. Sri Vijayâ continued as a vassal kingdom for another ten years. With the death of the figurehead rajah in 1212, all pretense was abandoned.

"The remnant of the dynasty remained in Temasik for eighty-six years. Then the Indians conquered Palembang in Saka 1297, driving out the Maja Pahít, who in turn conquered Temasik in 1298, driving out the last of the Sri Vijayâ."

Time to go. Ser Antonio rose to take his leave of Sri Tupas. Tupas cast his eyes about the room and asked him:

"Which of those did you like best?"

Ser Antonio was taken aback, but recovered quickly. Using sign language, he managed to convey his preference for the tallest girl, who was also the fairest of the three dancers. Tupas looked at me. I chose the darkest of them all, the orang asli slavegirl or Agtà, as they were called here. She was not a dancer but a gamelan player, the one who led the rhythm with her kulintang.

We were shown into separate but adjacent rooms. My Agtà girl was lying on a mat. She seemed to know what to do, what was expected of her. As I practically fell on her, her hand reached out and groped for me, to guide me.

"Hala, ka dakû," was all that escaped her lips.

I could not find the rhythm at first. Then I followed her lead...

I became dimly aware of Ser Antonio's voice coming through the thin wall.

"...in nomine Patrii, et Filii, et Spiritus Sanctii, amen."

He was baptizing the pretty dancer. Presumably with her consent, having converted her, through the language barrier, in that short time. He would not commit a mortal sin by indulging in communication with a pagan woman. He would fornicate only with a baptized Christian woman.

I had not bothered. Religion did not matter. Keeping the rhythm was all that mattered. My girl was good at it. The rhythm was perfect. We were in heaven.

Back in the *Trinidad*, we learned that Martín Barrena had expired while we were away. A Basque from Villafranco in Guipuzcoa, he had shipped as a sobresaliente on the *Santiago*. After that ship was wrecked he had sailed in the *Victoria*. Stricken with the escorbuto in the Pacific, he had now succumbed to it after a long illness...another human sacrifice claimed by the gods of the Kamaguyhang Laut.

The merino Juan de Aroche also looked moribund. El bachiller had all but given up hope on Juan.

The following day, Wednesday, April 10, the Captain-General sent Ser Antonio to request Rajah Humabon's permission to bury the dead man. I went along to interpret. Humabon was surrounded by most of his datus. We seemed to have interrupted a council of war. Ser Antonio was not aware of having barged into something important. He greeted Humabon and informed him of the Captain-General's request. Humabon expressed his condolences, and then said:

"If I and my vassals belong to you, how much more the land?"

I ignored the note of asperity in his tone. He pointed to a spot just off the market square, in the shade of a big tree. We could bury our dead there.

And set up a cross, too?

Yes, yes, whatever you like.

We went back to prepare for the burial, and to tell the gravediggers where to go, and learned that Juan de Aroche had breathed his last, too. A merino on the *Santiago*, he had been transferred to the *Victoria* after the shipwreck.

We buried Martín Barrena that afternoon with all the pomp we could muster. First in the procession was the cross, hurriedly fashioned by our carpenters that same morning. Five nails protruded from it, at the places that corresponded to the five wounds of the Christ Jesus, and at its top gleamed a brass crown plated with gold. Andrés de la Cruz, true to his name, had wanted to carry it to the square in the manner of Jesus bearing His cross to Golgotha. Several other men had then vociferously claimed they had as much right to carry the cross as he. But when it turned out to be rather heavy, the job had fallen, by default, on Petit-Jean d'Anjou's shoulders. Antonio de Basazabal, the biggest of the Basques, assumed Simon of Cyrene's role, ready to take over should Petit-Jean stumble and fall.

Padre Valderrama and Dom Fernão walked behind Petit-Jean and Basazabal, flanked by Andrés de la Cruz and Cristóvão Rabelo as acolytes. From what I knew of Christian rituals, someone should have been flagellating Petit-Jean, but this detail had been omitted.

Next was the coffin bearing Martín Barrena. Six Basques, led by Elcano were the pallbearers.

A skeleton crew stayed behind to guard the ships. Everyone who could attended the burial, the first chance for most of them to go ashore since our arrival three days ago.

The people of Sugbu watched us from a distance. It was only a few hundred feet from the wharf to the square, well within Petit-Jean's endurance. Basazabal seemed disappointed at not having had his moment to bear the cross.

Two holes had been dug, the large one for Martín's grave and the smaller one for the cross.

The cross was erected, and all knelt before it. The coffin was placed in front of it. Padre Valderrama led the congregation through the prayers for the dead. At one point the merinos, led by the alguacil, fired a salvo from their harquebuses.

Rajah Humabon was not to be seen, but later I espied him looking at Dom Fernão through a window. The two of them had yet to meet face to face, but this was not the right occasion.

Shortly after our men shoveled earth over Martín Barrena they dug a second grave, for Juan de Aroche.

In between the two burials our men mingled with the people of Sugbu. The natives were very friendly, and seemed to find our men's attempts at sign language quite hilarious. Every white man found himself the object of curious scrutiny. Two or three old women selling palm wine by the cupful soon were surrounded by our men.

We all regrouped for the second funeral, Juan de Aroche's. It was dark by the time we finished. The Captain-General went back to the flagship straightaway. Many of the men were in less of a hurry, drifting back to the ships in loose groups. The curious populace followed us around. There were quite a number of girls, none of them aware of the effect their exposed breasts had on our men.

The Captain-General sent out the alguaciles and merinos to round up malingerers, and soon most of us had returned to the ships.

Duarte Barbosa was missing.

The Captain-General sent the alguacil and two merinos to look for him. Taking me along as interpreter, Don Gonzálo searched for but failed to locate the *Victoria*'s captain. I queried some people near the market square. Barbosa had been dallying with some girls and had gotten loud and drunk.

Don Gonzálo gave up at that point. Barbosa could have been in any of the houses in the whole kampong.

Some of the men on the gravedigging detail were still in the vicinity of the square, drinking palm wine and engaging bystanders in banter.

I went off to a dark corner to urinate against a tree. Beyond was a field with gravestones: the local cemetery. I detected movement: two or three men somewhere among the graves. What were they doing in the cemetery?

Thursday, April 11, was given over to the transfer of our trade goods from the ships to the tents that had been set up in the market square. The Captain-General asked me to invite Rajah Humabon to the capitana for the ceremony of kasi-kasi. I informed him that Rajah Humabon expected him to go to the square and perform the rite there before the people of Sugbu.

"Ezpeleta tells me I am supposed to send the Rajah a drop of blood from my arm," he said.

This put me in a quandary. He was taking the Rajah literally, entirely missing the nuances of Humabon's request. Humabon had indeed asked to be sent a drop of blood as a sign of sincerity, leaving unspoken his preference for the personal encounter. He had suggested the less satisfactory way, that of exchanging blood through emissaries, in the hope that his visitor would rise to the occasion and gain face by insisting on the more obvious and much better way, that of a blood compact done face to face. The two had yet to see each other in the flesh. But the Captain-General was already bleeding himself and dripping blood from his right arm into a cup. Now I had the odious task of accompanying Ser Antonio and presenting this cup to the Rajah. The Rajah, I knew, would say nothing, merely bleed his arm and shake blood into another cup, to be sent back with us. Admittedly, in both cases the blood would be from the right arm. But it was all on the wrong foot.

38
〰️

ON FRIDAY, APRIL 12, the maestres opened shop in the market square. Most of the trade was by barter. The people of Sugbu insisted on using their own wooden balances.

"Those balances," said Juan Bautista de Punzurol, "remind me of the ones used in the Pardeza."

"You mean," said Bartólome Prior, "the par de ça de Loire."

The bar was held by a cord at its middle. At one end was a bit of lead, and at the other were marks showing the gradations of weight. The scales hung by three wires. The knot formed where the three wires met would be placed above one of the marks, and things were thus weighed quite accurately.

They offered livestock, fowl, rice, and bronzeware cast by the lost-wax method: lamps, hand gongs, condiment boxes for betel, pearls and gold. They also offered large seashells they called laghan and waxy masses that they said were squid beaks. Both the laghan and the squid beaks come from the bellies of whales. The laghan would be swallowed whole by the whale, after which the sea animal inside would creep out of the shell and eat the whale's heart. The whale would die, and fishermen would find the laghan inside the whale's body, near the heart.

"Jonah," said Bartólome Prior, "should have taken one of those shells when the whale swallowed him."

What about these balls of wax? Are they really the beaks of squid? They look too big.

These are the beaks of giant squid, one of which is as long as five or six men are high. When it is eaten by the whale everything is digested except the hard beak. The beak becomes coated with wax and is vomitted by the whale. The Sanglay pay good prices for those beaks.

What do they do with those?

He did not know. Perhaps the Xanglei knew how to make a soup out of them. They made soups out of birds' nests and sharks' fins and even monkeys' lips.

"I have seen this before," Bartólome Prior said. "It is called ambergris. It is used in the making of perfumes."

Following the Captain-General's instructions, our men pretended to be reluctant to take gold, accepting it only when no other merchandise was left.

For the goods of the natives our maestres and factors bartered combs, glass mirrors, knives from Flanders and Middle France; scissors, sewing needles, fishhooks; reams and quires of writing paper; bolts of cloth in different colors, red, green, yellow and blue; linen, canvas, velvet and satin; matamundo; alum; cumin seeds; saffron; and ingots of copper and iron. We also offered a few copper vessels containing azogue or quicksilver. We had brought quite an amount of mercury, about two thousand pounds. It could be used for medicinal purposes, if the pharmacology here had attained that high a level. We intended to use most of it ourselves, to separate gold from the impurities in its ore. Gold could be refined by mixing its ore with mercury and then burning the amalgam in order to evaporate the mercury. We doubted if this people knew that method. All gold in this region seemed to have been obtained by panning.

At the end of the day the factors reported that the locals were trading their gold for our iron at an utterly incredible price: 10 tahils of gold for 14 of iron.

Prior did some careful weighing, and determined that the Sugbu-anon people's unit of weight for gold, the tahil, was equivalent to $1\frac{1}{3}$ troy ounces. Gold was of course not measured by the avoirdupois scale, which divided the libra into 16 ounces, but by the scale used in Troyes, which allowed only 12 ounces per libra. One of the natives told him the tahil was the weight used by the Xanglei, and that it was $\frac{1}{16}$ of a kati.

On Saturday, April 13, the carpenters went to work building a platform in the square, where it would face the cross set up three days before, and in the shade of the tall trees.

Sunday, April 14, was the day for the Rajah of Sugbu's baptism. The ships fired their cannon as soon as our party was ashore. The people of Sugbu lined the streets from the docks all the way to the market square. Some of them followed us along the sidelines.

In the vanguard were two men in full armor, and the guidons carrying the colors.Next came Dom Fernão, in his Knight of Santiago's habit, Padre Valderrama beside him. Behind them marched forty of our men, dressed in doublets. Bringing up the rear were two harquebusmen.

When we drew up at the square the two riflemen fired their muskets, and were answered by the booming of the Armada's cannon. The Rajah of Sugbu, surrounded by his people, was waiting near the platform. We had been in Sugbu for a week, but this was the first time Dom Fernão and Sri Humabon were meeting face to face. They embraced.

"This is the royal standard," Dom Fernão said, pointing to the silken flag. "It isn't usually brought ashore unless escorted by fifty men in full armor, like those two, and fifty harquebusmen. But so great is the love I bear you that I have brought it, nevertheless."

"You flatter me," Humabon said.

But in his eyes I could see the mathematics his mind was doing. Rajah Kulámbò had doubtless made a private report to him, and he could calculate one fully armed white man to be worth 100 local warriors. There were 200 men, more or less, in the Armada. He would therefore need some 20,000 men in order to engage the Armada on even terms.

He did not have that many. From what I had heard, he could round up a thousand men at a moment's notice. His allies could contribute a few thousand more. The datus from all over the island, from Si-alo in the South to Bantayan in the North, were all in Sugbu. What were they doing here? Why weren't they home in their respective districts? Had he summoned them as soon as word from Kulámbò had reached him? That must have been why Rajah Kulámbò kept us in Masawa, harvesting his rice. The delay had bought Rajah Humabon more time to assemble his datus.But the forces of this island were not enough. Reinforcements from other islands, from Bu-ol, from Butuan and Kalaghan, and from the islands to the west, would be needed. Meanwhile, Humabon would humor the white leader and go through the ceremony of baptism and conversion. It would buy more time.

Padre Valderrama ascended the platform and bustled about the altar. The Captain-General and the Rajah sat down in front of the platform on chairs of red and purple velvet. The datus sat on satin cushions, and the others on mats.

The Captain-General praised God for having inspired the Rajah to become a Christian.

Humabon said he had indeed seen the light, but some of his datus did not wish to follow his example and convert, saying they were as good men as he.

"Are they here?" asked the Captain-General.

"Not all of them."

"Summon them."

Humabon issued orders. Underlings rushed about at his command. In a few moments several men, datus all, came before us and found places on the mats.

The Captain-General gave a short speech, the gist of which was that all who would not obey Humabon would be killed, and their properties confiscated. He then taught them how to make the sign of the cross. He instructed them to burn their idols, and set up crosses in their place. He told them to pray before the cross daily, kneeling and with hands clasped.

Then it was time for the baptism.

The Captain-General took Rajah Humabon by the hand and led him up the platform. Padre Valderrama poured water on his head, put a pinch of salt in his mouth, and elicited his replies to a few questions which, for me, were the devil to translate: "Do you renounce Satan and all his works?"

Sri Tupas was next, then Rajah Kulámbò, then the datus, then all the men they could find. Hundreds appeared. Each new Christian was given small gifts by our men.

It was high noon before the Mass began, so great was the crush of baptismal proselytes. Dom Fernão stood at the pulpit to deliver the homily, a stirring speech I had to translate at the top of my voice, all about the rewards of eternal life in Heaven, and the hellfire and damnation to which non-Christians were condemned. At the elevation of the Host harquebus shots were fired, immediately answered by broadsides from the three ships in the harbor.

Sugbu was now a Christian city. Rajah Humabon, with his baptism, had been renamed Don Cárlos, el rey cristíano de Çubú.

Sri Tupas had been christened Don Fernando, after the Emperor's brother, and Rajah Kulámbò was now Don Juan. The Siamese trader, Kulnarit Sungvornyothin, was now Cristóbal. Ser Antonio fondly referred to him as Cristóbal el moro, knowing it was much more difficult to convert a Muslim than a pagan to Christianity. He regarded the man's conversion as a personal victory.

The ranks of Christendom had been swollen; an entire city had converted. The exception was a datù from the island of Mat-an. He would of course come around and be converted, too. In due time. Merely a matter of persuasion.

A small detail nagged at the back of my mind. The Captain-General had sent the Rajah a drop of blood from his arm when he should have performed the kasi-kasi in person. Humabon had been too proud to send first bloood, and then too tactful to remark on the faux pas. Now the Rajah and the Captain-General were fellow Christians, but the two of them had not performed a proper blood compact. Was baptism the more important?

This was a change from the usual policy of conquest and slavery. My master was inaugurating a new epoch, an Age of Enlightenment, where man's humanity to man was paramount. No longer would a powerful nation exploit a weaker and for good measure commit genocide; this time the souls of those about to be exploited would be saved from eternal damnation and brought into the light of the one true faith.

The two other captains, Duarte Barbosa and Juan Serrano, said nothing, expressing disapproval with tight lips. They had served under da Gama, d'Almeida, and d'Alboquerque. They knew how a Portuguese Captain-General went about conquering a city. A massacre of the inhabitants was the rule rather than the exception. Rapine, looting, slavery...all these were normal. As for the typical Spanish Captain-General, everyone knew of Cortés...and what he had done in Nueva España. That was the way to do it. Indios were indios, whether brown men or black. They were inferior races all, so much vermin to be exterminated. This newfangled notion of conquest by persuasion, on the other hand, extended the dignity of Christian brotherhood to the indios. They did not deserve it. Such a policy was bound to fail, as it made no sense at all.

The Rajah and his datus escorted us to the wharves. Our parties took leave of each other, the Rajah and the Captain-General embracing, then everybody else too, the whole exercise punctuated by broadsides booming from the ships' cannon.

In the afternoon Padre Valderrama returned to the square, along with some page boys to act as acolytes, and myself as interpreter, to baptize Rani Humamay. Ser Antonio came along, too, bringing an image of the Virgin Mary and a wooden statue of the Christ Jesus as a child.

Bir-orang Humamay, with a retinue of some forty women, came to the square singing, and dancing a dignified sort of dance: shuffling left and right, a step back and several forward; a most graceful and elegant congregation.

I reflected on the Binisayâ words for the human female: "woman" was "orang parampuan," the same term in my language; a married woman was a "babaye," and a maiden was a "bini-bini." Women of rank were entitled to the honorific "Bir-orang."

The Rani's retinue included Humabon's three other wives, and the region's most prominent women. Among them were the principal wives of Rajah Kulámbò, of Sri Tupas, and of the datus, along with several of those men's lesser wives, and the most nubile of their daughters.

Humamay was rather younger than Humabon, and very beautiful. Fair of skin, bright of eye, red of lip, teeth neither stained by betel juice nor marred by gold spots, she wore a long flowing dress of black and white cloth. Her fingernails and toenails were of the same red hue as her lips. On her head was a widebrimmed hat of palm leaves cleverly woven to form a high crest on top, like a tiara. She was the only one who wore such a hat. Only nobles could wear hats like that. In the olden days the nobles, both men and women, carried white parasols given them by Xanglei traders, who wanted some way of distinguishing them from the common folk. Now they wore distinctive hats. The principal wives of Rajah Kulámbò and Sri Tupas wore similar hats, too, when in their own circles. For this occasion they had observed protocol and deferred to Rani Humamay.

Now, when had Rajah Kulambo's principal wife, Balud, arrived from Butuan? And who had she come with? Perhaps a whole contingent of fighting men from Butuan and Kalaghan?

I dismissed the thought. Fighting us was farthest from this people's minds. They had sized up our Captain-General as a religious man and they instinctively respected this, as Hindoos respect a sadhu, or Buddhists a monk. Here they were not content with having all their men baptized; their women, as good as their men in matters of the spirit, expected the same privilege.

Ser Antonio conducted Bir-orang Humamay to the platform and seated her on a cushion. He showed her the image of the Virgin and the statue of the Christ. She was quite enamored of the wooden child and asked if she could have it. Ser Antonio regretfully said he could not give it to her, as it belonged to the Captain-General.

Ser Antonio gave a little sermon on how all of us are born in a state of sin, how Jesus redeemed us by dying on the cross, how we should all accept the faith in order to be worthy of His sacrifice, and how we should resolve nevermore to sin again. I made a bad translation, but it must have been good enough. Humamay was quite overcome by contrition and tearfully asked for baptism.

Soon Padre Valderrama was ready. Humamay was the first to be baptized, with Ser Antonio standing as her sponsor. She was christened Juana, after the Emperor's mother. The name suggested itself, because of its similarity to her original name. There was no need to tell her Juana's epithet was La Loca.

After Humamay, Padre Valderrama baptized the women in her retinue, then other women as they came forward. Some three hundred women were baptized that afternoon.

Kulambo's wife was renamed Isabel, and Tupas's wife became Catalina. Padre Valderrama soon ran out of names and had to whisper to us to provide him some. All of us had to stop and recall the names of women in Europa: Beatriz, Ana, Conceição, Inéz, Rosa, Susana, Felippa, and many others.

Now that he had shown himself to the people of Sugbu, the Captain-General went ashore every day to hear Mass. Many of the newly baptized natives would attend, too, and after the Mass he would preach to them. I had to be at his side all the time, in order to interpret his sermons. I began to find the task unwelcome. Religious sermons tended to abound in words for which my language had no real equivalents. The Siamese trader was not always present, and I could not be sure how much of my pasar Malayu my listeners understood. But they always went away edified and full of zeal, as if they had understood everything perfectly. They made me wonder if the Holy Ghost had come down and given me the gift of tongues.

One day, before Mass, the Captain-General asked Rajah Humabon to put on his purple and yellow silk robe and his red cap, and to assemble all his datus. The Captain-General made them all formally swear allegiance to Humabon and to the King of Spain as their overlord. Then he drew his sword before the wooden statue of the Christ and renewed his own oaths to his King. He said he was giving Rajah Humabon one of the chairs, and asked him which he preferred. I thought Humabon would take the purple chair, but he chose the red. The Captain-General told him that whenever he went around he should be borne by four slaves in that chair, and showed him how the slaves should hold and carry the chair.

Rajah Humabon thanked him for that magnificent gift, and regretted he could not reciprocate at once with a gift of his own. However, he said he had ordered his smiths to fashion gold ornaments for the Captain-General: gold earrings for his earlobes, gold armlets to be worn above the elbows, and gold anklets.

Was he sending gifts to the Emperor as well, as a token of his fealty?

Oh, yes, said Rajah Humabon, he had ordered magnificent things for the Caliph too, a gold crown set with diamonds, rubies, pearls, and emeralds, and earrings, armlets, and anklets as well.

One morning Rani Humamay came to Mass. She wore a new dress of white silk and black taffeta; black and white seemed to be her favorite colors. A widebrimmed hat was on her head, and a silk scarf with gold stripes on her shoulders. Preceding her were three girls carrying three more of the Rani's hats. Following her were most of Sugbu's women, all barefoot and naked except for a cloth around the waist and a scarf on the top of the head. All of them had very long hair which they allowed to flow freely.

Only once before, in Río de Janeiro, had we attended Mass in the company of so many women with exposed breasts.

The Captain-General sprayed rosewater on Rani Humamay and the women nearest her.

After the Mass, Bir-orang Humamay asked the Captain-General to give her the wooden statue of the Christ as a child. He replied that he would give it to her, but that she must destroy whatever idols she kept in her house, and replace them with the Holy Child. She promised to. It was of course a much better crafted image than any of her own idols. Made in Flanders, it was the sort of icon that sold well in Europa. The type was called a Santo Niño, and I rather admired its artist's imagination.

Jesus was usually depicted as a babe in swaddling clothes, or as a bearded adult in a white robe. The maker of the first Santo Niño had decided to combine two disparate images, and show a little boy as a crowned king in full regalia.

The Santo Niño craved by Bir-orang Humamay, or Reina Juana as Dom Fernão called her now, was typical: a curly-haired boy dressed in loose brocaded robes, a velvet hat on his head, a scepter in his right hand, and a sphere of the world in the other. Two fingers of the right hand pointed up, while the thumb kept the other two fingers down: an ancient sign for peace, also used by the Hindoos. Implanted in the sphere was a cross.

A solid wooden base allowed the Santo Niño to stand upright, but in Europa he was always sold with a gilt crown and little cradle into which he could be laid at night, like a real baby.

Dom Fernão indicated that Pigafetta should do the honors, and so Ser Antonio graciously showed Humamay how the Santo Niño could be put to sleep in the cradle, and how the velvet hat could be replaced by the gilt crown. The change of headgear caused a magical effect, apparent only to the initiated: it transfigured Jesus from a little Flemish boy, holding a pair of toys, into the rightful King of the World, resplendent with the symbols of his authority.

"Halá, pagka-anindot!" chirped Bir-orang Humamay, taking the Santo Niño in her arms and handing the cradle to one of her ladies-in-waiting.

She made her exit from the square in the same way she had arrived, at the head of her group of barebreasted women, all of them singing their joyful tune and dancing their shuffling dance. She held up her Santo Niño for all to see, whirling around as if it were truly a living baby and she wanted him to enjoy a good view of everything around her.

Kulnarit Sungvornyothin, even after his baptism, was still called Cristóbal el moro. Vestiges of the special antipathy Iberian Catholics reserved for Muslims remained. My own feelings were quite the opposite. Having grown up in a Muslim town, I cherished the way Muslims lived by the five pillars of Islam. Then, too, I felt drawn to Kulnarit for his fluency in the pasar Malayu, even if he needed to work on his grammar. The first chance I could, I asked him if he had been to Melaka.

Four or five times, he said. It was quite different now, with the Portuguese occupying it and charging exhorbitant fees and taxes. But it remained an important center of trade, one no merchant willingly bypassed. He named the places he would stop at during a typical voyage out of Krung Thep: Vinh Loi, Kang Tau, Haifung, Khanfu, Sugbu, Sulu, Terrenate, Tidore, Amboina, Makasar, Palembang, Melaka, Kedah...

How far was is it then, I asked, from Sugbu to Melaka? Or from Sugbu to the Molukas?

He did not really know. He did not sail directly between Sugbu and either of those places. From Burnei to Sugbu was ten days, more or less, he said. From Melaka to Burnei was two weeks. That voyage could only be done in the season of the habagat...from Melaka to the Molukas was three weeks, if one did not stop at Makasar, or Amboina...from Khanfu to the place full of nilad weeds, on the mouth of a river called Pasig, was a week, if one sailed with the amihan...

What had he heard of Melaka's Sultan Mahmud Shah?

After the Faranghis took Melaka, he said, the Sultan went to Bintang, across the Strait in one of the Riau islands.

Mahmud attempted to win back his city, but was beaten off. The Faranghi fortress, A Famosa, the one built of Muslim gravestones, had proven well-nigh impregnable.

Mahmud Shah's eldest son, Muzzaffar, was in Perak. The second son, Mansur, was in Johor. Mahmud himself was often in Muhar, the village at the mouth of the Muhar River. All three were recruiting men-at-arms. After regrouping, they would again endeavor to retake Melaka.

I reported Kulnarit Sungvornyothin's remarks on the distance to Burnei and Melaka to my master...he said it tended to confirm his calculations: Sugbu was some 150 leguas northeast of the Molukas, and about 500 leguas northwest of Malacca.

He wrote down his observations in his derrotero. I noticed that he spelled Sugbu as "Çubú." Ser Antonio had spelled it either as Zubu or Zvbv. Among the escribanos and pages, it was Subuth, Çubio, Çibuy, or Zebv. In the derroteros of the pilots I had seen such renderings as Iubu, Zzeubu, and Çebú.

None of them had got it right.

None of their spellings acknowledged the presence of the *g* sound. The locals pronounced the name of their city very distinctly, and there was no mistaking that hard *g* in the middle. Something was wrong with the white man's ear.

39
≈≈

MONDAY, APRIL 15, moon a day shy of first quarter. The wind changed, the amihan yielding to the habagat. Was this the regular southwest monsoon, or a random shift? Kulnarit Sungvornyothin thought the latter. The habagat was fickle, he said. The amihan would return in a few days. I hoped he was right. The Spice Islands lay to the south, and it would be difficult to leave Sugbu while the habagat blew.

The next two weeks seemed to me like shadow plays, remembered in snatches, as one remembers dreams...

—a view of the city, seen from its heart: before me the harbor and behind me the mountains; the half-moon above, and to the left the river. How like Melaka, but with everything disoriented, facing east where Melaka faced west. A city converted, or at least baptized. A city with a familiar face: the face of someone I once knew very well. Did she remember me still? After all these years, would she know me if she saw me again? As in a dream, I saw her face: someone who regarded not the heart, but the liver as the center of feeling; someone whose soul could steal out of the body at will, and so look from the outside at her own self...

—Duarte Barbosa being hauled in, dead drunk, and clapped into the brig. The Captain-General deposing him and appointing Cristovão Rabelo captain of the *Victoria* in his stead. From page boy to captain was quite a leap, but by now everyone knew whose son he was. Besides, the promotion was seen as temporary. Barbosa always succumbed to debaucheries while in port, only to regain his senses when it was time to sail. He would probably be reinstated upon our departure from Sugbu.

—the sound of gongs summoning the people to the consecration of a pig in the square. Two priestesses, each carrying a bamboo trumpet:Bir-orang Mandalib-on and Bir-orang Dondonay. Humabon's sisters. They put double horns on their heads, then lifted their clasped hands to the sky. They danced to the sun, blowing on their trumpets, their melodies soaring above the rhythm of the gongs.

Bir-orang Mandalib-on pretended to drink from a cup of palm wine, five times raising it to her lips, then abruptly sprinkled it on the pig's belly. A lance was handed to her, which she aimed at the pig's neck, five times pretending to thrust it in. The gongs throbbed until the veins stood out on the drummers' necks; the singing and dancing grew frenzied. Suddenly Bir-orang Mandalib-on thrust the lance through the underside of the pig's neck. Its deathshrieks resounded throughout the square. Bir-orang Dondonay stopped up the wound with a fistful of grass. Bir-orang Mandalib-on took up a lighted torch, put it in her mouth and thus extinguished the flame. Both women dipped their trumpets in the blood. Approaching the spectators, each woman went first to her husband, wet a finger, marked her husband's forehead with blood, then went around the circle to mark the other men.

"Very similar to our Ash Wednesday rite," said Ser Antonio.

"What we do with ash," said Dom Fernão, "they do with blood."

"Pig's blood," said Duarte Barbosa. "Revolting to Muslims. I wonder if they've ever invited that Moro to this ceremony."

—women sighing after acts of love: "Oh, very good, but better when there is a palang." And so we asked some of their men to show us their palangs: the height of male vanity. Penis jewelry; metal implements fastened at the head of the circumcised penis. It was a bolt the size of a goose quill that pierced the utin near its ulok. At each end of the bolt, flanking the glans, was a spur, usually shaped like a star, with points.

One had to be circumcised to wear the palang, as otherwise its irritation of the foreskin would be unbearable. Most of the men of Sugbu wore the palang, which was invariably of gold; only the poorest of men were content with palangs of tin. All of the men in Sugbu were circumcised, even those of the Agtà race.

Ser Antonio was absolutely flabbergasted when he first saw a palang. He saw at once that it added a new dimension to the act of sexual intercourse.

"How is it done?" he wanted to know.

The woman has to help, the men told him, and guide it in. It has to be turned sideways and slowly inserted. And afterwards, it cannot be pulled out before it becomes soft. All our women prefer it this way, added the men, of which last detail Ser Antonio seemed doubtful. The women he had lain with had all assured him he was the best lover they had ever known, and he had taken it to heart.

—the strange case of Magiyu, Hari Palangga's son, stricken with an ailment that swelled his clubfoot, and left him quite unable to walk and unable or unwilling to speak. Dom Fernão, Padre Valderrama, and el bachiller Morales went to see him. The cirujano confided that the ailment was more in the mind than in the body; psychosomatic, he said, resorting to Greek words as doctors will. They baptized him and both his wives, and all ten girls in his household. Baptism restored the power of speech to Magiyu; in reply to the Captain-General, he said he felt better. They prayed with him, lit candles and incense, and fed him mandolata. The Captain-General gave him a mattress, a blanket, a yellow coverlet, and a pillow, and daily sent him mandolata, rosewater, oil of roses, and carne de membrilla.

After five days Magiyu got up and walked, a cure as miraculous as any in the Gospels. The people of Sugbu were much impressed, as their own priestesses had given up on Magiyu. It proved the power of the Christian god. Theretofore they had been reluctant to destroy their idols, old wood and copper statues, hollow and with no backs, with large faces and four tusks each, painted all over in gaudy colors, but now they set to it with a will.

"Castilla!" every man shouted as he smashed an idol, subsuming the new religion into its bringers' place of origin. None of them could pronounce the word right.

"Katjílà!" they shouted, some so loudly it seemed their voices rather than their blows had shattered their idols...

—the surreptitious trade in gold by several of the men, among them Serrano, all of the maestres, escribanos, and factors...one could see the gold fever in these men's eyes. But other men had other fevers, and among those worst afflicted with the delirium of hagiolatry were Padre Valderrama, Cristovão Rabelo, and the Captain-General himself; Ser Antonio, too, had a touch of it.

—returning to the house of Sri Tupas to interpret for Ser Antonio, who wanted to listen to the music of gongs and watch the naked girls. Ser Antonio took his quill and writing paper, and worked on his glossary of the Binisayâ language. He asked how the bodies of the dead were disposed of. Ser Antonio believed the way a race took care of its dead revealed much about its culture, and how it regarded the soul. He had yet to discover a culture that did not believe in an afterlife. Even the indios of Patagonia, the most primitive people we saw in the voyage, placed their dead in huts standing on posts the height of a man.

Sri Tupas said that the women took charge when a man died. The dead man was anointed with camphor and placed in a box, roped and curtained off, in the middle of his house. All the women wore veils of white cloth, for white was the color of mourning, and put porcelain jars about the room. They lit fires in those jars, and tossed in myrrh, storax, and benzoin, until those perfumes pervaded the room.

The principal wife of the dead man lay down upon his body, her mouth, hands, and feet upon his, as the wife next in rank slowly cut off the dead man's hair. Then, placing the dead man's prized possessions beside him, they covered up the box with logs, nailed these into place, and brought him to the cemetery for burial.

—by the light of the waxing moon, men digging up graves: the men our own, the graves those of long-buried natives of Sugbu, the moon gibbous. The people of Sugbu took many of their worldly goods with them to the grave, and certain of our men were desecrating tombs and stealing those goods: gold palangs, earrings, bracelets, rings, necklaces, porcelain jars. The Captain-General was informed of it, but none of the culprits were identified. He therefore said nothing. He would act when someone was apprehended in actual commission, not before; that was his way. The wanton acts of a few had brought shame on all of us, and he knew we would all henceforth police our ranks.

—the Captain-General joining a balairong, a council of Humabon and his datus, all of whom had converted and been baptized. All had agreed to pay tribute to the Captain-General. Most of them had actually paid: a few goats, a brace of fowl, a bahar of rice, articles of gold.

Discussion centered on the one datù who would not conform: Lapulapu of Mat-an, who ruled most of the island, leaving Sri Dula only the southern tip. A message had been sent to him, inviting him to recognize Humabon's authority, swear fealty to the white laksamana's Sultan, convert to the Nasiran faith, be baptized, and pay tribute to the Faranghi laksamana.

Lapulapu's reply:

"Walâ ako'y agawon gawas kanakò."

"I have no master save myself."

He had not stopped there. He had gone on to say more: "Walâ ako'y yukbo-an nga harì. Ang ako'ng alagad alang ra sa akong mga tawo."

"I bow before no king. I owe allegiance only to my people."

Finally, he had uttered words meant to cut to the quick: "Ang mga tabúnon walâ maka-ilá ug agawon'g langyaw ug dilì gayúd, bisan hangtud kanus-a."

"The brown races do not know any foreign master and never will, even unto the end of time."

If nothing else, he knew his rhetoric.

The Captain-General resolved to teach this Lapulapu a lesson. He would burn one of the villages of Mat-an. None of the datus objected.

—the burning of Buaya. Under the Captain-General's orders the alguacil, Don Gonzálo, led a force and sacked the village. Don Gonzálo's handpicked group of merinos, fourteen men, rowed the *Trinidad*'s batel at dawn on Wednesday, April 17, to the side of Mat-an that most needed chastising, its north shore. Buaya was put to the torch. The people of that town, rudely awakened, rushed naked out of their burning houses. A few men attempted to fight, but fled after seeing their spears glance off our men's armor. Don Gonzálo and his merinos planted a cross there, then rowed off in the batel. Not having inflicted casualties, they did not themselves suffer any.

Dom Fernão had a clear enemy now, not his but Humabon's. It was the conquistador's usual strategy. By defeating a vassal's enemy, he could consolidate his suzerainty over that vassal. Earlier he had offered to fight any enemies of Rajah Kulámbò, but the latter had said the season was not right. Now, standing beside Humabon, he had given notice to the enemy.

Without warning, the wind shifted again. Once more the amihan blew, a gentle but steady breeze from the northeast.

On Monday, April 22, a full moon rising over Mat-an, I sat with Sri Tupas in his house, enjoying the music his slavegirls made. I had brought trinkets for all of them.

A strange squealing sound came from above. I looked up at the rafters: the python had caught a rat and was leisurely swallowing it.

Sipping palm wine through thin reeds, I asked Tupas about the datu of Opong.

"Lapulapu Dimantag was named after a fish," he said, "two fishes, in fact. His surname, Dimantag, is the name of a large black fish. His own name, Lapulapu, is that of another fish. It's a rather big fish.Very tasty. One of the best there is.We don't eat that fish everyday. We reserve it for special occasions. Besides, it's very hard to catch. It's a wily fish that hides among the rocks underwater. The lapulapu is red, has small eyes, and thick lips. Datù Lapulapu looks exactly like that fish."

"I heard he's not from here?"

"No, he is not. He is an orang laut from Burnei. His father was an Arab, his mother a Dayak. He took afer his mother, and that is why he is daghagang, almost as dark as an Agtà."

"In what year was he born?" I asked.

"He has not attained his fortieth year. He's about 36 or 37; he was born in tu-ig Saka 1404. Don't ask me what Vikrama year that is."

I worked it out in my mind: 889 A.H. Then I computed it mentally for Ser Antonio, in case I later had to repeat the story to him: 1484 A.D. Or Vikrama 1619.

"I've heard his parents were Harì Mangal and Rani Bauga," I said.

Sri Tupas laughed.

"The real names of Lapulapu's parents were Aban and Magdangali.Of course, around here, people are more apt to remember silly nicknames. His father was an Arab trader who cut logs in Burnei before he became a bendahara to one of those rajahs in the Molukas. His mother was a Dayak...a typical jungle Dayak, dark as an Agtà, but one of high rank. She was a bagani in Burnei. Her epithet 'ba-uga' or 'baluga' means 'dark.'"

"Why is Lapulapu your uncle's enemy?"

"He is not our enemy.He is just someone with whom Humabon does not always agree. But he is a valiant fighter. He was a little boy when his family first came here.They were a boatload of orang laut from Burnei who settled in Bu-ol. After a few years they came to Pulaw Mat-an to be near Sugbu, the chief town in this region. Humabon had recently become the Rajah of Sugbu. He allowed the orang laut to live here.

"Lapulapu was twelve years old and living in the village of Opong when a band of Sanglay pirates came to attack Mat-an. The people of Mat-an met them in battle, on the beach. Lapulapu fought alongside the best warriors of the orang laut. The pirates were repulsed, many of them getting killed.Lapulapu accounted for two or three of the vanquished, including the leader, Chiong Li, of whom we had heard so much.

"Rajah Humabon commended the people of Mat-an for their stalwart defense of the island. He was much impressed with the twelve-year-old boy who had personally killed Chiong Li.

"When Lapulapu came of age, Rajah Humabon suggested that he go to Si-alo and act as manggugubat for my father, Sri Parang Bungdara. Lapulapu, however, demanded that he be named datù of Mat-an. Mat-an had no datù of its own. After all, it's only a small island.Mat-an was included in the area ruled by Humabon's brother, Sri Dula. The area included Bu-ol, Olanggo, Kalusu-an, and several other islands.

"Rajah Humabon placed Lapulapu in Mantawi, over Sri Magpanawan's objections, as a magalamag, or teacher. Pupils were assigned to him, and he taught them how to read and write. The harvests in Mantawi had been poor, and Lapulapu also taught the people new methods of planting. But when the harvests improved, Lapulapu abandoned Mantawi and moved back to Opong. He set himself up as a virtual datù. It was difficult to oppose him. He soon held sway over most of Matan, leaving Sri Dula only the southern part.

"More of the orang laut came from Burnei to live on Lapulapu's island. They sold fish at Pasil, the town just south of Sugbu. But the orang laut also took to preying on ships calling in at Sugbu.

"Rajah Humabon ordered Sri Dula to tell Lapulapu to stop these acts of piracy. Lapulapu defiantly said he and his men would do as the orang laut had always done. Piracy, you see, is a way of life for them.

"Rajah Humabon ordered his manggugubat to take his men, sail to Opong, and destroy every viray and prahu they could find, sparing only the fishing boats, their subiran or sakayan."

"He hasn't retaliated for that? Is he afraid of Rajah Humabon?"

"Yes, we were very much afraid he would retaliate. He is a fearsome manggugubat. But he respects Humabon. And he respects the number of fighting men Humabon can muster. He has said he regards himself as Humabon's guest in this region. He also said he is a very peaceful man. He does not seek quarrels, he says. He only fights when challenged."

The following day, I learned more from Kulnarit Sungvornyothin. Lapulapu was escorted everywhere by his shadows, stalwart warriors all: his younger brother Malingin, and three men known only as Balì-Alho, Sagpà-bahâ, and Bugtò-pasan. Those were not proper names, I learned, but epithets. "Balì-alho" meant "pestle-breaker," while "Sagpà-bahâ" was "flood-slapper."

A slapper of floods?

"Yes. He could turn back a flood with a slap."

"Bugtò-pasan" meant "puller-apart of bamboo cane." The "pasan" alluded to, said Kulnarit Sungvornyothin, was the sort of bamboo cane often made into fighting sticks. Any strong man could break such a cane by bending it across his knee, but this man would grasp a short cane by both ends and pull it apart with his bare hands.

As for Malingin, his name came from the name of an underwater hole off a beach in Mat-an. Not far from the shore, in two- or three-fathom water, was a round hole as wide as a balanghai is long, and as deep as a cocoanut tree is tall. That hole was called Malingin, or Round Hole, and Lapulapu's brother often dove in and swam to the bottom. He was said to be in favor with whatever creatures lived down there. Fishermen respected those denizens and always tossed, when passing overhead in their boats, offerings of food into the hole.

I repeated the stories Tupas had told me about Lapulapu's parents.

"Those are bad jokes," Kulnarit Sunvornyothin told me. "Mangal and Bauga are ordinary names here. No, I don't know what they mean. Perhaps they have no special meanings. Tupas just made up those bad puns out of their names."

"Is Lapulapu really such a redoubtable warrior?" I asked. "Did he really kill Chiong Li when he was only 12?"

"Oh, yes, he did. Everybody knows that. And he is second to none as a fighter. He and his men all know arnis."

"What is that?"

"A way of fighting with hands and feet and a bamboo rod. It is an art with them, almost like dancing."

"Ah, like silat."

They were also credited with mysterious powers, especially Lapulapu.

"Once a hawk was circling overhead," Kulnarit Sungvornyothin said, "ready to pounce on a brood of chicks. Lapulapu stared at the hawk. Suddenly, it fell from the sky. Lapulapu's gaze had killed it."

"Tales," I said.

"Another tale is that he and his group don't practice spear-throwing with real spears. Instead they use rice pestles."

"Pestles would make very heavy spears," I said. "I imagine they use pestles as spears in order to harden their muscles?"

"No, they really make better spears, if you're strong enough. It is said that a pestle thrown by Lapulapu can pierce the trunk of a cocoanut tree."

This was utterly unbelievable, of course, but the Siamese trader was merely repeating the stories told by the people .

"He almost doesn't sound human," I said. "Is he married?"

"Yes. His wife is Bulakna, the daughter of Harì Kusgan of Olanggo Island. That's the island on the other side of Mat-an, to the east. Bulakna has borne Lapulapu three children: two sons, Mangtas and Sawilik, and a daughter, Katahuman.

"You know, Sri Dula had wanted to marry Bulakna himself. In fact, Harì Kusgan had promised Rajah Bantug that he would give Bulakna to Sri Dula. She was still a little girl then. But after Rajah Bantug died, Harì Kusgan seemed to have forgotten his promise. And when Bulakna grew up into a very beautiful woman, she would take no other man but Lapulapu."

40
♒

A YOUNG MAN BRINGING two goats came to the capitana on Friday, April 26. His name was Sri Kubolukol, and he was Sri Dula's son. He had a message from his father: Sri Dula regretted that his tribute was so paltry. His island could produce much more, but he was hampered by the defiant attitude of the other datù, Lapulapu. He, Sri Dula, younger brother of Humabon and rightful Datù of Mat-an as well as of Bu-ol, Olanggo, and other islands, meant to wrest back control of Mat-an. He would attack Lapulapu on the following night. Could the laksamana of the Katjílà help him and send a boatload of men?

The Captain-General thanked Sri Kubolukol for the goats and gave him a message to take back to Mat-an: Lapulapu should recognize Humabon's authority; he should swear fealty to the King of Spain; and he should pay tribute, for which three goats, three pigs, three bahars of rice, and three bahars of millet would do.

Sometime that afternoon, a man purporting to be a vendor of eggs and oranges asked me to come ashore.

Sri Kubolukol was waiting for me. He was visibly disturbed. He feared facing the laksamana with such ill tidings. He quickly quoted the haughty words with which Lapulapu's henchmen had dismissed him: for each thing the Paranggi laksamana asked three of, they would send to him by twos. If he was satisfied with this, they would comply at once. If not, he might do as he pleased ("Bahalà na siya dihâ") but they would not give it.

I persuaded Sri Kubolukol to come to the ship with me. He stood dejectedly by while I repeated Lapulapu's words to Dom Fernão. The Captain-General charged Sri Kubolukol to tell Sri

Dula he would send not one, not two, but three boatloads of fully-armed men. And so, in that casual manner, to a man he had just met, he committed himself to the quarrel. I did not want to believe it, but he was spoiling for a fight.

Captain Juan Serrano attempted to dissuade him.

"It's not your fight, comendador," he said. "Lapulapu is Zula's problem. And Humabon's. Your intervention is hardly necessary."

"This cacique is the only one who has refused to accept baptism into the faith. Are we to shirk our Christian duty to show him the Light and guide him along the Way? No. Of course not. Remember the holy oath you and I swore in Sevilla, before our Emperor's flag. We must fight the good fight."

"Nothing good will come of it. Nada. This Lapulapu is merely a nuisance. Humabon can deal with him. Leave them alone. We've been here for three weeks now. The whole city is ours, and will remain loyal until we come back. Isn't it time we went on to Maluco? My brother Francisco, your own bosom friend, waits for us there. It's been ten years since either of us has seen him."

"A few more days won't matter. We must fight Lapulapu first."

"Nobody wants to fight Lapulapu, not even Humabon. Lapulapu is nobody's nemesis. You're only risking lives."

"Nobody is being ordered to fight who does not want to. I shall ask for volunteers. I shall lead only committed men, men who place the honor of their Emperor above their own comfort."

"It's not wise for a Captain-General to expose himself to such dangers."

"Do you think I have suddenly become an old woman? You know how I fought in Quilóa, in Cananor, in Goa. I nearly died in Diu. And after that I fought in Malacca...and in the Marruecos."

"Where you got lamed. Things aren't the same now, with that bad leg of yours. But I suppose there's no dissuading you. One favor. Release Duarte Barbosa. We'll need him to command your ship while you're off in the batel."

"Very well."

The Captain-General now spoke to the men of the Armada. He meant to fight the stubborn cacique Lapulapu, he said. He would not however order the alguacil and the merinos to assault Mat-an. In fact, he was declaring the alguacil and all the merinos *hors de combat*. He preferred to ask for volunteers, twenty from each ship. Twenty from the *Trinidad*, twenty from the *Concepción*, and twenty from the *Victoria*. Sixty in all. Clad in armor, and carrying *armas de fuego*, they would be more than a match for half-naked pagans with bamboo lances. Were there sixty worthy men left within the ranks of this Armada?

Of his own shipmates on the *Trinidad*, the sobresalientes and I were the first to come forward. The Portuguese noblemen Gonçalo Rodrigues and Luís Alonso de Gois stood up at once. Ser Antonio, Petit-Jean d'Anjou, and Juan Miñez of Sevilla stepped forward with them, as did I: my devotion to my master was second to none. Next came the four who had transferred from the *San Antonio*: the sobresaliente Antón de Escobár, the grumete Juanes de Segura, and Cartagena's erstwhile criados Rodrigo Nieto and Pedro de Valpuesta. The Portuguese grumetes João de Grijol and Luís de Beas volunteered, as did the Galician grumete Antón de Varela. Two grumetes who had originally shipped on the *Santiago*, Pedro Díaz and Hierónimo García, also came forward. They were followed by two more sevillanos, escribano León de Ezpeleta and pageboy Andrés de la Cruz.

The alguacil, Don Gonzálo, had been barred from volunteering, but now he looked at his criado, Pero Gomez of Hornilla la Prieta, and his slave, Antón *de color negro*. Both stood up. Then the marinero Francisco de Espinosa also stood up. Twenty of us from the *Trinidad* had now volunteered. Counting the Captain-General, this made up twenty-one from the capitana.

From the *Concepción* came all four of her sobresalientes: Martín Magallayns, Alonso Coto, Francisco Díaz de Madrid, and Juan de la Torre. After them came a number of the grumetes and marineros, including several of the Basques. The Flemish bombardero Roldan d'Argote also volunteered, as I had known he would.

From the *Victoria* came, first of all, her new captain, Cristóvão Rabelo. With him were the sobresaliente Hernan Lorenzo, originally from the *Santiago*, the bombardero Filiberto Torres, several marineros and grumetes, and the 16-year-old page Juan de Zubileta, the youngest crewman in the Armada—an orphan now. His father, the pilot Basco Gallego, had died two months before.

The volunteers went to the ships' stores and drew the armor they would wear. Of the sixty men in the party, twelve were to guard the batels and forty-eight to follow Dom Fernão in the actual attack. The twelve were issued cuirasses and pavises.

A few of the men, like Dom Fernão, Ser Antonio, Juan Miñez and Dom Luís de Gois, had their own suits of armor. The rest were issued plastrons, moriones, and pavises from the stores.

Twenty men were assigned to carry harquebuses, and another twenty to carry windlass crossbows. Every man was allowed to draw his own choice of other weapons from the stores: lances, darts by the dozen, Swiss pikes, and halberds.

The volunteers received instruction from the alguacil and the merinos in the use of the harquebus and the crossbow. Only the merinos had had much practise with these long-range weapons, but none of them had been allowed to volunteer.

Ser Antonio and I accompanied the Captain-General to Rajah Humabon's palace. The Captain-General told him how he was responding with three boatloads of men to Sri Dula's request. Humabon was impressed. He offered to supplement our forces with a contingent of one thousand men. The Captain-General thanked him, but declined the offer. Our strength was more than enough, he assured the Rajah. Even the services of Sri Dula's men could be dispensed with.

April 27 would be a Saturday, the holiest of days for Dom Fernão. The moon was now four days past full. It rose at 10:00 p.m. on Friday night, April 26, visibly on the wane. Out of habit, I computed for the tides: low water occurred at midnight with a new moon and thereafter occurred 48 minutes later for each day that elapsed. Checking the derrotero, I found low tide had been at 6:43 that morning and 6:49 that evening. That meant low tide the next morning, April 27, would be at around 7:30.

We set off at midnight, sixty men in the three batels. Accompanying us were two dozen balanghays bearing Rajah Humabon, Sri Tupas, most of the datus, and their men. The Armada's three ships were also coming, if only to fetch us after the battle. Both the wind and the current were contrary, coming from the northeast. The naos would have to tack laboriously in the narrow channel, or be rowed with the ashwood sweeps by men in the waists. They would take longer to reach the battle site.

We made quite a fearsome flotilla, but I found myself wishing the natives of Sugbu had not been expressly instructed by the Captain-General to stay out of the fight. They were coming along merely to be shown a display of the white man's prowess. This was to be a demonstration of Faranghi might.

We could have rowed straight across the channel and reached the village of Opong in half an hour. But the enemy lurked in Mat-an.

There had been some confusion here. The island was named Mat-an. Lapulapu's village was also named Mat-an. Rajah Humabon had carefully explained the difference between the words *pulau*, island, and *lungsod*, village. The part of Pulau Mat-an directly across the channel from Sugbu was Lungsod Opong. We had to go to Lungsod Mat-an on the north shore of the island. It lay east of Buaya. We had a longer way to go than Don Gonzálo and his merinos the week before.

It took us three hours of rowing to reach a point off the north shore. Mat-an, the village, showed hardly a light. We hove to. The lead balanghay, with Rajah Humabon aboard, came alongside. Kulnarit Sungvornyothin was there with Humabon, and the Captain-General requested him to go ashore with a message for Lapulapu.

"If you will obey the King of España," my master charged him to say, "recognize Humabon as your lord, and pay me tribute, I will be your friend. But if you do not want to do these things, wait and see how our lances inflict wounds."

Kulnarit Sungvornyothin was back within the hour. Lapulapu had listened to the message and then laughed.

"Tell the Paranggi laksamana," Lapulapu had said, "that if they have lances, we have lances, too. Our lances are only of bamboo, but they have been hardened with fire."

Kulnarit Sungvornyothin had been aware of something else: men waking up and coming nearer to see what Lapulapu was about. A veritable force of fighting men had been gathered. They were waiting for us.

"Let him attack anytime he likes," Lapulapu said. "But if he can wait until morning, so much the better. We shall have more men by then."

At about 5:00 a.m. the three naos arrived and anchored behind the balanghays. I knew that Duarte Barbosa was in command of the *Trinidad*, João Serrão of the *Concepción*, and João Lopes Carvalho of the *Victoria*, but none of them approached us. They could not venture too close to shore. We had all three batels. It was for us to approach them.

I thought the Captain-General would send one of the batels to the naos to arrange for supporting fire from the cannon, but he did no such thing. Nor did he discuss any tactics with Humabon. I thought there should be a provision for Humabon's men to jump into the fray should it become necessary. That possibility seemed not to have been considered.

I began to nurse misgivings. The Captain-General had already thrown away the element of surprise by sending Kulnarit Sungvornyothin to announce his presence. Now he was acceding to Lapulapu's wish and waiting for daylight.

The sky was lightening in the east. The batels rowed as close to the shore as they could, but the tide had gone down and the hulls scraped bottom while we were still some three crossbow flights, nearly a mile, from the shore.

Twelve men were left to guard the batels, four to each batel. They stowed their oars, and took up stations at the batels' serpentinas.

The Captain-General leaped into the water.

I jumped in along with him.

The water was thigh-deep. Ser Antonio splashed in next, and the others followed: the seventeen of us from that batel, and sixteen each from the other batels: forty-nine men in all.

I was on the other side now. I had been a Malayu watching the Faranghi row their box of a junk, its sides armored with teak, up the Melaka River. Impossible that the Sultanate should be conquered with that silly contraption. Our situation now looked just as foolish. But it had succeeded before, and it would succeed now. We would conquer Mat-an.

The enemy began whooping. They had seen us jump into the water, and they too waded in, to meet us. But they stayed near the shore. They would let us to bring the fight to them.

We could see them quite clearly now. We were in a bay, the land curving to our left and to our right, and they stood in three divisions, two flanking us and one in front of us.

"There are hundreds of them!" gasped João de Grijol.

"None of them have armor," Luís de Beas said.

Those with the harquebuses began firing.

Nobody seemed to have hit the enemy.

The gunners reloaded, and the crossbowmen loosed off some arrows. I saw a few fall short; the range was too great. I remembered Master Andrew saying the range of the harquebus was about the same as the crossbow's. If so, we were still out of range and would have to move in and close the gap. I realized too that the serpentinas in the batels would also be out of range.

"¡Non tirar!" yelled the Captain-General, but not everyone heeded him. Harquebuses went on firing.

We continued to wade forward. Suddenly the Captain-General sank into water up to his chest. He peered at the seabed, then stepped up again into thigh-deep water.

"They've dug a trench here," he told us. "Be careful."

A little later we came across another trench, and soon still another. The men of Mat-an had dug three trenches, and these would slow us down if we had to make a hasty retreat. It was not a comforting thought.

Past the third trench, we were still some two hundred yards from the shore. Many of the islanders were wading out to meet us, some of them throwing bamboo lances our way. Their lances flew surprisingly long distances, but at that range still fell short. They did not venture too far from shore; they were waiting for us to reach them.

"¡Non tirar!" ordered the Captain-General again, but many of the volunteers did not have the discipline of the merinos. Now I felt real fear. As the enemy lances plopped closer and closer to us, fear spread through our group.

"Don't fire until you see the whites of their eyes," Ser Antonio said, but no one was listening to him.

Coming into range, we found that hitting the enemy was not so easy. They kept darting around, like quick little animals, and had amazing reflexes: some of them actually caught our arrows with their shields. Many of our men were firing indiscriminately, without waiting for orders, and some of them had exhausted their ammunition. They still had recourse to their lances, halberds, and swords for hand-to-hand combat. As we were vastly outnumbered, retreat seemed the better option.

If only the men in the naos would rain cannon fire on the enemy! The lack of planning was becoming obvious. Lapulapu's men were bunched in thick groups near the shore, ideal targets for our artillery, but no such bombardment had been arranged. The only hope was that the men in the naos would see our predicament, take the initiative, and use the cannon. Here was the difficulty. The Captain-General had arrogantly told the crews that the sixty volunteers were all he wanted. The rest of the crew was not needed, indeed had been prohibited from interfering. His Protector, Dulce Maria the Queen of the Sea, would deliver the enemy into our hands.

I looked at the sky. Should we expect a sign? Were the words IN HOC SIGNO VINCES supposed to appear among the clouds?

We should have retreated here, but now the Captain-General decided to rally and launch a counterattack.

"Go ashore and burn the houses!" he commanded the men on the right flank, who were nearest a group of thatched huts near the beach.

"You! And you!"

The men he had indicated went off to the task. Both were in armor, but I recognized them.

It was all another strange dream. I was beyond horror now. Those two were good. With their crossbows they shot flaming arrows into the roofs of the houses, which burst into flame, one, two, three houses on fire, five, six seven...the flames spread easily. Thirty or more houses were burning. Of course it did not take long for a horde to surround, overwhelm, and cut down our two crossbowmen. I was devoid of emotion as I watched them succumb. I wondered merely if Cristóvão Rabelo and Juan de la Torre had accounted for any of the enemy.

The Captain-General ordered a retreat. The enemy forces waded out into the bay in pursuit. Dom Fernão looked back to see how far his men were from the safety of the batels. He could retreat now, along with the rest of his men, and stand a fair chance of reaching the batel. The risk was that, with everyone frantically rushing through the water for dear life, the retreat would turn into a rout.

There remained but a moment in which he could make that decision: run or fight. In that moment, while I waited to see what he would do, a wave of supreme sadness passed over me. His firstborn son had just been killed. His new route to the Spice Islands was too long and difficult: the Mar Pacífico had turned out to be too wide, and the Strait of All Saints too perilous. Because he had done away with all three of his Spanish captains, retribution by fair means or foul would be his lot in Sevilla. Cartagena's natural father, Bishop Fonseca, would hound him to the ends of the earth in pursuit of vengeance. No glory awaited Dom Fernão in Spain, only ridicule; no riches, only jail.

He took a stand, fighting off the natives, in order to cover the retreat and afford the men time to gain the batels. Eight of us stood there with him.

The enemy, a whole mass of men, moved in for the kill. We were vastly outnumbered, but they were too close. If we turned and ran, we would merely be presenting them our broad backs as easy targets. The decision had been made. Nothing for it now but to stand and fight.

The Captain-General's helmet was knocked off.

"There he is!" some of the natives yelled. The Captain-General was the prime target. They would cut us down, one by one, until they could get at him in the center.

Antón de Varela picked the helmet up and returned it to Dom Fernão, and in that moment a bamboo lance found its mark and pierced his leg. Antón fell into the shallow water and immediately a pack of natives was upon him like sharks, hacking at him with their kampilan blades. The water turned red with his blood.

I noted the fact dispassionately.

An arrow felled Francisco Espinosa. The Mat-anon men, some of whom were still hacking away at Antón Varela's body, turned their attention to this new casualty. Again the water at that spot turned red.

We fought on. The Captain-General again turned back to see if the others had made it to the batels. His helmet was knocked off a second time. Again we replaced it on his head.

Pero Gomez went down.

Rodrigo Nieto killed a man with his sword, only to be cut down immediately after by another man.

Only five of us remained. For the third time, the Captain-General's helmet was knocked off his head. The enemy men were aiming most of their thrusts at him. Yet once more, we put his helmet back on his head.

Two of the batels were already rowing off. Only the *Trinidad*'s batel remained.

Boom!

The sound of artillery. I craned my neck to see where it had come from.

The *Trinidad* had fired her cannon; smoke drifted downwind from the gunports. What had been hit? Then I saw it. A balanghay. But it was one of Rajah Humabon's. As it sank, I shuddered in sickening disgust. It was either a cruel joke, or very bad aim. From the look of it, several of Humabon's men in that balanghay must have been killed.

The Mat-an men were lunging and feinting at us. A man slashed at the Captain-General, inflicting a deep wound on the arm; the man's kampilan had cut through my master's chain mail. Dom Fernão reacted instantly, transfixing the man with his lance. The lance pierced through and protruded from the man's back.

Now Dom Fernão drew his sword from its scabbard. It came only halfway out. Blood was seeping through his chain mail sleeve, and although he heaved and cursed, try as he might he could not pull the sword out. I realized the deep wound had damaged his arm; he no longer had full use of it.

The natives saw it, too. The laksamana's helplessness was obvious, and it emboldened them. They rushed forward, all eager for the glory of dealing the death blow.

Dom Fernão was down in the water, and they were upon him. They were butchers, hacking away; they were madmen, thrusting their spears, for the sheer pleasure of it, into a body already dead.

They ignored us. The Faranghi laksamana was all they wanted.

There was nothing more we could do. We were all hurting from our wounds. The four of us, Ser Antonio, Filiberto Torres, Antón de Escobár, and myself quickly found our way back to the batel.

They took him with them, dragging his body through the bloodstained water like a log, holding him by his ankles and wrists. Sunlight glinted off his finger, off the gold ring Beatriz had given him shortly before their wedding. I recalled the words etched on its inside: *No tengo más qve darte.*

⚓

41
♒

SRI TUPAS, SENT BY A WEEPING Rajah Humabon to ransom the Captain-General's body, returned empty-handed.

"We will not," Lapulapu said, "give up this man for all the treasures in the world.For he fought most valiantly, and his courage shall ever be an example to all warriors. We shall keep him here, and make of him a memorial."

The maestres took down their tents in the market square, and began hauling their merchandise back to the ships. A vote was called, and Barbosa and Serrano were elected joint commanders, each to hold the rank of Captain-General. Barbosa was now captain of the *Trinidad*, while Serrão remained captain of the *Concepción*. Barbosa immediately appointed the sobresaliente Luís Affonso de Gois as captain of the *Victoria*. Dom Luís was qualified, certainly, but I wondered why Barbosa did not appoint the more experienced João Lopes Carvalho.

Duarte Barbosa made a count, and found there were only 166 of us in the Armada, including Juanillo Carvalho, the little boy from Río de Janeiro. We had set out from Europa with 264 men. Some 65 men had been lost together with the *San Antonio*. Another 34 had died, so that we now had 99 fewer men than when we started. The Indians we had taken from América had all died, except Juanillo.

Padre Valderrama went ashore to say Sunday Mass and most of the men dutifully attended. Andrés de la Cruz remarked that it seemed strange to be singing requiem without the bodies of our dead.

I lay on a cot, in sick bay, as did Ser Antonio, Antón de Escobár and Filiberto Torres.My wounds were not very serious, but Antón de Escobár's were quite grievous. His condition seemed desperate. Filiberto was not much better off. Ser Antonio's face was badly swollen from a hit by a poisoned arrow.

The next day, Monday, April 29, Antón de Escobár expired at dawn.

I did not feel like getting up, not even for breakfast. I heard words being exchanged between someone on deck and someone on the wharf. I could pick out a few words in the Binisayâ language: Humabon had apparently sent a messenger. Without me to translate, they could not understand each other. I turned over and went back to sleep.

Duarte Barbosa came to sick bay and brusquely asked why I was still abed. I mumbled something about my injuries.

"You lazy dog!" he said. "There is much work to be done, but you care only for your comfort. Just because you no longer have your master to attend to, you think you are now exempted from all labor? You are a slave, nothing more. Your cheeks should have been branded. So you think you're now free because Fernão manumitted you in his will? Oh, no, no. I'll deliver you to Beatriz. As far as I'm concerned you're still a slave. You'll be a slave for the rest of your life."

And so on, in that vein. I was not unaccustomed to verbal abuse, but this man had less right than most. Worse, he now had the power to do as he was threatening.

"I'll show you who's the master around here," he said. He had brought a whip along, the one used for floggings. He started whipping my legs. "Get up, demônio!" he shouted.

The pain stung me. I bolted out of bed and ran out to the deck.

Hatred was roiling around in my liver. It boiled up all the way to my head. Every fiber of my being cried out for revenge. I would go amok. Yes, I would go amok right now, kill Duarte Barbosa, then whoever got in my way next. Pull out my sheath knife now, slash and cut wildly. Best to get it over and done with.

I could not do it.

I did not have the courage, the raw fury of the amok.

I struggled with myself.

True, we Malays ran amok every now and then, but only out of sheer desperation. Only when there was nothing else to be done, when one's life no longer mattered.

But there were a few things I might still try. I remembered the ancient tradition of our tribe: a man who has been mortally wronged has three days to avenge himself. All Malays knew this. The people of Sugbu would know it, too, and would concede I was within my rights if I wreaked vengeance within three days.

I went off to see Rajah Humabon. I hoped he would offer me food. I had no stomach for breakfast in Duarte Barbosa's *Trinidad*.

Duarte Barbosa should have taken a more active part in the battle against the men of Mat-an. He should have rallied the bombarderos and provided comprehensive artillery support. Someone had indeed tried and fired the cannon, but it had not been the bombarderos. I never did find out exactly who. Their aim had been so bad they missed the Mat-an men and killed four of Humabon's men instead. But what had Barbosa done meanwhile? Doubtless he merely wanted to return to his carousing. That was all he cared for: women, drink, and trading in gold on the sly.

My mind was set. I had three days in which to act. I would make use of them.

Rajah Humabon was morose. I had thought only of my own losses, my own misfortune, but now I saw that he too had sustained enormous setbacks. He had been shamed by Lapulapu, and had lost enormous face with his own people. Now he looked foolish for having waived his docking fees. He was a dog who had paid tribute, a monkey who had accepted baptism.

I greeted him, and he said I had come at the right time and would I join him in a meal of leftovers?

A female slave brought in platters of food. The rice glistened; it had been fried in lard, as was usually done with rice left over from the previous night's supper. The stewed pork had been reheated. The slave, however, was fresh from a bath, her hair still damp, her nipples stiff.

Humabon said he usually drank water at breakfast, but if I preferred palm wine he would be honored to drink that with me.

I said yes, palm wine would go well with the stewed pork. Besides, it meant the slave would have to make another appearance to serve the tubâ.

She set the jug before us. I could not take my eyes away from her breasts.

Humabon said nothing as we ate. Every other mouthful was followed by a drink of wine. As was his custom, we drank it through thin reeds.

After the meal, his slave took away the dishes.

"I regret the necessity of bringing you ill tidings, Rajah Humabon," I began. "The Faranghis have evil designs on you."

"But that cannot be be true," he said in the Binisayâ language. "How so?"

"The new laksamana is Duarte Barbosa, together with Juan Serrano. Yes, both hold the rank of Captain-General now."

I let this sink in: he knew which one was Duarte Barbosa. He had observed Duarte Barbosa wallowing in debaucheries, and he had seen João Serrão's greed for gold.

"Those two have nothing of the lofty character Dom Fernão had. My master believed in converting you to his sacred beliefs, and in treating you as brothers in the faith."

Some of the words I was using were rather difficult, but it seemed he understood everything. So far the pasar Malayu had not been a problem for him.

"These two are different. When we were newly arrived here, and they saw what Dom Fernão was doing, I overheard them talking. They did not like the ways of Dom Fernão. They wanted him to do as Faranghi laksamanas have always done. You have heard of Melaka, have you not? And Goa? And Damão?"

He nodded.

"They wanted to do to Sugbu what the white man did to those places. Kill the strongest men, enslave the ones left alive. Do as they please with the women."

"They've already done that," he said.

"Yes, but mostly with slave women. They prefer raping the comeliest of the women, including your wives and daughters—and killing them afterwards. You must listen to me. They can still do it. They are planning to. That's why they've taken their goods away from the square, and folded up their tents. But their ships are still docked right here in your harbor, guns facing your town."

"What is the meaning of that?"

"They will attack Mat-an, if only to show how it should be done. But the real prize is your city. After Mat-an has been laid waste, they will take you by surprise. Do you know that they mean to abduct you first? They know this town will be thrown into confusion and be unable to organize a proper defense without you. They will attack at dawn, while everyone is asleep. You will have no warning. They will take you prisoner aboard ship, then bombard the town with cannon fire. Sugbu will go up in smoke."

He stared at me.

"You must do something," I said.

"They would not act in that way," he said. "I have been kind to them. I have treated all of them as honored guests. They would not turn against their host."

"They turned against their own Captain-General. They betrayed him when he needed them most. They did not lift a finger to help him. They did nothing when the tide of battle turned against him. They allowed him to be slaughtered by Lapulapu. If they had fired the cannon at Lapulapu's men, there might have been a chance. Dom Fernão might still be alive today. But they fired at your men instead. You think that was a mistake? No, they did it on purpose. They did it to make sure your men would not jump in and help Dom Fernão. They wanted him dead. They wanted him out of the way, so they could become Captain-General in his place, and do as they please."

"What should I do?"

"You can forestall them. You must not wait for them to carry out their plans. You must be the first to strike."

"But I have sworn a pact of blood brotherhood with them."

"Not with them. Only with Dom Fernão. My master was a man of honor, but these are scum. You saw for yourself that Dom Fernão would not touch a woman. He was married, and strove to remain faithful to his wife, though she be on the other side of the world. But these men are drunkards who fuck anything with teats. You know they had no scruples about trading in gold behind Dom Fernão's back. Some of these white men are so greedy for gold they've dug up the graves in your cemeteries, looted your dead ancestors. No, there is nothing honorable about these Faranghis. They will turn on you if you don't hit them first."

He sighed.

"You will help me," he said, speaking in the pasar Malayu.

I pretended great surprise. I had already guessed he knew my language very well, but for him it was a secret revealed only at great cost. I would give him his due.

"I'm utterly astounded," I said. "So I was right all along. You speak my language. You are a wily old harimau. Of course I'll help you."

"Why are you doing this?"

"They betrayed my master. And Duarte Barbosa thinks the brown man is inferior to the white man. I was loyal to Dom Fernão, but now I am just another brown man. There is no room for me in those Faranghi ships."

He sucked palm wine through thin reeds. He clapped his hands, and the female slave came in. He ordered her to bring him some turtle eggs. She brought a bowlful in at once.

"Here's what I shall do," Humabon said. "Don't worry, that slave doesn't understand the pasar Malayu. The gold bracelets and anklets I ordered to be made for your late master are almost finished. So are the crown and other things I ordered for the Caliph. I shall invite the Faranghis to come and receive the jewelry as a going-away present from me. At the same time, I will spread a feast for them."

"When will that feast be?"

"As soon as can be. Tomorrow. The day after tomorrow at the latest."

He meant Tuesday, April 30, or Wednesday, May 1. That was good. Both were within my three-day limit.

"What is your name? It's not Indiriki, is it?"

"No, it's not Enrique. They used to call me Harith, but that was long ago. The name my father whispered into my ear when I was 12 days old was Rintap. I have never used that name. Call me Indiriki if you like. Or Indra."

"Rintap," he repeated. "Doesn't that mean 'one who makes the world shake'?"

"I suppose it does."

"Harith, of Melaka. Kulámbò tells me your family came from Palembang. Perhaps I've heard of your father. Wasn't he the one they nicknamed Harimau?"

"Yes."

"Supposedly he was the image of a Sultan several generations removed from him, the one called Sri Harimau. Some have said he was actually descended from that Sultan, through an illegitimate son. How true is it?"

I shrugged.

"In Melaka the family tarsila means everything," I said. "Sons born on the outside don't always get included in tarsilas."

On Tuesday, April 30, Humabon firmed up his plans. The white men, when I told them about the jewelry, had pricked up their ears with interest. When, they asked, will the jewels be given? Soon, I said. The goldsmiths are still working on them. Perhaps by tomorrow or the day after.

Humabon had to do something, and not merely to regain his prestige. Lapulapu, cocky and insufferable, was threatening to come over and challenge him for the position of Rajah of Sugbu. Lapulapu, according to rumor, wanted to meet him on the field, in single combat. Ancient tradition accorded every datù the right to challenge his rajah thus, although the rajah had the privilege of sending a champion. The datu of course could not send a proxy but had to present himself personally, as proof of his readiness to do battle. No such challenge that anyone knew of had been issued in hundreds of years. How true was the rumor?

Humabon showed me into a back room. Inside, someone I had not seen for some time was waiting.

"What is this I hear?" Rajah Kulámbò asked without preamble.

"Kulámbò doesn't like it," Humabon told me. "He thinks the Armada should merely be asked to leave."

"True," Kulámbò said.

"I have to act," Humabon said. "I can't remain Rajah of Sugbu if I don't do this."

"It's a rotten thing to do," Kulámbò said. "Both of us have made blood compacts with them. And now, this..."

"You don't know how I feel," Humabon said. "They didn't threaten your datus with death for refusing to convert to their religion. They didn't levy tributes on you. They didn't dig up your graves. They didn't fuck your women...and your blood compact, like mine, was only with Pirnan."

"If that's how you feel, I can't stop you. Look, I'll even help you. I'll make my men available. If you like, we'll be the first to board their ships and fight those white men on their own ground. Or if not, I'll fight at your side *inig bahug-bahug na*, when everything becomes a free-for-all. Just don't ask me to kill anyone right after I have supped with him."

Soon the details were clear: dinner on Wednesday evening, at a warehouse near the shore, the only available hall large enough to accommodate all the guests expected.

I looked at it. It was not built on stilts, like the ordinary house, but had walls that reached the ground. It had no floor but bare earth. Because it was close to the shore, its floor was not hardpacked dirt, but sand. It had a door at each end, front and back, two windows grilled with bamboo bars, and two more doors that connected the hall to two rooms. Each room had one unbarred window; a man could go in or out of those windows if they were left open.

Humabon was extending a blanket invitation. It was up to the white men how many of them would attend. However, Humabon charged me with ascertaining their exact number. The hall could hold one hundred men, no more. That meant a maximum of fifty white men, as an equal number of Humabon's men were to join them.

I found Sri Tupas in his house and asked a favor of him. Should Ser Antonio attend the banquet, would he take him aside before anything happened? Tupas promised he would. I looked up. His python was curled around a roof beam. A rat was coming toward it. At precisely the right moment, the python struck and caught the rat in its jaws.

I extended Humabon's invitation to the men of the Armada. A farewell dinner. Humabon would present the gold ornaments originally intended for Dom Fernao as well as the pieces of jewelry wrought for the King. I described those in some detail, the better to excite their greed. Humabon had promised, I told them, gold pieces set with rubies, pearls, emeralds, and diamonds.

"Ah, emeralds," Duarte Barbosa said. "Emeralds have the richest lore among gemstones. Isn't that so, Gonzálo?"

"Yes," Don Gonzálo said. "If you look at an emerald long enough, you'll find its green color bewitching. Emeralds can counter magic spells, improve memory, reveal the infidelities of lovers, sharpen the wit, and make the wearer eloquent."

He flashed his ring for us to see. Set in it was a large green stone, cut in a square fashion that I supposed was called "hechizado."

"And emeralds," said Duarte Barbosa, "have divine glory, benevolence, and control of the planet Venus."

42

APRIL ENDED. Wednesday, May 1, began abruptly, with the stillness of dawn suddenly shattered by the death shrieks of pigs. There would be no shortage of meat at Humabon's feast. These pigs were not being slaughtered in the usual manner, with ceremonies conducted by the priestesses, but I doubted if the white men would notice the omission. Of course, it meant none of the Sugbu-anon men would eat that unconsecrated flesh. Perhaps that was the point.

It went without saying that officers and hidalgos had priority. The Rajah had expressed the earnest desire to entertain everybody, but unfortunately the dining hall could accommodate only so many, as there were the elders of the city to think of as well.

The white men assured of places at the dinner puffed up with importance. Names were advanced, and one of the pages ordered to draw up a list: Barbosa, Serrano, de Gois, Padre Valderrama, Don Gonzálo, Carvalho, Andrés de San Martín, sobresalientes Petit-Jean d'Anjou and Francisco Díaz de Madrid, escribanos Heredia and Ezpeleta, the two Francisco Martíns of the Trinidad, despensero Cristóbal Ros, licenciado Diego Ortigas, bombardero Guillaume Tañegui, and several others.

I counted them: two dozen men, perhaps more. Captain-General Barbosa and Captain-General Serrano, ex officio, would be leading the contingent. Ser Antonio, to my great relief, would not be attending. He would need at least a week to recover from his wound: the poisoned arrow had puffed up his cheek, and he sported a pair of black eyes. Andrés de la Cruz, Vasquito Gallego, Juan de Zubileta, and Juanillo Carvalho were not going either. I had one disappointment: Juan Sebastián de Elcano did not plan to go.

We all put on our doublets. Every man had his sheath knife, but that was all. I walked with the party from the ship to the warehouse. I knew them all very well indeed: Nuño Portugues, Juanes de Segura, Hernando de Aguilar, Simon de la Rochela, João da Silva, Francisco dela Mesquita, Rodrigo Macias, Francisco Picora, Francisco Paxe, Pedro Garcia de Herrero, Antón de Goa, Antón Rodriguez. White men, all of them.

The final count was twenty-nine men, including myself. This was little better than half of the fifty Humabon and I had planned for, but among that number were the highest-ranking men.

Rajah Humabon and his men greeted us at the door. None of them wore any weapons but their daggers. The sand floor of the hall looked clean. Fresh sand had been added, spread, tamped, raked smooth.

Everyone went inside and sat before the placemats. Rajah Humabon assigned the men to their places around the hall, white man next to Sugbu-anon man next to white man, and so on.

Jars of palm wine were brought in.

"This tubâ must be special," Duarte Barbosa told Humabon, "It has a finer aroma."

"It's laksoy," Humabon told the white men, pouring some into a cup and offering it to Duarte Barbosa. "Stronger than tubâ."

There were no thin reeds. For once, Humabon was going to drink like a mere mortal.

"What is it made of?" asked Barbosa.

"The same thing tubâ is made of. The sap of the nipà. However, no tungog is used, and after it has fermented it is distilled."

"What is tungog?" asked Cristóbal Ros.

"The bark of a certain tree," I told him.

"If you put tungog in the nipà sap," said Rajah Humabon told Cristóbal Ros, "after twelve days of fermentation you will have tubâ. But if you allow it to ferment without the tungog, you will obtain laksoy. Of course you have to distill it. Not just once; you have to distill it at least twice."

"Ah, like brandy," nodded Cristóbal Ros, taking a sip. "Yes, it's good. Very potent."

I went off and ducked into the back room, which was being used as the pantry.

Sri Tupas was there.

"Do we go through with it?" he asked me.

"Yes," I said.

The slaves began taking platters of steaming food to set before the company. I returned to my place between Barbosa and Humabon. At the sight of the food many of the white men hungrily licked their chops, but none of them made a move to help himself. To the host belonged the first bite, and they were all waiting for the Rajah to begin.

Humabon lifted a handful of rice to his mouth. That was the signal for the white men. Now everyone began eating. Duarte Barbosa gorged himself. He ate fast, but not too fast to exchange inane pleasantries with Rajah Humabon. Seated between them, I had to translate their prattle back and forth.

Sri Magiyu came into the room, went to Padre Valderrama, and whispered something to him. Valderrama got up. Sri Magiyu took him by the hand and led him out via the back door.

Don Gonzálo and Carvalho had seen the priest being taken away, and both suddenly became wary. They looked at each other. Carvalho muttered a few words under his breath. Don Gonzálo nodded assent. The two of them got up and left unobtrusively. Had they smelled something? Were they going off to fetch the others? It was now or never. I raised my clenched fist, then lifted my cup in a toast.

"Banat, mga Vijayâ!" I boomed.

Dashing down my cup, I dug into the sand at my feet and pulled out a sundang. All the Sugbu-anon men simultaneously plunged their hands into the sand and whipped out the weapons they had buried there; from the adjacent rooms, and from outside, poured in more men.

It was over very quickly. Dead or dying bodies were sprawled all over the sand floor. Some of the bodies were Sugbu-anon; certain of the white men had valiantly taken their murderers down with them.

I went outside and stayed in the shadows. I did not want to show my face.

Carvalho and Don Gonzálo should not have escaped; we had overlooked that possibility. The plan had been to capture the ships after disposing of the men at the banquet. Now that was no longer possible. The crews, alerted, were making frantic preparations for departure.

Men were hacking away at the cross in the market square. Those beams of wood, with five protruding nails to show where the bearded god had been transfixed to it, must have been too stark for the people of Sugbu. They preferred their idols well-portrayed, complete with fangs and horns; the bearded god's symbolic presence was too abstract for them. And why had that god, having miraculously healed Sri Magiyu, not interceded for the Faranghi laksamana in battle?

"Katjílà!" they shouted as their axes bit into the wood. Soon it was in pieces on the ground.

A group of men dragged João Serrão, his doublet torn and bloodied, his face bruised, to the wharf.

"Katjílà!" they called out to the capitana.

The *Trinidad* hove to, and Carvalho leaned out.

"O que quer?"

"Bayad alang ini inyong ka-uban."

The language barrier did not hamper them. The white men understood "lantaka" and that was enough. The Sugbu-anon men would ransom Serrão for cannon, the big ones, the ones that could be seen poking through the gunports.

Carvalho had a bombard lowered into the batel, and then another. Both were of the kind that took 32-pound iron balls of 6¼-inch bore at the muzzle. There was room for still another, but not enough buoyancy; a third bombard would have sunk the batel.

At Carvalho's order, Don Gonzálo took command of the batel.

They could not agree on how to carry out the exchange. Don Gonzálo wanted Serrano left at the far end of the wharf, alone. The Sugbu-anon men insisted that the bombards be rolled off onto the shore.

The smell of perfidy hung in the air. One side feared that the batel crew might simply spirit Serrano off the wharf and not unload the cannon. The other side was certain Serrão would be whisked away as soon as the bombards had been delivered. Neither side would give in.

"Don't do it!" Serrão yelled. "They're playing for time! They're delaying things until reinforcements come!"

Which was true. At the critical moment, when the batel docked beside the wharf and Serrão started getting in, there might open up a chance to rush them.

"Cast off now!" Serrão exhorted. "Go on without me! Save yourselves. Save the ships!"

A manggugubat punched him hard, perhaps meaning to silence him. The blow only made Serrão scream more maniacally. "João Lopes Carvalho, irmão sangue, I'll remember you to my dying day! If you ever come back, redeem my shrunken head and my tattooed cock from these indios selvagens!"

Someone threw a spear. Thunk! Still vibrating, its point buried in the side of the batel, it decided the matter. The white men hurrriedly rowed back to their mothership and clambered aboard, leaving the bombards to be towed astern in the batel. Carvalho bellowed out orders, and men in the waists rowed the *Trinidad* into the bay to join the *Concepcíon* and the *Victoria*.

Each ship now fired a broadside. The cannonballs made sickening thuds upon impact. Houses that were hit promptly fell apart like children's toys. The Armada was saluting the city of Sugbu in the most appropriate manner: with live ammunition.

I could barely see the ships in the dark. None of them had lit their farols. Their sails were patches of white; that was all.

They grew smaller as they moved away, and I knew the loss was mine. Having been left behind, I wallowed in the pangs of despair. Had it been thus for Cartagena and that priest the day we marooned them in Puerto San Julián? Should I now kneel on the sand, raise clasped hands to my crewmates, and with tears streaming down my cheeks beg their forgiveness, entreat them to take me back?

Too late for that.

I went off to look for Sri Tupas. I had lost my bearings, and was not sure which way led to his house. I would find it, of course. I would ask his Agtà slavegirl to dress the cut on my arm. Merely a flesh wound, but it was bleeding, the pain getting worse by the minute. Duarte Barbosa had managed to lunge at me with his Basque sheath knife. I had parried with my sundang and then rolled away, leaving him to the manggugubat who had been furtively eyeing him. I had then gone out of the hall. I could not stand the sight of blood, and would not lay a hand on my fellow crewmembers. Humabon's men had no such inhibitions.

I would repay Duarte Barbosa for the injury, of course. As I had repaid him for many an insult.

43

RAJAH HUMABON GRACIOUSLY TOLD ME I was welcome in his city for as long as I cared to stay, even unto the end of my days. If I wanted to marry a Sugbu-anon woman I could have my choice from among a goodly number of fair maidens, some of whom spoke the pasar Malayu. He would gladly grant me a piece of land, and I could build a house upon it.

Many thanks, I said, but I would be leaving soon. Having gone around the world and seen many lands, I did not think I could stay too long in any one place. I would seek a kampong where I could live quietly, in Palembang, Kedah, Samudra, or somewhere. From there I would travel, perhaps enter Melaka secretly, perhaps pass by places ibn Battutah had seen.

Here in Sugbu, he said as if he had not heard me, one could live out one's whole life without suffering from want. Besides, he would protect me—as best as he could—from men seeking blood revenge.

"You mean, in the event that I kill someone by accident?"

"No. From the kinsmen of the twenty men killed at Mat-an, and of the four Sugbu-anon men killed by the lantaka fired from your ship."

"But only fifteen of Lapulapu's men were killed, none by my hand, and I had nothing to do with the cannon."

"No matter. You came with the Faranghis. Many people here first thought you more of a Faranghi than a man of the tabunon race. You fought with the Faranghis at Mat-an, and by all accounts fought well. Fifteen Mat-anon men were killed in that battle, and five more died of their wounds later. You are here. You are visible. Inevitably, you will attract the wrath of the vengeful, as sharks are drawn to blood. I shall place you under my protection, and impose severe penalties on anyone who would harm you. However, there are those who might feel compelled, by the ancient codes of our tribes, to exact payment of blood debts in full. About such men I can do nothing."

"I have already said I will leave as soon as I can. I merely want a certain sum to sustain me in my travels. In gold, if that would suit your will."

Now that I had stated my demand, his haggling instincts became fully aroused. One could tell by the glint in his eye. At that moment, too, he must have recalled how scornfully I had once disdained, in behalf of the whole fleet, to pay his docking fees. Old debts were being discharged at last; it was that season. I had collected on some that were owed me. He still had a few scores to settle. He knew there were other debts I wanted to evade. He would drive a hard bargain.

"How much do you want?" he asked.

"As a seaman in the King's Armada," I said, "the Crown was to have paid me 1,500 maravedis for every month the voyage took. From the land of the Faranghis to Sugbu was twenty months. Al-Andalus lies at the opposite end of the world. The return voyage? Surely another twenty months. Therefore I have given up, for your sake, forty months' income."

I did not tell him I had received four months' salary in advance.

"Very well," he said. "Forty months' wages."

In Sevilla my 60,000 maravedis would have purchased, at 1,836 maravedis the quintal, some 32 quintales, 5 arrobas, and 24 libras of iron. At 12 troy ounces per pound, that meant some 86,455 ounces of iron, or about 65,000 tahils. At 14 tahils of iron for every 10 of gold, that worked out as 46,430 tahils of gold.

Or, Humabon said, 2,900 kati.

Too much, he declared, not for him but for me. Too heavy.

I checked my figures: about 7,200 libras, well over 3½ tons. He was right. That amount would present more problems than it was worth: how to load it covertly, how to distribute that weight on a prahu, what to do with any pirates who might smell it, where to find a boat crew who would not toss me overboard and run off with my gold.

We finally decided I should take only as much as I could carry on my person. I was about to demur, but he said he would throw in a handful of emeralds and diamonds. He asked that everything remain secret. He would pay me from the proceeds of the sale of the white men, ten of whom had survived the banquet. Not everyone had been killed; those who had surrendered had been shown mercy.

Kulnarit Sungvornyoth left when his ship returned for him. I had wanted to sail away with him, but there was the sale of the Faranghis to wait for.

Came the next trading season, the ships of the Xanglei blew in with the amihan. To them we sold as slaves eight of the white men. Padre Valderrama was not included, he being a man who had taken holy orders. Neither was João Serrão, as he was too old. Both were retained by Humabon, and treated as honored guests. Each was given his own house, where he could be kept within sight at all times.

Of the eight men, the one who fetched the highest price was sold under a non-negotiable condition: Duarte Barbosa was not to be disposed of to a master who might be inclined to manumit him for any reason whatsoever.

I asked the Xanglei men if it was their custom that a slave eventually buy his own freedom.

They laughed.

At his price, they said, no chance to happen. The bearded barbarian, he die a slave.

Before the season of the amihan yielded to the habagat, I left on a prahu bound for "the lands below the wind," as they called the regions to the south: Sarawak, Sulawesi, Burnei, Tiringganu, or whichever they meant. I bade no one goodbye, not even Tupas. In Sugbu one ate well, the staples of rice and millet being ample complements to one's meat and fish. I sought a kampong where rice did not grow and everyone lived on sago.

⚓

Epilogue

VOICES. From beyond the horizon. I hear them still: whispers of distant doings wafted on the amihan, rumors borne on the habagat. In turn, the waves chant mantras. As for my own voice, the sound of it startles me whenever I hear myself speak, which is seldom.

I pass whole days in silence.

I call this island Savai'i, after the mythical island the souls of blue-water navigators come home to. I sailed here by myself, earlier this year, in a sakayan, a one-man boat. An old man on his last voyage. I bade no one goodbye, told no one I was leaving. I did not know where I was going.

I could have died at sea, and it would not have mattered. But by following the swell I sensed through my scrotum, I found this tiny island. An isolated rock. In the middle of nowhere. Longitude unknown. Latitude, that of A'a, which the white man calls the Dog star. Here, Sirius attains the zenith when it passes overhead during the æquinoxes. From what I can recall of the white man's methods, this isle must then be at 16°S.

Here I built a crude hut.

I live off the land and the sea. At night, I sit on my beached boat and look at the stars. The year is 1570 but it could be 1705. Or 978. Anno Domini, Vikrama, Anno Hegiræ—who cares? It could be the first year of a great new era. Or the last.

I listen to the wind and the waves.

"Tupas and Makiyu are alive and well," the voices tell me. "And their sister Batungay, too."

"Tupas," replies a northwesterly, "is the Rajah of Sugbu now, having succeeded his uncle Humabon in due course."

"They received a fleet," says the first voice, "led by a man called Legazpi."

"A Basque name," the wind points out. "A Captain-General to reckon with. Perhaps a Knight of Santiago. Not a Castillian, and almost certainly not a dandy fop."

"Legazpi calls Tupas and 'Simaquio' sons of Sarripara."

"A garbling of their father's proper name, Sri Parang Bungdara, and nickname, Harì Palanggà. The nickname means 'Beloved King' and is at the same time a pun on the proper name, a nuance very likely lost on Legazpi."

"Tupas followed the ways of his ancestor, Sri Lumay. He burned Sugbu and all the crops, and fled with his people to the mountains. The white men nearly starved. They ate all the dogs and cats in the town. Legazpi had wanted to make Sugbu the capital of the Spanish colony now called Felippinas. After three years he gave up and sailed to another island."

A season ends, another begins. Now the habagat is at my ear with its questions. The waves, as if in answer, murmur indifferently.

"You live in a hut, yet seem always lost in the waves, or among the stars. Are you never again to see the world?"

"A ppalu's hut, the one he lives in when no longer sailing the sea and steering by the stars, is a universe unto itself."

"What is the shape of the hut?"
"A square."
"How long?"
"From east to west."
"How broad?"
"Between north and south."
"How deep?"
"As deep as the sea."
"How high?"
"Even as high as the heavens."

Afterword

A LETTER OF INQUIRY I SENT to Amnesty International was answered by one Nigel Mark Lovell-Smythe, who informed me that their file on Tristão Lopes-Pelea had been closed for years. Most of its contents were confidential, but he had been authorized to release the following biographical information:

Lopes, given name Tristão, maternal name Pelea. Born Oé-Cusse, 1946. Attended public school in Dilli, graduating with an AB in 1966. MA Lit., Universidade do São Paulo, 1968. Ph.D. Lit., Universidade da Lusitania, Coimbra, 1971. Postgraduate fellow at the Sorbonne, 1971-1972. Three-month stint as resident writer at Mishkenot Sha'ananim in Jerusalem, 1972. Professor of Portuguese and Galician literature, Dilli, 1972-1975. Presumed killed whilst attempting to flee East Timor in 1975.

I knew Oé-Cusse was an erstwhile Portuguese enclave within what used to be the Dutch half of Timor. Dilli was of course the capital of the Portuguese half. It was now·Dili; with the Indonesians had come spelling reform. Whether East Timor was an independent state after Portugal decolonized it in 1975, or a province of Indonesia after annexation in 1976 depended on one's point of view.

Lovell-Smythe ended his letter by thanking me for my concern. He regretted he could not be of more help. He however saluted my persistence in tracing the fates of unsung heroes, of whom Lopes-Pelea of glorious memory was another shining example. With warmest regards, he remained my obedient servant...

His elegant signature, a rare example of beautiful penmanship in an age when the advent of computers was causing many to forget the calligraphic arts, appeared to have been scribbled with a gold-nibbed fountain pen.

It wasn't until some time later that I realized it looked like the same hand that had written the manuscript.

I wrote another letter to Amnesty International, and in reply was informed with regret that anent mine of the 17th instance, their personnel records did not show anyone named Lovell, Smythe, or Lovell-Smythe to have ever been in their employ. As for Tristão Lopes-Pelea, the final entry in his dossier reported him to have disappeared from East Timor in 1975. There having been no further reports regarding him, the file had been reclassified as inactive in 1985 and closed in 1995. The signature at the bottom of this second letter was illegible.

♒

Gazetteer

1. Cabo Santo Agostinho.............Recife

2. Socopenapan...........................Copacabana, Rio de Janeiro

3. Paranapucu............................Ilha do Governador, Guanabara Bay, Rio de Janeiro

4. Bahia sin fondo........................Golfo de San Matias, off Patagonia

5. Puerto de San Matías...............Golfo Nuevo, off Patagonia

6. Bahia de los Trabajos.................Puerto Deseado on the Patagonian coast, at 47°46'S

7. Bahia de los Patos....................Cabo Dos Bahias

8. Islas del Sansón........................the Penguin Island Group (not the Falklands), off the Cabo Dos Bahias, at 47°55'S

9. Bahia de Virgenes.................. Bahia Posesión, off the entrance to the Strait of Magellan

10. Rio Sardinas................................Fortescue Bay in the Strait

11. Cabo Deseado............................ Cabo Pilar at the Pacific end of the Strait

12. Isla de San Pablo..................Puka-puka Island (14°38'S, 138°19'W) in the Tuamoto Archipelago, French Polynesia

13. Isla de Tiburónes....................Caroline Island (10° S, 151°W of Greenwich), one of the Line Islands of Polynesia

14. Quilóa.....................................Kilwa Kiswani, Tanzania

15. Sofala......................................between Beria and Nova Sofala, Mozambique

16. Calicut....................................Kozhikode, Kerala, South India

17. Dabul......................................Damão (Daman), West India

18. Cape Gaticara (Cattigara)....Kuta Radja or Acheh (Atjeh, Atjin),in Sumatra

19. Sumbit Pradit........................Antilia, or Septe Citade (mythical islands)

20. Temasik......................................Singapore

21. Lequieo, Ru Kiyu......................the Ryukyu Islands

22. Takubon....................................Himuquitan Island (Pigafetta's "Gatighan")

23. Pasihan....................................Pacijan, one of the Camotes Islands (Pigafetta's "Ticobon"—he apparently garbled "Pasihan" as "Gatighan" and then confused it with Takubon)

24. Pulao Kang Dayang (Tandaya)...Cebu Island

Endnotes

In a work of fiction telling the story is the prime consideration, not historical accuracy. Still, there was no avoiding the necessity of taking sides in certain scholarly debates that rage unabated to this day. Here are five of the most contentious issues, and the positions I took:

The accuracy of Magellan's landfall

Magellan has been accused of missing his target, the Spice Islands on the equator, by at least 8° of latitude, because his Samar landfall was at 12°N. While Maluco was indeed the avowed destination of the Armada, I believe that despite specific royal instructions Magellan was not aiming for the Spice Islands, but for an archipelago he knew existed at around 12° or 13°N.

Pilot Albo's log shows that in the Pacific the Armada consistently steered for 13°N after crossing the equator. They sailed at latitude 13°N for three weeks, until they came upon Guam. From Guam they maintained that latitude, more or less, all the way to Samar. Magellan knew the Spice Islands lay across the equator (they stretch from 4°N to 4°S). Had he been aiming for them, he would probably have steered between latitude 0° and 4°N.

An error of 12° of latitude, some 800 nautical miles, or even of 8° (550 nautical miles) is simply too large for any self-respecting Portuguese navigator of that time. Compare Magellan's Brazil landfall: an error of 3° there would have been disastrous, but he was was within a minute or two of the recommended latitude, 8°20'. Columbus had set the standard: "No one considers himself a good pilot and master who...makes an error of 10 leguas, though it be after a crossing of 1000 leguas." (Andrés Bernáldez, *à propos* of Columbus' second voyage, *Historia de los Reyes Católico*).

As far as latitude was concerned Magellan could be expected to err by no more than a fraction of a degree, or a few minutes of arc. Latitude was no problem for him; only longitude.

I am convinced Magellan was looking for the archipelago he knew would be found at 12° or 13°N. He must have planned to refit there, and proceed to the Spice Islands only after staking his claims to the new discoveries.

The location and date of the first mass in the Philippines

All the history books give this as Limasawa, Easter Sunday, March 31, 1521. I contend however that it was Homonhon, Passion Sunday, March 17, 1521. (These dates as in the Julian calendar with no adjustment for having passed the 180th meridian. To his credit, however, Pigafetta anticipated the invention of the International Dateline when he explained how they lost a day in going west around the world).

Pigafetta mentions the Easter Sunday Mass and no others previous to it, which does not necessarily mean none were celebrated. Canon law forbade Mass at sea, and so Homonhon was the first chance for Mass since South America. I think they would have taken that opportunity. They had every reason to. They were an Armada that kept up a show of devoutness and adhered to a strict schedule of prayers while at sea. March 17, their first full day on land after crossing the Pacific, was a Sunday and the Feast of St Lazarus. They must have felt obligated to hear Mass that day, the first time in a hundred days that no canonical impediments to it existed. A requiem Mass must have been said for the man who died of scurvy on March 21 and was buried there. On March 24, too, when they were still in Homonhon, it would have been unthinkable not to have a Mass on Palm Sunday. In sum, I find it highly unlikely of them to have delayed the first Mass until they were in Masawa.

I contend further that Padre Valderrama took his sacerdotal duties seriously and celebrated Mass every day. (That it was his wont to do so may be deduced from Pigafetta's statement that in Cebu, the Captain-General went ashore every day to hear Mass.) Allowing one Mass a day and discounting March 26 and 27, when they were at sea, there may have been as many as 12 Masses (9 in Homonhon and 3 in Masawa) previous to the Easter Sunday Mass of March 31. Pigafetta leaves many things unsaid in his book. When it comes to Masses the only ones he bothers to mention are those (1) attended by pagans; and (2) marked by the firing of guns during the Consecration. The Easter Mass in Masawa was so attended and so marked. Mass was governed by canon law; Pigafetta's mentions of them by Canon Law.

Compare the situation at Rio de Janeiro, where they must have celebrated Masses on Christmas Eve and Christmas Day. Pigafetta does not mention any such Masses, as contemporary readers would have taken it for granted that those Masses were said. He mentions only the farewell Mass of December 26—the one which had pagans Guaranis, Tupis, or Tamoios in attendance, and guns fired when the Host was elevated.

The identity and location of "Masawa"

The island called Mazaua by Pigafetta, Mazava by Albo, and Maçangar by the "Genoese pilot" is generally thought to have been the island now named Limasawa. The honor is disputed by an island close to Butuan, an island called Masao. I have accepted Sitoy's conclusion that Magellan's Masawa was Limasawa, not the Masao located off Butuan. Sitoy adduces these arguments:

1. Albo gives Mazava's latitude as nine and two-thirds degrees North, or 9°40'N. Pigafetta gives the same latitude ("nuove gradi et duo tersi") and adds that it is 25 leguas from Homonhon.

2. The "Genoese pilot" gives its distance from "Malhón" (Homonhon) as 20 leguas and says they sailed from Malhón to Maçangar without losing sight of Seilani (Leyte).

3. Albo gives two more details: firstly, from the summit of a mountain in Malhón, where they erected a cross, three islands to the west-southwest are visible; secondly, he describes Mazava as being long and narrow, and lying northeast-southwest.

Proponents of Masao's claim have preferred to translate Pigafetta's *nuove gradi et duo tersi* as "nine degrees and two-thirds [of a minute]" or 9°0'40" rather than "nine and two-thirds degrees" or 9°40'. Not only is such an interpretation ungrammatical, it is also ludicrous. The navigational instruments of the 16th century did not permit that sort of accuracy. Pigafetta in his book invariably expresses latitude as a whole number only, or a whole number plus a fraction, giving the degree and the minute. Nowhere does he give degree, minute, and second.

To my mind, the details mentioned above effectively eliminate Masao from further consideration. Masao lies at 9°N, is 130 nautical miles (149 statute miles) from Homonhon, does not have three islands to its WSW, and does not afford a view of Leyte, being too far from it.

Limasawa lies at 9°55'N, within sight of Leyte, and is some 80 nautical miles (86 statute miles) from Homonhon.

Morison[1] calculates the legua used by Columbus and Magellan to have been 3.18 nautical miles. Sitoy[2] relies on Navarrete[3], who reckons Magellan's legua to have been $3\frac{3}{7}$ statute miles—in decimal notation, 3.43 statute miles (2.98 nautical miles) where Morison's figure is 3.66 statute miles (3.18 nautical miles).

Note that a Homonhon-Masao distance of 25 leguas would be possible only with a legua of 5.9 miles. Of the many leguas in use in the 16th century, the largest I have found was one of 4.2 miles.

On Limasawa, too, one gets a fine view of three islands to the west-southwest.

I therefore consider Limasawa to have been the "Masawa" visited by Magellan. The "Li" comes from a mistake in transcription by a 17th-century Spanish priest: a small enough error to perpetuate. Declaring Masao to be the island where Kulámbo and Magellan made a blood compact would be a much larger one.

[1] Samuel Eliot Morison: author of *Admiral of the Ocean Sea*, now considered the standard biography of Columbus; an Admiral in the US Navy during World War II; Professor Emeritus of History at Harvard.

[2] T. Valentino Sitoy, Jr.: Professor of History at Silliman University in Dumaguete City.

[3] Martín Fernández de Navarrete: Spanish naval officer c. the late 18th and the early 19th centuries; historian; editor of a 5-volume series of books (Madrid, 1825-1837) on pre-16th century voyages of discovery.

Enrique's origins and native language

He was taken prisoner of war after the fall of Malacca in August 1511. Magellan acquired him as a slave shortly thereafter. Pigafetta says he was a native of "Zamatra," which suggests that Enrique had migrated from Sumatra. (In the novel Enrique is Malacca-born and -bred but as a typical Malay regards Sumatra as his traditional homeland.)

I accept Sitoy's conclusion that Enrique spoke the pasar Malayu, and that the Siamese trader translated his speech into the Visayan language of Cebu. Conversations between Magellan and Humabon thus required two interpreters. The Siamese was apparently not the only one who could speak the pasar Malayu, the trade language in that region of Asia. Kulámbò obviously spoke it well enough, and so, I surmise, did Humabon.

The use of the pasar Malayu would make complicated theories of Enrique's origins unnecessary. Enrique's effectiveness as an interpreter in Masawa and Cebu has been supposed to be due to his command of the Cebuano language. The theory thus arose—a case of the tail wagging the dog—that he was from Cebu and as a boy had been kidnapped and brought to Malacca. This line of thought also gave Enrique some claim to being the first man to have circumnavigated the world. I would hate to deny Enrique his claim, but there is no need for him to have been in Cebu during his childhood. It's much simpler to have Kulámbò and Humabon communicating with Enrique in the pasar Malayu.

All that can be shown is that Enrique travelled west from Malacca around the world to Cebu. For lack of further evidence I am constrained to leave him some 1500 miles short of a complete circumnavigation.

Magellan as circumnavigator

Like Enrique, Magellan fell short of a complete circuit of the world by 21 degrees of longitude. According to the official records, his farthest east was Malacca at longitude 103°E of Greenwich, while his farthest west was Cebu at longitude 124°E. However, sometime during his eighteen months as a Malacca-based caravel captain (1511-1512), he evidently sailed to points East. Morison says Magellan was the third captain in Captain-General Antão d'Abreu's flotilla seeking the way to the Spice Islands, and that they got as far as Ambon at longitude 128°E or Banda at 130°E. Other sources give the third captain as Simon Affonso, not Magellan. However that may be, Parr, citing the "chronicleer" (Argensola?) as his source, quotes another voyage, this one unauthorized, that lasted six weeks. Magellan is supposed to have entered the South China Sea and gone northeast. Parr hypothesizes that Magellan sailed to the Philippines, probably to Palawan or to the Kalamian group of islands, having heard about the archipelago from some of the 500 natives of Luzon who had settled in Malacca.

Either of those journeys, if true, would make Magellan the first to have encompassed the world, if in separate voyages. (If he accompanied his master, Enrique's claim is also strengthened.) Elcano's distinction as a circumnavigator is that he was clearly the first to do it in a single voyage. Another half-century passed before Drake became the first man to go around the world as Captain-General from start to finish.

Lastly, my apologies for the many gaps in my knowledge. Had I known how much there was to learn, I should never have started at all.
—C.C.

Bibliography

PRIMARY SOURCES

Albo, Francisco. *Diario ó Derrotero del Viage de Magellanes*. Included in Volume IV of *Colección de los Viages y Descubrimientos...desde Fines del Siglo XV*, Martín Fernández de Navarrete, editor. Madrid, 1837. Reproduced in part in Blair & Robertson's *The Philippine Islands*, vols. XXXIII and XXXIV.

Anonymous (probably Vasquito Gomes Gallego). "The Leiden Narrative." Unsigned manuscript, in Portuguese, of a relation of the entire voyage; in the library of the University of Leiden. Published as *Um Roteiro Inédito*, M. de Jong, editor. Coimbra, 1937.

The "Genoese pilot." (Leon Pancaldo? Juan Bautista de Punzurol?) *Roteiro*. Included in *The First Voyage Round the World, by Magellan. Translated from the Accounts of Pigafetta and Other Contemporary Writers*, Lord Henry E. J. S. Stanley of Alderley, editor & translator. The Hakluyt Society, London, 1874. Reproduced in part in Blair & Robertson's *The Philippine Islands*, vols. XXXIII and XXXIV.

Pigafetta, Antonio Francesco. *Primo Viaggio Intorno al Mondo*. Composed ca. 1525, original manuscript in the Biblioteca Ambrosiana, Milan, Italy. Translated by J.A. Robertson as *First Voyage Around the World*. In Blair & Robertson's *The Philippine Islands*, vols. XXXIII and XXXIV.

SECONDARY SOURCES

Abellana, Jovito. *Bisaya Patronynesis Sri Visjaya*. Cebu City, 1960.

Academic dissertation, 1965. In the Cebuano Studies Center, University of San Carlos, Cebu City.

Visconde de Lagõa. *Fernão de Magalhãis: com um estudo náutico do roteiro, pelo Almirante J. Freitas Ribeiro* (2 vols.) Lisbon, 1937.

Guillemard, Ferdinand H. H. *The Life of Ferdinand Magellan and the First Circumnavigation of the Globe.* London, 1890.

Gullas, Vicente. *Lapulapu: Ang Nakabuntog kang Magellan.* Cebu City, 1938.

Licuanan, Virginia Benitez & Llavador Mira, José. *The Philippines Under Spain: a compilation and translation of original documents. Book I (1518-1565): The Voyages of Discovery.* Manila, 1990.

Mitchell, Mairin. *Elcano: The First Circumnavigator.* London, 1958.

Morison, Samuel Eliot. *The European Discovery of America: The Southern Voyages 1492-1616.* Oxford University Press, New York, 1974.

Parr, Charles McKew. *So Noble a Captain.* New York, 1953.

Quimat, Lina. *Glimpses in History of Early Cebu.* Cebu City, 1980.

Ramas, Leonisa. *A Cultural Picture of the Visayans Derived from* [Blair & Robertson's] <u>The Philippine Islands</u>.

Sitoy, T. Valentino, Jr. *A History of Christianity in the Philippines: The Initial Encounter*, Volume 1. New Day Publishers, Manila, 1985.

Transylvanus, Maximilianus. *De Molvccis Insulis.* Cologne, 1523. Included in Lord Stanley's *The First Voyage...* as *The Moluccas Islands.* Reproduced in full in Blair & Robertson's *The Philippine Islands,* vol. I.

TERTIARY SOURCES

Brecht, Bertolt. "Kavalieren der Station D." Lyrics copyright © 1923 by Bertolt Brecht; English lyrics copyright © 1980 by Stepan Brecht. In Arthur R.G. Solmssen's novel *A Princess in Berlin.* New York, 1984.

Frazer, James G. *Totemism and Exogamy.* London, 1910.

Freud, Sigmund. *Moses and Monotheism.* Vienna, 1937. English translation by Katherine Jones, London, 1939.

Fuentes, Carlos. *Terra Nostra.* Mexico, 1975. English translation by Margaret Sayers Peden. Farrar, Straus & Giroux, New York, 1976.

Heyerdahl, Thor. *Kon-Tiki: Across the Pacific by Raft.* Translated by F.H. Lyon. Chicago, 1950.

Jennings, Gary. *The Journeyer.* Atheneum, New York, 1984.

Juergens, Sylvester P., S.M., S.T.D. *Marian Daily Missal. Compiled from the Missale Romanum, N 1564.* Henri Proost & Co, Turnhout, Belgium: 1934.

Lewis, David. "Wind, Wave, Star and Bird." *National Geographic* magazine, December, 1974.

Lockyer, Norman. *The Dawn of Astronomy.* London, 1894.

Ondaatje, Michael. *The English Patient.* Vintage Books, Toronto, 1992.

Rank, Otto. *Der Mythus von der Geburt des Helden.* Vienna, 1909.

Rosenstock-Huessy, Eugen. *Out of Revolution: Autobiography of Western Man (De Te Fabula Narratur).* William Morrow & Co. New York, 1938.

Watson, Lyall. *Heaven's Breath.*

Whitelock, Dorothy. *The Beginnings of English Society.* Penguin Books, Harmondsworth, Middlesex, 1952.

GENERAL REFERENCE WORKS

Blair, Emma Helen & Robertson, James Alexander, editors and annotators. *The Philippine Islands 1493-1898* (55 vols.) The A.H. Clark Company, Cleveland 1903-1909. Reissued by Domingo Abella, Manila 1962. Reprinted by Cachos Hermanos, Manila, 1973.

Chirino, Pedro, S.J. *Relación de las Islas Filipinas..., Roma, MDCIV.* Translated by J.A. Robertson as "Relation of the Filipinas Islands..., Rome, MDCIV (1604)." In Blair & Robertson's *The Philippine Islands*, vols. XII and XIII.

Clebert, Jean-Paul. *Les Tzingones.* Paris, 1961. Translated by Charles Duff as *The Gypsies.* London, 1963.

Colin, Francisco, S.J. *Labor Evangélica.* Madrid, 1663. Chapters IV and XIII-XVI from Book I translated by J.A.

Conrad, Barnaby. *The Encyclopedia of Bullfighting.* Boston, 1961.

De Bry, Theodor. *Tertia Pars, India Orientalis.* Frankfort, 1628.

Moorhead, F.J. *A History of Malaya and her Neighbours*, vol. I. London, 1957.

Morga, Dr. Antonio de. *Sucesos de las Islas Filipinas*. Mexico, 1609. Translated by Lord Stanley as *Events in the Philippine Islands*, London, 1874. Annotations by José Rizal and prologue by Ferdinand Blumentritt, Paris 1890, translated by Encarnación Alzona, Manila, 1958.

Morison, Samuel Eliot. *The European Discovery of America: The Northern Voyages, AD 500-1600*. OxfordUniversity Press, New York, 1971.

Robertson as a tract, *Native Races and their Customs*. In Blair & Robertson's *The Philippine Islands*, vol. XL.

Wallace, Alfred Russel. *The Malay Archipelago*. London, 1869.

Wheatly, Paul. *The Golden Khersonese: Studies in the historical geography of the Malay Peninsula before A.D. 1500*. Kuala Lumpur, 1961.

Winstedt, Richard. *The Malay Magician: being Shaman, Saiva, and Sufi*. London, 1961.

ART/PHOTO CREDITS

- outer cover/page ii: eccentric (ceremonial) Maya flint knife, from the September 1991 *National Geographic* magazine. Photo by Kenneth Garrett.

- page xx: the nao *Trinidad* leaving San Lúcar de Barrameda, from the June 1976 *National Geographic* magazine. Detail from painting by Björn Landström.

- page 1: the Moorish minaret topped by the belfry of the Seville Cathedral, showing La Giralda, from the February 1994 *Silver Kris* magazine. Photo by Habeeb Salloum.

- page 93: guanacos and chulengos, from the July 1981 *National Geographic* magazine. Photo by William L. Franklin.

- page 191: schematic representation of a Polynesian bamboo mattang. Illustration by M.V. Kapauan.

- page 299: Sarawak wall painting, from the 1995 *Insight Guide: Malaysia*. Photo by Hans Höfer.